JAM RUN

An Eddie Barrow Mystery

RUSSELL BROOKS

JAM RUN
An Eddie Barrow Mystery

By Russell Brooks

Copyright © 2023 by Russell Brooks

All rights reserved. No part of this book may be reproduced in whole or in part, scanned, photocopied, recorded, distributed in any printed or electronic form, or reproduced in any manner whatsoever, or by any information storage and retrieval system now known or hereafter invented, without express written permission of the publisher, except in the case of brief quotations embodied in critical articles and reviews. This book is licensed for your personal enjoyment. This book may not be re-sold or given away to anyone. If you would like to share this book with another person, please purchase an additional copy or copies. If you are reading this book and did not purchase it, or it was not purchased for your use only, then you should purchase your own copy.

Thank you for honoring the author's work.
This is a work of fiction. Names, characters, places, and incidents are products of the author's imagination or are used fictitiously. Any resemblance to actual events, locales, or persons living or dead is entirely coincidental.

13-Digit ISBN (print version):
978-0-9867513-8-7

13-Digit ISBN (ebook version):
978-0-9867513-9-4

Chicken merry, hawk deh near

—Jamaican Proverb

The chicken, unaware of the danger posed by the hovering hawk, makes merry.

Chapter 1

Citrusville Bar, Pegga Road, Irwin, Jamaica.

Eddie Barrow thrust a Jamaican five-hundred-dollar bill across the counter to the bartender before the other patron could utter a syllable. There was no way in hell Eddie was going to let someone else cut in front of him tonight.

This time it was a wire-thin *sista*, dressed in a crop-top, Harley Quinn shorts, and a Mary J Blige weave. To him, she looked like she must be thinking, "He ain't much of a man," but Eddie couldn't give a rat's ass what she thought. He may not have been born in Barbados like his parents, but he knew the rules of the Caribbean—that cut-ins were a way of life down here.

At five foot eight and a little over one hundred and seventy pounds, Barrow wasn't the most physically imposing *brotha* around, but it didn't mean that he didn't know how to stand his ground when he needed to.

"Two waters please," Eddie yelled as he competed with the heavy bass in the background that shook his internal organs, while keeping his hand on his money.

The bartender leaned closer. "What you say?"

"I said water." He held up two fingers. "Two."

Eddie loosened his grip on the bill as the bartender pulled it away and slipped it in the cash register. He reached below the counter, then placed two bottles in front of Eddie before moving on to the sista who'd tried to budge him.

With a bottle in each hand, Eddie navigated through the crowd. It was no different than trying to exit a packed subway car—especially getting elbowed and poked. He kept looking down, worried someone was going to step on his toes and dirty up his pristine pair of Air Max runners.

This was exactly the reason Eddie outgrew the club scene a year after he came into it, roughly seven years before. It didn't take him long before he realized that he wasn't missing anything. As for Corey Stephenson, his "brotha from anotha motha" from way back, clubbing and going out was more his thing. Eddie was the quiet one who always wanted to stay home with his head buried in a book or, up until recently, writing one to keep up with deadlines. If he went out, it was because Corey had dragged him.

The funny thing was that Eddie had always been told that Barbadians—Bajans—were the loudest, more so than Trinidadians. Corey was born in Trinidad and moved to Montreal when he was around eleven or twelve, not too long before he saved Eddie's ass from a bunch of skinheads who'd ambushed him in the park. At a solid six foot two with his Trini charm, he was always able to talk his way into a woman's panties, unlike Eddie.

But he'd since settled down a bit. Getting his girlfriend pregnant and then marrying her had changed Corey for the better. He'd once had an alcohol problem too. Those were moments that Eddie wanted to forget. One of those memories involved the two of them and Corey's then-girlfriend, Jordyn, being on the run from the police for a murder Eddie had been framed for.

Eddie didn't even wait to get back to Corey before he took a drink of his water to cool off in this sweltering Jamaican heat. Even though this section of the bar was outdoors, a bunch of brothas and sistas crowded together like sardines still made the mercury rise, especially since they weren't close enough to the ocean to catch the breeze.

They'd only arrived from Montreal earlier that afternoon. As expected, Corey had to drag Eddie out of the Airbnb to find the nearest party.

It was their first time in Jamaica. It was business for Eddie. Pleasure for Corey. In less than twelve hours Eddie would be signing copies of his latest thriller, which was why he didn't want to be out too late or drink anything alcoholic. Eddie was a lightweight. The last thing he needed was to be hungover during the book signing.

"Come on, it'll only be for a few hours. You'll have plenty of time to sleep," Corey had said earlier. Which only made Eddie sigh. He didn't have much of a track record in saying no to his friend.

Of all the areas Corey chose to drag him to, why did it have to be a ghetto on top of a hill? The only light aside from the headlights of their rental car came from the car graveyard to their left. Beyond that was pure blackness, as they drove on the two-laned road through an area of thick forest on either side. Even worse, the road was so neglected that they were forced to drive at a speed slower than one found in a school zone. Had they been ambushed by a street gang they'd have better luck escaping on foot.

As for school zones, the Irwin Primary School was adjacent from where they were. Eddie couldn't imagine a worse area to build a school. Hell, he couldn't believe he was at a party that could potentially be interrupted by gunfire at any moment.

Maybe he should've asked for a drink doused with rum to calm his nerves. All of this because Corey wanted to party in what he called *the real Jamaica*, and not the area that catered to tourists.

A sista caught Eddie's attention, clearly not hiding the fact that she was eyeing him. The woman's jet-black hair with blond highlights reached the top of her midnight dress—one which conveniently stopped just below her thighs. When she turned to the side it was as though the world moved in slow motion. Yeah, she wanted him to notice her, especially her peach-shaped booty. Eddie's eyes then dropped to her feet, and he nodded in appreciation. A wicked pair of stilettos. This sista had polished herself literally from head to toe. He no longer thought of getting a rum drink because his nerves were calmer than ever.

He gazed around now. There must be at least a dozen brothas there, all ready to jump her bones.

Eddie shook it off and found Corey—lost in his own world—doing the *Gully Creepa*. At least the crowd wasn't as dense, and the air was less tainted by the smell of sweat and perfume. He held out Corey's water bottle.

"Corey," yelled Eddie, but his friend didn't seem to notice.

Eddie tapped the bottle on Corey's shoulder, catching his attention.

"There you are." Corey took the bottle and unscrewed the cap. "What took you so long?"

"Don't ask."

Corey drank a bit and then nodded past Eddie. "You notice that girl staring at you?"

What a question to ask. How could he not? Eddie had always been the more observant of the two. He finished off his water in a single swig, giving Corey what Eddie hoped was a nonchalant shrug. "Yeah, I saw her."

"Why don't you go talk to her?"

"Oh sure, so that I look desperate."

"*Bwoy*, stop being a pussy and go talk to her." Corey shook his head and took a swig.

Eddie watched as three brothas—two of them solidly built—approached the sista. They weren't holding back, and one of the three reached under her skirt from behind. But she had already spotted them, anticipated his move, and slapped his hand away before striding off.

The brotha laughed as he casually ran his hand over the top of his durag. The other, who wore a bandana, bent over at the waist, laughing as he held onto his friend's shoulder. The third, who looked like the odd one of the three, bowed his head and looked away while covering his mouth. He, unlike the other two, didn't fit the tough-guy, macho type. In fact, he looked as though he was embarrassed by his friend's behavior.

"You see that?" Eddie asked.

Corey nodded. "She's waiting for you to make the first move."

Eddie knew when Corey was right, and this was one of those times. People around him were up on each other, sistas whinin' up on a brotha—bent over between six-fifteen and six-thirty—to music, whose lyrics at times even degraded them.

Eddie caught her smile as she ran two fingers across her brow to clear away the few strands of hair that fell over her eye. He approached her slowly, not letting go of her gaze. She gravitated toward him. The music stopped, and the DJ screamed something in Jamaican Patois that Eddie couldn't understand, right before bombastic dancehall music blasted around him. Eddie was caught off guard as the woman spun around and backed up into him—ass first—and performed the most energetic and wildest *Dutty Wine* he'd ever seen. She then followed through to *Bruk It Down*.

Damn, she has skills.

It was way more than Eddie could handle, and he struggled to keep up with her. She then turned around and looked into his eyes—their noses barely touching. He stared back, held her gaze, but something was off. It made him pause his dancing, a tiny voice in his head telling him to back up. But he was caught off guard when the sista grabbed him by the shoulders with a firm grip. Before he realized what was happening, she hoisted herself in the air and locked her legs around him just above the waist in a vicelike grip. Out of reflex, he quickly took a deep breath as he felt the pressure from her legs on his ribcage.

The jump's momentum knocked him off balance, and he stumbled backward before falling, nearly striking his head on the ground. The crowd went crazy, and all Eddie heard was howling laughter. For the next several seconds, the jarringly loud thumps of the bass from the speakers were reduced to background noise.

Eddie felt as though a nasty prank had been pulled on him as the back of his throat dried up.

But she wasn't done with him yet. She continued gyrating onto him as though nothing had happened while he lay on his back. She then spun around to face the opposite way—with her ass literally up in his face as she shook it. All Eddie saw was booty and thong. He couldn't help but watch—his neck hurt from holding his head up for so long. She then did a front roll into a handstand, held it, then gracefully let one leg fall after the next to form a bridge, and pulled herself up at the waist, with seemingly little effort, to stand on both feet.

Eddie couldn't hold his head up any longer, and let it drop as he breathed deeply, attempting to process what the hell just happened. Even before he sat up, brothas inundated him as they rushed to give him high-fives. He was slow to return them, considering that he was still recovering from the ordeal.

He couldn't tell if the crowd was cheering or laughing. It

sounded more like laughing—and at him. Twenty-seven years young, and he still felt like the odd one in the crowd. It reminded him of the times in elementary and high school gym class where he was always the last one chosen to be on a team.

The sista winked at him before turning to go. He felt the blood rushing to his groin as her ass bounced from side to side as she sashayed away.

"Wait," Eddie yelled as he scrambled to his feet. But she was already gone.

Where did she go?

Eddie heard Corey's long, drawling holler as his friend grabbed his shoulder. "Yooooooooo! Did you get her number?"

Eddie turned to him and saw Corey wiping the tears away with his towel.

"Naw, she took off too fast."

Corey shook his head. "Come again? You let her do all that, and you didn't even get her number?"

"I said she was gone before I could get up. By the way, I'm okay, considering that I nearly cracked the back of my head open."

"That ain't no excuse. Bwoy, I oughta slap you upside the head."

It was then that the DJ lowered the music and started yelling into the mic, announcing a dance-off, and that the participants should present themselves. Six army-vet-looking brothas, showing off their pecs by wearing tight black t-shirts with the word SECURITY emblazoned on the back, cleared a circle. As the area was being prepared, four young sistas—ranging from petite to thunder thighs—were already on the floor.

Corey beckoned Eddie to follow him quickly so that they could get a closer view. There was only one row of people in front, forcing Eddie to look between to see, while Corey, being the taller one, only inconvenienced the ones behind him.

It took just a few moments before Eddie spotted her again. She was on the opposite side of the circle, talking to another sista. It appeared that she was complimenting her on her dress. The woman then took out her smartphone, and they snapped a selfie. The smile was so irresistible. But something was still off, and a red flag was flapping in his mind. If only he knew why. The other sista, whom she took the selfie with, ran into the circle as the DJ blasted the music again.

Eddie tapped Corey's arm. "I'll be back."

"You leave, and you're going to lose your spot."

Eddie then nodded in the direction of the woman. "It'll be worth it."

When Corey looked away, Eddie saw what appeared to be a scuffle. He nearly pushed aside the person in front of him to get a better view. It was the woman. She was trying to leave, but some brothas and sistas were blocking her path.

A few seconds later, though, it appeared that they were persuading her to join the dance-off. It came to the point where the woman was literally pushed into the circle, where the other sistas already had a head start.

The look on her face—she was worried. It was as though she didn't want to do it or even be there anymore. But the crowd was not forgiving. One of the bouncers who helped clear the area came to her and said something into her ear. It was at that moment that she removed a stiletto.

Bedlam.

Eddie thought he would go deaf from the amount of screaming that erupted around him.

The second stiletto came off, and she handed those, along with her purse, to the bouncer. She relaxed, and her smile came back. It was contagious enough that it even made Eddie smile. After she started to move, he knew that the contest was already over after the first twenty seconds. It was evident by the amount of noise the crowd made that she was the winner. Two of the other competitors seemed to know they didn't stand a chance of winning, and they gave up and bolted in a New York Minute. She clearly had more energy and endurance than the remaining competitors. However, it was the backflip ending in ground splits that sealed the deal for her.

Game over.

The music came to an abrupt stop, and the DJ called out the names of the remaining contestants one at a time to let the amount of noise the crowd made determine the winner. He came last to the woman Eddie had danced with. The DJ had to ask for her name.

She must be new. How else would the DJ know the others and not her? Eddie thought.

The woman was handed her belongings along with a cordless mic. She then turned to the DJ. "My name's Shenice."

Chaos.

Eddie was bounced from both sides and from behind as everyone around him completely lost it—jumping up and down, swinging towels, obviously not caring who they knocked into. It was soon after that the DJ announced her as the winner.

"You better get her number. That's wifey material," Corey shouted into Eddie's ear. Eddie didn't answer. As blown away as he was, he still couldn't help but feel that there was something off about Shenice.

As she slid her feet back into her stilettos, a brotha walked to Shenice and handed her an ultra-wide gold-colored column trophy and an envelope. Eddie assumed the latter was either a cash prize or a gift card.

Thunder-thighs and the selfie-sista both gave Shenice congratulatory hugs while the other two women scowled and stormed off.

Eddie forced his way past the people in front of him, but others crowded back inside the circle, creating enough obstacles to slow him down. When he got to where Shenice was, she was gone again.

Shit, man!

He jumped in the air a few times, hoping to see her above the crowd. The sixth time he spotted the blond highlights at the back of her head.

"Shenice," Eddie yelled, only for his voice to be lost among the dozens. He went to the spot where he last saw her and found himself next to a line to the ladies' room.

A line this long, she couldn't have gotten in so quickly. "Excuse me. Anyone see Shenice?"

"Who yuh call Shenice? Which Shenice is dat?" answered one

woman in a heavy Jamaican accent.

"She just won." All Eddie saw were shaking heads.

"Me no see yar pass tru." Eddie assumed she said: *I didn't see her pass through here.*

How does Shenice keep going ninja on me? He went back and found Corey waiting where he had left him.

"And?"

Eddie furrowed a brow and shook his head. He tugged at his own collar. "I'm going out to the parking lot for a bit. It's too stuffy here."

The sound of tiny gravel crunching under his feet was a relief from the jarring bass from the subwoofers. As he walked between two rows of cars, all he saw were Toyotas, Mitsubishis, and Hondas—not an American or European car in sight. The ringing in his ears wasn't as bad as he had expected.

His phone buzzed in his front pants pocket. He grabbed it and saw the envelope icon indicating that he had received a text message. Eddie held his thumb on the monitor in the fingerprint display to unlock it. The message was from Corey, asking if he'd found Shenice.

Eddie replied with a "No." A few seconds later, the phone buzzed again. He checked it out, expecting to see Corey's answer. Instead, he noticed that his text didn't go through. It bounced back, accompanied by a red exclamation mark. *Damn.* A slashed zero replaced the phone signal bars and the Wi-Fi icon at the top of the screen.

No signal.

Eddie stopped and walked backward a few steps while raising the phone above him to catch the signal. Still nothing.

That was odd.

Eddie slid the phone back into his pocket. He tapped the other one—the third time he'd done so this evening—and still felt the thin pouch. The pouch was too obscure to be visible to a would-be pickpocket but large enough to just hold his ID and a few dollar bills. No sense checking it too often, or he'd tip off someone that he had something of value on him. As for his wallet, he'd left it in the glove compartment of his car.

His thoughts drifted back to Shenice. *What kind of sista whine-up on a man so and don't even talk to him after?* But she was gone. Either she caught a taxi, was picked up by a friend, or she drove herself. Who knew? Again, the thought came back to him that there was something unusual about her. It was killing him that he couldn't figure out what it was.

Eddie was startled by shouting that came from several cars away, and he turned to see what appeared to be fighting among three people. Two brothas held onto a sista by the arms and threw her facedown onto the hood of a car. Eddie's walk turned into a jog so that he could get a better view. He paused when he saw that it was Durag and Bandana. Eddie couldn't see the sista's face but caught a glimpse of the back of her head and saw the blond highlights, sending his heartbeat into overdrive.

Holy shit, they're going to rape Shenice.

"Hey!" Eddie yelled, catching the attention of Shenice's attackers just as he was about to rush them. "Leave her—"

The cuff to the back of his head sent a shock that penetrated Eddie's brain. The world spun around him, seconds before he fell forward, striking another solid object before he hit the ground. He scrunched up his face as he forced his eyes shut, crying out from the agonizing pain. But he only heard his cries internally. Something—no, *someone* was forcing down hard on his mouth with what felt like a damp cloth with a noxious-smelling chemical. Whatever it was, he had already inhaled too much of it that he was left disoriented.

He felt the crook of an arm under his chin, pulling him backward. His body fell limp as his heels dragged across the ground. He didn't even have the strength to turn his head to see his attacker before his eyes got very heavy.

***

The choking startled Eddie awake. He rolled on his side, only to inhale a mouthful of dust, making things worse. He got onto all fours as he tried to take deep breaths in between violent coughs. He turned around and into a seated position with his back to one of the cars beside him. The right side of his forehead throbbed. He put a hand to it. Things started to come back to him. He had bumped his head. And right before that, he was hit from behind. And that was right before...

Shenice.

Standing was a struggle, but he held onto the car next to him for support. Once up, he heard the banging cacophony coming from the bar. He let go of the car to see if he could walk on his own but ended up stumbling forward. Eddie braced himself on the car again to stop himself from falling.

He did his best to maintain his footing as he headed to where he had seen Shenice being attacked.

"Shenice?" Eddie yelled. Nothing but the slow-jamming reggae in the background. He grabbed his cell and called Corey, holding the phone to his ear as he searched the area.

Come on, pick-up. It suddenly hit him that the phone signal was down earlier. Eddie took a quick glance at the screen and still saw the slashed zero.

The loud sliding of tires on dirt and gravel startled him—freezing him where he stood as the shock took over, preventing him from jumping out of the way of the oncoming vehicle. The car still slid but luckily came to a stop, within inches of striking him.

Eddie's nerves unlocked, allowing him to breathe again.

With the headlights shining below his waist, he was able to see the visible BMW insignia on the hood of the car, and who was inside. Bandana was in the passenger seat, but there was something wrong with his eyes. He was clearly in pain as he was rubbing them with his hands while howling. The driver was one of his friends, the odd one of the group. He then saw Durag in the back seat, staring between both of them and straight at Eddie.

"Delroy, Laawd Jesus! How yuh slam pon de breaks so? Why nuh kill me?" yelled Bandana.

"It's dat *bloodclaat* who shout at us," said Durag. "Move out at de road, yuh damn idiat. Bumboclaat!"

The driver wasn't among the two who attacked Shenice. At least, Eddie didn't remember him being there. But the fear was all over his face. When his hand slammed on the horn, it startled Eddie enough that he jumped to the side.

Eddie raised his hands in surrender. "Yo, my bad."

The accelerator was floored, causing the tires to spin wildly, gravel ricocheting out behind the car. As they passed, Eddie saw Durag point at him while imitating a gun. He then lowered his thumb to touch his index as though he was pulling the trigger. This was done slowly, and Eddie knew that Durag was making a point.

Eddie shielded his eyes with his forearm as a dust cloud emerged from under the spinning tires. The tiny pebbles became projectiles, stinging his arms and legs as the car cut left, causing it to fishtail. It then sped off and exited the parking lot. Once it hit the road, Eddie heard the screeching of tires and the accelerating roar of the engine.

Even though it was impossible to catch the license plate number, he already had two clues: the driver's name was Delroy, and he drove a BMW—the only European car he saw in this lot so far.

"Ed."

Eddie turned to see Corey running toward him.

"I was looking all over for you." Corey slid to a stop, a bit out of breath. "Didn't you get my text?"

It didn't take long for his best friend to notice his injury. "Bruh, what happened to your head?" Corey reached out to touch the bruise.

Eddie moved his head to dodge his hand. "That's nothing."

"What happened to you?"

Eddie continued searching for Shenice. "I wish I knew."

"What?" Corey put his hand on Eddie's shoulder to get his attention. "Were you fighting? Who did this to you?"

"Shenice."

Corey tilted his head. "*Shenice* did that to you?"

"No, she was being attacked," Eddie answered. "It was those same guys we saw earlier."

"They did this to you?"

Eddie began to wander off. "No, not them."

Corey moved quickly to catch up to him. "You ain't making any sense."

"We have to find her." Eddie picked up the pace—looking left and right. "I think they raped her."

"You serious? Where?"

"Over there, I think." Eddie pointed to the spot where he'd last seen her. "I saw Durag and Bandana dragging her, and I yelled at them. Then someone jumped me from behind. That's when I fell and hit my head. I tried texting you, but the phone signal's out."

"I know," said Corey. "When you didn't reply, I texted you again, but it bounced back. So I came out here looking for you."

An object on the ground caught Eddie's attention. It was a shoe, more specifically a stiletto—and it looked like one that Shenice had been wearing. Eddie darted right for it and picked it up. The heel was broken and dangled from its attachment like a shoelace. He showed it to Corey, who raised his eyebrows.

Shenice could've been running for her life.

They both frantically searched, looking underneath the cars in anticipation that she was on the ground, all while yelling her name.

A loud, frightening scream came from the entrance to the parking lot. Eddie jumped to his feet, and his mouth dropped in a gasp. A human torch ran blindly in zigzags and circles with both arms flailing. The person fell but continued to kick and thrash on the ground, screaming as the bright flames seared through fabric to flesh.

Eddie rushed to the victim while pulling off his shirt, then swung it as hard and fast as he could to beat out the flames. He didn't care that his hands were getting singed. This person's life was at stake. Moments later, he noticed that Corey was doing the same. They yelled for help as they lashed the victim and furiously kicked dust and gravel from the ground to help smother the flames.

Eddie's shirt caught fire, forcing him to throw it on the ground. He grabbed his phone ready to dial 110…or was it 119? He went with his gut and dialed 110 while kicking as much dust as he could onto the victim. Still, the call wouldn't go through. This didn't make sense. Emergency calls always worked, whether there was a phone signal or not.

But Eddie's gut told him they were already too late. It was the first time that Eddie had smelled burning human flesh, and it brought on a brief wave of nausea. He still didn't stop kicking gravel onto the victim even though the flames had died down.

"Hey, do you hear me?" Eddie yelled.

No reply.

"Please answer. Can you hear me? Please say something."

"Ed," said Corey.

"Come on," Eddie's voice died down. "Say something."

Eddie felt a hand on his shoulder. He turned to see Corey shaking his head.

"Help! Somebody help!" Gritting his teeth, he ran toward the bar. He continued yelling for help, but it was as though no one heard him.

Eddie turned and ran back. "Did they say anything?"

Corey sighed and shook his head.

Eddie dropped to his knees in front of the victim and noticed they were missing their shoes. He then saw what remained of the dress. No long hair with gold highlights, which was most likely a weave that had completely burned away. It was definitely Shenice.

"Fuck!" Corey yelled as he stomped on the ground.

Eddie often read about Jamaica's high homicide rate. He just never imagined that he would witness one within the first ten hours of his arrival. He didn't know what had suddenly come over him as he stared at the smoking, charred body. Was it fear, shock, or both?

It wasn't long before one of the patrons noticed what had happened. It began with one, then quickly became a few. Word spread swiftly, and others began showing up. As expected, cell phones were up as the mob suddenly became the paparazzi. They practically smothered him, Corey, and Shenice.

"Who dead?"

"Who do it?"

"Move outta de way. Put it pon Facebook."

The last comment pissed him the fuck off. Eddie jumped up and spun in the direction of the person who said it. "Who said they're putting this on Facebook? Don't you have any respect? Jesus!"

The crowd went silent for a moment, then they resumed what they were doing as though they hadn't been interrupted.

Eddie turned to look back at Shenice's body. Most of the burns were from the neck down.

There was enough light from the flashlights on the patrons' cell phones that allowed Eddie to notice that Shenice had suffered a skull-fracturing blow to the side of her head—maybe from a rock or a bat. But something was still off, and he was reminded of the red flags that hit him earlier. Something about Shenice's body caught Eddie's attention. He took out his smartphone to activate the flashlight so that he could get a better look.

What Eddie saw made him tense up while stifling a gasp. He quickly pointed the flashlight away from the victim.

So that's what was bothering me.

"Clear outta de way!" Eddie heard a few brothas yelling. He turned to see that the crowd was being physically dispersed by the bouncers. They made it through, grabbing Eddie and Corey, then shoving them back.

"Bumboclaat!" yelled one of them as he turned his head away in disgust.

Another pointed his finger toward Eddie and Corey. "A two a uno do it?"

"We were trying to save her," Corey answered. "We even lost our shirts trying to beat out the flames."

Eddie didn't understand a word the bouncer said. But after Corey answered him, it was obvious that the bouncer asked: *"You two did this?"*

The same bouncer eyed them while shaking his head.

"If we did this, why would we hang around to get caught?" Eddie couldn't believe that this idiot would have the gall to accuse them of killing Shenice.

The bouncer then sighed and pointed to a spot away from the crowd. "Stay ova deh so, and no botha move!"

Move over there, and don't bother trying to leave! Eddie understood that part.

Both Eddie and Corey obeyed and went to where they were instructed.

"That's some straight-up bullshit," said Corey as they looked at the gathering. "Those guys not only raped her, but they killed her too. What kind of sick fucks do such a thing?"

Eddie shook his head. "I have my suspicions, but I don't think they raped Shenice. And if it's possible, a medical examiner will confirm that."

Corey turned to Eddie and tilted his head. "I thought you said that those guys attacked her."

"Yeah, before someone jumped me." Eddie turned to his friend. "I don't know what happened while I was knocked out or how long I was out for."

It was then that Eddie saw two of the bouncers talking into their mobile phones. He checked his own and saw that the signal was back.

"It's good that we're over here because I don't want anyone to overhear us."

"Overhear what?" asked Corey. "That you don't think Shenice was raped?"

Eddie shook his head as he continued watching the crowd. "Whoever that person is, their real name isn't Shenice."

"How do you know that?"

"Because I got a good look at the body before the bouncer shoved us away. I think this may be a hate crime." Eddie then turned to Corey while he thumbed in the direction of the deceased. "Shenice is a brotha."

Chapter 2

Freeport Police Station, Montego Bay, Jamaica

"Please state your full name," said the sergeant while he typed on his laptop. The officer introduced himself as Sergeant Henry. Eddie noticed how he barely made eye contact with him when he spoke. That, combined with his lazy attitude, was indicative that Henry did not want to be here. He slumped over the table, leaning on an elbow, while holding his wrist just in front of his mouth. For the first time, he looked Eddie in the eyes.

Eddie tugged the collar of the oversized t-shirt that the station gave him to replace the one he lost. He kept his facial expression neutral while staring back at the sergeant.

Eddie didn't need to read the sergeant's thoughts to know what was on his mind. His condescending mannerisms said: *This brethren is clearly from overseas because he's about to snitch. No average West Indian would do that.* And it was the only thing that made Eddie forget about the annoying rocking of his chair, as it kept teetering on its uneven leg.

Eddie dragged his chair forward, never taking his eyes off Sergeant Henry. "My name is Edward Barrow Junior."

"You don't need to lean in so close," barked the sergeant as his wrist swung out and changed to an open palm—pushing toward Eddie. "I'm not deaf."

Eddie snapped back to dodge Henry's hand. Not even thirty seconds passed since Eddie sat down and he'd already pissed the man off.

"What brings you to MoBay, Mister Barrow?"

"I'm here for a book signing."

"Book signing?" Henry sat back in his chair with his head cocked slightly to the side. "What kind of book signing?"

"I'm on tour for the release of my latest novel."

Henry's lip curled upward as he typed. "You're a writer?"

"Yes, I'm an author."

Henry stared at him a few moments with his head cocked. Eddie had gotten used to others not accepting him for what he did for a living—even other Black people, and the sergeant was one of them. It reminded him of the first signing for a book fair in Barbados. One out of five visitors to his booth didn't appear to accept that he was *the* Eddie Barrow. They were probably wondering how a young Black man could solve a murder for which he was framed. Corey often said had Eddie been white, his credentials never would've been questioned.

Eddie got tired of waiting for Henry to respond. "I thought I was here to give my statement. Is there something else you need to ask me, Sergeant?"

"How many books have you written, Mister Barrow?"

What the hell does this have to do with Shenice's murder?

Eddie bit back his annoyance. "I've just released my sixth."

"Your sixth?"

"Yes."

"So, you write books on the side. What's your *real* job?"

Eddie resisted the urge to roll his eyes. "This *is* my real job. If you want, I can put you in touch with my agent, Nancy Bevins. Or would you prefer I show you my tax returns?"

"Look. There's no reason for this attitude. Just answer the question."

"I just did. You're the one speculating about what my real job is, while I'm giving you the facts."

Just control your breathing, Eddie. This guy's trying to rattle your cage.

The door to the room swung open, catching Eddie's attention. A massive man, who towered at around six foot four, walked in. He looked like a retired Olympic shot putter who traded his tights for the two metal bars on the shoulder straps of his broad shoulders, ones that supported the bulky arms and large hands that could've crushed Eddie's neck with little effort.

"Mister Barrow." The way he accentuated Barrow was a blatant attempt to exude authority. "I'm Detective Inspector Leighton Ellis."

"Good, then maybe you can explain why your colleague's treating me like a suspect."

"Should you *be* concerned about being treated like one?" asked Ellis.

"No. I'm more concerned with you guys wasting your time trying to build a case against me, while letting the real killer, or killers, get away."

Henry turned to Ellis. "I was questioning him, and he got defensive."

"Your questions had nothing to do with the murder I witnessed," Eddie shot back. "It's as though you're trying to build a case against me."

"Who said that we're building a case against you?" asked Ellis.

"It's obvious that your sergeant doesn't believe anything I said." Okay, that was a bit too aggressive. Eddie closed his eyes, inhaled deeply, and glanced at the nametag pinned to Ellis's right breast pocket. "Look, Detective Inspector, I told your colleague that I'm a full-time author. I was going to say that I'm also the co-owner of a coffee shop back home in Montreal, with my friend, Corey Stephenson. You probably met him since he's also giving his statement."

Ellis looked up with raised eyebrows. "Montreal? Like in Canada?"

"Yes."

"Is that near British Columbia?"

Eddie shook his head. "BC's a province on the west coast. Montreal's in the province of Quebec—a good five-hour plane ride away."

"Yeah, I've heard of Quebec," Ellis said as he turned his head briefly, rolling his eyes. "I have a colleague whose son works in a paper mill in BC. Jamaica gets its paper from Canada, but demand has dropped because *you* young people prefer playing on your phones instead of reading a newspaper."

"Some of *us* young people see it as a way of saving trees."

Keep the control. Just breathe.

"Anyhow, according to my colleague, the mill his son worked at caught fire about nine months ago, and production in BC has gone down, only for Quebec to pick up most of the business."

Great. Now, this guy has another reason not to like me.

"Listen, as I said before, it was my understanding that you're questioning me because I'm a witness."

"How well did you know Shenice?" asked Ellis.

That was a reasonable question. "I met her at the bar tonight."

"You know you were dancing with a man, right?"

"No, I didn't know that Shenice was a guy. However, my gut was telling me something wasn't right. I didn't know what it was until after she was killed."

"Why you keep calling that man a *she* when you know he's a man?" scoffed Henry.

"I'm doing so out of respect for the victim." Eddie clenched his jaw. It was taking everything in him not to respond condescendingly to this homophobic asshole.

Eddie did not know what to make of Ellis, but he tolerated him. For now. He retold everything that happened from the moment he danced with Shenice to after he and Corey tried to save her. It was also a way for him to ignore Henry, who eyed him suspiciously.

"If I understand you correctly," said Ellis, "you went to the parking lot, saw two men attacking Shenice, right before someone attacked you from behind."

Eddie nodded. "That's what happened."

"You don't think you tripped, fell, hit your head, and knocked yourself out?"

Oh, for Christ's sake. "No, because right after, someone—and I'm assuming that it's the same person who hit me—dragged me up from behind. He held me in a way that made it impossible to move before he shoved a chemically soaked rag in my face. It knocked me out."

Henry dropped his head as he stifled a laugh.

Eddie turned to him. "What's so funny?"

"You'll have to excuse my sergeant," said Ellis. "But it's not very often we get stories like yours. Maybe you really are an author."

Maybe I'm really an author? "It's not a story." Why was he wasting his time here? These guys didn't believe him. Even Ellis seemed like he was looking to poke holes in what Eddie had told them.

"Moving on," said Ellis. "What can you tell me about the three men you said were trying to get away."

"After I regained consciousness, I searched the parking lot for Shenice, only to nearly get run over by the car they drove. I noticed right away that one of them had a problem with his eyes. The first thing that came to mind was that he'd been pepper sprayed. The other in the back seat formed a gun with his hand and pointed it at me before they sped off. Those two were the guys I saw attacking Shenice."

"And what about the third?"

"I saw him earlier in the club with his two friends, then later while he drove."

"Just to be clear, you didn't see the third man—the driver—attacking Shenice."

"I didn't see him with Shenice in the parking lot." Eddie shook his head. "Come to think of it, right after he nearly hit me with his car, his friend—the one who got pepper sprayed—called him Delroy."

"Did you get the make of the vehicle?"

"Yeah, a silver BMW."

Eddie noticed how Henry's eyes widened before he and Ellis exchanged glances. They couldn't make it more evident that those brothas were known to the police.

Ellis tilted his head with a slight twist toward Eddie while narrowing his eyes. "Are you sure?"

"I'm positive."

Ellis nodded to his sergeant, who then stopped the digital recorder. He turned to Eddie. "You can go."

"Just like that?"

"Is there anything else you want to add?"

Eddie shook his head. "Not now." He got up without pushing the chair back under the table. He didn't even bother acknowledging Ellis as he passed him on his way out.

"Just some advice, Mister Barrow."

Eddie turned around to Henry's voice.

"We don't tolerate no battyman. You're not in Canada, so just watch what you say and do around here."

Henry's words jolted him like a centipede's sting to the neck. "What did you just say?"

Henry sighed. "I said that you're not in Canada, so you need to be careful down here."

Eddie whipped out an index finger and walked back toward him while shaking his head. "Who's this *we* you just referred to?"

Ellis stretched out his massive arm in front of Eddie. "If we have other questions, we'll call."

Eddie turned to Ellis. He knew what he just heard, and he knew that Ellis heard it too. He sighed and shook his head. "I should've known. You're not going to take this investigation seriously just because the victim was gay."

"Go home, Mister Barrow. It's late," said Ellis.

Eddie sucked his teeth, turned, and walked away moments before he heard the door close behind him. It had been roughly twelve hours since he and Corey arrived, and now Eddie had this to deal with. The murder he witnessed three years before had traumatized him to the point that he needed almost five months of weekly therapy appointments after it was over. Seeing someone charring in front of him wouldn't help.

Why were Delroy and his friends known to the police? Were they in trouble with the law before, or were they related to well-known people in the community?

Among those who sat in the waiting area, Eddie saw Corey, just as the sleeping man sitting next to him fell to the side, his head landing on Corey's shoulder. Corey nudged the man in disgust—startling him awake.

"Bumboclaat!" said the man.

Corey swatted the air in front of his nose while scrunching up his face. "You ever hear of breath mints? Goddamn!" Corey got up as though to get away when he saw Eddie. "I thought you'd never get out of there."

"I couldn't get out soon enough." Eddie tossed his head toward the exit, and the two headed out.

"What happened? They kept grilling you for answers?"

Eddie pushed open the front door ahead of Corey, and they walked down the few stairs to the parking lot. "I don't want to talk about it."

As they walked, he saw that Corey was looking at him.

"You're not going to let this ruin our trip, are you?" asked Corey.

A few seconds went by when Corey put a hand on Eddie's shoulder to stop him.

Eddie turned to him. "What?"

"You know what," said Corey. "I know that look."

"What look?"

"The look that says you're going to keep thinking about this and not let it go."

"I don't have that look."

"Bullshit."

"Are we going to do this now?"

"Yes, we are. You're going to swear to me that you will let this go. You're going to focus on your book signing, which is…what time is it?"

"About a quarter to five."

"In a few hours," continued Corey. "Then we're going to have some fun on the beach, do a little sightseeing, go to your next book signing in Kingston, head back to the beach, do some more sightseeing, then party again if possible—"

"I can't believe you still want to go out partying. After what we saw tonight?"

"There's your problem, Eddie. You keep thinking about the past. If you keep doing so, you're going to screw up the book reading portion of your tour."

"I ain't going to have a problem reading my own book."

"If you won't let go of what's bothering you, you will."

"I'll be fine."

Corey chuckled.

"You don't think I can handle myself?"

"Not the way you are right now. I know how you can get."

Eddie walked around to the passenger side of their rental car and looked at Corey above the roof as he opened his door. "Once I'm standing in front of the mic, I'll be in my sanctuary. I'll be so immersed in what I'm reading I won't even be able to think about what happened tonight."

Corey smirked and nodded before getting in. "If you say so."

"I say what I know." Eddie got in and closed the door.

Corey drove out of their spot to exit onto Alice Eldemire Drive. "I have an American twenty in my wallet that says you'll fall apart tomorrow."

Eddie turned to his best friend. "You're on."

Chapter 3

Coral Reef Village and Suites Resort, Montego Bay

Vincent Lee Weiss had been in love with Jamaica ever since PennSteel held their first conference. These yearly events were retreats that served to award the company's top salespersons. He recalled when he started on the plant floor thirty years before, becoming the company's executive vice-president—a position he held for the past eight years. Today, he had managerial control over the Braddock, Pennsylvania-based company, which traded on the New York Stock Exchange for the past five years.

Last year, under 's leadership, it became the third-largest steelmaker in the United States. He was also instrumental in bringing the company back to the same resort each year. There was an endless supply of booze, multiple swimming pools, jet-ski rentals, and parasailing activities. This was topped off with a breathtaking ocean view and a white sandy beach that went on for miles.

As a ritual, Vincent woke up around six-thirty to do his morning run. The beach was his preferred spot, and he always timed it around sunrise. It wasn't the most straightforward task, as the sand made for extra resistance—the equivalent to running with ankle weights—but it beat running indoors on a treadmill on a rainy day. Sure, there was a fully equipped indoor gym, but he could always wait until he got back home to work out indoors.

He was near the end of his run when he checked his iWatch. His heartrate had slowed down. Weiss's run was three minutes slower than when he first arrived a week ago, with his wife and daughter for their annual after New Year's family trip. While they flew back home two days before, he stayed, as the conference was in the exact location.

"Damn," he mumbled.

The stress over an incident three nights ago was still eating away at him. And even though his attorney helped settle the problem, he couldn't get it out of his mind. Thank God his wife and daughter weren't around.

Weiss walked from the sand and onto a stone pathway through the bush. A security guard he knew as Calvin greeted him. As Weiss continued walking, three women were on their daily routine of sweeping away fallen palm leaves.

One after the next, they nodded, speaking a predictable refrain, chanting, "Good morning, Mister Weiss," as he passed them. Sure, the average guest got the "good morning" or "good afternoon" greetings, but *he* got the personalized greetings. Of course, they were pandering for tips, gifts, or both.

Unlike the central building, he had more privacy in a separate gated home, which he stood outside of, while he kicked off his beach shoes, then shook out the sand. He then swiped the key card against the door's sensor and let himself in. All he wanted was to lie down across his bed and catch a few *ZZs* until breakfast was ready. That thought disappeared once he saw that one of the oak double doors at the back was wide open. He knew he didn't leave any doors unlocked when he left his home. The first thing that came to mind was to find the nearest object he could use as a weapon.

"Relax, Vincent, come out and join us."

The words startled him. It was a woman's voice, not one he knew. The fact that she knew his name didn't sit well with him. And her accent did not sound Jamaican. It sounded American. Then again, she may have dropped her accent for his benefit.

The second oak door was pulled open from outside, revealing a Black woman sitting with her legs crossed at the table where he usually ate breakfast. She could've passed for being in her mid to late fifties. But it was her jaw-dropping, bare-shoulder, ruffled, cream-colored top that demonstrated that she was a woman of high authority. Not to mention how the color of the blouse accentuated her toned, dark arms. Her legs, however, were hidden under the matching wide-legged pants and flat sandals. If there were a clone produced from the genes of Alfre Woodard and Viola Davis, it would be her.

Standing next to her was a much younger, athletic Black man—dressed in an unbuttoned blue polo with beige slacks. He had his arms crossed, while leaning against one of the pillars that supported the edge of the roof that hung over the patio. He must be the muscle.

To his right, Weiss sensed movement. He looked there, and saw a henchwoman, around the same age as the henchman outside, sitting near the bottom of the staircase.

Weiss turned back to the older woman. "Who are you, and who let you in?"

The brotha grabbed the back of the basket-weaved chair and dragged it from under the table.

The woman narrowed her gaze. "Take a seat."

The icy tone in her voice made his throat go dry. He swallowed and turned to the creaking sound from the stairs as the henchwoman stood. Without taking her eyes off him, she nodded toward her partners. He glanced back and forth between the henchman and the henchwoman. It was as though they dared him not to comply. Seeing that he did not have a choice, he went out to the patio. The male muscle did not release the back of the chair until Weiss was seated.

"Does running every morning help clear your head?" asked the woman as she scooped out the teabag with her spoon.

"It helps…somewhat."

He studied her. He still wanted to know who they were, but he had the feeling that it would anger them if he were to ask. Weiss didn't want to test their patience—especially the hired muscle, who stared at him while leaning against the pillar, his arms crossed, with a fixed gaze.

"You must have many questions." The woman took a sip of her tea. "I hope you don't mind. You didn't have any tea, so I brought my own."

They rifled through my belongings? "Are you going to tell me what this is about?"

"I just thought we'd pay you a visit so that you could have a chance to meet the ones who cleaned up your mess."

"What mess?"

The woman gave him a shady glance. "Don't be coy, Vincent."

Weiss noticed that she paused, maybe to give him a chance to think about what she said.

The woman sighed. "You need to do a better job choosing whose panties you get into."

His hand shot to his mouth as he sat back in his chair and crossed his leg while looking away.

"Ah, you didn't think anyone else would find out, did you?"

"What did you do?"

"Your partner didn't think that your way of handling things would keep your secrets airtight. That's why we're here, to clean up your mess permanently."

"You…you killed…?"

"We had a job to do, and we did it. You ought to show a bit more gratitude," the woman said as she drank the last of her tea.

"Oh my God."

"Don't worry. It'll blow over soon."

"Really? Murder isn't something that I can forget."

"The police have way too many murder cases to solve," the woman answered. "They won't have resources left over for this case—considering who the victim is."

Weiss sighed and shook his head. "I didn't want any of this."

"Then you should've chosen a better hobby," the woman spat. "And if you don't want the situation to get any worse, I suggest you keep your hands to yourself and your pants on. Do I make myself clear?"

Weiss hesitated for a bit, then nodded.

"Good." The woman smiled and then stood. "I'm glad that we understand each other."

Chapter 4

*Daynea's Book Haven, Whitter Village Mall,
   Montego Bay, Jamaica*

Eddie knew that he had just lost twenty bucks to Corey. He felt his drawers clinging to him as he faced his audience. Even the book he held in his hands was slippery. What did the bookstore do with his book that it wound up like this? And that damn ringing in his ears wouldn't go away—another reminder why Eddie did not like nightclubs.

So much for this place being his sanctuary.

There was no fooling Corey, who sat in the front row with his arms crossed and his head cocked to the side, staring at Eddie, wide-eyed with the *I told you so* look. The audience of forty to fifty, around and behind Corey, couldn't have noticed that Eddie was losing control, so he began to read out loud. Three pages in, he realized that the paper was sticking to his fingers. It was him. His palms were sweaty. This didn't usually happen, and it shouldn't. He wasn't overdressed, just an oxford short-sleeve shirt with some khaki shorts.

Eddie paused as he glanced over everyone, both seated and standing. He grabbed the water bottle he left on the stool behind him and took a swig. No, he couldn't fall apart, not now.

Just get through this, then get to a liquor store to grab some overproof rum and head back to the Airbnb.

There he could hang with Corey and let a bottle of Coruba chase away last night's troubles. He glanced briefly at Corey in the front row, who gave him a nod as though to say, *You got this.*

"Sorry about that." Eddie scratched his right temple and cleared his throat before continuing.

He didn't know how many noticed that he was slipping, but if anyone did, it was difficult to tell with the applause he got in the end. As he did with every book signing, he took a selfie where he stood in front of everyone while they held copies of his book above their heads.

Before the reading, Eddie's interview with one of Jamaica's top media personalities had been easier. He was not asked too many controversial questions—unless one counted the time he and Corey were fleeing the authorities in the dead of winter after being framed for murder, all while dressed as a dom. Eddie was just relieved that he was not asked about last night's incident. Besides, he didn't go public with what happened. Hopefully, no one who was at Citrusville was sitting in the audience right now.

The interviewer poked fun at Corey by bringing up his infamous viral audition on a singing competition program. Corey responded by standing and turning to the audience, then he sang three flawless verses of a popular Machel Montano song—complete with his Trinidadian accent. The cheers he got put to rest any doubts about his singing ability.

The reading was rocky, but Eddie was happy sitting behind a table and signing books his fans brought. There were more selfies, smiles, a very short chat, then onto the next person.

But it was the thirteenth individual—a teenage girl—that gave Eddie a sense of Déjà-Vu. He didn't know why, but something about her made him study her facial features a bit more than the others. She was definitely among the youngest in the group—the oldest being probably in their sixties. This one couldn't be much older than fourteen. She was chubby, around five feet tall, with form-fitting jeans and a short-sleeved tunic. She took out all four of Eddie's books from the plastic bag she held and placed them on the table.

Eddie smiled. "Hey there, what's your name?"

"I'm Jalissa. Nice to meet you at last."

"My pleasure. It's always great meeting my readers," he said as he opened to the title page of his first novel. "Is your name spelled with one S or two?"

"Actually, I'd like you to make it out to myself and also to my brother…my…"

Eddie waited for her to continue but sensed something was wrong. She blinked rapidly before her eyes welled up with tears.

She shook her head and dropped the plastic bag on the floor. "I'm sorry." Jalissa ran away but stumbled and fell.

Eddie jumped out of his chair to see if she was hurt. It was apparent that she hit the floor hard. The incident didn't go unnoticed as a few patrons and staff rushed to her aid.

Eddie politely asked the others to let him through, and they obliged.

She was on her hands and knees by the time he got to her. "Are you okay?" He was curious to know what brought on that reaction.

She shook her head as she sobbed. She was near deadweight in his arms as Eddie helped her stand.

"My brother, Dwayne, was a big fan of your books. He was murdered last night at a bar."

There were several gasps in the background as Eddie looked to the side.

A Bar? "By any chance, was he at Citrusville?"

Jalissa nodded with a bowed head.

No wonder she looked familiar. She had Dwayne's—Shenice's—eyes, and lips.

He looked around, seeing the mixture of emotions from everyone. How could he continue the book signing? He glanced at Corey, who was just as surprised as he was.

Daynea the owner rushed to see them. "It's okay, young lady." With her big arms, she hugged Jalissa, cushioning her cries. She then turned to Eddie. "Don't worry. I'll take care of her. Go back with your other fans."

"I'll stay with her too," Corey said to Eddie just as one of the patrons passed him a small stack of tissue paper wrapped in plastic.

"I'll come and see you after." Eddie handed the tissues to Jalissa. "Is that all right?"

She pulled out a tissue, dabbed at the tears, then nodded. The crowd was at least supportive, applauding as Corey and the store manager walked Jalissa over to a chair and sat with her.

Eddie was another ten minutes into the signing when one of the store employees walked up to him behind the table.

"I'm sorry to interrupt," she said as she handed him a business card. "But there's someone who insists on speaking to you."

Eddie's eyes bulged when he saw the name. "Is this a joke?"

She shook her head then gestured toward the entrance where the man stood. "He's standing right over there."

Eddie looked where she pointed and saw a Caucasian man. He was around five nine, had a slight gut, and dressed as though he was about to play golf against Tiger Woods. It was Dennis Denton, one of the biggest names in Hollywood, who then waved to him. Could this be happening? A filmmaker knew who Eddie was and wanted to speak to him. It took everything to contain his excitement as he stood and turned to the employee. "I'll be back."

"No problem, sir."

As Eddie got up, he glanced briefly to the next woman in line. He nodded to her as he raised an index finger—signaling that he'd be away momentarily. As he walked off, the same employee announced to the crowd that Eddie would be back in a few minutes and thanked them in advance for their patience.

A section of the store was cordoned off with a velvet rope where Eddie met Denton.

Denton already had his hand out. "I can't believe it. This is my lucky day."

He grabbed and pulled Eddie toward him so hard that Eddie nearly lost his balance. "I...I...can't believe it myself," Eddie answered. "It's an honor."

"I guess it's just one of those moments where we're at the right place at the right time," said Denton. "Normally, I would've had my assistant contact your agent to set up an appointment. But when I read the paper and saw that you were in the area for a book signing, I'm like screw the formalities, I should just show up."

Eddie was still at a loss for words—he was on cloud nine. "I'm sorry that I'm so tongue-tied, but this is a big surprise for me. When I got your business card, I was like, yeah, right. And then I saw you, and then I was like holy sh—well, you know."

"I think you meant to say, *Bumboclaat!*" chuckled Denton.

"That's what you all say, right?"

Eddie cringed but caught himself, hoping that it wasn't so obvious. "Uh...no. My origins are Barbadian. We don't speak Jamaican Patois."

Denton's eyebrows rose suddenly. "Oh my God, Eddie. I'm sorry for the assumption, I shouldn't have said that. By the way, you don't mind me calling you Eddie, do you?"

Eddie shook his head.

"Good." He patted Eddie on the back. "Look, I don't want to hold you back any longer. I'm scouting locations for a future project, so I'll be here for the next few days. Call the number on the card so that we can meet for lunch. My assistant is expecting your call. I see some huge potential in your novels."

"You've read them?"

"Don't be naïve." Denton nodded. "Why else would I want to see you?"

Eddie was feeling a bit faint, and it was as though the air conditioner in the store suddenly malfunctioned. "Wow, I don't know what to say."

"Just say that you'll call the number once you're finished with your book signing, and we can take it from there." Denton grabbed Eddie's hand. "Deal?"

Eddie couldn't hold back his joy and shook Denton's hand. "Deal."

Denton patted Eddie on the back again. "We'll talk soon."

After Denton left, Eddie made his way back to the table, when Corey intercepted him. "Who was that?"

Eddie grabbed his best friend just below his shoulders. "That was Dennis Denton."

"Who?"

"What do you mean, *who*? You know the *Galaxy War* series and the *Hudson Valley Stalker*?"

"*He* did those?"

"Yeah?"

"I thought those were Dennis Denton flicks?"

Eddie rolled his eyes. "I just told you that's who I just met."

Reality seemed to hit Corey finally. "No."

"Yes."

"No way."

"Way."

"And he wants to turn your books into movies?"

"He said he wants to have lunch."

Corey slapped both palms to Eddie's shoulders in excitement. "Shit, that's amazing. I'm happy for you, bruh."

"But we can't tell anyone, okay."

"Got it." Corey nodded.

Eddie then went back to the table to continue signing more books and taking selfies with fans, while Corey went back to sit with Jalissa.

The crowd slowly dispersed over the next half hour as the signing came to a close. In the end, it was only Corey and Jalissa sitting near the back. Her books were still on the table, so Eddie brought them as he took the empty seat beside her.

Eddie took Jalissa's hand, only to remember how sweaty his palms were. He released her hand and swiped his on his shirt. "Please accept my sympathy. What happened to your brother was despicable."

"Thank you," her voice cracked as she replied with a nod. She appeared to be holding it together much better than earlier.

"Were you at the bar last night?" Eddie asked.

Jalissa shook her head. "No, my parents would never allow me to stay out that late."

Corey gave back Eddie's mobile. He had been holding onto it for the duration of the signing. "Jalissa was telling me about Dwayne. He obviously recognized you last night, which is why he danced with you."

"He *really* wanted to be here," said Jalissa as she gestured to the surrounding chairs. "This event was all he's been talking about ever since he learned that you were coming to MoBay. I got into your books because of him."

"Again, I'm so sorry about what happened to him," said Eddie. "I would've loved to have seen him here, you know, again. How are your parents?"

Jalissa closed her eyes tight as she shook her head. "Life goes on for them."

Eddie leaned back. "How so?"

"My parents disowned Dwayne four years ago. My father was harsher on him than my mother—whom he blamed for turning my brother gay by teaching him how to sew." Jalissa sat back in her chair and sighed. "My brother was gifted. And he was often teased and bullied by his classmates because he was…different. It got so bad that he dropped out in his last year of secondary school to maintain his sanity. He only had to endure more of it at home."

"In other words, your father saw him as being too effeminate," said Eddie.

"He never stopped berating him for it," said Jalissa. "While most boys in his class were into the so-called 'manly' activities, Dwayne was more interested in drawing."

"He wanted to be an artist," said Corey.

"A fashion designer," said Jalissa. "That was his dream. It's just that it was hard for him to get started. He used my dolls to practice making dresses. He even made me a dress for my birthday—one that I could wear to church."

Eddie noticed as she clenched her eyes shut and looked away. Something about what she just said had upset her. "Did Dwayne go to church also?"

"He did." Jalissa nodded. "Despite what was said about him, he still went."

"Let me guess," said Corey. "The minister often spoke about homosexuals going to Hell, right?"

"Worse. That man would say things like that while looking at Dwayne. He even invited a guest preacher named Pastor Green. He's very popular down here. When it comes to attacking gays at the pulpit, that man's the worst of them all. Radio and TV stations broadcast his church services. All he talks about is how gays are going to burn and that they must repent. When he attacked my brother during that particular service, it took me everything not to jump up and scream at him." Jalissa grabbed another tissue and dabbed it below her right eye. "People say that Jesus speaks through our pastor. But I never knew Jesus to show anyone so much hatred."

"Your parents forced Dwayne to go to church?" Eddie asked.

Jalissa shook her head. "No, Dwayne liked going to church. After that incident with Pastor Green, he went to another church."

"You were saying earlier that he made you a dress—one that everyone liked."

Time to bring back the conversation from off a tangent.

"Yes, with a matching hat, purse, and shoes. I wish I never told everyone that." Jalissa let her head drop into her hands for a moment. She then turned to Eddie. "Dwayne made the dress in secret, then asked our Aunt Amancia to gift it to me in front of our parents as though she made it. That way they wouldn't suspect Dwayne made it. But stupid me, people at church asked me where I got it and, by mistake, I told them that Dwayne made it. It didn't take long before Daddy found out. And when we got home, he stormed into Dwayne's bedroom, grabbed his scrapbook, and tore it up. He began throwing things everywhere. Dwayne tried to stop him, but Daddy just began to beat him, over and over and over. I pleaded with my father to stop. But all that happened was that he slammed Dwayne's bedroom door. My mother then scolded me for encouraging his so-called 'girly' habits."

"But wasn't she the one who taught him how to sew?"

"My mother stopped teaching him once my father intervened. So, Dwayne taught himself in secret. My parents didn't know this, but one of his friends had a sewing machine. That's where he'd go. I knew this but never told my parents."

"For obvious reasons," said Corey.

"It wasn't fair. My brother had a passion, and he should've been allowed to express it. But in the end, it didn't matter," said Jalissa. "The way Dwayne cried in agony. I thought my father was going to kill him. The next thing I knew was that Daddy stormed out of Dwayne's room with a suitcase and threw it out the front door. He then went back for Dwayne, dragged him out of the room across the floor by his legs, and threw him out onto the street." Jalissa sniffed to clear her nose while wiping away a tear. "It's all my fault."

"Don't blame yourself." Eddie put a hand on her shoulder. "You didn't do it on purpose."

Eddie did his best to hold back the frustration that built up inside. He'd heard numerous stories where gays and lesbians in Jamaica were continuously persecuted. Gay-bashing stories were commonplace in Jamaica, but to learn that this happened to someone he was briefly acquainted with was beyond devastating.

"That wasn't all," Jalissa continued. "The entire village came down on him with taunts and insults. Calling him names such as 'batty bwoy, girly man.' He was pelted with all types of objects—mostly empty cans and bottles. The last I saw of my brother that day, there was blood and bruises all over his face, and his eye was swollen shut, and that was before he faced the village."

That's when the tears flowed once more. "I had no choice but to watch from the window, begging the neighbors to stop. My parents wouldn't even let me go out to help him or even say goodbye. He had no money, no help. I was worried about how he would survive. I picked up the pages from his scrapbook and spent over an hour taping them back together. I was going to give it back to him so that he wouldn't need to start over from scratch. He called me several days later to tell me that two drag queens let him stay with them. I was going to bring him his scrapbook, but he told me that he had memorized his designs and had already reproduced them."

Jalissa sighed. "Designing clothes was the one thing that made him happy. It helped distract him from the problems he faced regularly."

Eddie rested his elbows on his legs as he leaned forward. He stared ahead at the table where he sat, just thinking that nearly forty minutes earlier, he was entertaining a group of his fans. He never thought that he'd be consoling one of them.

He turned to Jalissa. "I can't say that I got to know your brother. I have to admit that I thought that I was dancing with a woman."

"You and everyone," Corey reminded.

Eddie closed his eyes and nodded once. "All I can say is that the person I was with last night, well, he wasn't someone who appeared to hold any pain, or any grudges. Dwayne was happy, and he didn't look as though he was oppressed in any way. He was free."

More tears formed in Jalissa's eyes as she reached over to hug Eddie. "Thank you."

He looked over Jalissa's shoulder at Corey and made a facial expression that said: *Come on, join in. You know the drill.*

Corey understood the message and leaned, stretching his arms past Jalissa to Eddie. The hug lasted a few seconds when Jalissa cleared her throat.

"Just to let you know," said Eddie, "Corey and I went down to the police station after the party and gave full statements to what we saw."

Jalissa rolled her eyes. "As though that's going to change anything."

Eddie raised an eyebrow. "What's that?"

"You can go back and give a hundred reports, and the police still won't do anything."

Eddie looked at Corey, and then back at Jalissa, who nodded.

"That's right. Nothing's going to be done." She glanced at them. "I'm sure you're the only two who came forward. Those parties usually have upward of two hundred people. You can't convince me that nobody saw who attacked my brother."

"Don't lose hope," said Eddie. "Just because more people didn't show up at the police station yesterday doesn't mean that they won't come forward later."

"Not likely," said Corey. "People ain't going to talk. They don't want to make themselves targets."

"Listen to your friend," said Jalissa. "People are afraid of reprisals. And now that everyone knows that Shenice is a man, you can be sure that none of them will want to come forward. I mean, did you see the nasty things people are saying on Facebook about him? I couldn't even listen to the radio because of all the horrible things callers said. They're assassinating his character, and they never knew him."

"The first thing you need to do is change the settings on all your social media accounts so that people can't leave comments or contact you directly. You know what? You're better off deleting your account totally and staying off social media."

Jalissa wiped away a tear. "Okay."

"I...I wish there was more that I could do. I don't know what else to say," said Eddie.

"You can start by autographing her books." Corey pointed to the bag on the chair beside him.

"Oh yeah, right." Eddie grabbed the first book and wrote a sympathy message to her, while addressing Dwayne. He did the same with the rest, when Jalissa spoke.

"Come to think of it. There's something you *can* do."

Eddie moved on to the next book. "Anything."

Jalissa paused to swallow, then took a deep breath. "I want you to find out who murdered my brother."

Eddie nearly dropped the pen. "Come again?"

Jalissa took another deep breath as she glanced ahead at the stage. She then looked Eddie in the eyes. "I want to hire you to find my brother's killers."

The request alone felt like being shot with a rubber bullet. Eddie rubbed the back of his neck. "I...I...wasn't expecting this sort of request. I don't know how—"

"Weren't you once framed for murder?" asked Jalissa.

Eddie tilted his head to the side. "Well yeah, but—"

"And despite the odds, the police, witnesses, with little to no money to your names, you," she quickly glanced at Corey, "and you, with your girlfriend, found out who the real killers were, exposed them, and cleared your names."

"She's my wife, actually," said Corey.

Eddie struggled to find the words. "Well, we did, but..."

"But what?" asked Jalissa. "You had no help, no encouragement, and the whole world was against you. Yet you managed to expose a conspiracy that could've fleeced millions from people."

"It was more or less a billion," Corey added.

"We lucked out," said Eddie.

"Whatever," said Jalissa. "The point is that you solved a murder on your own. I don't think you lucked out. I refuse to believe that. You probably don't remember what you did or how you did it. But considering that you sent many bad people to prison, you had to have done *something* right. Tell me I'm wrong?"

Eddie had run out of excuses. He was supposed to be in

Kingston tomorrow for his other book signing. Even if he investigated things for Jalissa, he and Corey would never have the time. Their flight back to Montreal would leave in two days.

Eddie gestured to Corey. "We need to talk."

Eddie excused himself from Jalissa as he and Corey walked into one of the aisles between two bookshelves, where they were alone.

"How are we going to let her down easy?" asked Corey.

Eddie made a face. "What do you mean, let her down? We have to do something, I mean, isn't there something we can do?"

"We *did* do something. We gave a police statement, which was probably too much because we probably made ourselves marked men."

"Come on. Can't we at least give Jalissa some peace of mind that we did all we could?"

"We've already done that. Come on, bro, you're not Sherlock Holmes, and I sure as hell ain't…uh…"

"Watson."

"Yeah, him."

"Or *her*, depending on the version of the story."

"Whatever. We're neither one."

"No, we're not. But how *did* we solve a murder on our own last time?"

"Well, that time we went into it already knowing stuff in advance. What do we know so far?"

Eddie shrugged. "I know that the same guys who tried to mess with Shenice-slash-Dwayne in the club nearly ran me over in the parking lot while I was looking for her."

"Yeah, and?"

"Guys looking to grope someone they thought was a woman? You think they were *only* there to enjoy the music?"

Corey shrugged his shoulders. "So, they were looking to fuck. Practically all the guys at the party were thinking about getting some. I'm sure you were too."

"Except the ones I saw were ready to take it a step further. I know what I saw last night."

"Did you mention this to the police?"

"Yeah," Eddie said. "And seeing how they reacted after I called out one of the suspects by name, I know they know who they were."

"Then it's solved. Dwayne's attackers will be questioned, arrested, then hopefully charged."

"And you believe that?" asked Eddie. "I didn't get a good feeling from those two officers who took my statement. I'd like to know more about those three guys. I just don't know where to start."

"Whoa." Corey gestured with a downward palm. "Why don't we wait for the police to do their jobs first. Besides, Jalissa's grieving. The last thing you want to do is start making promises you know you can't keep."

"We can't just sit here and do nothing."

"Think about how much more you'll hurt her if you come up empty handed."

"I'll pay you." Eddie and Corey were startled as they didn't notice Jalissa standing beside them. "I don't know how, but I know Dwayne had lots of friends. I could start a GOFUNDME campaign online. I'm sure that I could raise money to pay you."

Eddie looked back at Corey, who was just as much at a loss for words. Eddie then turned to Jalissa. "It's not about the money."

"Don't get us wrong. Money's not a bad thing," added Corey.

Eddie elbowed Corey, then turned to Jalissa. "I…I wasn't prepared for this."

"Can't you just take a look?" She then gestured to Corey. "Earlier, you told the interviewer that Eddie's capable of spotting things that most people won't see, and that it's sort of like a sixth sense to him—Oh, I almost forgot." She reached inside her handbag, took out what appeared to be a scrapbook, and held it up in the air. "This is all that I have left of my brother."

"What's in it?" asked Corey.

"Some of my brother's fashion designs." She turned to Eddie. "There are others, but I didn't have time to find them because I didn't want to miss my bus ride over here. Dwayne had big dreams, just like you. He worked very hard, and even though he was robbed of an opportunity, he still didn't give up—right up until the point that his life was cut short."

Jalissa then put the scrapbook back in her handbag and looked at Eddie and Corey. "All I'm asking is that you take a look. Go back to the nightclub and see if you spot something. Something *has* to be there."

Eddie dropped his head into his hand while reflecting on what he was about to tell Jalissa. She was asking a lot, especially considering that he wasn't a private investigator.

He then turned to her. "This is a tall order you're asking. The truth is, I'm not a detective. What happened a few years ago, well, it just happened. Corey and I were lucky to come out of it alive."

"I see." Jalissa nodded her head, while she sniffed. "You're not going to help. That's okay, I mean, I knew I was asking for too much. I'll just have to accept that."

Eddie pinched the bridge of his nose as he lowered his head. "I didn't say that." He sighed, then held her shoulders with both hands, and looked at her. "Corey and I aren't doing anything this afternoon. I'll take a look at the crime scene and see if I spot anything. But I'm not making any promises."

Both Jalissa's eyes and mouth widened. "You will? I mean, of course. Thank you for doing this." She then smothered Eddie with a hug. She did the same with Corey. "What now?"

"Let me and Corey worry about that."

"Yes, of course," she answered.

"I'm going to need your number," said Eddie. "Do you have a cell phone?"

"Yes, but I have to top up every so often, so I have to be careful with my usage."

"Got it," said Eddie.

"Let me ask you," said Corey. "Do you let anyone else use your phone?"

"Well, from time to time, I may let a friend use it, but not too often," Jalissa answered.

"Don't let anyone use your phone," said Corey.

"And be sure to clear your call list frequently," said Eddie. "Are your parents the hovering type?"

"Hovering?" asked Jalissa.

"Yeah," answered Eddie. "Are they always checking up on everything you do?"

"Sometimes, but not too often."

"Meaning that I can send you a text message without worrying that they'll be reading them?" asked Eddie.

"Yes, I'll be extra careful."

Eddie shook his head. "Then we're good. Corey and I'll see what we can find. As I said earlier, I'm not making any promises. But if we learn something, we'll forward it to the police. Hopefully, they'll take us seriously."

"Okay, got it," she said as Eddie took out his mobile.

"Are you on WhatsApp or Signal?" asked Eddie. Given the situation, he did not want to leave anything to chance that someone would hack their phones to spy on them. WhatsApp and Signal apps had end-to-end encryption to prevent that.

Jalissa nodded. "WhatsApp."

Eddie handed her his phone. "Give me your number."

She dialed her number into it and pressed the send icon. Jalissa then handed it back to him as her mobile buzzed, displaying Eddie's number. Eddie saved the number she dialed under her name.

"Save my number too," he instructed, "but don't use my real name in your contact info. Whenever you need to text or call, only do so with WhatsApp."

"Got it."

"Also, it's important that you don't tell *anyone* what you asked of us. For your safety and ours."

"I understand." Something on her cell phone caught her attention. "Oh, I've got to go." She reached over and grabbed the bag of books. "Thanks again. This means so much."

Eddie and Corey nodded in response.

Just as she was walking away, Eddie called out to her. "Jalissa."

She stopped to face them.

"You have to keep this between us. I can't stress that enough. Not even your closest friends."

"Oh yes." She nodded. "I won't make that mistake."

She then left the store.

Making sure that no one else was around, Corey turned to Eddie and sighed. "What do we do now?"

"Easy," answered Eddie. "We're going to go back to where it all started."

Wan han wash de oda

—Jamaican Proverb

One hand washes the other.

Chapter 5

"Dennis Denton? You met him in person?" It was Eddie's agent, Nancy Bevins, whose excitement partially muffled her voice through the car's Bluetooth. Corey lowered the volume slightly from the controls on the steering wheel as he drove.

Eddie reached for his wallet and took out Denton's business card. "I couldn't believe it myself."

"I have to say, this is great." Eddie heard the mixture of disbelief and excitement in her voice. "I tried shopping your books around to my contacts in the film industry for the past two years, and they kept on telling me the same thing, that your stories aren't what they're looking for right now. Do you have his contact info on you now?"

Eddie had the business card. "I'm holding it."

"Just a second, let me get a pen and paper." There was a short pause, then, "All right, go ahead."

Eddie gave her Denton's digits and put away the card.

"Let me speak to him and set up the appointment," said Bevins. "We'll set up a teleconference, while you meet him to discuss things."

Eddie smiled. "Sounds like a plan."

"Great, I'll get on it later today," said Bevins. "By the way, what's this about a drag queen being murdered in Montego Bay last night?"

"The police actually called you?" Eddie couldn't believe that Detective Inspector Ellis or the sergeant took him seriously when Eddie told him about Ms. Bevins—considering that neither asked for her number.

"No, I was having lunch with a friend who works for one of the local LGBTQ organizations, and he told me about it. Why would they call me?"

So they hadn't called her. "Well," Eddie began, "Corey and I were there. It happened right in front of us, so the police questioned us." Eddie then summarized the events from the night before.

"My God, how are you both now?"

"We're good, just a bit shaken," Eddie answered. "Corey and I gave our witness statements, but if you ask me, they're not going to take this murder seriously."

"Why do you say that?"

"You should've been there. The officers didn't even bother to hide their homophobia."

"I've read about that sort of thing," said Bevins. "But you're not going to be able to change that. Just cooperate with them if they call you."

Eddie sighed. "Yeah, sure."

"Is that a hint of sarcasm in your voice?"

"Yes, it is," said Corey. Eddie shot him a stare.

"Eddie?" asked Bevins.

He still scowled at Corey, who ignored him while he drove.

"Eddie."

"Yes."

"Please don't tell me that you're thinking about snooping around for clues."

"I…I'm just curious about some…things."

"Oh my God! Don't you remember what happened the last time you got involved in a murder investigation?"

"I was framed. It's not like I had a choice," Eddie rebutted.

Bevins was referring to when he and Corey were the prime suspects in an S&M-related murder of a VIP. The provincial-wide manhunt was front-page news all over North America.

"You know what I meant," continued Bevins. "Just promise me that you won't get involved."

"He already promised the victim's sister that he would," said Corey.

"Goddammit, Corey!" Eddie slugged Corey's arm.

"Jesus, Eddie, you already questioned the victim's sister?" said Bevins. "Are you out of your mind?"

"It's not like that," said Eddie. "She showed up at the book signing and literally begged me to look into her brother's murder. I couldn't say no to her."

"Do you realize what you've just done?" Bevins paused as though to gain her composure. "I know you mean well, but this is the victim's sister we're talking about. She's in shock, and she's grieving."

"I know, but what would you have me do?" said Eddie. "She was devastated. I couldn't say no to her. I told her that I would look around, and if I learned anything, I'd share it with the police. But I didn't make any promises."

Eddie pictured Bevins sitting at her office desk with her head in both hands, shaking it from side to side.

"Just promise me that you two will stay out of trouble."

"We will," said Corey.

"Eddie?" said Bevins.

"I promise."

"Good. I have everything set up for the Kingston book signing. You two take care."

"We will." Eddie was about to turn off the phone app when he remembered the fundraiser. "Oh, by the way. I'm setting up a crowdfunding campaign to help cover the funeral expenses. I'll send you a link to give to your friend."

"That's a great idea," said Bevins. "I'm sure I can find a few donors. Talk to you soon."

Eddie tapped the screen to turn off the phone app.

"She's right, you know," said Corey. "Us snooping around isn't a good idea."

"We won't be doing much," said Eddie. "No one will know what we're up to."

"I hope so."

Seconds later, a radio talk show was on, and, coincidentally, the topic was Dwayne Pottinger. Corey raised the volume via the controls on the steering wheel. He didn't get a chance to catch the host's name. Still, Eddie heard her introducing her two guests—Dane Lewis, the former executive director of the Jamaica Forum for Lesbians, All-Sexuals & Gays, otherwise known as J-FLAG. Her second guest was Pastor Benedict Green, who was well known throughout the Caribbean. He was also very outspoken in his strong stance against homosexuals. The two debated back and forth over Dwayne's choice of dress and the rights of homosexuals. To no surprise to Eddie, Pastor Green brought up Sodom and Gomorrah and how Jamaica is a Christian nation.

"Ain't that the same pastor Jalissa spoke of earlier?" asked Corey.

"It must be," answered Eddie.

A few people who called in expressed their sympathy for Dwayne. But the majority attacked him, tossing out hate-filled statements.

"Good riddance, he brought this pon heself."

"Judgement under he backside. Bun out the boom, bye-bye, battyman."

"Lightning, lava, brimstone, and fiya pon mud fishes. God done set example with he a Sodom and Gomorrah so who don't take heed will feel."

Eddie sucked his teeth and turned off the radio. He knew that Pottinger's death would bring out the worst in people down here. But the harshness of those comments made him want to call the radio station and cuss out the host for not screening these calls.

"You could've asked me to change stations," said Corey.

"Go ahead." Eddie logged onto GoFundMe.com with his smartphone. At the same time, Corey turned back on the radio, but switched the station to music instead.

Eddie took a few moments to set up the funeral fund for Dwayne Pottinger, and shared it with his email mailing list, his blog, and his social media platforms. He then wrote a press release and emailed it to Bevins. It was only a draft, but Eddie expected her to polish it and submit it.

He then logged onto Facebook. It wasn't too long before he found videos related to Dwayne's murder. On Twitter, Dwayne Pottinger was trending. Eddie never cared to watch videos of people fighting or making fools of themselves on social media. However, for Dwayne Pottinger, he made an exception. Not only were there videos of the crime scene, but there were also videos posted throughout the evening.

"What are you looking at?" said Corey, who obviously heard the noise coming from Eddie's phone.

"We still have about five minutes left before we get to the bar," said Eddie. "I thought I'd check out some of the stuff others posted from last night."

Corey glanced at him briefly before looking back to the road. "Why? You're just going to see a bunch of sympathies or hate comments."

"I know," Eddie answered. "But I'm looking to see if any of the three guys I saw left comments. And if they have their actual picture in their profile, it'll help me identify them."

"You think they'll be that dumb?"

"You never know." Eddie scrolled through one hate-filled homophobic comment after the next. "A few years ago, a North Carolina bank employee stole over eighty-eight grand from the vault. He was then dumb enough to post pictures of himself holding large sums of cash on social media."

Corey turned to him and chuckled. "Are you serious?"

"I'm not making this up," said Eddie. "I'm sure the FBI's still laughing about it."

They arrived at the bar, Corey drove into the lot, stopping halfway between the bar and the entrance, and parked. Eddie got out and scanned the area. The area was less intimidating than the night before since there was still daylight. Plus, the lot was empty. He breathed in the rich vegetation and earthy aroma in the air surrounding them as they baked in the humidity—the remnants of the rain that fell the night before and earlier in the day.

Corey shut his door. "What are we looking for?"

Eddie looked around and then shrugged his shoulders. "I don't even know." He glanced at the entrance to the bar, which, from what he saw at this moment, could use a new paint job. All he could hear were the chirping of the birds. He was surprised that there weren't any mosquitoes.

Eddie turned toward the entrance and walked in that direction. Perhaps he would remember something that he hadn't mentioned to the police.

"I think this is a waste of time. What else do you expect to find?" Corey asked. "The police already combed over this area. They wouldn't have left anything behind."

"Don't be so sure." Eddie stood a few feet away from the building. "Sometime around two thousand and three or two thousand and four, a Jamaican gay-rights activist was found murdered in his home. Even though there was an investigation, his friends found two other murder weapons at the crime scene on the same day, where over a dozen officers had visited the scene hours before."

"How's that possible?" asked Corey. "Shouldn't the crime scene have been taped off so that things couldn't be moved around? We can get in trouble for this if we're caught."

"I believe you're referring to contaminating a crime scene. I thought the same thing." Eddie gazed around him.

"It makes you wonder why there isn't any crime scene tape here, doesn't it?"

Corey took a moment and surveyed the area. "You're right. But to be fair, the police did block the entrance and diverted everyone else to leave through a makeshift exit."

"I don't know what difference that made." Eddie scanned the entire lot from one side to the next. "Last night's rain would've washed away most of the physical evidence."

Eddie glanced at the clock on his cell phone and saw that it was close to four. The sun would set roughly at a quarter to six. Throughout the year, the average sunset was around six o'clock. It was not like Canada, where seasonal changes affected what time the sun would set.

"Why are you starting here? The body was found over there." Corey pointed toward the parking lot entrance.

"Because I want to see this from a different perspective," Eddie answered. "Dwayne didn't simply teleport from the club to the street." Eddie strolled a bit slower than the pace he initially walked and stopped near the spot where he had nearly been struck by the BMW.

Durag and Bandana were about to rape Shenice—most likely not knowing she was a brotha—before Eddie showed up and interrupted them.

He turned to Corey and tapped the spot on the back of his skull where he was struck. "Stand behind me and pretend to hit me but do it gently."

"Any preference?"

"Start with your fist."

Eddie felt Corey's knuckles pressing the back of his head. That wasn't it.

"Try another hand attack," said Eddie.

Eddie felt Corey's palm and fingertips. Something was off, but he was warmer.

"Do the same thing, except this time focus more on the heel of your palm."

Got it! "That's it. That's what I felt. A palm-heel strike."

"Like in karate?"

"I think so. I had a karate teacher collaborate with me on my last novel. This was one of the moves he told me about."

"This means that your attacker had martial arts training."

"Possibly. The average person may have struck me with an object. But my attacker smothered my face with a cloth that was soaked with a knock-out toxin. Who walks around with that?"

"Didn't you say that out of the three guys we saw on the dance floor, you only saw two attacking Shenice?"

"Yeah."

"Perhaps the third was the lookout," said Corey. "Maybe he was the one who knocked you out."

"The driver, Delroy?" Eddie tilted his head from side to side, weighing the idea. "To be honest, I see more Durag and Bandana being into martial arts. I may be wrong, but somehow Delroy doesn't fit the profile."

"How can you be sure? You don't even know him." Corey nodded to the bar behind them. "With the amount of background noise, you couldn't have heard anyone sneaking up behind you."

"Exactly. It could've been anyone."

"But if Delroy was the lookout, then he'd have a reason to attack you."

"There was just something about the look on his face when he stared back at me from inside his car," said Eddie. "Something was bothering him. I'd say he looked scared."

Corey shrugged his shoulders. "Duh. Didn't you say that one of his friends looked like he got pepper sprayed? He knew what his friends were doing and was trying to get away."

"Of course, he'd be bothered by that. But him knocking me out, then incapacitating me with some chemical? It seems too farfetched."

They walked for roughly forty meters, when Eddie stretched out his arm in front of Corey to stop him. "This is the spot. This is about where Shenice was attacked."

"All right. What happened next?"

"I don't know. I was knocked out, remember?"

"Then it's time to be creative," said Corey. "Imagine you're being attacked. Then your attackers pause because they realize they're being watched. What do you do next?"

"I fight my way out and run," Eddie answered. "I grab my pepper spray and use it on one, which turns out to be Bandana. While he's in pain, I threaten to use it on the other, who then probably chooses to let me go while he rushes to his friend's aid. He'd be struggling to breathe, coughing, and most likely crying out for help."

"And Durag would be left with the choice of either beating up Shenice or helping his friend before he drew too much attention to them."

"But Shenice could've gotten away because I found her shoe," Eddie turned to point to the spot, "over there."

They walked to where Eddie had found Shenice's shoe. They continued walking until he felt his chest tighten as the hard-braking sound of tires across gravel still echoed in his mind.

Eddie stopped. "This is where I was nearly run over, or about this spot."

"What happened next?"

Eddie turned as though he were facing the car and looking inside at the passengers. He then stepped to the side, just as he had the night before.

"They drove off."

"But where was Shenice?" asked Corey.

"She was..."Eddie pointed to the entrance to the lot. "She had to have been somewhere out there."

They walked toward the entrance, and Corey pointed to the darkened, scorched area on the ground. "This is where Shenice died."

Eddie stared at the charred area before him, then closed his eyes to focus. Both he and Corey were beating the flames. He felt the fire searing his hand, as Shenice flailed helplessly on the ground—the odor of burned flesh was still fresh on his mind. The flames were out, people started crowding around them, smartphones out as patrons rushed to be the first to post videos and pictures to social media. But something was off.

Eddie held his head with both hands as he turned his lips inward and spun around like a top, slowly on the same spot.

"Bruh, what's the matter?"

"Something's not right, and I can't figure out what it is."

"Calm down, relax, don't force it."

Think, Eddie. Think...

A dead body with a missing shoe, wearing a singed dress, wig mostly burnt away. He caught a glimpse of genitals—confirming that Shenice was a man. Men don't regularly wear dresses... unless they're in drag. They put on lipstick, makeup, just as women do. They pick out a lovely dress with matching shoes. Jewelry is optional. Come to think of it, it's often a must. Women always go to the bathroom to freshen up, so they wouldn't leave home without a...

"Purse," Eddie shouted, letting go of his head as he stopped spinning. "Shenice didn't have her purse when we found her."

"Are you sure?"

"Positive. We looked everywhere, even under the cars, we didn't find one."

"It was dark. We wouldn't have seen much."

Eddie ran in a slow jog toward the road, leaving Corey to catch up.

"Another thing," said Eddie. "Those three guys, I don't think they killed Shenice."

"But you saw two of them attacking her."

"Attacking her, yes. Killing her, very unlikely."

"How are you sure?" Corey followed his best friend onto Pegga Road, where they had seen Shenice emerge from after she'd been set on fire.

Eddie walked through the area of Pegga Road that was surrounded by dense forest. As the road sloped downward, Eddie saw that low-hanging branches obscured a rockface to his left. The opposite side was bordered by tall weeds and grass, with the dense forest a few feet in.

"Shenice came from here when she emerged into the parking lot. She was set on fire out here."

"And this was after the attackers fled, right?"

Eddie thumbed behind him. "The BMW took off that way, so they wouldn't have passed Shenice." Two cars drove toward them, one from the front and the other from behind. Eddie instinctively moved farther to the side, as both cars passed each other at the precise spot where Corey and Eddie were. While minding the oncoming car, which was less than a foot away when it drove by, Eddie stepped into a pothole and stumbled. He felt two hands grab his triceps, which saved him from falling on his face.

"Be careful, bruh," said Corey.

"Thanks," Eddie said with a sigh of relief. He was momentarily staring into the woods when something caught his eye.

"Check this out." Eddie motioned to a set of broken twigs that were either hanging from their branches or had been broken off completely. "It's as though someone had been in here, maybe hiding."

He cleared the branches from the side as he went deeper inside the bush. An object, partially covered in soil and fallen leaves, stood out from its surroundings.

Gotcha!

The soil was damp as Eddie's feet sank in with each step. He grabbed his hand towel that hung from his back pocket. Eddie reached down and used the towel to pick up the purse, then turned to Corey. "Look familiar?"

"You're sure that's Shenice's?"

"It looks like the one I saw." Eddie nearly stumbled while

stepping out of the bush.

Corey glanced where Eddie exited. "So, she was hiding in there."

"She must've been scared shitless, and that branch must've hooked the strap of her purse as she ran in. I imagine Shenice waited in here—crouched down as low as she could, waiting until it was safe to come back out. When she did, she left her purse behind."

Corey looked around. "There aren't any streetlights. We drove through here last night. It was pitch-black. Shenice wouldn't have been able to find it."

With the towel separating his fingers from the purse, Eddie opened it and sighed when he noticed that some water had gotten inside. "We were right about the pepper spray."

He turned the purse over to drain it, while partially covering the opening to catch its contents. Eddie sighed when he took the phone. "Ugh, this isn't good. It's wet."

"Is it working?"

"It's off," said Eddie as he held the phone upright. "I assume that Shenice, in her panic, didn't turn it off. "Did you bring your hand towel with you?"

Corey pulled it out from where it hung from his back pocket and handed it to him.

Eddie reached out and exchanged the purse for it. He was relieved that the towel was dry as he wiped down the phone's exterior.

"We need to get it in a bag of rice," said Corey.

"That won't do anything."

"Sure it will. I've heard that's what you do to save a wet phone."

"That's a myth. Dry rice can't absorb water that's inside a phone. Let's go." Eddie walked back toward the parking lot in a brisk pace, with Corey next to him.

"What are you going to do with it?"

"We need to ship this phone to Colorado."

"Colorado?"

"Yeah. I once spoke to a guy, Craig Beinecke. He's the best

when it comes to repairing smartphones."

"How'd you hear about him?"

"I stumbled on one of his interviews while researching a story idea. His store has a device that can safely get rid of the water without damaging the phone."

"I'm surprised you're not turning this over to the police."

"You're kidding, right?"

"I'm not. What were the chances of us finding Shenice's purse? If a dozen officers searched this area, they would've had an easier time finding it. What does that tell you about how seriously they're taking this investigation?"

"I hear you."

In little time they arrived at their car. Eddie's phone buzzed. He checked it and saw that Jalissa had texted him: "Did you find anything yet?"

Damn, she was quick.

Corey was already inside, while Eddie took a moment to reply: "Will let you know as soon as I learn anything."

He got in, and in a few moments, they were on the road, when Eddie's phone buzzed again. It was Jalissa replying with an "okay" text. Just then, it dawned on him. "My phone was working back there."

"Yeah, so?"

"Remember when we tried texting each other, and there wasn't a signal. And you tried doing the same after you couldn't find me?"

"Right. I guess the cell phone tower was out last night."

"Whenever a cell phone tower's down for any reason, our phones communicate with the nearest one. The whole network would've had to have been down."

Eddie did a quick search for the customer service number of the local phone carrier. After being on hold for a few minutes, a pleasant woman answered him.

"Digicel customer service. This is Denisha. How may I be of assistance?"

"Hi, Denisha," Eddie answered. "I need your help. Early this morning, I was in the Irving area outside of Montego Bay. My friend and I lost our phone signals. Can you tell us why?"

"I don't know why that would happen. Let me put you on hold to find out if there was a problem with the network. Around what time did this happen?"

"Sometime between one and two in the morning."

"Okay, please stay on the line while I put you on hold."

Eddie was jerked forward and he nearly dropped his phone, as Corey slammed on the brakes to avoid ramming a car that pulled out of a side street at the last moment. "Damn it, Corey."

"What the hell are you blaming me for?" Corey pointed to the car ahead. "You ain't see this idiot pull out?"

"Just slow down."

"All right, bruh. Do what you need to and let me drive."

Before Eddie could make a comeback, he heard Denisha's voice. "Hello, sir, thank you very much for holding. I just checked with my supervisor, and she confirms that there wasn't any problem or disruption with the network service during the time you mentioned."

"Okay, thanks."

"Is there anything else I may help you with today, sir?"

"Not at the moment. Thanks."

"Thank you for choosing Digicel, and have a wonderful evening."

Eddie tapped the screen to end the call.

"What did they say?" asked Corey.

"Nothing wrong on their end."

"But of course you're thinking this is odd, aren't you?"

"Of course," said Eddie. "You think that it's a coincidence that our phone signals are dropped around the same time Dwayne Pottinger is killed. I forgot to mention this to the police."

Before Corey could answer, Eddie's phone rang. He didn't recognize the number but answered regardless. "Hello?"

"Mister Barrow. It's Detective Inspector Ellis. How soon can you come down to the station?"

"What's this about?"

"We need you to ID some men from a line-up," Ellis answered. "We may or may not have the men you witnessed last night in custody."

Chapter 6

Freeport Police Station

Eddie watched eight brothas walk into the adjoining room, each around five feet nine with bald fades, sporting jean shorts and buttoned-down shirts. Each man held a card with a number on it, while Eddie watched from behind the one-way glass. Eddie had already identified Durag and Bandana from two previous line-ups. As for Delroy, Eddie identified him the moment he entered the room.

"Number four," Eddie said without taking his eyes off him. Leaning against the wall with his arms crossed to Eddie's left was Detective Inspector Ellis. There was also a man in a suit, whom Eddie assumed was an attorney for the accused. There was a third—a sista with peppered hair, from the Canadian consulate, stood behind Eddie. It was standard procedure that a representative from the consulate be present since a Canadian citizen was assisting with a police investigation. She was the only person in the room that gave Eddie some level of reassurance that matters would be done properly.

"Are you sure?" asked Ellis.

Eddie nodded. "That's him, number four."

Eddie noticed that Ellis closed his eyes for a moment, and then looked away. Was he upset that Eddie picked out the wrong men? Or was Ellis worried about consequences of him making three consecutive positive identifications?

The man in the suit left the room, while Ellis turned to Eddie, gesturing toward the exit. "That's all, Mister Barrow."

A few moments went by as Eddie walked through a room full of stories to tell. A brotha tried to expose himself while as many as four police officers struggled with him. The others were forced to distance themselves from the melee—including two skinny brothas, both of them were holding ice packs to their faces. They were both being yelled at by a sista weighing north of three hundred pounds, dressed in form-fitting pink leggings, a matching t-shirt, and too much make-up. Based on her insults, it was clear that it was a love triangle gone horribly wrong.

He had nearly reached the exit when he heard his name being yelled above all the noise.

"Mister Barrow."

He turned to see Ellis walking toward them holding a file folder.

"May I have a moment with you?"

Eddie felt as though he did not have a choice. He walked toward Ellis and was led inside what Eddie assumed was an unoccupied room. Ellis stood next to the doorway, gesturing inside with a nod.

Eddie entered and took a seat at the table while Ellis closed the door, shutting off the noise from outside.

"Thanks again for showing up so quickly." He walked around and tossed the file folder on the table. When it landed, a few of the papers partially spilled out. Rather than sit, Ellis leaned, with outstretched arms, on the back of the chair opposite Eddie.

"I get the feeling that there's a *but* somewhere," said Eddie.

"There are some matters I'd like to discuss again with you."

Something wasn't right. "Such as?"

"Please tell me again what is your relationship to the men you identified?"

Eddie's eyebrows arched. "None. I don't know them."

"Okay." Ellis paused as though he were attempting to ask the question again, but differently. "In your initial statement, you said that you danced with Shenice, correct?"

"Yeah, because I thought that I was dancing with a woman."

"At any moment during the party, were you in an argument or confrontation with the men you alleged attacked her?"

"Never." Eddie shook his head as he sighed. "*Shenice* came over to dance with me."

"Just to be clear. You're saying that you never fought over Shenice with anyone?"

"I never mentioned that in my statement because that never happened. Why?"

"Here's the thing," said Ellis. "The three men you identified have lawyers who are claiming that you were aggressive and confrontational with them *inside* the bar on the night of the murder. And that your allegations are simply a way of getting even with them."

"That's nonsense," said Eddie. "My friend Corey and I saw the guy wearing the durag walk up to Shenice from behind and reach under her skirt. But she slapped his hand and moved away. Both he and his friend laughed about it."

"So, you're saying that you weren't competing over her? Shenice chose you, end of story?"

"I already gave my statement, and I'm not changing it."

"Fair enough," said Ellis. "And I assume that you're sticking to your statement that you saw two of the three men attacking Shenice?"

"They were dragging her, and she was resisting. Durag had his hand over her mouth so that she couldn't scream."

"Their lawyer is saying that all they did was follow her outside so that they could talk to her. Instead, she attacked them by pepper spraying them."

"And you believe that?" asked Eddie. "Without the stilettos, Shenice was around my height, doesn't matter that she was really a dude. Why would she try to pick a fight with two men who could physically overpower her? The first thing she would've done was try to get away. Using the pepper spray would've been a last resort. I was running to help her, until someone knocked me out from behind."

"Did you see the person who attacked you?"

"Didn't you already ask me that?"

"Do you have *any* idea who'd attack you?"

"Again, you already asked me that. Why are you asking me questions to which you already know the answers?"

"If I understand correctly, you only caught a glimpse of what you alleged was the victim being attacked by the two men you identified."

Eddie saw where this was going. He closed his eyes and shook his head. "Yes."

They were interrupted by a knock at the door.

Ellis held up a finger in front of Eddie before heading to the door. "Hold on."

Eddie looked over his shoulder as he watched Ellis open the door and close it partially behind him. It was enough to obstruct his view of to whom Ellis was speaking. He looked back to the file folder in front of him, but more specifically, the set of papers that had partially spilled out. They must be Ellis's files on the suspects.

Eddie glanced over his shoulder to see that Ellis was still engaged with whomever he was with. Eddie then leaned closer to the table and lifted the folder enough for him to peek under it. It was a file on Delroy. His headshot alone spoke for itself. Eddie scanned the document and learned that his last name was Stewart. He was the assistant branch manager at the Scotiabank on Market Street. A yellow sticky note at the center of the document made Eddie's chest tighten and his eyes bulge.

Eddie heard Ellis's heavy footsteps, signaling him to release the folder and lean away from the table. Ellis returned to where he stood earlier.

"Where was I?" Ellis looked away as though he were in thought. "Oh yes. As I was saying, the defense is going to argue that your testimony's inaccurate due to you missing the interaction because, by your own admission, you were knocked out. They're also going to argue that you're using your imagination to fill in the blanks. With what I have so far, I don't see how a jury will convict those men of a crime."

"You can start by telling your officers to do a better job searching the crime scene."

Ellis squinted his eyes shut. "Mister Barrow."

Eddie slammed his fists on the table while leaning forward. "Why is it that I was able to find a near-empty can of pepper spray in Shenice's purse."

Aw, shit!

Ellis's eyes widened as he leaned forward. "What did you just say?"

Eddie sighed and slumped back in his chair. "My friend Corey and I found Shenice's purse."

"When?"

"This afternoon." Eddie could see that Ellis was going to pry. The detective inspector may be looking for a way to get something on Eddie.

"Why?"

Think fast. "I lost one of my house keys. I thought it'd be better if I go back to look for it rather than pay an extra fee for the Airbnb to replace it."

"Really?"

He didn't sound convinced.

"Did you find it?"

"Yeah, it was close to the spot where Corey and I tried to save Shenice," Eddie answered. "It obviously fell out of my pocket while I was beating out the flames."

"Then how did you let yourself in when you got back to where you're staying?"

"Corey unlocked the door with his key," said Eddie without missing a beat. "He was walking ahead of me when we got back to the Airbnb."

"And you just happened to find Shenice's purse lying around?"

"How is it that we found it before the police?"

"Don't dodge my questions."

"I'm stating the obvious. When Corey and I went back there this afternoon, we didn't see any police tape or barriers, meaning that *anyone* could've contaminated the crime scene." Eddie stood and paced back and forth behind where he sat. He then turned to Ellis. "If I didn't know any better, I'd say that you aren't interested in making an arrest. The moment I mentioned Delroy's name and that he drove a BMW, I saw the look on your and your sergeant's faces. Who is he? I'm curious. Is he from a rich family you guys are afraid to piss off?"

Ellis closed his eyes as though his patience was running out.

"Mister Barrow."

Eddie stopped behind his chair and held onto it while staring at Ellis. "To you guys, it's just another gay-bashing and that Dwayne got what he deserved, isn't it?"

Ellis slammed his hands on the table so hard that the file folder bounced. "That's enough."

Eddie grabbed the back of his chair and watched as Ellis shook his head.

"You Canadians may think that we Jamaicans don't know what goes on in the rest of the world because we're a smaller nation. But I know all about the shenanigans that got you framed for murder a few years back. My colleagues and I took an interest in the developments of the case you solved—especially the fallout that happened afterward."

Ellis then sighed. "I admire the fact that you made something of yourself after such an unfortunate incident. However, you're not a detective, nor do you work in law enforcement. So, I'm going to have to tell you to leave the police work to the police. Do you understand me?"

Eddie didn't answer him immediately. Then again, he couldn't hide his anger from him either.

"Mister Barrow?"

Eddie sighed. "Yes, I understand."

Minutes later, Eddie walked through the parking lot behind the precinct. Corey, as he expected, was standing outside with the windows rolled down—music blaring from inside.

"Can you play that music any louder?" Eddie shook his head.

Corey reached inside and lowered the volume. "What's up with you?"

"Guess." Eddie circled the car from the back to the passenger side. "Ellis isn't going after the suspects I picked out of the lineup."

"What? Why'd they make you come down here then?"

"They lawyered up." Eddie opened the door and reached inside to the back seat where the purse was, while he told Corey what happened inside.

"That's bullshit."

"You think?" Eddie grabbed the purse.

"Where are you going with that?"

"We have to give it to them."

"Why?"

"Because I don't want to get locked up for withholding evidence."

"How did they find out about it?"

"I...may have accidentally mentioned that we found it."

"Way to go, genius."

"It's all right. I didn't say anything else. Besides, the phone's already miles away somewhere above the Atlantic. I can't turn over what we don't have, right?"

"I don't think a lawyer will agree with you."

"Don't sweat it," said Eddie. "If my guy can save Shenice's phone, he'll return it via overnight shipment."

Corey shook his head. "I hope you know what you're doing."

"Another thing," said Eddie. "I was right about the three suspects—well, one of them."

"What about them?"

"Ellis stepped away for a few moments, so I may have peeked inside a folder he'd been carrying. A file on Delroy—the guy who drove the getaway vehicle. Get this. His grandfather's a judge."

"Are you sure?"

"There was a sticky note on Delroy's file."

Corey shook his head. "No wonder Ellis doesn't want to go after him and his friends."

"That's possible, but I have to admit that part of what he told me is true. I don't know what happened while I was unconscious. And the truth is, their lawyer could possibly use me as a witness to sway a judge or jury to decide in their favor if ever there was a trial."

"If you say so." Corey seemed to notice Eddie's mood was off. "What's wrong?"

"Dwayne's murder, something's not adding up."

"Like what?"

"For starters, he had to have known that he was taking a huge risk showing up at a party dressed as Shenice. He avoided contact with almost everyone—except for the contestant he took a selfie with, and me. Then he left right after being pushed to participate in the dance-off?"

"What are you getting at?"

"I think there's more to this than what we've seen." Eddie took out his phone and called Jalissa. "And I have an idea where we can find out."

Chapter 7

One kilometer away from Dwayne Pottinger's House, Bogue Village, Montego Bay

"Turn it down." Eddie had to shout above the din of the bombastic reggae tune as he pushed the arrow button to drastically lower the volume.

Corey slapped Eddie's hand away. "You want us to blend in or stand out?"

"We don't need to have the music this loud for us to blend in," said Eddie.

"Two guys our age, driving together after sundown, enjoying dancehall. What's so suspicious about that?"

"We don't need to draw attention to ourselves. Do you want Wesley staring out the window as we park?"

Wesley had been Dwayne Pottinger's roommate, and Eddie and Corey were on their way to see him.

"Fine." Corey lowered the volume from the controls on the steering wheel. "Is that better?"

"Much."

It became silent between the two of them. Little time went by before Eddie noticed that Wayne Wonder and Buju Banton were on. He couldn't remember the name of the song, just that it was a classic. It didn't take long before he started singing along.

"'Because I love you in every way…I don't know why.'"

Corey then joined in. "'Oh whyyy?'"

They both sang together to the end of Wayne Wonder's part, which then switched to Buju. "'Woman don be wealthy but drive your Fiat car, but mi can leff yuh cause I come from far.'"

"Yo, bruh!" said Corey.

"What?"

Corey shook his head as he glanced at Eddie briefly while eying the road. "Uh-uh. Stop imitating Buju."

"What's wrong with me wanting to sing like Buju."

"Because listening to you trying to imitate Buju is like listening to Steve Urkel trying to imitate Lil Wayne."

Eddie gave Corey a side-eye. "You're just being savage."

"Robert Downey Jr. could've done a better job."

"Now you're being facetious."

"You don't even know the words. Not once does Buju sing about a woman driving a *Fiat*. It's driving a *fast* car."

"Never mind." Eddie looked to the side of the house, which Jalissa had described to them. "We're here."

"You think this is the place?" asked Corey.

Eddie motioned to the house opposite it, which had a car that was in dire need of a new paint job. "There's the busted car Jalissa told us about. Plus, she also said that the numbers were missing from Wesley's house."

Eddie was grateful for the landmark, considering that all the houses looked similar. They were all single homes in an area that appeared to be sub-middleclass. Each house had a front yard outside a veranda. Walls made from wood or concrete separated the road from the front yard. Many homeowners preferred having a metal grill or even a hybrid of concrete and grill. Fortifying the homes was a priority for the residents. It forced any visitor to wait outside the front yard before being let in.

Corey drove to the side of the road and parked in front of the house next to Wesley's. Eddie was the first one out and led Corey to the grill. He was about to ring the doorbell only to notice that none was there. With no alternative, he shook the padlock on the grill, then stepped back two paces. Corey did not budge. It dawned on Eddie that he was in a predominantly Black country and shouldn't have to worry about a white occupant freaking out and calling the police at seeing two Black strangers after sundown. So, he approached the grill again.

Corey glanced at him briefly, then looked back at the grill. "You just remembered there aren't any white people around to call the police, didn't you?"

"I...don't know what you're talking about."

"Yeah, sure." Corey nodded mockingly. "Come to think of it, Wesley's not expecting us. How are we going to play this out?"

"Just follow my lead." Eddie banged on the padlock again.

The front door to the house opened, and a brotha with short, twisted hair walked toward the grill on the veranda holding a cricket bat, swung that gate open, and stepped up to them. "Weh unu want?"

What you all want. Is that what he was trying to say?

Not being sure, Eddie played it cool. "Good evening, Wesley—"

"How yuh know mi name. Who yuh be?"

"My name's Eddie. I was acquainted with Dwayne, your roommate." Eddie gestured to Corey. "This is my friend Corey."

"I don't know no Dwayne, and I don't know yuh."

"You're saying that Dwayne never lived here?" Eddie pointed to the rusty car across the street. "His sister told us—"

"Yuh betta goweh from mi yaad." He raised the bat for them to see. "Unless yuh want mi fi lik yuh wid mi bat."

"We're not looking for trouble." Eddie made a slight retreat. "We just need your help with—"

Corey sighed loudly, then stepped around and in front of Eddie. "Look. We know Dwayne lived here, so cut the bullshit and let us in. We just want to talk."

"Mi no have nuttin fi seh—"

"Wes!" Corey yelled as he turned around, his voice cracked as though he was heartbroken. "Wes, how can you leave me? I thought you loved me."

Eddie's mouth dropped as he watched Corey do the unthinkable. He then turned back to Wesley to see him staring back and forth between Eddie and Corey with widened eyes and a hanging jaw.

"Please don't leave me, Wesley. Mi loooove yuh, and mi don't care what others say."

Catching on, Eddie thumbed toward Corey. "He's not going to stop."

Wesley fumbled to unlock the grill then swung it open outward—barely missing Eddie. "Shut up and come een!"

Corey stopped yelling as though someone had flicked an *off* switch and turned to them with a smile. "Cool." He passed Eddie, who did not waste any time hurrying up to get inside as Wesley slammed the grill shut.

"Yuh bloodclaat. Yuh a ideat?" shouted Wesley once they were inside the house. He stormed past them through a beaded curtain into the living room. "Yuh'll get us all killed."

"My friend needs to talk to you." Corey followed him into the living room. "You going to get us a cold drink, or do I have to fake an orgasm?"

Eddie hurried to step around Corey and get between him and Wesley. "Sorry about my friend. He tends to get a bit impulsive at times. We came here as a favor to Dwayne's sister, Jalissa."

Wesley walked over to a recliner and leaned the cricket bat upright against it while he sat down. "Yuh two trying to link up wid Dwayne?"

Eddie and Corey shook their heads vigorously.

"It's not like that," said Eddie.

"I'm married and have a son." Corey paused for a second before smirking and pointing to Eddie. "He's single, though."

Eddie shot a grimacing glance at Corey. "As I said," he then relaxed his face before turning to Wesley, "it's not like that."

"Den why yuh deyah?" asked Wesley.

"As I was about to say," Eddie and Corey sat on the adjacent sofa, "we got a chance to meet Jalissa at my book signing this morning."

"Book signing?" asked Wesley.

"I'm an author."

His indifference was evident as he turned to Corey. "What about yuh?"

"I'm his business partner."

"Getting back to Dwayne..." Eddie noticed Wesley's head dropping down into his hands.

"Mi tell dat bwoy no fi to de bar dress lakka dat. Yuh jus a ask fi get yuhself dead."

The Patois was too much for Eddie as he struggled to interpret what Wesley was saying. "Sorry, Wesley. I'm not from around here, so I can't understand everything you're saying."

"So yuh want mi fi chat betta?" Wesley cleared his throat as though he were about to make a speech. "How does this sound?"

Eddie nodded. "That I can understand."

Wesley then raised his chin, sat more upright while rounding his shoulders. "Or would you rather I sound more British?"

Eddie gave Wesley a side-eye after being mocked in a British accent.

"As I just said," said Wesley in broken Jamaican-English. "I told Dwayne not to go to the bar dressed like that because he's just looking to get killed."

"Why do you think he went to the club dressed as a woman?" asked Eddie.

"He was headstrong and do what he want."

Eddie let his back sink into the couch. He saw that he was able to engage Wesley in a conversation. "Did he usually go out at night as Shenice?"

"No, mon," said Wesley. "He only come up with that getup a few weeks ago. The ones he live with before dress up as girls too, but they do it for money."

"Was Dwayne broke?"

"No, mon." Wesley raised his head. "Money was never a problem for him. He always pay he half of the rent on time. Especially in the last few weeks."

"What do you mean?" asked Corey.

"We have a common friend, Candace. She was the one who asked me to let Dwayne stay. I tell her no because I don't want him to draw attention to me."

"You were scared that him being in your house would make people think you're gay," said Eddie.

"Mi ano battyman," Wesley snapped. "You obviously not from around here. And you sound Bajan."

Eddie grinned, flattered that Wesley recognized his accent. "You've been to Barbados?"

"No, but I know a Bajan when I hear one."

"I was actually born in Montreal. My parents are from Barbados."

"You still a Bajan."

For Eddie, his Bajan accent became more prominent whenever he was among West Indians.

Wesley got up and went to the kitchen, which was the adjoining room. "Dwayne kept to he self. And as I was saying, you're obviously not from here because if you were, then you'd know that they don't like no fish around here."

"Really? I thought Jamaicans love fish just like us Bajans," said Eddie. "Flying fish is my favorite. You can get plenty in Barbados—"

"No." Wesley scrunched up his face and shook his head at Eddie. "Here, we call gay man a fish. You know, like battyman or chi-chi man."

Corey turned to Eddie. "Seriously? You didn't know that?"

"How am I supposed to know every Jamaican gay slur?"

Wesley opened the fridge, reached in, and grabbed three beer bottles. He held two by the necks in one hand and one in the other. He pushed the door closed with his foot, then walked back into the living room and placed the bottles on the small table. "Here, they kill you just for being gay, and the police don't do nothing."

"If that's so, then why did Dwayne risk his life going to a straight party in drag?" asked Corey as he was handed his drink.

"Because he think that he's invincible," Wesley answered. "Dwayne was just stupid for doing that. Anyone could have told him that he was asking for trouble. Ask around, and you'll see that no one felt sorry for him and that he got what he deserved. I tell he, don't go dressed like that, and he don't listen to me. He just say that he wouldn't be out too late, but it'll be worth it."

"What do you mean, *worth it?*"

"He wouldn't say. I assume he was looking for a man to link up with." Wesley took a long gulp and dropped the bottle down on the glass portion of the table with a loud bang. "When he moved in, I told him that he could do so on the condition that he doesn't do anything to draw attention to this house. You don't see them, but there's always someone watching because people nosey around here, always wanting to know everybody's business. And as soon as they hear that two men are fucking, you'll find a mob gather outside your house, ready to stone, shoot you, even both."

Eddie and Corey allowed Wesley to vent. He rambled on about the number of gay men who were either stabbed, shot, stoned, or run over by cars that the local newspapers couldn't even keep up. Eddie suspected that these incidents were underreported as to not give the island a bad reputation. Such news could devastate the tourism industry—which the island nation and all Caribbean islands depended on.

Eddie didn't mind Wesley's ramblings. In fact, he encouraged it as the discussion was a sign that Wesley was lowering his defenses. He even got up for another beer, and though he tried to act tough, Eddie clearly saw that he was grieving as it was apparent that he wasn't over Dwayne's death.

Eddie cleared his throat. "You told us earlier that money wasn't a problem in the last few weeks. What did you mean by that?"

"When he first came here," Wesley answered, "he didn't have no money. Normally I wouldn't have taken someone broke and flamboyant as a roommate because I would just be asking for trouble."

"You took him in as a favor to your friend. What's her name again?"

"Candace," said Wesley. "She works at one of the resorts and was good friends with Dwayne. She's the only reason why I let him stay here."

"I imagine he didn't have any money when he first arrived." Eddie wanted to bring Wesley back to the subject of Dwayne's finances.

"Not really," Wesley answered. "He brought home his first paycheck after two weeks."

"Dwayne had a job?" asked Eddie.

"Yeah, mon. He got one as soon as he moved in, and he brought home a sewing machine. He'd be in his room all day sewing. The lady he worked for, she name Milly, would always pass by after midnight once or twice every two weeks and pick up the clothes. She'd always leave some more material or other clothing items that needed fixing."

That's right, thought Eddie. *Jalissa said that Dwayne was a tailor.* "Are any of those clothes still here?"

"Yeah, mon."

"May I take a look?"

"Sure, mon, come see." Wesley stood and crossed the hall into one of the two bedrooms, with Eddie and Corey following. After Wesley flipped on the light switch, Eddie saw the sewing machine on its table next to the wall, adjacent to a single mattress, which he assumed was what Dwayne had slept on. There were plastic boxes with different types of material and many different colors. Stacked against the wall were bristol boards—Eddie assumed Dwayne had used these for his drawings.

Wesley walked to the closet and opened the door. He grabbed one of the outfits, still inside its clear plastic covering. Eddie could've sworn that he was looking at a three-hundred-dollar woman's pantsuit.

"You're kidding." Corey was fixated on the pantsuit. "Dwayne made *this*?"

"Yeah, mon," said Wesley. "When I leave for work, Dwayne would be at the sewing machine and when I get home, he still on the machine. As I told you, he worked hard all day."

"Dwayne should've had his own clothing line," said Corey.

"I heard that he tried, but it didn't work out," said Wesley.

"But he still kept himself busy?" said Eddie.

"Always," said Wesley. "Milly paid him well. I guess it's because he was so good at his job. In fact, I also heard that business picked up for her ever since she hired Dwayne."

"Was Dwayne's involvement with Milly a secret?" asked Corey.

"Yeah, mon," said Wesley. "Dwayne didn't want to take credit for helping Milly with her dresses. He thought that would be best for both him and Milly."

"Because she and her store may become targets." Eddie walked over to the sewing machine.

"Of course." Wesley sat down on the mattress. "That's why she'd pass by after midnight or around four in the morning to pick up the dresses or the other clothes that Dwayne made or fixed. She couldn't afford to let anyone catch him working in the store because people would be wondering how a young man be so good at making clothes unless he was gay."

Corey shook his head. "Dwayne was lucky. It's not often you hear about someone's boss going out of their way to accommodate them."

"Milly liked Dwayne," answered Wesley. "She has a big heart and wanted to give him a chance. Very few people would've hired him."

Eddie went to the mattress and checked around it. "Where's Dwayne's computer?"

"What you want with his computer?" asked Wesley.

"Dwayne's cell phone was damaged when we recovered some of his belongings," said Eddie.

"We think that he may have filmed whoever attacked him," added Corey.

"So why do you need his computer?" Wesley repeated.

"Because if he recorded anything or took pictures, they may have been automatically backed up in a cloud," said Eddie. "We should be able to access them from his PC."

Wesley gestured to the chest of drawers. "It's in there, top drawer."

Eddie crossed the room, pulled open the top drawer, and moved some socks and underwear to the side. The laptop was underneath. "Why would he keep it in here?"

"I guess he didn't want anyone to steal it," said Wesley as Eddie took it out, with its adapter, and opened it.

Wesley stood from his seat on the mattress. "Come plug it in the other room."

Eddie and Corey followed Wesley back into the living room. Eddie handed the adapter to Wesley, who plugged it into the outlet on the wall. Eddie pushed the opposite end into the computer, then turned it on. Once at the password prompt, Eddie was about to text Jalissa to ask if she happened to know Dwayne's password, but then a thought came to him. He entered a password that came to mind. To his surprise, it worked.

"How'd you guess the password?" asked Corey.

"A character in one of my books hid a second laptop in a sock drawer, just like Dwayne. Since he's a fan, I used the same password *that* character used, and it worked."

He clicked on the File Explorer icon, and a window opened on the screen. There weren't too many files, but Eddie glanced over them as Corey and Wesley sat on either side of him. There was a file named Essis that he clicked on, but it was empty.

"What's Essis?" asked Eddie.

"I dunno," answered Wesley. "I never heard Dwayne talk about that."

Eddie moved onto the following file folder, which contained videos. He clicked on one, and it was of Dwayne. The video was dated two days ago, and judging from the amount of sunlight, it was filmed sometime during the day. There was dancehall music in the background, and Dwayne was right where they were sitting. The only difference was that the furniture was moved to give him room.

"So, this is what he's been doing while I'm at work." Wesley shook his head.

"He could've been taking a break from sewing," said Eddie.

Corey pointed to other videos that were posted on earlier dates. "Those look like other videos. Did he regularly do dance contests?"

Wesley looked upward as though in thought. "No, not that I know of."

They glanced at other pictures going back several days. Most of them were predominantly of the dresses that Dwayne made as they were fitted on the mannequin in his room. Others were of him with his sister, Jalissa, and another young woman.

Wesley pointed. "That's Candace, the girl I was telling you about."

"They look like they're tight," said Corey.

"They're very close friends," said Wesley. "You'd think they were siblings."

"Have you spoken to her lately?" asked Eddie.

Wesley shook his head. "No, mon, I tried to call her since yesterday, but she won't answer. I even swung by her place this evening after work. No one home. Even the landlord hasn't heard from her."

"That's strange," said Eddie. "Dwayne's killed, and his best friend just disappears into thin air?"

"Wherever she is, I hope she's all right," said Wesley.

Something occurred to Eddie. He couldn't find a folder containing any of Dwayne's dress designs. Maybe he didn't make copies and store them on his computer in JPEG or PDF files. Perhaps he kept the original drawings.

He turned to Wesley. "Did Dwayne keep a scrapbook?"

"Scrapbook of what?"

"Did you ever see Dwayne with a book where he kept drawings of his designs?"

Wesley looked up to the side as though in thought. "I think so, you know. Hold on."

Wesley left the living room and went into Dwayne's room. While Eddie heard Wesley searching through Dwayne's belongings, he went on Google, which had already been logged into Dwayne's profile, and clicked on *photos.* The most recent picture was of the selfie he took with the contestant right before the dance-off.

Eddie formed a fist and hammered his thigh once.

Damn it!

There weren't any videos or photos of Dwayne in the parking lot that could reveal what happened to him after he was jumped. Eddie was then interrupted by Wesley, who came back with a large three-ring binder.

"This all I found." He handed it to Corey, who then passed it on to Eddie. "This what you want?"

Eddie handed the laptop to Corey and took the binder. He glanced through the first few pages. "Yeah, thanks."

He flipped through the drawings, then stopped when he came to an illustration of a fish—a flying fish, in fact, and it was a 3D drawing. He showed it to Wesley, who was still standing. "This isn't one of Dwayne's clothing designs. Any idea why he drew this?"

Wesley shook his head. "No, mon. I don't know anything about what he drew."

Eddie was about to flip the page, but there was something

about the drawing that kept him fixated on it.

"What's wrong?" asked Corey.

"I don't know," said Eddie. "This is a three-D drawing of a flying fish."

"Do you think that it's part of something else?" asked Corey.

Eddie looked at him, cocking his head. "Maybe." He turned a few pages, then paused. He lifted the page while he stared at the drawing of a dress. He turned to the next page. It was the same dress, but different.

"Hold on a sec." Eddie grabbed the edge of the laptop while it was on Corey's lap and turned it toward him, then quickly brought up the selfie of Shenice and the contestant. "She's wearing Dwayne's dress."

Staccato gunfire erupted from outside, blowing out the living room window, sending shards of glass exploding inside. Eddie and Corey quickly reacted as they shoved the coffee table to the side and dove to the floor.

Eddie turned in time to see Wesley thrown back into the recliner, flipping over with it. They all covered their heads as more gunfire ravaged the living room, shattering picture frames and blowing out chunks of bare walls.

The gunfire ceased.

"Wesley's hit," yelled Eddie.

Eddie placed his palms on the floor, then turned his head and saw Corey staring in Wesley's direction. Eddie then shuffled across the floor away from the window using his elbows and forearms.

"Help me with Wesley," yelled Corey as he shuffled the same way toward Wesley.

Eddie's ears still rang with the reverberations from the gunshots rattling inside his head. "Are they gone?"

Corey threw his arm out. "Don't get up."

There was a loud crying close to him. Eddie looked across the floor from where he lay to see the recliner flipped over with Wesley lying beside it, his shirt soaked red with blood.

"Call an ambulance. I think the number is one-one-zero," Eddie said as he saw Corey tapping the screen of his smartphone.

"Yes, someone's been shot," Corey yelled into his phone. "We need help, quick...What? I don't know the address. Just trace my phone and look for a shot-out house."

That's when Eddie yelled out the address, hoping the operator heard it.

"You get that?" yelled Corey to the operator. "Hurry."

Corey shoved his phone in his back pants pocket and crawled over to them. "You think they're gone?"

"Like hell they are." Eddie turned to Wesley. "Do you have any weapons? A gun? Anything?"

Wesley couldn't respond as he was still crying in pain. Eddie noticed now that Wesley had taken two bullets—one to the chest and one close to his left shoulder.

A bright flash in Eddie's peripheral vision caught his attention. He looked toward the window just in time to see a fireball hurling toward them. It smashed through the window and crashed into the inner grill—exploding into several smaller ones that scattered all over the living room. He immediately felt the blast of heat.

"Shit," cried Corey. "Grab his legs."

Eddie scrambled to grab Wesley's legs, while Corey caught him by the armpits and lifted as the fire began to spread fast.

The laptop.

Eddie spotted it, but it was too late. It was too close to the fire. There was no way he could get to it and save Wesley and himself. As for Dwayne's scrapbook, it was already feeding the flames that had begun to climb the living room walls to the ceiling.

"How do we get out?" yelled Corey.

"Washroom...di washroom," Wesley coughed.

"What?" yelled Eddie.

"He means the laundry room," shouted Corey.

"There it is." Eddie nodded just as they were about to pass the doorway. The smoke stung his eyes to the point that it was too painful to keep them open. Holding Wesley's legs, he led them into the laundry room, where he let go of one leg to open the door and the grill. Flames erupted behind Corey as the draft of fresh air gave them new life. They didn't waste any time hauling ass into the back yard just as a hot shockwave blast scorched them, throwing them onto the lawn.

Eddie didn't know how long he had been knocked out, but the stinging in his throat from the smoke shocked him back to consciousness. He was on his stomach surrounded by burning debris. He swallowed hard to soothe the pain in his throat.

Corey. Wesley.

Wesley was to the left, on the ground between Eddie and Corey.

"Corey," Eddie yelled as he cradled Wesley's head in his lap. "Bruh, get up."

Corey was in a coughing fit as he got up onto his knees. "What the fuck just happened?"

"You okay?" asked Eddie.

Corey nodded and then looked at Wesley. "How's he doing?"

"He's still breathing."

"Fuck! That was a stupid thing I did."

Corey was obviously referring to the silly stunt he pulled earlier that scared Wesley into letting them in.

"We can't be sure you brought that on."

"Why do you say that?"

"There's something I saw in Dwayne's scrapbook that set off some red flags." Eddie gave a single nod toward the burning house. "If that was a clue as to why he was killed, we just lost it."

Chapter 8

Cornwall Regional Hospital, Montego Bay

"Yuh family or not?" This smart-mouthed nurse was really trying Eddie's patience. "We're friends of his."

"Den yuh can't see him."

Corey leaned in. "We were nearly gunned down and blown up with him. He's alive thanks to us."

"Aww, you want a medal? Go tell the police to give you one."

Eddie patted Corey's arm and motioned for them to walk away. "Forget it. That bullfrog nurse ain't letting us through."

"Who yuh call a bullfrog?" yelled the nurse as Eddie and Corey ignored her.

Corey shook his head as they walked down the hall. "You think Wesley knows something else?"

Eddie stepped aside as a nurse rushed past him. "I'm sure he knows more than what he told us."

"Then why don't we wait awhile. Maybe they'll let us see him."

Eddie sighed. "Not while he's in post-op. Only the police will be able to see him if they're lucky."

Ahead of them, three men exited the elevator. Two were in blue uniforms while the other was unmistakably Detective Inspector Ellis, wearing his khaki uniform.

"Speaking of which…"

Eddie sighed. He really didn't care to see this man, but it was too late to jump into another room or hide in the bathroom. They had already been spotted.

"You two just can't stay out of trouble, can you?" Ellis still had the same arrogant tone he displayed from the night before.

"We're not the ones causing trouble." Eddie stopped along with Corey as the officer approached them.

"I never said you were the cause," Ellis quipped. "Should I change my opinion?"

"Are we suspects or not?" Corey was clearly frustrated. As usual, he was not afraid to show it.

Ellis pointed his finger at Corey. "You watch your tone, young man."

Eddie held out an arm in front of his best friend as though to hold him back. "Look, we've had a rough evening and just want to go home."

"You can go once you answer a few questions." He motioned to a room that appeared to be a staff rest area. "In there."

Eddie turned to the room, while Corey shook his head and sighed. Ellis was the last one in as he closed the door behind him.

"What were you doing at the victim's home?"

"We were collecting some of Dwayne's belongings for his sister," answered Eddie.

"Where, when, and how did you end up meeting his sister?"

"At my book signing."

"Book signing? Oh yes, you're a fiction writer."

Eddie rolled his eyes.

"And she, Mister Pottinger's sister, just happened to be there?" Ellis sighed while he shook his head. "What a coincidence."

"Why do you have a problem believing that my friend is good at what he does?" asked Corey.

"Excuse me?" said Ellis.

"He already told you why we're here, and you had plenty of time to Google his name and see that he's a bestselling author," said Corey. "So why do you keep belittling him? Had he been a white guy, would you be looking down on him?"

"Mister Stephenson!" yelled Ellis. "We've had a murder and an attempted murder in less than twenty-four hours, where both of you were the last ones in contact with the victims. I'll conduct this investigation, and question witnesses and suspects at *my* discretion. And I don't care for some foreigner, like yourself, implying I'm a sellout. I don't care if you are white, Chinese, Indian, or Black. You'll be treated the same. You understand?"

"Detective Inspector, if you must know," interrupted Eddie, remaining calm, "Dwayne was a fan, according to his sister, and would've been at the book signing had he still been around. She came instead and introduced herself."

"And she asked you on the spot to get Dwayne's belongings, just like that?"

"We offered," said Eddie.

"Really? And you didn't find it odd that she'd ask you first before asking a family member to help her?"

"No, because Dwayne—as others like him—was disowned by most of his family," said Eddie.

Ellis paused, looking away from Eddie briefly as though the question that was meant to stump Eddie embarrassingly backfired on him. He turned back to Eddie. "What did you manage to pick up?"

"Nothing, considering that the house burned down. But I thought that you would've figured that out already."

The way Ellis was looking at him, Eddie could imagine steam blowing out of his nose and ears.

"What can you tell me about the shooting?"

"I didn't see anything," said Eddie.

Ellis looked at Corey. "You?"

Corey shook his head. "Nothing."

"You're just like the neighbors," said Ellis. "Nobody saw a thing."

"Because we dove for cover," said Eddie. "Wesley was the only one standing at the time. That's why he got shot."

"Hmmph," grumbled the detective inspector. "And you were *only* there to collect Mister Pottinger's belongings?"

"We already answered that question," said Eddie.

"I know. But I find it hard to believe that his sister—whom you only met this morning—would be asking two complete strangers to get her brother's belongings."

"Eddie already told you that we offered," said Corey.

"I was also going to write an article on Dwayne. I wanted to get Wesley's input."

"An article?"

Eddie saw that Ellis didn't believe him. "Yes, I have a blog."

Ellis rolled his eyes.

"What else would you like to know?" asked Eddie.

"I just find it odd that two nights in a row, you two are at the scene where somebody's getting killed," said the detective inspector in a less angry tone. "Did you make any enemies while you've been down here?"

"None, unless someone tipped off the guys I identified in the line-up."

Ellis sighed as he gave Eddie a hard stare. "Let us do our jobs. We'll question whomever we feel." He then turned and walked to the door, pulled it open, and stopped to look over his shoulder. "And that means you two. I find out that you're interfering with this investigation, I'll arrest both of you myself." He stared at Eddie. "And you can add *that* to your blog."

He disappeared down the hall.

Eddie saw that Corey's bottled-up anger was about to be released as he slapped the wall hard with the palm of his hand. "That sonofabitch."

"Let it go," said Eddie. "It's not worth it."

Corey paced to the window and back, shaking his head. "Had you been an older white man, do you think he would've spoken to you like that? Of course not. He would've treated you like a king."

"Let it go."

"I'm not letting this go!"

"Keep your voice down."

"We…" Corey lowered his voice, "we were nearly killed tonight, and Ellis didn't even ask us how we're doing. No 'Did you suffer any burns? How did you escape?' How about 'Let me get you some bottled water because of the smoke you may have inhaled?' None of that."

"You think I didn't notice that?" Eddie suddenly felt thirsty for more water. "I also observed that Ellis didn't want to entertain the possibility that this incident may have been payback."

"You think? He's not interested in going after the ones who attacked us. I'll bet he's just going to play it off as another gay-bashing because Dwayne once lived there. End of story."

Eddie leaned with his hand against the wall. "You won't get an argument from me on that one."

"Too bad Wesley was standing. He may not have been shot had he sat."

Eddie nodded. It *was* a shame that Wesley wasn't sitting beside them at the time. "Shots fired into the living room. Wesley's hit as we dove to the floor. We stay on the ground, crawl to get Wesley, then the Molotov cocktail crashes through the window."

"It's a good thing they didn't just blast through the front door with guns and spray the living room," said Corey.

Eddie shook his head. "That would've taken longer. Don't forget the grill surrounding the veranda. It would've slowed them down, giving us a chance to get away. Unless...Wesley was the target."

"Wesley?"

"Think about it. Dwayne's killed, and then his roommate gets shot. What are the odds?"

"Do you think it's the same person?"

"Perhaps," said Eddie. "In that case, the attacks may be connected."

"Didn't you tell me that you thought Dwayne's killing may have been a hate crime?"

"Yes, that's what I thought. Then I saw his scrapbook." Eddie held his head with both hands. "I don't know what it is, but there was something I saw that bothered me. It pisses me off that I don't know what it was."

"What were you looking at?"

"I was looking at two dresses Dwayne designed."

"And what does that have to do with Wesley?"

"I don't know. I wish I could ask him some more questions about them."

"But you can't right now," said Corey. "Even if you could, you no longer have Dwayne's scrapbook to show him. Maybe their friend Candace has some answers."

"Except she's…missing." Eddie's eyes widened as he turned to Corey, who was staring right back at him.

"Are you thinking that she may be a target too?"

"It would explain why she disappeared." Eddie rushed out into the hallway with Corey right behind him. "And if so, whoever tried to kill Wesley will most likely try to finish him off right here."

Chapter 9

Eddie and Corey skidded to a stop at the nurse's desk. The same obnoxious woman from earlier jumped back in her chair so fast that her reading glasses fell.

"Yuh a try fi gimmi a heart attack?" she yelled.

"Where's Detective Inspector Ellis?" huffed Eddie.

"Who?"

"Big guy with broad shoulders," said Corey. "He was supposed to question Wesley."

"Bwoy, yuh jus miss him. And that's a shame because mi wudda jus mek him lock yuh up."

Eddie sighed. Wesley's life may be in danger, and this nurse was only interested in seeing him and Corey in jail. This was pointless.

The double doors that led to the restricted post-op area opened as an athletic looking brotha in scrubs exited with a patient in a wheelchair. The hallway was only accessible by swiping a keycard.

"Corey, go get Ellis, quick." Eddie ran toward the doors as they were closing.

"Hey!" Eddie heard the nurse yelling just as the doors closed behind him.

He slowed down as he came to an intersecting hallway. He looked to his left and saw a large room with empty beds. None of the curtains were drawn to separate them, which made sense considering the beds were unoccupied—except for one. Eddie hurried toward the closed curtain and skidded to a stop, where he saw a male nurse in scrubs had his back to him while standing next to the sleeping patient. There was no mistaking that it was Wesley.

"Is he all right? We need to get the police to stand…watch."

The attending nurse glanced over his shoulder at Eddie, then continued to do what appeared to be inserting a needle into Wesley's IV.

This isn't right, Eddie thought. *The brotha should be ordering me to leave the area...unless...oh shit!*

Eddie's instincts took over, and he lunged toward the imposter with outstretched arms—aiming for the syringe.

The imposter dropped the needle on top of Wesley moments before Eddie felt the inside of his right arm being grabbed and forced outward. Eddie then felt five rock-solid fingertips crushing his facial bones as he was swung around in a semi-circle. He saw black and red as the back of his head slammed into the wall, followed by stars and a spinning room as he fell to the floor.

Eddie was barely conscious as a damp cloth was pressed over his nose and mouth.

That smell...I know that smell...It's him...The guy from Citrusville who jumped me.

The assailant's attack took everything out of him, leaving Eddie to the mercy of whatever drug he inhaled. He felt as though his brain went numb and he gradually began to lose his eyesight. He then felt his entire body go limp before everything went dark.

***

Corey had just exited the hospital lobby and was outside by the main parking lot. Where was Ellis? He couldn't have taken off *that* quickly. When he didn't see him, Corey ran back inside to where he had left Eddie.

The same mouthy nurse looked in his direction. "You again?" She slammed her palm on the counter. "Security!"

"Where's my friend?"

"Who dat?"

Corey shook his head rapidly. He didn't have time for this bullshit. "Is Wesley okay?"

"Who?"

"Your patient? We came here to see him. The one who was shot."

"Me nuh tell yuh already, yuh kyan go in deh."
I told you already that you can't go in there.

A Code Blue blasted over the PA, seconds before Corey saw about eight people, he assumed were nurses and orderlies, hightailing down the hall. The obnoxious nurse suddenly forgot Corey and ran after them.

No, this can't be.

Corey followed the nurse through the double doors to the post-op area. He didn't care that he wasn't supposed to be there. With the bedlam that followed no one even noticed Corey.

"The patient's going into cardiac arrest."

Corey saw doctors and nurses crowding around what he assumed was Wesley's bed. One barked orders as they hooked him up to a defibrillator.

"Clear!" yelled the man seconds before Corey caught a glimpse of Wesley's feet spasm. A few more seconds passed before the same voice was shouting again, "Clear!"

Five more seconds of cacophony passed before he heard the single prolonged sound of a flatline. Corey closed his eyes and turned away while the doctor who appeared to be in charge announced the time of death.

Eddie!

He looked up and down the hall and couldn't see him anywhere. "Eddie?"

Corey continued walking quickly down the hall. It was mostly empty beds. "Eddie."

"Don't move."

Corey turned to see two men in uniform.

He stayed where he was as the two men slowed down from a run and stopped a few feet from him.

"My friend's missing. He came to see Wesley."

"If he's here, we'll find him. You're coming with us," said the security officer.

There was no use in arguing with them. Corey sighed and walked with the security officers on either side.

***

The surface was rough and bumpy below Eddie's head. At least, that's the first thing he noticed when he began to open his eyes. He sat up slowly, holding his head with one hand while the other was palm down on a metal surface. It felt as though he had a hangover, except he didn't remember drinking. When Eddie turned his head, a shockwave of dizziness struck him.

"He's awake." It was a Black woman's voice—one without a trace of a Jamaican accent. The first Eddie had heard since he arrived on the island.

Eddie's limbs were so heavy that he let himself fall flat on his back. He glanced from side to side without moving his head. There were at least two lights on. Wherever he was he did not see any windows. The surface rumbled below him, accompanied by what sounded like an engine. Was it a truck? If so, then he might be in the cargo area.

A moment later Eddie felt the vehicle slow down and stop. As his vision became more focused, he realized that something was being pointed at him. Eddie closed his eyes hard as the last bit of nausea subsided. When he opened them, he was staring into the business end of a gun, held by a woman wearing a clown mask.

Startled, he gasped as an adrenaline surge caused him to scramble backward until he hit a wall. His heart pounded rapidly as his breathing was reduced to short, quick breaths. His hands shot up as his eyes bulged.

Eddie turned to the sound of a door being dragged on a set of tracks attached to the ceiling. That's when he saw two others wearing clown masks standing outside the back of the truck he was in. He turned to the woman in front of him, moments before she lowered her gun and tucked it away.

Eddie still didn't drop his hands as he scanned his surroundings. Things were clearer. He was sitting in the back of a moving truck—a ten-footer at most. The Molotov cocktail, the hospital, being attacked and drugged. It all came back to Eddie.

"You're very nosey, Mister Barrow." It was another Black woman. She also spoke without a Jamaican accent. By her voice, she sounded older than the one standing next to him. She climbed inside first, followed by the other individual who got inside with a single vertical leap. Eddie recognized him as the brotha who attacked him. Eddie clenched both fists simultaneously as his chest tightened—the brotha held a machete.

The woman standing next to Eddie backed away as the older woman approached. He glanced back at the sista, then the brotha, then the older woman.

"Gretel...Hansel...the evil stepmother," Eddie mumbled the first names that came to him. "How do you know my name?"

"Because *I'm* in control, that's how I know your name. As for the aliases you just came up with, not bad...I think I'll use them."

Eddie couldn't care less if this woman stole his nicknames for them. He had more important things to ask. "Did you kill Dwayne?" Eddie turned to the brotha. "Did you kill Wesley too? You're the one who jumped me in the parking lot, aren't you?"

The brotha didn't answer but slowly approached him, scraping the tip of the machete against the wall of the truck. The sound of metal on metal made Eddie's nerves quake as he squirmed away—only to back into the sista's legs.

Stepmother held out her hand to Hansel. "Hand me the machete and hold his legs open. We need to teach Mister Barrow a lesson."

Eddie squirmed as both Hansel and Gretel grabbed his legs, then dragged him by the ankles from where he sat to the center of the cargo bay, where they made him face the exit. They yanked Eddie so hard that he was off balance, leaving him next to no control over his own body, and tugged, stretching his legs wide open and then kneeling on each leg. Eddie struggled to sit up just as he saw the leader get down on one knee and hold the machete slightly above her.

"I hope you weren't planning on having any children."

Eddie shook his head violently as he hollered for help. Sweat rolled down his forehead as he struggled to shake himself free. These people were undoubtedly professional assassins, and they were going to mutilate him in the worst possible way.

Stepmother swung the machete down, and Eddie heard a loud clang against the metal floor surface.

He didn't feel anything. Maybe she sliced his genitals in half, and the adrenaline surge masked the pain. He didn't want to look but couldn't stop himself from breathing hard. The three of them held their positions as they stared coldly at him. Eddie glanced down between his legs, only using his eyes, to see that the tip of the machete barely missed his crotch. Eddie then looked at Stepmother.

"Looks like I missed." Her attention then drifted to Eddie's left arm as her eyes widened behind the mask. "Nice veins."

Gretel then backhanded Eddie in the face, making him see flashes of black and red as he fell back to the floor. He was winded when Hansel crawled up to his chest and rested the total weight of his knee on him—distracting Eddie long enough for Hansel to grab his forearm. Eddie gritted his teeth as he tried to resist. He felt the jab, and then Hansel got off him.

"I don't want to see you again, Mister Barrow. Consider this a warning…I don't miss twice."

Eddie clamped down on the spot where he had been punctured as he stared at it. His breathing intensified as his fingers dug into his skin. He then turned to Stepmother. "What did you put in me?"

"You'll find out soon," she answered, then exited the truck. As though they were on cue, Hansel and Gretel grabbed Eddie's legs and tugged him so hard that he fell flat on his back. They then spun him around and pushed him headfirst toward the door. Before Eddie knew it, the floor disappeared from beneath him, followed by a brief moment of being in freefall before striking concrete. The momentum caused Eddie to flip over once before he wound up resting on his side, facing away from the truck into darkness. He heard the back door slam shut and footsteps walking away from him.

It took a few moments for Eddie to catch his bearings before he turned toward the truck, just as a plume of exhaust fumes blasted into his face—forcing his eyes shut and sending him into a coughing fit. He stopped hacking in time to see the taillights of the box truck disappear around a corner into the bush.

He felt his crotch area again and sighed with relief, knowing he didn't lose his manhood. His heart raced, and he felt the adrenaline surging through his body. He stood and looked around, clueless.

There were bushes on both sides of the road, and he could see the city lights in the distance. He had no idea where he was, given that there weren't any streetlights on this road. The city lights below, several miles away, were his guide. As long as he remained on the concrete, he'd find his way. His arm began to itch in the spot where he had been injected, and he started scratching it as he walked down the winding hill toward the city.

So far, everything seemed normal. Eddie needed to get help, and he went to grab his smartphone.

Damn it, they took my phone.

His pace picked up to the point that he was running. Eddie didn't know why. He just felt good.

Get a hold of yourself!

He slowed to a walk. A few moments had passed, and he had not seen a single vehicle. All he heard were the crickets and the grasshoppers. Maybe tree frogs were joining in the chorus.

His eyesight...something was off. Things were beginning to get blurry. Bright lights streamed by him, with horns blasting as they flew by. Shit, how hot is it out here? The temperature must have jumped to around fifty degrees Celsius, not that he would know what that felt like. These clothes. He had to get out of these clothes. First came the shoes...another horn blast startled him and he looked all over to see where it was coming from, then where it went...only for him to hear another.

What the fuck is going on? Spaceships...they're all around me...aliens...the aliens have landed.

It wasn't too long before he was fully naked, but he was still burning up. He needed water, and lots of it.

The aliens? Them, with their big swollen gray heads on top of their ultra-thin bodies. I think they're reading my thoughts. Why are they laughing? Are they laughing?

There was another horn, but this one sounded different, followed by a set of lights in his face. It was a spaceship with wheels. The lights were so bright that they blinded him, and his first instinct was to run away in the opposite direction. He didn't make it too far before he stumbled and fell. Within the sea of flashing lights around him, two dark figures emerged above him. They were saying something. Eddie couldn't understand their language. It was inaudible, considering the amount of noise around him.

"Stay away!" Eddie yelled. "Don't touch me. I don't want to go on your ship."

Eddie covered his eyes as he screamed. It was all he could do as he curled up into a fetal position—just as he felt himself being grabbed by the arm and flipped onto his stomach. Both arms were pulled behind him, and then suddenly, he realized he couldn't move them. It must've been some form of alien technology that caused his hands to be stuck together at the wrists. Eddie kicked and thrashed as he was forced to stand and then was dragged toward the alien ship.

Chapter 10

Cornwall Regional Hospital

Eddie's vision was a bit blurry when he first opened his eyes. His whole body felt heavy. It was as though he'd run a marathon. He turned to the sound of a machine and felt a sharp object stabbing him in his right forearm. Why was a plastic tube taped there, and was this a hospital gown? When he followed it, he saw that it was connected to an IV bag on a stand. Something was taped to his chest, and he felt for what it was with his left palm. They were electrodes, and he was connected to what appeared to be a heart monitor.

"Hey."

Eddie's head swung in the direction of the voice.

"What's going on?" Eddie scanned the room. "How did I get here?"

"You were brought in about three hours ago," said Corey. "Before that you were yelling and screaming about aliens and an invasion."

"Aliens?" Eddie looked at Corey with slanted eyes and a furrowed brow. "Why would I be screaming about an alien invasion?"

"Not only that," said Corey as Eddie watched him tapping away at his Android. "You also put up quite a fight. It took four officers to hold you down long enough for the paramedics to sedate you."

"That's ridiculous. How small were these officers? Hobbits?" Eddie looked toward his legs where he saw that the straps were undone. The same thing with his arms.

"I undid the restraints, if you're wondering." Corey handed him his smartphone.

"Thanks." Eddie took it and saw that Corey had queued up a

video on Twitter. His jaw dropped when he realized that he was watching cellphone footage of himself—completely naked, while jumping on and off the hood of a car, screaming, "Aliens, they're here! They've always been here. We need to call the military. We need to call the FBI. For god's sake, will someone call the Jedi council!"

"What the fuck?" Eddie jumped up and then winced in pain—forgetting that there was a needle still in his right forearm. "How did this happen?"

"Would it be a bad time for me to tell you how many times this video's been shared on social media?"

Eddie raised the phone with his left arm—remembering that the needle was in his right arm—ready to toss it, when Corey jumped up from his chair and caught his arm. "Easy, bruh. That's my phone you're about to throw."

Eddie gave Corey back his phone. He then crossed his arms, gnashed his teeth, and let out a long, drawn-out sigh. "How am I going to explain this to my publisher?"

"Don't think about that right now."

"Easy for you to say. This video could wind up on WorldStar. Or worse yet, PornHub."

"I'm sure Nancy's already on top of this. The videos will be taken down soon."

"Nothing really disappears once it's been on the internet." Eddie sighed and let his head fall into his hands. He pictured Bevins doing her best to remain calm over the phone then going on a cussing rampage the moment she hung up. It was ironic that she'd be helping him to bury this scandal, considering that he and Corey had met her following a previous one they were partially responsible for.

"How did this happen?" asked Eddie.

"I was hoping you could tell me." Corey shook his head. "You were clearly drugged. The doctor believes that you were high on PCP. They drew blood from you, to be sure. What's the last thing you remember?"

Eddie sighed as he looked up at the ceiling. He closed his eyes as he tried to playback the events of the evening in his head. All he remembered was being in the back of a truck with three strangers.

Eddie turned to Corey. "It was them."

Corey leaned forward. "Who?"

"The ones who did this to me. They're the same ones who killed Dwayne."

Corey took a quick glance to the door and then back to Eddie, as though he was worried about who may be listening in. "You actually came face to face with Dwayne and Wesley's killers?"

Eddie's stomach tightened. "Wesley's dead?"

Corey nodded. "He died earlier this evening. The doctors said that it was a heart attack."

Eddie shook his head. "They're wrong. He was murdered, and I saw who did it. I tried to stop him, but he threw me into the wall, then made me inhale some knock-out drug. It was the same thing that happened to me last night at Citrusville."

Corey stared at him with wide eyes and raised brows. His face remained that way for the next few seconds.

"It got worse," continued Eddie, as he told his best friend everything up until the point where they threatened him with the machete. The last part was too much for Corey that he stood and paced around the room.

"Did you get a good look at them?"

Eddie shook his head. "They wore masks." He let his head drop into his hands. "They were sending me a message. They want us to back off."

"Which means that we're onto something."

"You don't think I know that?"

They turned to a noise at the door and saw a sista, mid-forties, with her hair shaved very low on top of her glowing round face. It accentuated the warmth of her smile. "I see you're up, Mister Barrow. You had quite the adventure."

Corey backed away while the woman picked up the clipboard that hung from Eddie's bed.

"I'm Doctor Sharon Nelson," she said as she replaced the clipboard at the foot of the bed. "I want to keep you overnight, just to make sure you don't develop any other symptoms."

"What happened to me?" asked Eddie.

"You were doped up when you were brought in a few hours ago. It was a cocktail containing phencyclidine, otherwise known as PCP," she answered as she glanced at Corey. "I'm not going to ask how you came across such a dangerous drug, nor how you wound up so far away in Bogue Heights."

"You wouldn't believe me if I told you."

Doctor Nelson paused as she looked at Eddie's feet, then his arms. "Who untied you?"

Neither Corey nor Eddie answered.

It did not take long before Doctor Nelson stared at Corey. She then turned to Eddie. "You were tied down for your own protection."

"I don't think that'll be a problem, Doc," said Corey.

"You're lucky," said Doctor Nelson. "You don't appear to have suffered any serious injuries. I can't say much about your reputation, considering that several videos of you have hit the internet."

"I know what that's like," Corey mumbled, being reminded of a previous embarrassing experience he'd like to forget.

"But you should know that the police have some questions for you," she said, then left.

The GoFundMe account.

"Pass me your phone." Eddie reached out to Corey for it.

Corey handed it to him. "Just don't throw it."

Eddie logged onto the GoFundMe account he set up in Dwayne's name. What he saw didn't surprise him.

"Shit, man!"

"What's wrong?"

"The GoFundMe I set up for Dwayne," answered Eddie. "There was over twenty thousand dollars, US. Now it's down to zero."

"What?"

"I knew this would happen."

"How much were you aiming for?"

"My goal was five grand US because that's how much it costs for a decent funeral down here. The plan was to give the rest to Jalissa."

Corey shook his head as he let it drop.

"Just look at the comments," continued Eddie. "Everyone wants their money back because they think that I'm going to use the money to buy drugs. And GoFundMe's now claiming that my fundraiser's a violation of their policy."

"Why don't you write a blog to let everyone know your side of the story?"

"Who's going to believe me?"

"You never know."

"You think anyone back home saw the video?" asked Eddie.

"Quit beating yourself up," said Corey. "It's not your fault."

"They drugged me and dumped me on the street."

"I know, bruh. Just be glad that you're still alive."

"They could've killed me. They threatened to chop my dick off."

Corey cringed and squeezed his legs tightly together. "You're safe now. Stop overthinking it."

"I'm not overthinking it."

"You overthink a lot."

"Really? When?"

"Hmm, you once thought that *Shaft* was a porn flick."

"I was a kid back then, and we never saw a lot of African-American movies in Canada."

"We were eighteen."

"I don't care. Anyone could've made that mistake. With a title like that…anyway that doesn't prove that I overthink things."

"You also thought Nene Leakes was African-American slang for a penile discharge."

Eddie shot Corey a glance and made a face. "Anyone born outside the United States could've made that mistake."

Corey rolled his eyes. "Sure, Eddie."

Eddie and Corey turned to the sound of movement at the door. Eddie rolled his eyes when he saw that it was Detective Inspector Ellis.

"When are you two going to stay out of trouble?" asked Ellis, who then turned to Corey. "Step aside. Your turn is coming soon."

Corey made a face as he looked at Ellis. "Turn for what?"

Ellis's facial expression didn't change, and it made Eddie even more uncomfortable.

"Eddie Barrow, you're under arrest for indecent exposure and for being under the influence of a controlled substance." Ellis showed Eddie a pair of handcuffs. "I must advise you that you're not required to tell me anything else from this point on."

Chapter 11

Somewhere in Saint James Parish

The sixty-six-year-old retiree took a large swig of his Appleton Estate rum, then rested the glass on the side table. He drank so often that he no longer noticed the way it burned on the way down. He closed his eyes, inhaling deeply then letting himself sink into his recliner. It must have been at least forty years old, and he would never replace it. It had too much history. The television set in front of him, however, was less than ten. He'd had no choice but to throw out the old one with the rabbit ears…though, its life span had been impressive for something purchased twenty years before. He didn't like having to adapt to the new technology. It may have had its benefits of making life easier, but today, nothing was built to last. He counted the days until this flatscreen television decided to call it quits on him.

But the house he was in, it had been in his family for over two generations. It was built to last, and he wouldn't let anyone do the repairs. Even though he was in his sixties, a few nosey neighbors insisted that he hire professionals to renovate the place. Still, he felt that as long as he could walk and bowl a cricket ball, he'd do what was needed to keep the house standing.

However, that was the least of his concerns. A news report featured the author Eddie Barrow, who had been arrested for indecent exposure and was suspected of using drugs. He sucked his teeth while shaking his head. He then grabbed the glass and drained the rest of the rum.

On the same table was a landline phone. He picked up the receiver and dialed a number, then lowered the TV volume with the remote while he heard ringing on the other end.

"Yes?"

"Ellis, it's me."

"What's going on, Karlos?"

"I just see this Barrow youngster on the news. You were telling me about him from the other night."

Karlos heard Ellis sigh loudly. "He's a damn nuisance, but I took care of him."

"You sure of that?"

"He's going straight to jail once he leaves the hospital. Of course, I'm sure."

"I'm not convinced of that," said Karlos. "He was at two crime scenes already, and now your men pick him up because him a stocky and running around naked. I'm sure you know that something ain't right."

"Of course I know that."

"Then you know that he's been trying to find out who killed Dwayne Pottinger."

"He won't be playing detective any longer, that I can guarantee," said Ellis. "With what happened to him this evening and with what's going to happen to him, he won't be a nuisance after tonight."

Karlos swatted away a fly that buzzed around his face. "I doubt that. He's a celebrity and will most likely be back out by morning. I'd keep an eye on him if I were you."

There was a moment of silence on the other end.

"You still there?"

"Yeah, I'm here," said Ellis. "Is there anything else?"

"No, just keep a close watch on Barrow."

Chapter 12

Freeport Police Station, 12:11 PM the next day

"A publicity stunt?" Eddie shoved the front door and stormed out of the building with Corey next to him. "I could've been killed, and the prosecutor thinks that I pulled a Jussie Smollett to sell more books."

Eddie straightened the oversized gray shorts and shirt that he wore. "Again, they gave me clothes that don't fit. I think the police did this on purpose."

"I know that it sucks that the prosecutors used your past experience against you. You're lucky that you were let off with a fine," said Corey. "They could've kept you in jail a lot longer and make you face trial."

"Yeah." Eddie stopped to tighten the drawstring of his shorts. "A fine plus lawyer's fees."

"Fees paid to a good one whom you'll have to thank Jordyn's father for."

"That's not the point. I was set up, and they don't want to believe me."

"You and I both know that," said Corey as they walked through the parking lot. "Your lawyer managed to convince the prosecutor that you wouldn't have abandoned me because you don't know the area well enough. Besides, after what we went through earlier—being shot at and nearly set on fire—wandering off on your own to take drugs didn't make sense. Besides, the police found your phone and wallet in the area you described."

Fortunately, his phone was protected with a thumbprint lock—making it less attractive to a would-be thief. As for the wallet, everything was still there except for some cash and his credit card.

"It doesn't help that the hospital's CCTV footage experienced technical difficulty around the time Wesley died," said Eddie as they walked to their car. "That's not a coincidence."

"I know. Just be happy that you're out," said Corey. "By the way, how bad was it in there?"

Eddie stopped and looked at his friend with his head cocked to one side. "I spent the last three hours sharing a cell with six guys who thought I was a male prostitute."

Corey winced. "I hope they don't think I'm your pimp."

"It ain't funny."

Corey stifled a chuckle. "I'm just messing with you."

They got back to their car, which Corey had parked under a tree.

"Did you bring me some clothes, my laptop, and battery charger as I asked?" Eddie turned on his phone. It beeped to alert him that the battery was down to fifteen percent.

"They're all in the trunk."

Eddie stood behind the car and waited while Corey popped the trunk. He then lifted the lid and grabbed the laptop bag. Eddie closed the door and then climbed into the passenger seat, joining Corey up front.

"You're not going to let this go, are you?"

"How can I, knowing that my naked Black ass is all over the internet."

"I guess that it's not a good time to tell you that *Eddie Barrow* is trending on Twitter for the wrong reasons."

Eddie sucked his teeth.

He connected his phone to the portable battery with the USB cable just as it rang. It was Bevins.

Eddie answered, listened, and finished the conversation with an "I understand" before hanging up.

"That didn't sound good." Corey started the engine and shoved the gear into reverse.

"Forget about Kingston. My book tour's been canceled," said Eddie. "My publisher's considering breaking ties with me. Bevins said she'll fight for me. She's also trying to salvage the meeting with Dennis Denton."

Corey glanced at him, then turned to face the road, shaking his head. "Cancel culture, bruh. I don't know what to say."

"Are you surprised?" Eddie tapped the screen to set up the mobile hotspot feature before opening the laptop.

"What are you looking at?" asked Corey as he drove onto the street.

Eddie did not have to answer him since Corey soon saw him looking at pictures from Citrusville.

"Are you kidding me, Eddie?"

"Something's been bothering me the whole evening."

"Besides being in jail?"

"It doesn't mean that I lost focus."

"Then maybe you should," said Corey. "I know that you feel you owe Jalissa, but getting involved in Dwayne's murder has been a disaster. We were nearly killed last night."

Corey's last words flew over Eddie's head as he continued examining each picture.

"Eddie? Are you even listening to me?"

Eddie was about to scroll to the following picture when one jumped out at him. For the first time in several hours, he grinned.

Gotcha!

"Remember when I told you that one of Dwayne's drawings looked familiar?"

Corey shook his head and sighed. "Yeah, what about it?"

Eddie soon found the Facebook profile of the contestant who had taken the selfie with Shenice. He scrolled through it until he stopped on a pic she had taken of herself at home a few hours before she arrived at Citrusville. The comment she left with the picture made Eddie smile even more. "I knew it."

Corey turned to him briefly before looking back at the road. "Should I even ask?"

"I found something," said Eddie as he looked up Jalissa's number.

"You're unbelievable," scoffed Corey.

Eddie dialed Jalissa's number using WhatsApp. After three rings, there was an answer.

"Jalissa?"

"I don't know why I thought you could help."

"Before you say anything else, I was kidnapped and drugged last night."

"What?"

"Those videos of me on social media don't tell the whole story."

"I trusted you when I asked for your help. Now, I don't know what to believe."

"Please give me a chance to explain, but not over the phone. By the way, have you downloaded any apps, music, or videos on your phone lately?"

"No, why?"

"Under no circumstances must you do so," said Eddie. "Don't accept any friend requests on social media nor click on any website links."

"Why not?"

"I'll explain later. We need to meet."

"I don't know. I'm not sure if I should be seen with you right now. I think this was a mistake."

"Had you asked anyone else to look into your brother's murder, they would've walked away by now—especially after Corey and I were nearly killed last night," said Eddie. "I know that I'm onto something, but I really need your help. Is there a secluded spot where we can meet—one that's not in the MoBay area where we won't draw any attention to ourselves? I'll reimburse your cab fare."

Jalissa sighed. "Like where?"

"How about a church?" Eddie noticed Corey glancing at him.

There was a short pause. "Okay. Do you know the Unity Hall Open Bible Church?"

"As long as it's on Google Maps, I can find it."

"It should be. Meet me there in an hour."

"Oh, another thing. Do you still have Dwayne's old scrapbooks?"

"Of course. Why?"

"Bring them with you. There's something I want to check out. See you in an hour."

Jalissa hung up, and Eddie put down his phone.

"Are you going to tell me what's on your mind?" asked Corey.

Eddie turned to Corey. "You remember when you told Wesley that Dwayne should've had his own clothing line, and Wesley replied that he heard that Dwayne tried it, but it didn't work out?"

"I think so."

"Trust me, you did," said Eddie. "I think Dwayne may have found out that he was a victim of intellectual property theft."

"Are you sure?"

"I'm pretty damn sure," said Eddie. "It would explain why he risked his life showing up at the club as Shenice."

Chapter 13

Unity Hall Open Bible Church, Unity Hall, Jamaica. 4:05 PM Monday

"Anything suspicious back there?" said Eddie as he made his third detour.

Corey glanced in his rearview mirror from the passenger side. "For the sixth time, no. Aren't you being a bit paranoid?"

"I'm making sure we're not being followed." Eddie turned off the main highway and drove uphill on a much narrower road. Narrow in the sense that half of one side was so badly damaged that it was missing in certain parts. They arrived at the church, which was located at the corner of the road they were on and another road that was in a similar condition. After turning onto the side road, Eddie reversed into one of the four available parking spots.

"I know, but you don't need to be asking me the same question every three minutes."

Eddie didn't care that Corey found him to be a bit paranoid. After they left the courthouse, the first thing Eddie did was buy a burner phone. He also made Corey do everything to lose or expose a potential follower. An extra turn here, driving down the wrong road deliberately, only to make a U-turn and go back to where they came—all ideas Eddie picked up from reading a spy novel. After what happened to him the night before, there was no such thing as being too careful.

They got out and made their way to the front entrance. As expected, the front doors were left wide open like many churches in the Caribbean. Not only to welcome everyone but also to keep the inside cool—especially in this thirty-eight-degree heat.

The church was not the traditional Anglican church that dated back to the colonial period but a more modern one. The exterior was a faded orange with white French windows. The size of the building—in comparison to the neighboring homes, in Eddie's opinion—put it out of place. Perhaps it was because there wasn't a sidewalk, or that it should've been built farther away from the road.

What concerned him was that he only saw one way out. If Stepmother, Hansel, and Gretel were to show up, they'd be trapped.

The second-floor entrance was accessible by two mirroring exterior staircases that led onto a terrace. Once Eddie and Corey made it to the balcony, Eddie stayed inside the doorway to get a good view of the parking lot, while Corey searched for another exit, just in case of an emergency.

Eddie expected Jalissa would be taking a taxi. If he saw that she had been followed, he would text Corey immediately to leave and meet him outside at the back of the church. He would also text Jalissa and tell her not to get out but to head back home.

He looked at the time on his smartphone and saw that she was running late—fifteen minutes to be precise. The only thought that came to mind was that her parents learned what she was up to and stopped her from leaving the house, but then he remembered that she would've been leaving school. She was mature for her young age, determined and perseverant from what he saw the last time they met. He felt like texting her but then thought otherwise as it may compromise her.

Just be patient.

His phone buzzed, making him look away from the area below: "How much longer are we waiting? You sure she's coming?" It was from Corey.

"We're staying. She may be caught in traffic," Eddie answered.

A few seconds went by before his phone buzzed again: "I have to go to the bathroom."

"Can't you hold it?"

"Too late, I'm already at the john."

"You couldn't drain yourself before we got here?"

"When? You made so many detours and not one of them close to a gas station."

"You could've told me you had to go. And how are you pissing and texting at the same time?" Eddie clicked SEND, then began typing again. "Never mind."

Eddie looked out and saw a taxi enter the parking lot and stop near the bottom stairs. He then saw Jalissa exit the cab, carrying the same bag she had at the book signing. He texted Corey: "She's here."

Corey should hopefully be making his way back by now. Eddie waited a bit longer and watched the taxi drive off. From what he saw, there wasn't any suspicious behavior from any motorists who passed. This was a very low-traffic area, making it the ideal spot.

Just as Jalissa got to the top of the stairs, he turned to see Corey approaching from the opposite direction.

"Thanks for coming," said Eddie as Jalissa joined them. Eddie counted twenty seconds to make sure no one followed her before joining Jalissa on one of the back pews. Corey sat sideways on the pew in front of theirs to look back.

Jalissa turned to Eddie. "What were you looking for back there?"

"I wanted to be sure that you weren't followed."

"Not followed?" Jalissa shrieked. "Why would I be followed?"

"It all comes down to what happened last night," said Eddie.

Jalissa's eyes widened as she leaned closer. "What the hell was that all about?"

"I was attacked and drugged by the same people who killed Wesley," said Eddie. "They came after him in the hospital to finish the job."

"What? Is this what you didn't want to discuss over the phone?" Jalissa paused to lower her voice. "Then why did I hear that Wesley died from a heart attack? People are saying that both he and Dwayne were selling dope and that his place was shot up by rivals."

Eddie turned to Corey, who appeared to be as surprised as he. "Wesley didn't die from a heart attack. He was murdered, and I walked in on the guy who did it."

Jalissa's hands went straight to cover her mouth. "Oh my God. You saw who killed him."

Eddie nodded. "And I believe he was one of the people who killed Dwayne."

"People?" gasped Jalissa, who paused as though to remember to keep her voice low. "Who are they, and why would they want to hurt Dwayne?"

"We don't know yet," said Eddie. "This is why I asked you to make sure that you're not being followed and to *only* contact me on WhatsApp because those texts and phone calls cannot be traced or hacked. Are you sure that Dwayne didn't have any enemies? Did he owe money to anyone?"

Jalissa paused as though in thought, then shook her head. "Not that I know of. As for enemies? Other than those who say gay people should be killed, no. I don't know who'd want to kill him."

Jalissa grabbed her phone. "What about when you told me not to download anything? What was that about?"

"WhatsApp isn't entirely hackproof," said Eddie. "Whenever you click on a website link that leads you to a pop-up window, or when you download an app from an unfamiliar website or play any games that require you to share personal details, you're setting yourself up to be hacked."

"What?"

Eddie nodded once. "Sure, they look harmless. But it's a way for a hacker to slip some malware onto your phone which will give them backdoor access to all its content—even on a secure app such as WhatsApp."

Jalissa turned away as she covered her mouth with her palms.

Eddie knew that what he said would spook her. He felt the same way when he read about an Israeli company developing spyware called Pegasus. It worked so well that it managed to reveal all WhatsApp chats to the person or persons operating it.

"Should I throw away my phone and get a new one?" asked Jalissa.

"I wouldn't go that far," said Eddie. "Just remember what I said, and you'll be fine."

"Getting back to last night," said Jalissa. "You're lucky to be alive."

"You ain't kidding," said Corey.

"As for the dope allegations," said Eddie, "that doesn't make any sense."

"I don't care what people are saying," said Jalissa. "I know that my brother's not a dope dealer. I'll never believe that."

"I believe you," said Eddie. "I think whatever drugs the police may have found at Wesley's house were planted."

"But now they came after you." Jalissa looked away, shaking her head. "I feel bad about this."

"We don't think that we were among their targets," said Corey. "But we can't be too careful."

"Which is why they chose to threaten and then humiliate me instead."

Jalissa turned away from them. "I'm so sorry. I shouldn't have gotten you involved in this. I'm so sorry that I almost got you killed."

"It's not your fault." Eddie put his hand on top of her shoulder. "I ain't stopping now if that's what you're wondering. Which comes to why I asked you to bring Dwayne's scrapbooks."

"Yes." Jalissa reached inside her bag. "Here they are."

Eddie took the one she handed him and flipped through a few pages. Most of them were badly stained, and the drawings were damaged from water. Many were taped together, but some remained torn. He stopped on two familiar pictures. They were dirty and discolored, but he was sure they were the same ones he saw at Wesley's home. Eddie then showed it to Corey. "See what I was talking about?"

Corey already had his smartphone with the photo app open to Dwayne's selfie, dressed as Shenice, taken with the other contestant. "Yeah, I see what you were talking about."

"Show that photo to Jalissa," said Eddie.

Corey handed his phone to her.

She glanced at the selfie and then at the drawing. "This woman's wearing one of Dwayne's dresses." Jalissa slapped the top of the pew in front of her. "I knew my brother was right. He was *always* right. How'd you figure it out?"

"I looked for a pattern and found it." Eddie glanced at the drawing before turning to Jalissa. "When did Dwayne first tell you that he suspected that someone had stolen his designs?"

Jalissa fell back in the pew and sighed as though a long and very distasteful memory had come back to annoy her. "Two years ago, Dwayne had two scrapbooks filled with his designs. He wanted to create his own fashion line. But to do so he'd need to get his designs featured in a major fashion magazine. Fortunately, we have our own local fashion queen who he hoped would pull some strings for him. You may have heard of her, Vanessa Pusey."

"Vanessa Pusey?" Corey answered as he looked away, then back at Jalissa. "The Jamaican track star?"

Jalissa closed her eyes and shook her head. "Yeah, that one."

Corey turned to Eddie. "You should've seen her back in the day. She wore the most bomb-ass outfits, big muscular legs and booty, and long-ass nails. She used to tear up the track at the Olympics."

Eddie was suddenly reminded of such an athlete. "The name rings a bell." He didn't watch sports as much as Corey. Still, Vanessa Pusey's flamboyant personality was hard to miss, even if one wasn't a regular fan. "So, she became a designer?"

"Second best to Dwayne," spat Jalissa. "I used to be a fan of hers until what she did to my brother."

"Yeah, tell us what happened," said Corey as he rested his elbow on the top of the pew in front of them.

"As I was saying," Jalissa continued, "after a lot of running around, Dwayne managed to schedule a meeting with Pusey to show her his work. He had a lot of respect for her and literally begged her to give him a chance at getting his foot in the door."

"Let me guess," said Eddie. "She told him that she'd look at his work, sent him on his way, called him back, then told him that the designs wouldn't sell. Right?"

Jalissa looked at Eddie with large eyes.

"It's something us independent artists fear if you were wondering," said Eddie.

"Dwayne was devastated when she told him that she showed

them to several fashion magazine editors, and none were interested. He was so upset that he talked about giving up designing and making dresses." Jalissa then pointed to herself. "I was the one who pushed him to continue and not to give up. A year went by after that meeting with Pusey, when some of his dresses appeared in one of the top fashion magazines. Dwayne was livid when he saw them."

"Pusey stole his designs and claimed credit for them," sighed Eddie.

"She's a damn thief." She shouted so loudly that Eddie had to make a downward hand gesture to remind her that they were in a church.

Jalissa closed her eyes and held her forehead. "I'm sorry about that. It's just that I get so mad when I think of what she did to my brother. Montego Fashion Week started yesterday. I heard that Pusey's showcasing her so-called clothing line."

Jalissa took out a tissue from her pants pocket and dabbed at her eyes. "It was Dwayne's ticket out of here. Imagine how he felt, knowing that the woman—Jamaica's own track queen—whom he held in the highest regard, stole from him. A fellow Jamaican betrays and deprives him of his opportunity to shine."

Corey took a handkerchief and wiped off some sweat from the back of his neck. "What did Dwayne do next?"

"He fought back as best he could," Jalissa replied. "He confronted her—or at least tried to—when he marched into her office, only for the police to show up and throw him out."

Jalissa flipped through Dwayne's scrapbook and stopped at a partially torn picture. "Dwayne snatched *this* before Pusey had him removed from her property."

Eddie saw that the torn picture was juxtaposed with another.

Jalissa first pointed to the partially torn picture. "Here's hers, and there's Dwayne's. He then went on social media and posted a video of himself blasting Pusey for the thief she is. Dwayne even showed his original drawings to prove that she stole them." Jalissa dropped her head in her hands.

Eddie leaned forward. "But…"

She held her head up again. "Pusey fought back. She held a

press conference where she showed her copied drawings and claimed them as hers. Pusey then acted as though *she* was the victim. Through her lawyer she sent Dwayne a *cease-and-desist* notice. He had no choice but to give up. No one wanted to believe him because she was too famous. According to everyone else, Dwayne was just a village fish—a nobody."

"Listen," Corey nodded, "Dwayne was somebody. Others just didn't know it at the time."

She turned to Corey and smiled as a tear came to her eye. "Thank you."

Eddie put a hand on her shoulder to console her. "We're not giving up yet."

Jalissa turned to Eddie. "Even after everything you went through?"

"We came this far." Eddie looked back in the scrapbook to the same picture. He studied it bit by bit.

"You're seeing something else?" asked Corey.

"Naw," he said as he turned to Jalissa. "I just don't know what Dwayne hoped to accomplish from taking a selfie with the girl who wore this dress. Even with this drawing, it's so badly mangled there's no way that he could prove that it was his."

"Maybe it wasn't the dress," said Corey.

"Why do you say that?" asked Eddie.

Corey shrugged his shoulders. "I don't know. You just said that he'd never be able to prove that the dress was his from just taking a selfie with the woman wearing it."

Jalissa looked at Corey's smartphone. "May I see that?"

Corey unlocked it. "What do you want to see?"

"The same picture you showed us earlier."

Corey brought up the photograph and handed the phone to her.

Jalissa sighed. "That's Pusey's niece, Shantel. I guess the apple doesn't fall far from the tree in that family."

"So, her niece wore Dwayne's dress." Eddie shrugged. "I don't see what Dwayne hoped to prove."

"But that's the only selfie he took that evening," said Corey. "He had to have done it for a reason. Maybe there's something else."

"Like what?" asked Eddie. "She's wearing a similar dress to what Dwayne drew, but there's no way of proving that it's his because his original drawing is next to destroyed and barely recognizable."

"So, what do you suggest we do?" asked Corey.

Eddie turned to Jalissa. "Does Dwayne have other drawings? Maybe they're hidden someplace?"

"I don't think so." Jalissa shrugged. "What I've brought you is what I've been able to save. The rest he would've had with him."

"Then we're at a dead-end," sighed Corey.

Eddie looked to the stained-glass window ahead, behind the alter. He stared at it as he heard Jalissa grumbling under her breath about everything being a lost cause. He then turned to her. "Not yet."

Jalissa's face lit up as she grabbed his hand and squeezed.

"Don't worry yourself," Eddie answered as he looked at Dwayne's scrapbook. "Is it all right that we hold onto this for a while?"

"Sure," Jalissa answered. "Keep it as long as you'll need it."

"Great." He then looked to the door. "Do you want a lift?"

"Sure, but not up to my front door, you know—"

"Right. Your parents."

"Exactly."

"May you wait for us outside?" asked Eddie. "We won't be long."

"Sure." Jalissa got up and left.

Corey turned to Eddie. "I think you already know what I'm going to say."

"We can't stop now," said Eddie. "We're onto something. I know it."

"You also have a career to think of," said Corey. "Or is that no longer important for you?"

"I know," said Eddie. "But I can't ignore what's going on."

Corey sighed.

"Look, I just want to do one more thing," said Eddie. "Who knows, this may end up being the lucky break we need."

"And what's that?"

"We need to find a way to meet Vanessa Pusey."

"You're crazy." Corey shook his head. "She'll never meet with you."

"One celebrity to another? I'm sure I can find a way to set that up. Nancy can talk to her agent and set up the meeting."

"And you expect her to come out and admit that she stole Dwayne's designs? She most likely saw your nude celebrity video and will do everything to avoid you."

"I don't care. And no, I don't expect Pusey to admit to anything. But I'm sure that I can get her to slip up."

"How?"

"I don't know yet," said Eddie.

"Nice," said Corey sarcastically.

"But in the meantime," said Eddie, "why don't we pay Dwayne's ghost-employer a visit. She may know how to find Candace."

Chapter 14

Milly's Dress Store, Church and E Street, Montego Bay

Eddie saw that Jalissa could not hide how upset she was after he and Corey dropped her off. It was official. Drugs were found by authorities around Wesley's home, inside a fireproof safe. Unfortunately, Eddie couldn't change the radio station fast enough before that part of the report was mentioned. She was adamant in her claim that Dwayne didn't peddle dope. Even though Eddie didn't want to believe that Dwayne may have used or sold drugs, the report raised more questions. What kind of trouble were Dwayne, Wesley, and Candace into?

While Corey drove, Eddie went online to look for the website of Dwayne's employer. He did not find one, except a location that was marked on Google Maps. He imagined that she must have a very loyal clientele, depending heavily on word-of-mouth. Most small businesses operated this way.

Corey dropped Eddie off outside the store since he had a plan that would allow them to approach the case from another angle.

It was a few blocks shy of the high-traffic area of the city. The store was on the ground floor of a two-story building near the intersection. Compared to the Witter Village Shopping mall, each building—including Milly's store—had grills on the windows and doors. Eddie watched Corey drive off slowly on the pothole-filled E Street. There wasn't any visible signage. This led Eddie to believe that Milly's business clientele may have already been well-established and boosted by word-of-mouth.

Like in other parts of the Caribbean, Jamaicans used landmarks to find places. Even the mail carriers didn't need numbered addresses to know where to deliver.

Eddie pushed open the front glass door and was greeted with a door chime and a cool Arctic blast. Standing where he was, he already felt cramped. Eddie wouldn't be surprised if this store could fit inside one of Oprah Winfrey's bedrooms—or even one of her walk-in closets. The racks holding different varieties of women's clothing barely gave one enough room to pass in between.

Eddie turned to the sound of footsteps, and through a doorway in the back, a relatively large woman—both in height and weight—emerged. Eddie knew from the measuring tape hanging around her neck that it was Milly.

"Good afternoon, son, how are you?" she said with a smile as she slid her glasses onto her forehead. "This is your first time here, isn't it?"

Eddie returned the smile. "I'm visiting from overseas."

"Well then, welcome to Jamaica. I'm Milly." She then put her hands on her hips while looking at Eddie suspiciously with her head turned slightly. "You look familiar. Should I know you?"

Oh shit! She saw the video.

"My name's Eddie Barrow," he answered while holding his head up high. "You probably saw my picture in the paper for my book signing yesterday."

Milly's face lit up as her eyes and smile widened. "Oh, Mister Eddie the author. I knew I saw your face before. I knew someone who read all your books and always spoke of you."

Eddie sighed with a smile as a crisis was averted. It was at that moment that her facial expression switched from excitement to sadness.

"Lord!" She was clearly fighting back the tears. He had struck a nerve.

"I hope that I didn't pass by at a bad time." Eddie wasn't planning on leaving, but it was necessary to show empathy to maintain the appearance of a random tourist who was passing through.

"No, no. It's okay," Milly answered as she shuffled between racks to the cash register, where she pulled open a drawer. Eddie didn't see her reach inside but only saw her dabbing her eyes with a tissue seconds later. "How did you hear about my store?"

"A friend recommended you to me." It was at that moment that he took out dress pants from his bag. "The hem on one of the pant legs came undone. I was hoping that you could fix it."

Milly reached out for the pants then slid her glasses down onto her nose. "Let me see."

Eddie handed it to her, holding up the pant leg that needed to be hemmed. She took one look and nodded.

"I can fix this. Are you in a hurry?"

"No, I can wait," Eddie answered. "Do you need me to put them on?"

"No, that won't be necessary." She looked at him. Her spirits returned. "It's not often I have celebrities passing through. Come with me to the back."

Eddie followed her through the same door that she emerged from earlier. The back store would've been less cramped had it not contained so many stacked boxes. Some of them weren't sealed and some of the material was visible.

"So how much longer you're staying in Jamaica?" she asked as she sat down in front of the sewing machine. She gestured to the wooden chair. "Pull up the chair, sit down, please."

Eddie took a seat next to her. "I was going to leave tomorrow, but a few things came up, so I'll be here for a bit longer."

Milly lined up both pant legs to measure the lengths to see where the old hem was stitched. "I see. Will you be back soon for another book tour?"

"That depends on what my agent and publicist can arrange, as well as how soon I can write my next novel."

"Am I too late to get an autographed copy?" She removed a pin from the pincushion and fastened it into the hem she made.

"Which book would you like to have autographed?"

She looked up at him with glowing cheeks. "You'll do that for me?"

"Of course."

"I'll go to the store and buy all of them."

"How about I gift them for you instead."

"Nonsense. I'll buy your books first, then you can autograph them." She was clearly adamant. "I love to support young Black people in their endeavors. Besides, you made an impression on my friend."

"Who's your friend?" He already knew to whom she referred, but the more relaxed she was with him, the more comfortable she'd be in answering his questions.

"He died in a fire." She was swift to answer, in fact, a bit too quick. It was as though she was trying to avoid going into detail.

Eddie faked his gasp. "I'm sorry to hear that. You have my sympathy."

"Thank you, dear." She ran the pant leg under the sewing machine. The noise went on for a few moments before she stopped and turned to Eddie. "He was very young and ambitious. Very hard working too. He spoke a lot about you, the mess you and your friends got into, and how you were nearly killed." She talked about her *friend*, all without mentioning his name, while pausing a few times to run the pant leg through the sewing machine.

She was done a few minutes later, and she held up the pants for him. "There you go."

Eddie reached out to take them. "Thanks."

"You're welcome," she answered as she removed her glasses, then turned to face him. "But there's something else, Mister Barrow."

"What's that?"

"I get the feeling that you already know who my friend is and that you didn't just come over here to get your pant leg hemmed. Am I correct?"

Eddie sighed with a smile, while he held his hands up as though in surrender. "I'll be honest with you, Milly. I know that Dwayne Pottinger worked for you in secret—but don't worry, I won't tell anyone. I have nothing against Dwayne or anyone who's like him. My friend and I witnessed part of his assault."

Milly's hands shot up to cover her mouth. "Lawd, Jesus."

"We did our best to save his life, but it was too late."

She slammed a palm on the table. "I don't care what they say about Dwayne. He was a Godsend. He was a kind and very caring person. And those who say otherwise don't know him."

"I've heard as much."

"And, unfortunately, most people around here don't want to accept that." She rested her elbow on the table while she covered her mouth as though in thought. "I really wanted to tell my clients that those beautiful dresses that they're wearing are thanks to Dwayne."

She gestured to the stacked boxes that crowded the room. "You see all of those? *All* of them are Dwayne's work. The demand was just too high for me to do it all on my own. He was the reason why I was able to keep up. He even came up with better designs than what I came up with when it came to creating an outfit from scratch—yet he never took the credit for them. That's how generous he was."

"It's my understanding that he didn't want you to lose any business because of him."

Milly nodded. "This store is all I have. If I lose this, I don't know what I'll do."

"As I mentioned earlier," said Eddie, "your secret is safe with me."

"Please tell me you saw who killed him."

Eddie bit his lip briefly. "I can't say for a fact I saw who did it. As I said before, I only witnessed a part of the assault."

"Whatever you hear on the news about Dwayne being a dope peddler, it's not true. I won't believe that. I refuse to accept that." Milly then motioned to the stacks of boxes. "Look at all the work Dwayne did. Where would he find the time to be selling dope? That doesn't make sense. And from what I know about Dwayne, he'd never live with anyone who was selling dope."

Eddie decided that it was time to use a different tactic. He took out his smartphone and brought up the photograph of Dwayne—dressed as Shenice—in the picture with Pusey's niece, then showed it to Milly.

"I was looking over some of Dwayne's sketches from his scrapbook. The dress that this woman wore looks like one of his."

Milly sucked her teeth and raised her voice. "That horrible Pusey woman tief Dwayne's designs. She tief di whole a dem."

She stole all of them, is what Eddie understood.

Milly lowered her head and shook it with her eyes closed. "That part I figured out."

"And she gets away with it because she's famous, got money, and she's a former Olympian. Nobody's going to believe that a young boy from the ghetto would've come up with those designs."

"Unfortunately, that's how the world works," said Eddie. "However, I believe that Dwayne thought that he could prove that the dress this woman was wearing was his. Based on what I've seen so far, it would've been tough to prove. Is there anything unique about the dress—or is there anything in the picture itself that you find suspicious?"

Milly took the smartphone and studied the photo for a few moments, then shook her head. "No, I'm afraid not. I wish that there was something I could see because I just want that tiefing woman fi get exposed fa wha she be."

She then glanced behind Eddie's shoulder and nodded in that direction. "You see that?"

Eddie turned around and saw a small desk that included a drawer. Boxes containing clothes Dwayne had worked on sat on top of it. "You mean the desk?"

"Yes." Milly nodded. "Dwayne drew patterns on that desk. I'll never get rid of it, no matter how unsightly it looks. Once my clients come to pick up their items, that's all that'll be left to remind me of him. He was like a nephew to me."

This wasn't going anywhere. It was time to attack it from another angle. "How did you and Dwayne meet?"

A smile lit up her face. "I was introduced to Dwayne through a friend, Delva. She and I go way back to our school days."

"What does she do for a living?"

"She used to be a caregiver, but she's retired," said Milly. "One of her Alzheimer's patients attacked her. It's a very terrible disease, and it makes you do things you don't normally do, you know?"

"I've heard."

"But then her husband passed away, left her a bunch of money, but she never told anyone. Only her closest friends and I know."

"Why? Did she suddenly become a big spender?"

Milly shook her head. "No, not at all. I don't know what bills she had to pay. The mortgage on her house was paid, and she didn't have any children of her own. But after she retired, she was always baking and cooking for those children who live on the street."

"She'd have them over to her house?"

"Oh no." Milly smiled. "She'd invite them, but they'd refuse. So, she made sandwiches, packaged them all nice to give them. Dwayne used to be one of them she brought sandwiches to, but he was living with his two friends in a run-down house in Albion."

"In other words, she was an—" Eddie imitated quotation marks with his fingers, "ally."

Milly nodded. "Um-hum. Those wicked excuses for parents kicked him out. I don't know how anyone could do that to their own flesh and blood."

Eddie saw that he may lose her, so he redirected the conversation back to Delva. "So did your friend Delva offer Dwayne a chance to stay with her."

"No, like the others, Dwayne didn't feel comfortable. He didn't have a job, nor any money. But that's when he offered to fix a dress she wore."

"And what happened?"

"She let him do it. He also did some more work on some of her other clothes. It wasn't too long before she told me about him and asked me to give him a chance."

"But couldn't Delva have brought her clothes to you, considering that you're friends?"

"She did. But she knew that I was overwhelmed. And with my arthritis acting up, it slowed me down even more. Soon after, I hired Dwayne, and he moved in with that boy who just got killed."

"You mean Wesley."

"You know him too?"

"We were briefly acquainted."

"I tested Dwayne by giving him one dress to fix up. Boy, was I surprised at how fast he got it done."

"I heard he was very talented."

"Talented? More like extremely gifted," said Milly. "Not only did he fix up the dress, but he handed it back with two designs that would make it look even nicer."

"Really?"

"I'm not making this up. Dwayne drew the designs on that table—right here on the spot. He then asked me to show them to the owner and ask if he could alter them into one of the designs. Within three days, he created a new dress."

"And all this time, the customer never suspected that it was anyone else but you."

"No, as I said earlier, Dwayne wanted to keep a low profile," said Milly. "Anyhow, that client showed up two days later with two friends of hers who wanted to know if I could design new dresses for them. They were big women, so it was difficult for them to shop for clothes in their size. To make a long story short, I bought the material, took their measurements, and Dwayne did the rest. I wound up with two new happy clients. My business kept taking off. The demand was so high, I had no choice but to hire Dwayne full time."

"That's really something."

"When one door closes, another will open, as they say," said Milly.

"You ain't kidding." Eddie decided to then switch the subject matter. "Did any of Dwayne's friends stop by?"

"Oh yes, every once in a while," said Milly. "Those boys on the street had nowhere else to go for their fashions."

"Fashions?" Eddie was puzzled. "They had money to buy clothes?"

"They didn't have much," she answered. "But any cash they got, they had to earn it by…other means. And I'm not talking selling drugs."

"In other words, they were providing certain *services* which their clients didn't want their wives or anyone to know about."

"Um-hmm." Milly nodded her head. "I can't tell you if Dwayne did any of that before I hired him. But I kept him so busy that he wouldn't have been able to find the time. Besides, it's not in his character."

Eddie took out his phone, logged into Dwayne's Google

account, which—not to his surprise—he was able to access using the same password he had guessed back at Wesley's home. He then accessed his online photo gallery. He found one of Dwayne with Candace and showed it to Milly.

"Do you recognize her?"

Milly took the phone to examine the photo. "That's Candace. She was one of the few who knew that Dwayne worked here."

"Do you know where she is or how to find her?"

"Mi can't tell you dat, yuh know," she replied as she handed back his smartphone. "I haven't seen har in a while."

Just then, Eddie heard the chime of the front door opening.

"Milly?" It was a woman's voice, sounding like she was around the same age as Milly.

"Delva, mi a come," Milly yelled back excitedly as she turned to Eddie and got up. "Just the person you should talk to."

Eddie followed her out front, where he saw a very petite woman around five feet five. She had white hair that had been cut short to about half an inch. Behind the thick lenses of her glasses were a set of warm, joyful eyes that would draw attention away from the bags under them.

"I was just passing through," Delva said. "How are you keeping?"

Milly sighed as she gestured to the merchandise. "You know, mi a hol on."

You know, I'm hanging on.

That's when Delva spotted Eddie. "Who's this handsome young man? You have a grandson that I don't know about?"

Milly stepped aside as she turned to Eddie. "This is Mister Barrow. He's visiting from Canada."

Delva's face lit up. "Canada. I hear it's a beautiful place. Are you here on vacation? My name's Delva, by the way."

Eddie told her what he did for a living and why he was visiting. She appeared to be more impressed with him the more he spoke.

Milly then directed the conversation to what they were discussing before. "You remember Dwayne's friend, Candace?"

Delva looked up as though she was trying to recollect who she was. "Candace, Candace, uhh, I believe so. But I don't know all of Dwayne's friends. Speaking of which, I can't believe what they're saying about him—that he was dealing dope and such nonsense."

"I told Mister Eddie the same thing," said Milly. "People just waan spoil him name."

"I guess the police believe that because they don't know that he was working for you," said Delva. "Maybe you should tell them."

"I don't think that's such a good idea, at least, not right now," said Eddie. "You've already suffered a loss. The last thing you need is for you to become a target. Timing is everything. But the choice will always be yours."

"I know." Milly nodded.

Delva then looked at Milly. "What you want to know about Candace?"

"It's just research. I'm writing an essay for my fans. My goal is for my readers to know the real Dwayne Pottinger, hoping to change public perception of him. I thought that the best thing would be to speak to his closest friends."

Just then, a thought came to him as he turned to Delva. "Didn't you used to provide lunches for the children on the street?"

"Oh yes, somebody has to help those poor children," Delva answered. "I can't stand by and let them starve. I wish I could do so much more."

"I'm curious," said Eddie. "Would you be able to introduce me to them? In return, I'll help you deliver the lunches while I'm here."

Delva appeared to be unsure. "I don't know. Those children like to keep to themselves. I don't know how they'd feel about being interviewed."

"I'll think of something to give them in return."

"Hmm," said Delva. "Let me talk to them first and let me get back to you."

Eddie handed her his business card. "That would help enormously."

It wasn't too long after that Eddie left the store. He was comfortable knowing that Delva was there to keep Milly company as the conversation drifted back to Dwayne. It was apparent that Milly did so much to hold back the tears. That poor woman. It was as though a part of her had died with Dwayne—a major, yet invisible, contributor.

Chapter 15

Scotiabank, Sam Sharpe Square, Montego Bay

"Just a reminder that we're closing in twenty minutes," said the security guard to Corey as he entered. Fortunately for him, the banks were open later than usual. It could be due to the fashion event Jalissa spoke of earlier. He was about to stand in line when he doubled back to the guard.

"Hey, is Delroy working today?"

"Mister Stewart?"

"Yeah, he's one of the managers here."

"He's over there," said the guard as he gestured to the tellers.

Corey turned and recognized him right away.

"You want me to get him for you?"

Corey shook his head as he walked to the back of the line. "Don't worry yourself."

He was surprised to see Delroy working behind the counter since he pictured branch managers and their assistants working behind closed doors where they couldn't be disturbed. He thought that perhaps Delroy wasn't so busy and decided to work with clients to speed up the line, which extended outside.

An elderly woman left, leaving him available to assist the next person in line. The man at the front of the line went toward Delroy, then stopped midway. Corey noticed Delroy crossed his arms and his eyebrows curved downward.

"What are you doing here? You're bold." Delroy then looked toward the entrance. "Security."

The man was already backing away with his hands raised as the guard rushed over.

"I'm sorry," said the man. "I didn't know that you worked

here."

Delroy slammed his palm on the counter. "Get away from me."

A bald, bearded man with an overhanging gut showed up next to Delroy. Corey assumed that he was the bank manager.

"Is there a problem?"

"Forget it," the brotha said as he backed away. "I'm sorry, I don't want no trouble." Soon he had walked past Corey, but not before Corey surreptitiously snapped a picture of him while holding his smartphone at waist level. He got a good look at him, about five feet ten, some facial hair with a semi-afro, early to mid-forties. His build suggested that he worked out regularly. Corey watched as the guard escorted the man out. Once he exited, he rounded the corner at the intersection. Corey looked at the photo he took to make sure that it was a clear shot, considering it was done on the fly. It was not the best, but good enough.

Corey glanced toward the counter and saw Delroy speaking to his supervisor. To Corey, it appeared that the supervisor had asked him if he was all right to continue working for the rest of the day. He couldn't read lips but saw that Delroy responded with a nod as they walked away, with his superior patting him on the back. Moments later, the same man replaced Delroy at the counter. Corey's first assumption was that Delroy's boss just told him to go home early and that he'd take over.

Corey immediately left the bank, crossed the cobblestones to a black, green, and gold fence roughly two car lengths away that separated the pedestrian area from the vehicle traffic. He leaned against the fence, choosing a spot that was partially obscured by a nine-foot-tall palm tree. From there he could keep an eye on the entrance. Less than ten minutes passed when he saw Delroy exit the bank with a laptop bag slung from his shoulder.

He then paused. Stiffened. He took on the appearance of a deer frozen in headlights. Corey saw that he wasn't looking at him, but past him. Corey looked over his shoulder. Besides a taxi that drove by and the pedestrian traffic in front of the museum, nothing strange stood out.

He looked back just in time to see Delroy bolt right and around the corner onto Market Street. Whatever spooked Delroy would have to wait. Corey took off after him. Even though Delroy had a significant head start, Corey still saw him ahead as he turned right at the next intersection.

Corey passed several vendors.

Delroy made a right onto Orange Street. From what Corey saw, it didn't appear that Delroy noticed him yet. Delroy crossed the street at the second intersection at Church Street—just a few blocks from Milly's store—and entered a peach-colored two-story building.

Corey picked up the pace, as he could easily lose Delroy. It was a small shopping plaza. He used the same entrance as Delroy. For the most part, it appeared to be nearly vacant, with many unused shops. However, he heard the faint music above him, which drew Corey to the stairs. When he looked up between the adjoining staircases, he caught a glimpse of Delroy heading to the top floor.

Corey ran up the stairs, taking two at a time. The music grew louder. At the top he saw more vacant store fronts with the exception of one—narrowing down where Delroy went.

Corey pushed the door to enter. There wasn't much of a breeze, just a space with cigarette smoke and sweaty men in tank tops. He first walked through a room with three pool tables, all occupied. The loud reggae music almost drowned out the ringing of the slot machines and the boisterous pool players at each table, and those who watched from the sides. A woman at a teller's booth sold lottery tickets—what locals referred to as a cash pot. But there was no sign of Delroy.

As Corey kept walking, he saw that the arcade/pool area was connected to a separate room, one that was much brighter, with a few packed tables and a bar. The sight of the liquor bottles on the wall stands brought back some terrible memories of a painful period of his life a few years back. It was when his then-girlfriend, Jordyn, worked as a barmaid in a strip club. He'd hang out there often, blowing whatever money he had left over, while Eddie worked his ass off at the bookstore—a job that barely kept a roof over both of their heads. Eddie had every reason to kick him out, and Jordyn could've left him for the same reasons. Hitting the bottle was a way out for him. Now that he looked back on that time, Corey could only be glad that he hadn't gone back to what he was before.

The loud voices to his left caught his attention. He turned to see Delroy sitting at a table with the same two guys, Bandana and Durag, he'd seen at Citrusville. A fluffy waitress in short-shorts and a top that barely contained her bouncing breasts was at their table. Delroy's friends talked about her big bumpa and how it would eventually destroy her shorts. She snapped back at them with a comment of her own about them not being able to handle it. The exchange was short, but enough for him to learn Durag and Bandana's names—or nicknames as it were—as Scuba and Jucee respectively.

Corey noticed that Delroy didn't say anything. That's when one of them shuffled the dominos on the table. There were only three players. A fourth one could easily fit in if he could convince them to let him join.

He walked over, knowing that they'd most likely play the best out of six—after which they may not play anymore.

Corey grabbed a chair on his way over, put it down backward at their table, and sat down. "Best out of six?"

His introduction caught their attention as they all looked at each other before staring back at him.

"Ah who yuh?" asked Scuba.

"I'm the one who's challenging you all. You're missing a fourth player."

"Who tell yuh seh wi miss sumadi?" said Jucee.

Who told you that we're missing someone?

"A cut-throat," said Corey, meaning that this game would be every man for himself. "My girl gave me a hard time because I lost my job. I need something to take my mind off her."

The three of them looked at each other, then Scuba turned to Corey while he said to the others. "Mek mi give unu six love."

I'm going to let you watch me win this in six rounds.

Corey was dealt seven dominos—better known as *bones* or *cards*. Delroy played the first bone as he had a double-six. Since he was sitting to Delroy's right, everyone played their hand before Corey got his turn.

"I ain't see you here before," said Scuba as he played a bone.

Corey played his. "I'm from out of town."

Delroy played but didn't say anything. Jucee followed through, and then Scuba.

"Out of town?" asked Scuba. "You sound like a foreigner."

"You can say so." Corey didn't have a bone to match either end of what was on the table and knocked, indicating that he was passing. He was down to two.

"What's this?" Scuba grinned. "You knocking already?"

Delroy knocked, and so did Jucee.

Scuba played his last bone and grinned at Corey. "One-love."

"Don't get ahead of yourself," said Corey. "I'm just adapting to my new environment."

The fluffy waitress returned with the beers and put them down on the table for Corey's adversaries. She then turned to him. "What can I get you?"

"The same as these guys," Corey answered without taking his eyes off Scuba. She left, just as Delroy shuffled the bones. They each took their seven from the boneyard.

Scuba played the first. "You sound Trini."

Corey played next. "I'm from there."

Delroy couldn't play and knocked on the table.

Jucee then placed a bone to match Corey's. "What you doing here?"

"As I said, I just want to get away."

After Scuba played a bone, Corey followed with one of his own.

They each played a hand, and the waitress brought over Corey's drink. He ended up having the upper hand and was able to win the round a few minutes later.

After the bones were dealt, Corey—the winner of the last round—placed one down on the table. He played on while keeping an eye on Delroy. He didn't look like he was concentrating. It was as though he wasn't sure if he wanted to be there or not. Unlike the other two who sat with them, he lacked drive and confidence. No doubt this guy was affected by what happened the night Dwayne Pottinger was killed. The other two didn't seem to care less, but the incident was clearly still on Delroy's mind, if not something else also related to it.

It was Corey's turn to play, and he did. Delroy wasn't budging. It was as though he had forgotten where he was.

"Delroy!" yelled Scuba, startling him. "Yuh playing, or yuh passing?"

Delroy fumbled his bones and dropped one on the floor as though he had lost his train of thought. He slammed the other pieces facedown on the table and scrambled to pick up the other one off the floor before anyone else could see what it was. However, Corey had already glimpsed it as well as three of his other dominos beforehand. There was no way Delroy could play on what he had put down.

When Delroy picked up his piece, he rechecked his bones and shook his head.

"You've been passing quite a few times already," Corey said mockingly.

Without looking at Corey, Delroy answered. "Bad hand."

Jucee knocked, but Scuba played—giving Corey a better idea of what the others had. He knew he could win this round. He played again while keeping an eye on Delroy, who passed again.

"You sure it's *just* a bad hand?" Corey then eyed Delroy's two friends. "You look like you're carrying more than that."

"Bwoy, play di caad, bumboclaat!" yelled Scuba.

"It's cool, brethren." Corey smiled as he looked at Scuba, then back at Delroy, placing a bone on the table. "I'm going to play… and you're going to pass…again."

Delroy's eyes narrowed as he stared into his hand, then knocked.

Corey nodded to the other two, one after the next. "You're going to pass, and so are you."

Corey played another piece and ended up blocking the game. He then placed his remaining bones faceup on the table. He had a double blank and an ace-blank—a blank on one side and a one on the other. A game is blocked when no other player can match either end with the dominos that they have. As a result, the players flip over what is left in their hands, counting the dots. Considering that Corey had only one dot, he won the round.

Since Delroy had the highest number of dots on his last set, he again had to shuffle the dominos.

Corey nodded to Delroy. "You're going to end up building the muscles in your arms from all that shuffling."

Corey chuckled but soon realized that his opponents didn't even give the suspicion of a smile. Delroy then scattered the dominos for everyone to select. Corey noticed that they had all finished their beers. It was then that he called the waitress over and ordered beers for the three of them. His bottle was only half full.

Sore losers. They weren't keeping their cool—especially Delroy. Just keep after Delroy...got to break eventually.

Corey went first as he looked at each of his opponents interchangeably. "I hear things got a bit heated for some boy a few nights ago."

"What bwoy?" asked Scuba, as the waitress put beers in front of them, except for Corey.

"The one who dressed as a girl at a party." Corey took a swig of his beer. "Someone or some people beat him then set him on fire."

"He should've known better than to show up dressed like that," said Scuba. "He got what he deserved."

"That batty-bwoy was trying to wine-up on other men, trying to trick them into bringing him home," said Jucee.

"Trick people into bringing him home?" Corey laughed as he placed a domino on the table. "He must've known who was ready to go home with him."

"No one knew that they were dancing with a man," said Scuba. "He was looking for trouble."

"But with whom?" asked Corey. "No one ever came forward to admit that they danced with him."

"He danced with someone, a guy," said Scuba as he slammed a domino on the table. "Then he went and danced in the contest and won."

"He fooled everyone," said Jucee as he slammed a domino. "We all thought it was a girl. Nobody did tink him a fish. Him style di whole a dem an tief di prize money."

No one thought he was a guy, tricked them, and stole the prize money. Corey wondered what other excuses they would come up with.

By this time, both Scuba and Jucee had drunk all their beer. However, Delroy remained silent and had barely touched his.

Corey could tell that the alcohol was working on them, as he could get them riled up to the point that they talked casually. Corey gently slid a domino into place. "So, this guy won the contest, danced with one person. What happened next?"

Delroy knocked the table, so did Jucee, and the turn went to Scuba, who answered. "You ask too many questions." He then knocked while shaking his head.

Corey placed another bone on the table. "From what you've all told me, that boy brought it on himself. There must be other parties he and other people like him could've gone to."

"That's what I tell you before," said Scuba. "He led us on to the point that we joined him in the parking lot."

"To do what?" quipped Corey.

"We thought she want to give us di pumpum," said Jucee right before Scuba knocked.

Corey passed, and the turn went to Delroy, who quickly said, "Pass."

This surprised Corey because he knew that Delroy must've been able to play on what was in front of him. Both Scuba and Jucee must've learned by now that Delroy's head wasn't in the game.

"And did you get it?"

Scuba knocked again. "Get what?"

Corey nodded to Jucee while looking at Scuba. "He just said she was ready to give up the pumpum to all of you."

"We thought she was a teeza," said Scuba.

They thought that Shenice was playing hard to get? Bullshit, Corey thought. "So you decided to teach her a lesson, right?"

"We wouldn't have done anything had we known it was a batty-bwoy." Scuba's voice got louder just as Jucee placed a card. "Wi shoulda kill him den—"

"I wasn't there! It's not what you think," screamed Delroy as he slammed the rest of his dominos on the table.

The only sound that Corey heard in that room was of the music that played through the speakers. There was an extremely uncomfortable pause from all three of them as they stared at each other. It was as though they suddenly realized what had just happened.

But it was too late for them. Delroy got up so quickly that something fell from his pants pocket. Corey reached down and picked it up and saw that it was a parking stub.

"Hey, you dropped this." He held it out for Delroy.

Delroy turned and saw Corey holding it but still stormed away. Corey had already glanced at it and saw that it read Seaview Group Home. The date and time stamped on it were from the night before. Corey then realized that the others were waiting on him to play.

"Oh, is it my turn?" Corey broke the silence as though he suddenly remembered that he had one bone left. He flipped it over and placed it on the table. "Looks like I win again. And it looks like I got to six wins first, too. It's a good thing we ain't playing for money, or else you'd be broke."

"A wonda if yuh did tief," said Scuba.

"How could I have cheated?" asked Corey.

Scuba grabbed his beer bottle by the neck as he stood, knocking his chair over, and smashed the bottom end on the edge of the table.

Corey knew what was about to happen next and jumped out of his chair just as Scuba lunged at him with the jagged edge, missing him. Scuba flipped the table over, spilling the dominos and bottles, which all smashed on the floor, then lunged at Corey again.

Missed.

Corey went on the offensive, grabbed his chair, and swung it at Scuba, striking him in the chest with one of the legs. The impact sent him stumbling and he tripped over the table he had flipped.

Jucee threw himself onto Corey from the side, sending them both to the floor. Their hands were clumsily trying to grab the other. Still, Corey managed to jab his opponent in the throat, disorienting him, then shoving him backward. He then got up, grabbed Jucee by the front of his shirt, and pushed him in the direction of Scuba, who then tripped over him and fell.

A set of hands grabbed Corey from behind as he was then shoved to the side. He caught his balance and saw that it was one of four male patrons. The other three had surrounded Scuba and Jucee.

"Yo, cool it!" yelled an older man who showed up from nowhere with a cricket bat. Corey figured that he must either be the manager or maybe the owner. "Get out, all three of you, or I'm calling the police—that's if I don't beat your asses first."

Corey raised his hands in surrender. "That's okay, boss." He looked at Scuba and Jucee as they got up off the floor. "I'm done."

It wasn't long before Corey was back on the street. He didn't see Delroy anywhere but figured by the way he'd taken off that he'd most likely head home and lock himself in his bedroom for the rest of the evening. It was clear that both Scuba and Jucee didn't show any empathy for Delroy. They didn't even ask him what the problem was after his sudden outburst. Corey didn't have to be a detective to know that Delroy definitely saw something the night Dwayne Pottinger was killed, and it freaked him out.

As Corey crossed the street to head back to where he had parked, he grabbed his phone—glad it wasn't broken during the fight—and called Eddie.

Eddie answered after the second ring. "Yeah?"

"Where are you?"

"I'm in a cab heading back home," said Eddie. "Hurry up. I managed to get some VIP tickets to a fashion show Pusey's putting on tonight."

"How'd you pull that off so quickly?"

"Ms. Bevins hooked me up."

"That's a ballsy move, bro," said Corey. "You really think you're going to get something out of her?"

"There's always the chance that she'll slip up."

"What am I supposed to do there?"

"Just be yourself. I can always use a second pair of eyes."

"If you say so. By the way, did you learn anything new?"

"Naw," Eddie answered, sounding down. "Nothing that could get us closer to finding out what happened. You?"

"Not sure, but I just had a game of dominos with our suspects."

"What? How'd you do that?"

"I followed Delroy from work to their hangout." Corey turned the corner, checking to make sure that he wasn't being followed. "I managed to get them to talk, after a few beers. I think you're right. These guys didn't kill Dwayne. But I have a feeling Delroy saw more than what he wanted to."

Chapter 16

Crab Key Resort, Montego Bay

"You think that Delroy's been holding back?" asked Eddie as they got out of their car and crossed the parking lot.

"Hell yeah. I'm surprised he didn't drink something stronger, especially when I mentioned Dwayne," Corey answered. "The other two are definitely homophobes and would've beat up, if not killed Dwayne. Delroy's a puppy dog. He won't hurt anyone."

"How are you so sure?"

"You got book smarts, and I've got street smarts. The other two attacked me while he stood on the side before taking off."

"Why would Delroy hang around with guys like that?"

"I guess he's one of those guys who just wants to fit in."

"Makes sense."

Corey grabbed the parking stub from his back pocket and handed it to Eddie. "Delroy dropped this."

"What's this?"

"According to Google, it's a home for the intellectually disabled."

"Who does he know there?"

"Beats me, he didn't say."

Less than thirty seconds later, they were walking through the hotel lobby. There were posted signs directing visitors toward the fashion show. Although helpful, the music and the MC were loud enough to lead them toward the show's beach. Not too long after, they were at the back of the resort, where a colorfully lit stage, catwalk, and chairs were set up among a backdrop of palm trees. The sound system drowned out the crashing waves of the beach but did not block the ocean breeze—a pleasant relief from the scorching heat coming from the bright lights around the stage area.

"What was the point of coming?" asked Corey. "The show's practically over."

"Right, as though you wanted to sit through the whole thing."

"Not with these fine ladies who are wearing next to nothing and flaunting it on the catwalk."

"I'll be sure to let Jordyn know that."

"And when she kicks up a fuss, I'll remind her of all the times I've been competing against Lenny Kravitz."

"I don't know why you're jealous of him. The man's old enough to be our father—Jordyn's too."

"I ain't jealous, just annoyed."

"Whatever."

Corey then looked past Eddie. "Isn't that—what's her name—Pusey's niece?"

Eddied turned and looked over his shoulder. "Yeah, that's her. Why don't you use your street charm on her and see what you can find out?"

"Sure." Corey reached into his wallet. "You got any cash?"

"For what?"

"Just in case, you know, I need to buy her a drink. That's how you get 'em talking."

"Why don't you get a credit card," grumbled Eddie as he took out his wallet.

"Jordyn worries that I'll run it up."

Eddie handed him some cash. "Which is why you're always coming to me."

Corey rolled his eyes before walking away.

Eddie took out his mobile phone and turned on the voice recording app as he saw Vanessa Pusey on stage, lined up with all her models. He snapped a few photos of them before Pusey left the stage. The DJ toned down the music to the point that Eddie could hear the voices of people around him.

Pusey made her way toward Eddie as she shook hands with various VIPs, while photos were being snapped all around them.

It wasn't long before they made eye contact. She flashed a set of flawless teeth and ruby red lips as she walked over to him with her hand extended.

"Hello, you must be that writer. What's your name again?"

Jesus, this is starting off well. "Eddie Barrow. Nice to meet you," he said as he shook her hand, amazed at how soft it was. "You can call me Eddie."

"That's a cute name. How'd you enjoy the show?"

"I wish I saw more of it."

"Aww, that's too bad. But I'm glad that we had a chance to meet."

"Likewise. Actually, I was hoping to interview you. I'm researching subject matter for an upcoming novel. It'll only take a few minutes."

"Right. We'll have to do this quickly because," she gestured to the surrounding crowd, "as you can see, I have many people waiting on me."

Eddie raised his smartphone and tapped the audio recorder app with his thumb. "First off, the clothes the models wore are amazing. What inspired these designs?"

She laughed. "Oh, I get this a lot. A little bit from everywhere. For instance, the swimsuit collection from this evening was inspired by numerous scuba diving trips. I also visit art galleries whenever I'm in New York, London, or Paris. I even get some of my ideas from things I see on the internet."

"Interesting." Eddie nodded as she went on bragging about herself and what was last year's style versus what is in for this year. Listening to her speak, he gathered that Pusey was used to commanding an interview—even back in the days when she ran track. The few interviews posted on YouTube from her 200- and 400-meter victories demonstrated that she was a woman of confidence. Pusey wasn't afraid to show some attitude to journalists whenever they got a bit too testy. He'd have to take charge, or else she'd end the interview before he got a chance to get to the serious matter.

"Before I got here, I read an online article about you in Vox magazine. You were once considered *the fashion designer to watch*, then your designs appeared less and less in fashion magazines. It was rumored that the editor of Prance Magazine, Lady Grace, walked out on one of your presentations." Eddie brought up the article which he had saved to his smartphone and read from it. "However, there was a miraculous turnaround, and your dresses appeared in Prance Magazine. You even had a show during Paris Fashion Week. How do you explain your comeback?"

"Wow." She chuckled, one that sounded forced. "I never did anything different than what I normally do. I spend hours at the drawing boards. And just like when I ran track, I would sometimes have a false start or stumble, but in the end, I always recover."

"Really?" Eddie nodded. "It's the same with me, sometimes I may go through six to eight weeks of writer's block, then overhear a conversation, then *poof,* an idea—"

"I forgot to ask you, sorry," Pusey cut him off. "What do you write about again?"

"Adventure, suspense, even a little science fiction."

"Ah, okay." She sounded like she was trying to divert the conversation. "What's your last name again?"

Seriously? "It's Barrow. Getting back to what I was saying before. Was there something specific which suddenly brought on this sudden spike in sales?"

She shrugged her shoulders. "I can only say that my latest designs came up at the right time. Timing is everything in this business. But I'm curious. It's not every day that I'm interviewed by someone who writes fiction. I would've thought that non-fiction writers would be more interested in what I do."

She's smart. Trying to figure me out. Eddie smiled. "What can I say? I'm here also looking for inspiration for one of my characters."

"And you travel all the way from Toronto for this?"

"I'm actually from Montreal, and I came for a book signing." *She's still trying to deviate from my questions.*

She put a hand to his shoulder. "My apologies. Were there a lot of people at your event?"

"It was well attended, given the amount of space at the venue, such as your event. Which brings me to my next question…"

She removed her hand from his shoulder as she slowly backed away. "You know, I'd love to stay and chat. But I really need to get going. How about you get in touch with my assistant, and we can continue this another time. Enjoy the rest of your stay, and thanks for coming."

She waved a tiny hand gesture and turned to walk away.

You ain't getting away that easy. "You know, I recently learned that Dwayne Pottinger was one of my fans. You *do* know, Dwayne Pottinger, don't you?"

Eddie said this loudly, perhaps a bit too loudly. Not only did Pusey stop dead in her tracks, but she also turned around slowly to face him with her head slightly cocked to the side. Others had also taken notice.

She leisurely walked back to him, staring off into space as though she were in thought. "Dwayne Pottinger, Dwayne… Pottinger." She then gave the appearance that she suddenly remembered to whom he was referring. But Eddie wasn't fooled. "Ah, that guy who frivolously claims that I stole his designs. I heard that he was killed. That was so awful what happened to him."

"Yeah, about that." Without pausing the voice recorder, he opened the photo gallery on his phone until he came to the selfie that Dwayne Pottinger—dressed as Shenice—took with Pusey's niece, Shantel. He turned the phone around and held it up for Pusey to see. He spotted a slight moment of trepidation from her once she saw it. "I came across this. I was always trying to figure out what would possess any gay man to show up at a straight party in drag. After all, we're in one of the most homophobic countries in the western hemisphere."

He faked an itch and scratched the top of his head as though he was perplexed. "It then hit me. Maybe, just maybe, Dwayne wasn't there to dance or to socialize. Perhaps his goal was to get close enough to get a picture of this dress." He flipped the phone around briefly before turning it back to Pusey. "By the way, this *is* your niece, isn't it? You made this dress, didn't you?"

"Yes, I did," said Pusey. "My niece showed up at my office last week. After she left, I noticed that one of my dresses was missing from the clothing rack. I later found out that she borrowed it without my permission. Typical of her."

"That's interesting." Eddie smiled as he turned the phone around and flipped through a few more images, stopping at a video that he'd transferred from Dwayne's Google cloud from the same evening. He showed it to Pusey. "It turns out Dwayne filmed you while you were confronting your niece. I imagine that it's about the dress. I just found it odd that you mentioned that you *heard* about Dwayne's death, when in fact, you were there."

She unleashed an exasperated sigh. "I didn't know at the time that Dwayne was there. As I'm sure you know, no one could tell that he was a man dressed as a woman."

She had a point.

"From what I know," Pusey continued, "Dwayne was dirt poor and needed the money. That's why he was so desperate to falsely accuse me of stealing his drawings. He was never able to prove that I stole anything from him because I didn't."

She raised a finger and looked upward as though she remembered something. "Wait a minute. Didn't the police recently find drugs at his house? In fact, they believe that his roommate's house was shot at and firebombed by rival drug dealers. May we not assume that Dwayne was looking for money to fuel a possible drug addiction?"

Eddie chuckled in disbelief. "Please don't tell me you buy that."

"Speaking of drugs," Pusey approached Eddie to stand arm's length away, "weren't you caught wandering the street, naked, all doped up last night?"

Pusey then paused while pretending to stare into space briefly before she pointed to Eddie with a grin. "How was your night in jail?"

"It was only a few hours. But I'm sure your three friends who took me for a ride last night could've told you that."

Pusey tilted her head and furrowed her brow. "What? What three friends?"

"I don't know," said Eddie. "Perhaps ones who do *special* favors for you."

She tilted her head slightly more. "Special favors? I wish I knew what you're talking about."

Eddie shrugged both shoulders. "Yeah, so you say. But I'm sure we can agree that Dwayne Pottinger having the reputation of a drug user helps you. In fact, there must've been something about the dress your niece wore that Dwayne felt he could use against you, something that he'd risk his life over."

"I had to get my lawyers after Dwayne to get him to drop that nonsense," Pusey said. "And if any of that rubbish finds its way into one of your books, rest assured my lawyers will come for you too."

"Yeah, I can understand that you'd use your lawyers to intimidate and bully a young talented designer. Both of you, no doubt, agreed to an out-of-court settlement. How convenient for you that Dwayne's death now prevents him from using this photo against you. I imagine if he could prove that you profited from his designs, it could jeopardize your business relationship with Lady Grace. You could also be sentenced up to seven years in prison for violating Jamaica's Intellectual Property Act. It's like you said, 'Timing is everything in this business.' Dwayne getting killed right after he took a selfie with your niece wearing this dress, I'd say that's some damn good timing. For you, that is."

Two broad-shouldered, towering, muscular men dressed in tight black t-shirts and matching pants emerged from the crowd and accosted them.

"Is there a problem, ma'am?" asked one of them with a deep voice.

"Yes," Pusey answered. "Mister Barrow needs to be escorted out. Give him the *Jazz* treatment."

Eddie saw one of the bouncers bend slightly to grab him behind the legs. Instantly he was flipped over the bouncer's shoulder, backward, where he hung. The move was so quick that it left him disoriented.

Smartphones were up and recording him as he was carried through the lobby, until he felt himself being lifted over the man's head and heaved into the air. Eddie crashed onto the concrete and rolled over until he settled onto his back. He sat up with a pain on the back of his arm where he had scraped it from the fall.

Then it hit him. *The Jazz treatment.* Pusey referred to episodes of *The Fresh Prince of Bel-Air* where Uncle Phil would physically throw Will's friend, Jazz, out the house.

My phone. Where's my phone? Eddie looked around frantically, only to see it a few feet away from him—in pieces. He then looked up to see the two giants walking away, while hotel guests gathered near the entrance and filmed him with their phones. Now it would be two nights in a row that a humiliating video of him would find its way onto the internet.

"Eddie."

He saw Corey pushing through the crowd and yelling at the gawkers to get a life. He managed to scare most of them off, then turned to come to Eddie.

"You all right?" Corey asked. "What happened back there?"

"I ruffled Pusey's feathers." Eddie nodded toward what was left of his mobile. "Look what they did to my phone."

"The security did that?"

"It's not a total loss. All the photos and my recording were automatically backed up in Google cloud."

"Do you think you have something on her?"

Eddie shook his head. "I'm not sure. Unless she put on an Oscar-worthy performance, I don't think she was involved in my kidnapping last night."

"You don't think she killed Dwayne?"

"Stealing his designs, yes. Killing him over something he may have found out about, not so sure anymore."

"What's next?" Corey helped Eddie up.

"Do what we can to find Candace before Dwayne and Wesley's killers do."

Chapter 17

Tangle River, Saint James Parish (next morning)

The climb through the hills was done eighty seconds faster than yesterday. The roughly eight-hundred-meter run wasn't Tarone's full workout. He was currently running downhill to complete it. It'd been far too long since he had worked out in this area, but it did not take too long for him to readapt. The average person would've been limping from cramping in the calf muscles if they attempted what Tarone did.

Over twelve years ago it was running on the road, the track, and the beach for his early-morning workouts—a relic from his early years in the Jamaica Defense Force. His elder brother, Garfield, was always convinced that Tarone needed protecting.

Lord, he lost one fight when he was seven years old to a bully named Marlon. He was a ten-year-old who always called Tarone names he didn't want to think of. Garfield wouldn't have it, ambushed Marlon outside his home, and placed two blows to his ribs and a fist to his eye. Marlon was too scared to tell anyone. Not even his parents. From what Tarone recalled, Marlon's father laid a few more floggings across his ass, just for getting beaten up. Tarone never knew why until now. And he felt sorry for him, knowing that his bully was himself a victim of child abuse.

Garfield wanted Tarone to *'man up'* so he could give licks to others more than he took them. But Garfield wasn't a professional fighter. He just got his inspiration from old Jet-Li movies. And he had Tarone run, taught him how to box, he threw everything at him that he could come up with. Was it too much? Yes. But Tarone never lost another fight again. Often, Tarone just had to give anyone who challenged him a stare, and it was enough to make them walk away.

But Garfield rubbed off on Tarone, which was why he enlisted. His mother was against it at first, but then she accepted his decision. It only took two years. As for his father, he had passed away while Tarone was in lower school. The heart gave up on him in his sleep.

Tarone remembered how he and Garfield ran to their parents' bedroom door after being woken up by their mother's screaming. And there she was, cradling their father's head in her arms, only to yell at them to call 1-1-0 for an ambulance.

But the army wasn't his thing. He stayed in long enough to become a Regular Force Soldier and was out after he turned 23. He'd surprised so many when he got employed as a teacher at Queen Mary's School for the Intellectually Disabled. Why name the school after Queen Mary, someone from the land of the country's oppressors? He always thought that Jamaica ought to get rid of all symbols of the British Monarchy and replace them with Jamaican heroes like Marcus Garvey and Samuel Sharp. And it hurt like a centipede's sting to drive past the school's sign.

If the school's name wasn't bothersome enough, he found himself in a set of handcuffs six months into his first year, after he was accused of raping one of his students. He was in a catch-22 because he couldn't say to the police where he *really* was the night the alleged rape was to have taken place. His live-in girlfriend at the time didn't hang around after he was sent away for a crime he didn't commit. She didn't even visit him in prison. And the thing was that he knew who probably did it but couldn't say anything. The police set him up good.

It had been seven years since Tarone's release. Those fifteen years couldn't end fast enough, always having to watch his back because he couldn't depend on others to do so. Everything changed, even Delroy, whom he had bumped into at the bank yesterday. He didn't need any more trouble with the police for violating the restraining order. He'd had that bank account since he got out of prison. How was he supposed to know that Delroy would end up working at the branch he visited. It was as though he was cursed—and the reminder of the crime he didn't commit would follow him for life.

Tarone ended his run near Tangle River Road, where he had parked near a local corner shop. He slowed down to a walk and then bent over to catch his breath. He wiped the sweat from his forehead with the back of his arm, briefly feeling his hair, which had grown to half an inch. About ten seconds later, he reached into one of his socks to remove the car key from inside, walked up to the driver's-side door of the taxi he drove for a living, and got in.

Tarone popped the hood of the used Nissan, took out a USP-Tactical .45 he had hidden under the spare, tucked it into the back of his waistband, and pulled his shirt down over it. He walked downhill through the bushes to a flatter area where the bamboo grew three to four inches a day for six months straight.

The area was cooler and much quieter, except for the whistling sounds from the bamboo. He stopped at a spot roughly fifty meters away and stared at four empty beer bottles he had fitted inside four different bamboo joints. It was customary for locals to cut bamboo for rafts or arts and crafts, leaving an empty joint in its wake.

Tarone held the gun straight in front of him, gripping it tightly with both hands. As a lefty, it had always been awkward turning the safety off by reaching around the gun with his left shooting thumb. But old habits die hard. He pointed the gun straight at the bottle and popped off a single shot—striking his target and leaving it in shards. He repeated the same with the bottles on the subsequent fence posts.

Tarone heard footsteps in the nearby bushes. He glanced over his shoulder once and saw Garfield before focusing back on the remaining bottles.

"Why yuh set things up so easy?"

Tarone squeezed the trigger and popped another bottle. "You want to stand out there with a bottle for me to shoot at, then go ahead."

"You know Mum worry about you?"

"And why's that?"

"Because you act like you're preparing to go to war."

"Prison does that to you."

"You were released long ago, but it seems like your mind's still there."

"I'm not in the mood to argue with you."

"Good, because I don't want no quarrel."

Tarone shot the last bottle, then slid the USP in the back of his pants as he walked toward his brother. "I'll call Mum sometime today."

"She just want to hear your voice," said Garfield as Tarone passed him. "You don't want her to get worked up."

"How did you know I'd be here?"

"You forget that I'm your brother?" They approached Tarone's car and Garfield's scooter. "Once I see your car, I knew you'd be down here."

Garfield was soon back on his scooter and was gone, leaving Tarone behind.

Tarone was soon behind the wheel of his car, the windows fully lowered because the air conditioner needed replacing. He would head back home to shower before getting back on the road—driving strangers for pay. Perhaps he would call his mum before heading to work. Maybe he needed to hear her voice as much as she wanted to listen to his. Or so Garfield said.

He wished that she wouldn't bring up the gun, but he knew that she would, so he may as well get it over with.

Chapter 18

Dwayne Pottinger's Funeral, Cain and Son's Funeral Services, Pitfour, Saint James

Eddie took another swig of the water he brought with him as he watched Jalissa struggle through her eulogy. Her Aunt Amancia stood close by with a hand on Jalissa's shoulder. There was one moment where Eddie noticed that she was ready to catch Jalissa, as it was apparent that the girl's legs were about to give way. Although she cried for the most part, she made it through, ending with a stop to her brother's flower-adorned, closed casket before returning to her seat.

Even though he had only met Dwayne briefly, Jalissa made Eddie feel like he was part of the family. Both he and Corey were pallbearers, and they both had seats in the front row in the reserved section—an area typically closed off for family. It was sad listening to testimonies from Jalissa and Amancia. Not to mention Charlene and Shirley—Dwayne's former roommates who were both in drag. More tragic was that Dwayne's immediate and extended family—a dozen of which, Eddie had learned, were on the island—did not attend. Dwayne's parents did not even claim their son's body. Only Dwayne's Aunt Amancia, and four other relatives, including an aunt, uncle, and two cousins, came to pay their respects.

Amancia, Milly, and Delva contributed to cover the balance of the funeral costs, while he, Corey, and what was left over from the GoFundMe account covered the rest.

Eddie felt the anguish grow inside the chapel as each person spoke. The weight of it forced a tear from him—one that he was quick to catch as it fell onto his cheek. The chapel had around thirty people in attendance, including Dwayne's friends and others in the LGBTQ community, with some advocates too. It was clear that even though they were strangers, Dwayne was still one of their own who died because of who he was.

Like an itch that needed scratching, Eddie kept turning to check on the front entrance every so often.

Corey nudged him and whispered, "You've been looking back there a lot. You expecting someone?"

"I was hoping that Candace would show up."

"Forget it. She's obviously hiding."

***

Less than two hours later, Eddie and Corey returned to their role as pallbearers and helped lead the procession outside, down the four stairs, then to the semicircular driveway where the hearse was parked. Eddie saw Corey talking to the other pallbearers, when he turned to the sound of his name being called.

"Eddie." He turned and saw Jalissa running to him with open arms. "Thanks again."

"Don't mention it," he said as he hugged her back.

Jalissa released Eddie but kept holding his hand. "I didn't want to bring it up earlier, but I heard what happened last night. Are you okay?"

"I'm fine," Eddie answered. "I don't think Pusey slept too well last night."

"I can't believe that you actually confronted her."

"You sound surprised."

"I am," she answered. "You're really committed to finding Dwayne's killer. What did you say to her?"

"It's not so much what I said. It's more what I showed her that put her on edge."

"You think she had something to do with Dwayne's death?"

"She had a motive, but my gut says that she didn't. But from what I've learned, and her reaction, I believe that she stole your brother's designs. I just can't prove it yet."

"What are you going to do now?"

"I'm working on something." The truth was that Eddie didn't

know what the hell to do, and he felt terrible misleading Jalissa. But he could not let her lose hope. Not here of all places.

He looked over at the front entrance and saw Amancia talking to everyone as they exited. Eddie turned to Jalissa. "You better go and tend to the guests. I'll hang around so we can talk later."

Jalissa nodded and left to join her aunt.

Corey, who was conversing with the other pallbearers, left them to join Eddie. "How's Jalissa?"

"She's hanging in there," said Eddie. "She wanted to know how far we are with Dwayne's case."

"She's grieving and wants justice. You can't blame her," said Corey. "You're lucky Bevins still managed to hook you up with Dennis Denton—even after what happened last night."

"She's good at what she does. What can I say?"

The jarring noise of blasting car horns caught their attention as they turned to see a caravan of vehicles drive slowly past the funeral home.

"What the hell?" said Corey.

Eddie watched the lead vehicle, which parked close to the exit to the driveway. The others in the convoy parked before and after it—blocking both the entrance and the exit. A plump, sixty-something balding man wearing a cassock emerged from the passenger side and led his followers in a chant.

"No gays. Keep the sodomites away."

It was Pastor Green. Eddie recognized him immediately.

Others exited their vehicles holding placards with anti-gay rhetoric, Bible quotes from Leviticus, and other hateful messages. One of the signs was handed to the priest, who joined the hostile protest, hogging all the sidewalk and the street space. The response was swift, especially from the LGBTQ crowd, who engaged them in a counter-protest.

Eddie saw the anger and frustration that was building on both sides, and his hand shot to his forehead. *You can't be serious. He's actually doing this?*

"Eddie," yelled Corey.

"What?"

"We better get out of here. It's not going to take much for a full street brawl to happen."

He was right. "Where's Jalissa?"

"She was just here a moment ago," said Corey.

Eddie's chest tightened as he scanned the area. "We better find her, and fast."

As they both looked around, something occurred to Eddie. "Why do I get the feeling that most of the people who showed up aren't part of Pastor Green's church?"

"Just as I said," Corey answered. "I think most of these people just came to disrupt the funeral."

A few moments went by when Eddie felt Corey tap his shoulder and point toward Pastor Green. "There she is."

Eddie and Corey rushed toward Jalissa, but the crowds had grown too immense for them to move with haste. Above the heads of those who stood in their way, Eddie saw Jalissa in what appeared to be a very heated argument with Pastor Green.

By the time Eddie got there, he was able to catch the tail end of the argument.

"You must understand, young lady, that your brother lived a very ungodly life. He impersonated a woman and misled men into dancing with him. He tricked good Christians into sinning."

"You acting as though you don't know what else goes on at these parties. How dare you say such things about my brother," screamed Jalissa. "He never hurt anyone. The only people who were doing the hurting were the ones who killed him. And you dare bring your hatred on the day I just want him to rest in peace."

Eddie grabbed Jalissa by the shoulder. "Jalissa, it's not worth it." He pulled her into his chest, as she bawled her tears onto his shirt.

"Oh, and here's the devil's apprentice," called out the pastor as he pointed at Eddie. Jeers and insults were hurled his way. "You use your celebrity status to help fund Satan's cause."

Corey did not waste time stepping between Eddie, Jalissa, and the pastor. "Who the fuck you think you are?"

The pastor didn't appear to be fazed by what Corey said.

"Why do you resist the Lord's calling, my son?" said the pastor. "You are young, blind, and cannot see the mistakes that Dwayne

Pottinger made that brought on his own demise?"

"The only one who's making a mistake is you if you and your sheeple don't get out of our faces."

"Corey," said Eddie.

"A young girl's trying to bury her brother in peace, and you want to interrupt his funeral."

"Corey."

Corey waved a hand behind him toward Eddie. "Naw, I got this."

"Do not lie with a man as one lies with a woman," yelled a woman behind the pastor. "To do so is an abomination." It was Leviticus 18:22. The crowd on the church side erupted into applause and cheers.

"Oh, you want to use Bible verses. Then let's go with Bible verses." Corey formed a steeple and held it to his face for a moment. He smiled and dropped both arms with his index fingers pointing at the woman. "Were you ever sold into slavery? Because the book of Exodus makes it okay for daughters being sold into slavery. And you're definitely someone's daughter, so I guess you're cool with being the pastor's bitch."

There were loud cheers and even laughter from the LGBTQ crowd. Boos from the church side.

Corey waved his arms as he faced the LGBTQ crowd to rile them up for a bit, then waved downward to calm them before turning back to the church group.

"Corey," said Eddie in a warning manner.

"It's cool, bruh," said Corey. "I'm just getting warmed up."

Aww, shit, Eddie thought. *This is a disaster waiting to happen.*

Corey said he would quote from Leviticus 21:40. "It says that none of us may approach the altar of God if we have a defect in our eyesight." Corey began pointing to people in the crowd. "But I see that you, you, you, you, you, you, and you are wearing glasses. I'm curious if your optometrist is here with you guys."

The LGBTQ crowd roared in laughter, and the church side started chanting hate slogans as a counter.

"Corey!" Eddie let go of Jalissa and grabbed his best friend's wrist. "Stop it."

"Yoooo, bloodclaat!"

Both Eddie and Corey turned to the voice to see that it was Scuba, with Jucee beside him.

Oh shit. Just what we needed. "We don't want any trouble," said Eddie.

"So, all dis time wi play domino wid a fish," said Scuba as the crowd parted to let him and Jucee walk through.

This set off a red flag for Eddie, as he saw how much influence Scuba and Jucee held over the crowd.

"Corey?" asked Eddie without taking his eyes from Scuba. "What did you do to piss this guy off?"

"I just whooped their asses at dominos."

"In other words, you pissed off a sore loser."

Scuba stopped a few feet away from Corey with Jucee and what seemed to be a small posse in tow. "Yuh tief me and mi frien di otha night an yuh attack mi. No fish no do dat to mi."

"Bruh, I won fair and square. I didn't have to cheat." Corey laughed. "And you think I'm gay? If you're coming back for another beating, you must have enjoyed it."

Eddie looked to the side and noticed Pastor Green was backing away into the crowd and moving toward the back—another red flag. Nah, something wasn't right.

The scuffle to their left caught their attention as someone snatched the wig from one of the funeral guests. Fists flew between the two, and like a wave, the brawl spread.

That's what it was. Pastor Green brought in outside agitators to start the melee. And there must have been a specific time for this to happen too.

Eddie ran to grab Jalissa, but their side was being pushed back. Someone bumped into her hard enough that she was knocked over. Eddie immediately grabbed her by the armpit and pulled her up so fast he thought for a moment that he dislocated her arm. But that would be the least of her problems if he didn't get her out of here soon.

"Get inside," Eddie yelled, barely capable of hearing himself above the cacophony of screams. He saw her run toward the front steps of the funeral parlor when he spun around to look for

Corey. He could've sworn Corey had been right behind him. But the brawl was out of control. Someone grabbed him by the shirt. Out of reflex, Eddie brought both arms under his assailant's and upward to pry them off him, ripping his shirt. He lunged forward and shoved the guy, whom he didn't get a good look at before Eddie got pushed by someone else.

Someone fell to the ground a few feet away. It was Corey, scrambling to get back up, but Jucee kicked him back down.

Aww, shit!

Eddie bolted to his friend's aid just as he saw a shiny object in Scuba's hand. Eddie reacted without thinking as he charged Scuba, ignoring that he was taking on someone taller and more muscular than he. Scuba didn't see Eddie coming, which made it easier for Eddie to slam into him from the side. Scuba was knocked off balance and stumbled into someone else, who bumped him hard enough that he fell to the ground. Scuba rolled onto his back with his jaw hanging open.

Eddie knew that something was wrong. He then saw that Scuba was bleeding. He must have fallen on his own knife. That's when Jucee rushed to his aid, ignoring Eddie.

Eddie hurried to Corey just as he was getting up. Eddie grabbed Corey's forearm and pulled him up. He may have nearly been stabbed by Scuba, but the melee could be much worse. They shoved their way through the crowd toward the funeral home entrance when they heard broken glass behind them, followed by a large explosion. They turned to see the hearse burst into flames. More screams erupted as the crowd scattered. There were loud cheers—clearly from the church side.

This would be the second time for them to see Dwayne attacked with fire. There was a loud scream from behind, and when they turned, they saw Jalissa fall to her knees at the entrance to the chapel.

"No, no, no, no, no! Look away," Eddie yelled as he and Corey attempted to block her view. She wouldn't listen as they had to pull her back to her feet and literally carry her inside the chapel as she kicked and screamed, with sirens wailing in the distance.

***

Several minutes had passed before Eddie and Corey set foot outside the funeral home. Most of the crowd had scattered by the time the police arrived. As of now, Eddie saw ten people sitting on the front lawn with their hands zip-tied behind their backs. Paramedics were with twice as many, tending to their injuries, and the hearse was a total loss. He watched as the firemen removed the coffin, severely scorched and barely intact.

Eddie heard the door open behind him, and when he turned to see who it was, he saw Jalissa's eyes welling up.

"Jalissa, wait," cried Amancia, running after her, obviously failing to prevent her from going outside.

Eddie turned to block her view, but it was too late. He let his arms drop to his sides. "I'm so sorry. I never meant for any of this to happen."

Jalissa shook her head. "All I wanted was to celebrate the life of my brother with his closest family and friends. Why did this happen?"

Amancia hugged her from behind. "I'm here for you, as I was for Dwayne. Don't you forget that."

Eddie looked at Corey as he sat at the top of the four steps shaking his head.

"I'm sorry too," said Corey. "I should've kept my mouth shut."

"No, young man," said Amancia. "You did the right thing and let those wicked people know that you weren't going to let Pastor Green's people bully us. He incited those ruffians. You had nothing to do with that."

"She's right," said Eddie. "Pastor Green had agitators within this crowd. He planned this."

"And when the police question you, what do you say?" asked Corey.

"I'll tell them what I saw," said Eddie. He let a few moments pass before turning back to him. "By the way," he started, informing Corey it was Leviticus 21:20, not Leviticus 21.40.

"Huh?"

"You quoted Leviticus earlier. Right chapter, wrong verse."

"Oh." Corey nodded once, then turned to Eddie. "Do you think they knew that?"

Eddie shook his head. "Nah."

Jalissa sniffed and wiped her eyes with the back of her hand. "There's no love, just so much hate. Why?"

"There's love here," said Eddie. "We saw it inside the chapel."

"That's right," added Amancia. "There were many strangers who came. I'm sure most of them never met Dwayne."

"And I'm sure they wished they had," continued Eddie. "I wish my encounter with him hadn't been so brief."

Jalissa cleared her nose and nodded. "Dwayne had such a rough life, even though he brought so much joy to everyone—especially to those who didn't even know it."

She looked up at the sky, then back down, while she shook her head. "All I wanted was for him to have a peaceful send-off. I thought that I could at least get that for him."

Eddie sighed. "I'm going to do what I can to make this right."

"Jalissa!" It was a baritone voice that yelled from at least forty meters away. All three looked up to see a bearded man with a small afro heading their way.

Eddie looked in the man's direction. "Is that—"

"It's my father," answered Jalissa.

"What are you doing here?" yelled Mister Pottinger as he stood in front of them. "You had your mother and me worried sick. You had to come to this blasted funeral and nearly get yourself killed."

Amancia released Jalissa and stepped from behind her. "She was safe with us."

Pottinger pointed a finger at Amancia. "You stay out of this." He then turned to Jalissa. "You're coming home right now. Enough of this nonsense."

Jalissa looked at Eddie, Corey, then to Amancia.

"Now!" yelled Pottinger.

Jalissa shrugged her shoulders and sighed. She clearly had no choice.

The longer he waited, the more of the redness Eddie saw in the man's eyes. He appeared to be at the breaking point, where he might grab Jalissa and beat her.

"Mister Pottinger," said Eddie, hoping to defuse some of the tension. "I'm truly sorry for your—"

"Sorry about what?" he snapped. "That you nearly got my daughter killed just so you could do some blasted publicity stunt for your stupid books?"

"Lamont!" Amancia gasped.

"I told you to stay out of this," Pottinger yelled.

Wow.

He turned back to Eddie. "And you, importing abnormal behavior from overseas."

"I was actually—"

"I don't want to hear anything from you." He grabbed Jalissa and roughly pulled her behind him. "Just stay away from my daughter."

Pottinger then looked over his shoulder at Jalissa. "Get in the car."

"Daddy," cried Jalissa. "It's not Eddie's fault. He was only trying to help."

"Get your bumboclaat in the car now," he yelled.

Jalissa shrugged her shoulders as though to apologize, then turned and ran away crying.

Mister Pottinger turned to Eddie and Corey. "If I find out you've been talking to my daughter again, forget me calling the police and having them arrest you for harassment. I'll come after you myself. So go back to where you came from. No one wants you here."

He stormed off.

Eddie let his head drop into his hands.

"Don't mind him." Amancia put a hand on Eddie's shoulder. "He's who he is, and that can't be changed."

Corey shook his head. "Bruh, don't tell me you let that man get to you."

"I didn't let him get to me."

"You could've fooled me. I know you're blaming yourself for this, and you shouldn't."

"It's hard not to feel complicit."

Corey stood and paced in front twice before turning to Eddie.

"Even if you didn't fundraise for Dwayne's funeral, there was enough press coverage of his murder. That fake pastor and his dumbass followers would've still shown up."

Eddie didn't answer.

"And you wouldn't have been able to protect Jalissa from that mob had you not been here." Corey pointed to the burned-out hearse. "You didn't do that. *They* did."

"Eddie?"

They both turned to a familiar voice. Walking quickly toward them was Delva.

Eddie faced her. "Are you okay?"

"Yes, son." She looked around her as tears fell. "This is so terrible. I can't believe how people can be so wicked." She covered her mouth and turned back to Eddie. "I'm just thankful that you're okay. Did you see Jalissa?"

"Her dad came and got her," Eddie answered.

"He was here? I didn't see him at the funeral."

"He wasn't," said Corey.

It was then that Eddie realized that Delva had not yet met Corey. "This is my friend, Corey."

"Hello," she said with a nod as she wiped away the tears with a tissue she dug out of her purse. "Sorry, I'm a complete mess. It's not that I don't want to shake your hand."

Corey nodded. "That's okay."

"I'm just glad that nothing bad happened to all of you."

Eddie's phone rang. He looked at the call display and saw that it was marked *PRIVATE*. "Hello."

"Mister Barrow?" The man's strong accent made Eddie's heart skip. That was all it took for him to walk away from the group.

"Who's this?"

"Get out back now. And come alone."

Hansel. One of my kidnappers, thought Eddie as he saw him in his mind. His heart skipped another beat as thoughts of being watched made him spin around and quickly scan the area.

There's fewer people than earlier. I should be able to spot him easily. Policeman, policeman, friends of Dwayne's...

"Where are you, and what do you want?" Playtime was over.

He was going to stand up to this guy, whoever he was.

"Yuh deaf?" he shouted. Eddie spun around, expecting the man to be standing somewhere behind him. No one appeared to fit the profile. "Yuh waan info and mi boss waan talk to yuh."

His boss wants to give me information? Something isn't right. Stepmother—if she's the boss—was ready to castrate him two nights ago. Why would she want to help him in exchange for info? The thought grabbed his attention to the point that he unwittingly stopped looking for the brotha who'd kidnapped him.

"Who's your boss?" Eddie threw confidence behind his voice. "What does she want? I've had too many rough days since I got here, so I don't like the idea of some stranger calling me. I want to know—"

"All mi waan know if yuh agoh do weh dem tell yuh?" The force behind the stranger's voice extinguished a large chunk of the fire that had built inside Eddie. "Maybe you'll understand me better when I speak like you foreigners do? Don't bother calling for help. Those police officers that showed up, they work for my boss, you understand? He got eyes and ears everywhere. So don't try his patience, and get your bloodclaat to the back now."

There was a click, and Eddie lowered the phone. His mind was capsized at the thought that this stranger was watching him. But it couldn't be the same people who had kidnapped him. The two women, Stepmother and Gretel, weren't Jamaican—at least they didn't sound as though they were. And even though Hansel didn't say anything in his presence, chances are if he did, he would likely talk the same way.

He turned and saw Corey staring at him with his head slightly tilted, and his eyes narrowed.

"Who was that?" Corey asked.

Eddie slipped his phone into his back pocket. "Wait here. I'll be back."

"Where are you going?"

Eddie walked away. "I won't be long."

He saw it all over Corey's face…his best friend knew he was holding back on him. There was just no fooling Corey. He knew Eddie too well. But he couldn't risk putting Corey in danger—

and possibly Amancia, Delva, Milly, or even Jalissa. He hoped that Corey would not follow him.

He hurried to the back by following a tiled path around the side of the building, which was bordered by a thick bush that was seven to eight feet tall. When he emerged from the side and into the parking lot, there were two men in suits and shades—one leaning against the hood of a diagonally parked black Mercedes-Benz SUV. At the same time, his partner stood adjacent to him with arms crossed.

"Mister Barrow." It was him, the one who just called. He stepped away from the car with both hands at his side. "My boss is waiting on you."

Eddie saw the second suit pull the back door open. Eddie's stomach tightened, and he irrationally took a step back before he bumped into a solid mass. He turned around and saw a massive, bald brotha glaring down at him. The man was reminiscent of Deebo the neighborhood bully from the Friday movies, and he acted like him too, as it took only a shove from one of his hands for Eddie to stumble and fall. Eddie tried to scramble away backward on his hands and feet, but he kept slipping. Meanwhile, the giant approached him, cracking his knuckles as though he was getting ready to break Eddie in half.

Eddie backed into something. Before he could turn to see what it was, he felt two strong hands grab him by the armpits and yank him to his feet. Eddie turned to see that it was the man who had called him.

The caller did a quick pat-down of his backside, where he felt the smartphone. He snatched it from Eddie's pocket and threw it to the concrete, where he stomped on it with the heel of his shoe. The crunch that Eddie heard was enough to convince him that the phone was lost forever—as well as any means of tracking him to wherever they were taking him. Not even twenty-four hours had passed, and his replacement phone was destroyed too.

"Mi aguh shoot yuh bloodclaat if yuh no get inna di car." The caller shoved him toward his associate. Eddie's arms were then pulled behind him and held together at the wrists before he felt them being zip-tied.

"Go," he said, as he turned Eddie to get inside the back seat of the SUV. Eddie was soon sandwiched between the same guy and Deebo. Had the kidnapper to his left not been thin, the three of them would never have fit in the back seat. That was Eddie's last thought before a black bag was pulled over his head.

***

Corey didn't know why he listened to Eddie. He knew that Eddie was spooked by whoever just called him, or else he wouldn't have been looking around the area as though he was trying to catch his caller. And now it had been over two minutes since Eddie had gotten away. Amancia and Delva had already left, leaving Corey to watch as police still questioned the few leftover witnesses who were brave enough to give statements.

Fuck it.

He called Eddie's phone as he hurried to the back parking lot, only for it to go straight to voicemail. When he was prompted, he said, "Eddie, I don't know what's going on, but you need to call—"

The sight of an empty parking lot, apart from their own rental car, made him pause as he slowly lowered his phone without finishing the message.

He saw a pair of skid marks and a black object on the ground that appeared to be broken. "No." Corey rushed ahead to get a better look at what he just saw. "Don't let it be this."

It was a broken mobile phone, definitely Eddie's, explaining why his call went to voicemail.

"Eddie?" he yelled as he scanned the area. There was no mistaking what just happened. He'd just been kidnapped. Again. Corey grabbed his head at the thought that it was the same ones from the hospital.

"Eddie," Corey whispered to himself. "What have you done?"

If you get your han' in a debil mout' tek time an draw it out.

—Jamaican Proverb

*If you put your hand in the devil's mouth,
take it out carefully.*

Chapter 19

Guava Hill

"Do I need to have this hood over my head?" asked Eddie. "I can barely breathe."

"Shut up, nuh bwoy," said the man to his left.

"My nose is getting stuffy. Can't you at least lift it above my mouth?"

"Yuh hear weh mi seh?" *You heard what I said?*

There was no negotiating with these guys, whoever they were. Kidnapping him was a two-man job at most. They didn't need Deebo unless they wanted to intimidate him into complying.

Eddie doubted this was the driver's first time kidnapping someone. The first clue was that he kept the music turned loud enough that Eddie couldn't hear any identifiable sounds that would allow him to trace his way back. It was the first time he heard very old-school hip hop since he had been in Jamaica. Currently blasting through the speakers was the song "Back to Life" by Soul II Soul. Listening to a tune he liked was the only pleasant part of the trip.

However, playing the music loudly may be an attempt to disorient him. As hard as he tried, it was impossible for Eddie to hear any sounds outside the vehicle that could help him identify where he was. All he knew was that the drive was mostly uphill, indicating that they were driving away from the coast and toward the island's hilly interior.

The SUV stopped at the top of another incline. The doors were opened, and he felt Deebo's large hands pull him outside. The ground below his feet was soft, indicating that he was on a muddy surface, which eventually changed to concrete. Soon he was indoors, and by the echoes everyone's feet made from walking, he knew that he was inside a room with high ceilings.

Someone else's hand grabbed his left shoulder to make him stop, just as he heard what sounded like a wooden chair being dragged across the floor toward him until it hit the back of his legs. They made him sit, lifting his zip-tied wrists around the back of the chair. The black bag was ripped from his head to the side, causing Eddie's head to snap in that direction too. Looking around, he saw that he was inside an unfinished basketball court—where the hoops and floor patterns were missing.

Eddie turned to his captors. "Are you going to tell me who you are or what?"

A hard slap to the back of his head was his answer.

"Ow!"

"Yuh waan to seh supem else, bwoy?"

"Yeah, I'll say something else. You're clearly a lackey for the person in charge. So where is he, and what does he want?"

"Yuh like fi get slap nuh true."

"Slap me? I don't think your boss would like that," Eddie retorted. "If he wanted to hurt me, you could've chosen many isolated spots to do so instead of driving me all the way here."

"Aah, so yuh tink yuh smaat?" He lifted a backhand.

"Wha di rass ah gwaan yah?" *What the hell is going on here?*

Eddie felt the thunderous voice rattle his bones as he heard footsteps approaching from behind. The presence of the individual caused Eddie's captors to back away simultaneously—all without taking their eyes off the man who entered.

"All this noise," said the man as another wooden chair was handed to him. He put it down to sit opposite Eddie. The man was around five feet ten, mid-to-late forties, sky blue pants with a matching light blazer. He was more casually dressed than the others and didn't bother to wear a tie. Instead, he kept the upper part of his shirt unbuttoned—exposing some of the peppercorn-shaped chest hair. Then there was his face. Eddie knew that he had seen this man before.

"You know I don't like all this noise," the man said as he sat. His sudden dropping of the Patois was a dead giveaway that he knew who Eddie was and wanted to make sure that he was understood.

"I'm sorry, sir," answered one of the kidnappers. "Dis bwoy ah dis mi."

Eddie turned to him. "I'm being disrespectful? You keep calling me *bwoy*."

"Enough," said the boss as he crossed his legs and exhaled slowly. "Do you know who I am?"

Eddie's jaw slow-dropped as he remembered where he had seen him. "Yeah." His eyes widened at the thought that he was sitting across from Jamaica's most powerful drug lord. He swallowed hard as he wanted to look away but didn't dare to. "You're Brutus."

Eddie then looked back and forth to the henchmen. "And these guys are part of your 'Spray Boys Posse.'"

"And do you know why they're called that?"

Eddie took a deep breath and exhaled. "They're known for *spraying* your enemies with bullets."

Brutus nodded once as he smiled. "You know a lot for someone who's not from around here."

"I do my research."

"Research? Or is it that you just like snooping?" asked Brutus. "I'm going to cut to the chase. Why are you looking for Candace?"

Damn, how long has he been watching me? "I think her life's in danger."

"And *you* think you can protect her?" Brutus turned to his henchmen and chuckled with them. "Or were you going to call the military, the FBI, or the Jedi Council?"

More laughter.

Eddie grinned as the laughter died down, knowing that he had to play it cool with them. "I see that you saw the video."

"It's not what I expected from you."

"It's not every day that I get kidnapped, threatened, drugged, then released so that I can make an ass of myself in public. Who's responsible? Something tells me that they aren't friends of yours."

"No, no, no." Brutus shook his head while wagging a finger. He then pointed to his chest. "I ask the questions here."

Brutus then uncrossed his legs and leaned forward. "What do you want with Candace?"

"My friend and I were almost killed by the same people who killed Candace's friends. I just want to know why."

"Oh yes, you're the curious writer who likes to solve murders on the side." Brutus stood with his hands in his pockets.

Eddie kept smiling, just to keep up the act. "Actually, I was only doing someone a favor. I didn't—"

"Favor for whom?" Brutus circled around the back of Eddie's chair before he approached him on his right and played with Eddie's earlobe. "For Dwayne Pottinger's sister, Jalissa. Correct?"

"You know all the answers, right down to the name of the victim's sister," said Eddie. "What? Do you receive intelligence briefings every morning? Is that why they call you Mister President in these parts? Or do they just call you Presi?"

"Not exactly." Brutus let go of Eddie's ear as he circled in front of him and gestured to the wall. "Outside these walls is my village, my own personal kingdom. None can keep secrets from me here. Whenever one of my people says someone robbed from them. Whether it's their jewelry, TV, or anything, they can go to the police—who'll take a report which will get stashed away without any investigation. Or, they come to me, and I'll have their belongings back to them within one to three days."

"And what do you do with the thief? Chop off his hand to make an example of him?"

Brutus looked at his henchmen. "You hear what this Bajan say?" He and his henchmen laughed. "You watch a lot of TV, don't you?"

To keep up the act, Eddie chuckled along with them. "I also read."

"And I guess yuh one of those people that believe everything they read in the paper."

"I prefer paperless," said Eddie with a smirk. "It saves trees."

"Then you're *still* not getting the whole truth," said Brutus.

"How so?" said Eddie. "That you're wanted by both the FBI and by MI5? Your father ran a drug empire that spanned throughout the Caribbean, the US, and the UK. You took over when he passed away—adding guns to the list of items you traffic. How am I doing so far?"

"What the papers don't mention is how much I've given back. Do you think everyone in Guava Hill pays their electric bill? They can't, and the government knows this. So, I pay it for them." Brutus gestured around him. "Even this indoor facility, I built this for everyone to use at no cost."

"Are you saying that everything I've read about you hacking an embezzler to pieces with a machete isn't true?"

"Not quite." Brutus shook his head. "I've since upgraded to a chainsaw."

Eddie turned his head to the side and swallowed.

"But I take nuff care of mi people," said Brutus, drifting into Patois. "I should've had mi men remove that mask from your head so that you could see how good things are here. There ain't no crime here in Guava Hill. People don't need to lock their doors. I invested in a space where the residents grow their own fruits and vegetables. No one steals from each other because we're family. Them tiefs come from yonder, and I catch them all. Everyone knows the law around here: No tiefing, no raping, and no killing. Yuh come through every day without doing none of dem things and you're good. No one in mi village complains because dem see me as their protector."

"Like Candace?" quipped Eddie, remembering to smile. "It was important for you to mention that you take care of your people. I assume that it's from local threats. But all I've done was ask a few questions about Candace, and you sent your men to kidnap me."

"Stop saying that you were kidnapped," said Brutus. "You're my guest...for now."

"Nonetheless," said Eddie. "You brought me here claiming that you want to know why I've been asking about Candace, but I get the feeling that there's something more about her that you're not telling me."

Brutus smirked. "How so?"

Eddie closed his eyes as he let his thoughts flow. He shook his head slowly and tilted it up while keeping his eyes closed as though in a trance. "As I was saying, you claim to take care of *your* people from threats. You asked me why I'm looking for Candace…you've shown concern for her…as though she's one of *your* people…" Eddie stopped swaying his head and opened his eyes with a gasp, then followed with a smile. "She's here."

Brutus's eyes widened as he crossed his arms.

I'm onto something. Don't stop, thought Eddie as he focused on Brutus's eyes. "Which could mean that she's possibly a former resident of Guava Hill. She probably reached out to her parents or some relative because of her predicament. And either one or all her relatives reached out to you to bring her here safely. Or perhaps…" Eddie paused as he grinned. "She's one of *your* relatives. Tell me I'm wrong."

Brutus stared at him without saying a word. Roughly five seconds later, he raised his hands and clapped, slowly at first and progressively faster as he smiled.

"Very good, Mister Barrow." The clapping stopped. "But I'm sure that brain of yours would've told you that's not the only reason why you're here."

"I figured as much."

Brutus stood, turned the chair backward and sat—resting his elbows on the back.

"My sources tell me that you were at Wesley's place before it burned down. Why were you there and what did you find out?"

"My friend Corey and I went there looking into Dwayne's death, but only found weak evidence that may prove that he was a victim of copyright theft."

"Keep talking."

"Everything pointed to Vanessa Pusey. She had a motive to kill him. At first, I suspected that she was the one who hired the hit squad to kill Wesley and kidnap me to tie up any loose ends. After all, she has the means. But that all changed now that *you're* in the picture."

"Why's that?"

Eddie closed his eyes to drift back into his zone. "Candace came here for your protection because she felt that whoever killed Dwayne was also after her. This means she may know who the killer is. Had she suspected that Pusey was behind Dwayne's death—" Eddie opened his eyes, popping out of his zone. "Then you would've sent your Spray Boys after her."

"So far so good. Now tell me what you saw at Wesley's place."

Eddie tilted his head slightly while narrowing his eyes. "You know who killed Dwayne and Wesley."

"Focus, Eddie. Focus. What did you see at Wesley's place?"

Eddie closed his eyes again. "Wesley showed us Dwayne's scrapbook…the outfits he made…we looked at what was on his computer…just a video of him dancing…pictures of him and Candace, his sister…nothing from the night he was killed. Wesley didn't know what Dwayne was up to…he was an innocent bystander…or maybe not because one of the assassins showed up at the hospital to finish the job…he had to have known something, but what?"

"Think, Eddie, think. Was there something in Dwayne's bedroom that stood out?"

Eddie heard Brutus in the background while he stayed in the zone. He shook his head. No, Brutus ruined his concentration. Got to get back in the zone. "Scrapbooks…a dress stood out… there was a picture of a flying fish…but there was something on Dwayne's computer…pictures…a video of him dancing…the furniture was moved to give him space…what could Dwayne possibly have that you'd want? No, something you need… why? You could send the Spray Boys to take out the people after Candace, but you haven't because…they may be just as powerful as you are, if not even more so, but something Dwayne possessed could possibly give you leverage or maybe take them down…I know there has to be something. What am I missing?"

There was a loud bang as the double doors to the gymnasium flew open, startling Eddie.

"Stop this!" yelled a young woman Eddie could not see. The anger was not only in her voice but also in the sound of her footsteps as she approached. He gathered by the sound from each step behind him that the woman was of average height and build.

"Oh rass!" Brutus mumbled to himself as he closed his eyes and shook his head. "Don't you ever listen? I was handling this."

"Don't touch me," the woman said.

"Mister President, I try to stop her," came a man's voice, another one of Brutus's henchmen, no doubt.

Brutus slapped his leg while sucking his teeth and stood, just as Eddie saw a woman in a tunic and short, form-fitting jeans walk past him. As for her Senegalese twists, she wore them on top of her head like a crown. There was no mistaking that it was Candace, just like she appeared in the photo of her and Dwayne—minus the Senegalese twists.

"Why are you doing this? He doesn't know anything."

"Candace?" asked Eddie.

"Shut up!" Candace and Brutus said simultaneously, turning their heads at the same time, then turning back to stare each other down.

Eddie's head snapped back a nudge, not seeing that one coming.

Brutus threw an index finger in his direction. He turned back to Candace. "He was about to talk, and then you burst in here and spoil everything."

"He has no business here." Candace pointed her finger toward Eddie.

"That's for me to decide."

"And did he talk?"

"Jesus Christ!" Brutus slapped both hands to his side.

"You didn't," said Candace. "He doesn't know anything, so send him back."

"At this point, I'd rather not," said Eddie. "But I'd appreciate it if you send your men to pick up my friend if you're convinced that here's a safer place for the time being."

Candace turned to Eddie. "You want mi uncle to bring your friend here. You mad?"

"No, he's smart," said Brutus. "He knows that if I send him back, he'll be targeted, especially if his would-be killers find out that he was here. They may want to know what he told me. And they'll likely torture him and his best friend to make him talk."

Eddie sighed as he held his head. He didn't need to threaten Eddie with a chainsaw. He only needed to help Eddie realize that his life would be in greater danger if he sent him back. And by not remembering what he may have seen, or most likely *not* seen at Wesley's place, he was endangering Corey's life even more.

Damn it! Why did he have to be in this dilemma?

Eddie saw that something had caught Brutus's attention, the drug lord had looked over his shoulder and turned around.

Candace faced Eddie and threw her index finger in his direction. "You should've minded your business. Now, look what you got yourself and your friend into."

"Shh!" said Brutus as he appeared to be staring into space. It did not take Eddie long to hear what sounded like helicopter propellers—more than one.

Five men ran into the gym. "We need to evacuate, and quickly, Mister President."

"What's going on?" asked Brutus.

"The army was spotted approaching."

"What?"

"There's no time to explain—"

Rapid gunfire was heard in short bursts a short distance away as the helicopters drew nearer.

"Cut him loose," Brutus said, pointing to Eddie.

Eddie felt something slice through the zip ties, freeing both hands.

"If you want to stay alive," said Brutus, "then you better keep up."

Chapter 20

Cain and Son's Funeral Home, Two Hours Earlier

The two officers took a single gaze to each other as Corey recounted the moments after the brawl and up to when Eddie disappeared. One crossed his arms and turned to Corey. "Are you sure your friend didn't run off with the brawlers before we got here?"

"I'm telling you he was kidnapped." Corey closed his eyes hard as he took a deep breath. "He wouldn't just take off without telling me and leave behind a broken cell phone."

"What broken phone?"

"The one in the parking lot." Corey threw his arm out in its direction. "Aren't you guys listening to me? I already told you about it. You should've found it by now."

"Please calm down, sir."

"Don't tell me to calm down when you don't believe me."

"Nobody said we didn't believe you."

"Then why aren't you writing anything down?"

The same officer looked down, closed his eyes as he pinched his nose twice. He looked back up with his eyes open. "Does Mister Barrow have any enemies?"

"A lot," Corey answered.

"May you be more specific?"

"He was kidnapped two nights ago."

"By whom?"

"How am I supposed to know?" Corey stopped to sigh. "You should've heard about it because you guys found his clothes and phone after he was caught wandering the town."

"Missing clothes?" The two officers stared to the side in thought.

"You mean you're friends with the man that was wandering naked around Bogue Heights screaming about some alien invasion?"

"Yes, that's him."

"I'm not aware of any kidnapping."

Corey shook his head as he hit it with both hands at the temples. "Look, are you going to look for him or not?"

The first officer reached into his back pocket and took out a small notepad, then grabbed his pen from his breast pocket. "What's your friend's name again?"

"Eddie Barrow."

"Do you have any pictures of him on your phone you could send to us?"

Corey took out his phone and scrolled through the pictures. He skipped over a few showing them boarding the plane at Trudeau to their arrival at Sangster airport. Corey stopped on one of Eddie as he faced him once they'd collected their luggage. He then held up the phone to the officers. "Is this good enough?"

"That's fine," he said as he gave Corey his card. "Just email it to the address below and include the file number. Can you give me your name and your phone number, and a second we can reach you at if the first doesn't work?"

Corey gave him his cell number. "That's the only way to reach me."

"Someone will call you," said the officer as he flipped his notepad shut.

"How soon?"

"In time," said the officer before he and his partner walked away, leaving Corey standing where he was.

How could Eddie be so careless as to just wander off on his own? Then again, Corey wondered how he could've been so stupid as to let him walk off by himself after the brawl they were caught up in.

"Stupid, stupid, stupid," Corey kept saying to himself as he started walking in circles.

The same people who kidnapped Eddie last Sunday came for him again. And according to the funeral director, there weren't any closed-circuit cameras in the lot—making the kidnapper's job easier.

Come on, think like Eddie. What would he be thinking and doing had the situation been reversed? He'd be overthinking it... maybe, or maybe not. Okay, Eddie would be thinking, what if this were planned? Then the kidnappers would know to lure Eddie back here. They'd also have to know Eddie's phone number. But who would have that knowledge? Jalissa, Milly, Delva all had Eddie's phone number. Could they have shared it with anyone?

He had Milly's mobile, so he called her.

"Hello?" She answered after three rings.

"Milly, it's Corey, Eddie's friend."

"What's the matter, son?"

She must've sensed the anxiety in his voice. "Eddie's been kidnapped."

"What?"

"Listen, I don't want to talk on the phone. I can't think of anyone else to turn to." Corey knew Eddie would be this paranoid.

"You want to see me?"

Corey sensed that she felt scared for him. "That would be great."

There was a moment's pause as though Milly was hesitating. "Okay, meet me at the store. I'll try to leave the house soon."

Corey hung up and ran to his car, and in no time was turning onto the road. About twenty minutes later, he was parked in front of Milly's store. It wasn't too long after when he saw her drive by in her tan Corolla.

He got out and walked around the front of his car to join her on her passenger side. He leaned sideways to look in the window, just as she lowered it.

"We'll talk here," said Corey as he saw Milly fidgeting with the door handle, only for her to realize that it was still locked. Corey heard the click as the door was unlocked and he then got in.

"Did you hear anything yet?" Milly asked.

"No. The police wrote a report and went on their way." A truck roared by, belching out diesel smoke as he closed the door. Milly flicked a switch to automatically roll up both front windows to block out the street noise.

"You know, I wish I could help. I really do."

"Maybe you can." A thought came to Corey. Milly didn't look like the person who'd be friends with people in the underworld. But maybe one of Dwayne's friends could connect him with someone who may be able to find out who took Eddie and why. "Eddie said that you knew some of Dwayne's friends—the ones he made dresses for."

"I know of them, but I don't know each one personally that well," said Milly. "But why you ask this for? I hope you don't think of trying to find him."

"I don't think I have a choice."

Milly looked ahead as though in thought, then nodded. "Yes... yes, I know a few, but not that well. But you shouldn't be trying to find your friend. Leave that to the police."

"I'm tired waiting after the police. Besides, I'm not convinced that they'll use all their resources to look for Eddie. Don't forget that they think he takes dope."

"You mustn't say that, son. They work hard to keep some of the wicked people locked up. Mi can't have another rob mi cash register."

"They haven't been helpful so far," said Corey. "I wouldn't be surprised that Eddie's done more to find Dwayne's killer than they have, or else he wouldn't have been kidnapped. That's why I'm asking for your help. Can't you just take me or give me directions to one of Dwayne's friends?"

"But mi don't know how to reach them." She paused as though something had come to mind. She took out her phone and dialed a number. "Hold on."

Corey sat and listened to her as she spoke. The conversation went on for about two minutes before she rested the phone on the middle tray. Milly then reached between the two front seats to the back, where she grabbed her handbag from the floor. She dug around inside with both hands and took out a used envelope and a pen, then jotted down something on top of it. She handed it to Corey.

"Har name Lucille. Go to this address. She'll be expecting you," said Milly. "She may be able to find out something for you.

But I hope that you're not bothered by her...orientation."

"I don't care about that." Corey shook his head. "I just need to find my friend." Corey glanced at the envelope, then folded it in his hand before getting out.

"Just go there." Milly lowered the passenger window. "She might know who to send you to. I wish I could do more."

Corey leaned sideways to look through the open window. "Don't worry."

He walked back to his car and got in. He rested his hands on the steering wheel to reflect. He understood. People witness many things, but they'll never talk to the police because they don't trust them. If she's one of Dwayne's friends, Lucille had probably had run-ins with them, thus wouldn't have any reason to want to help them.

He got into his car, entered the address into the GPS on his smartphone, and followed the directions. For the thirteen-minute ride, he had the radio tuned to the news, hoping that he wouldn't hear an announcement about Eddie's body being found. There was another murder in the MoBay area, which appeared to be the forty-fifth of the year. At the moment, the police wouldn't release any information on the identity of the victim. Corey's worst fears came to mind that the police would call him to give him the news he didn't want to hear.

It was then reported that the prime minister had authorized a preemptive military strike on the home of Brutus. Apparently, he was given a chance to surrender peacefully while the town's residents had ample time to vacate.

The address the GPS brought Corey to was in a well-to-do neighborhood called Coral Gardens. The A1 highway separated the residential area from the five-star resorts that lined the coast. The fairly large area was built on flat land that consisted mostly of one- and two-story houses. To drive farther from the coast, one would encounter the steep, hilly area with more lavish homes and villas.

The road had a few potholes Corey had to dodge. He didn't see anyone else besides the two men he drove past. One would've been the homeowner engaged in chatter with his neighbor as they stood on opposite sides of the concrete border wall. They paused to turn to Corey as he drove by, obviously curious to know who he was.

Corey's GPS brought him to a cream-colored one-story cottage. Everything from the concrete border wall to the home was that color except for the red roof. He pulled up beside the wall and parked his car slightly off road. There weren't any sidewalks, so Corey parked halfway on the grass, roughly a foot away from the grilled entrance. He got out, walked up to the gate, and rang the doorbell on the side. Corey was surprised to hear the buzzer less than ten seconds later. Perhaps Lucille was already next to the front door.

Corey pushed the grill and closed it behind him as he walked to the veranda of the one-story house. He noticed the absence of a vehicle in Lucille's driveway, which made Corey wonder how she got around. Bus, taxi, or walking he presumed.

Corey knocked on the door, which was located inside the doorless extension of the house—for him it seemed the closest thing to a garage. About fifteen seconds later, a plump, nearly bald woman in her early- to mid-forties answered.

"You Corey?" she asked.

"Yes," he answered.

She stepped aside and held open the door wider. "Come in."

She closed the door behind Corey and gestured to his feet. "Yuh caan lef yuh shoes pon di mat."

She walked to the living room while Corey took off his shoes and left them on the mat as she asked.

"Yuh caan sit in deh," she gestured to the living room. "Yuh waan sumpen fi drink? Mi nuh have no beer, but mi caan bring some soda or juice."

"Soda's good," Corey answered.

Corey walked into the living room where the ivory-colored curtains flapped in the sea breeze, a major contrast to the Airbnb he and Eddie stayed at, where they depended on air-conditioning.

Corey heard clapping on the floor, and when he turned to the sound he saw a frail, elderly woman with a walker moving toward the living room. She had a very warm smile, as though she was excited to see him. He stood out of politeness.

"Hello. You must be Corey. Milly was telling me about you." Corey assumed that it was Lucille. "Did you have any trouble finding the house?"

Corey shook his head. "No problem."

"Why are you standing for? I'm not the queen." She laughed as she made her way to the living room sofa, sitting opposite him on the other side of the glass-surfaced table. He lost count how many times he'd seen similar tables in the homes of older West Indian families.

It was then that Corey saw the scarring on her arms and the side of her face. They appeared to be defensive wounds from what may have been a knife attack.

"Milly told me to expect a tall young man, she forgot to tell me to also expect someone very handsome."

Corey shook any idea that this woman had horny thoughts about him—given her disability. "You're flattering."

"I've been known to tease young men and women, but not so much anymore," she said with a sigh. "But I don't want to bore you with too much chat. Milly told me that you're looking for your friend."

"You know how to find him?"

"That depends." She took a short breath. "I understand that both of you were looking for a woman named Candace who mysteriously disappeared."

"We were, but I'm more concerned about my friend Eddie. I think he was kidnapped."

"And why's that?"

"We were both there when Candace's friend, Dwayne Pottinger, was murdered. Eddie was looking into who would've killed him since he's convinced that the police have it all wrong."

She laughed as she shook her head. "Tell me something I don't already know. And the men who were suspected of killing he, we don't even see them on the news."

Corey took out his cell phone, searched through the pictures that Eddie had saved and found the photos of the three he had lifted off the net.

He held up the phone to her. "These three?"

She leaned forward and adjusted her glasses, nodding. "I know of this one, his name's Delroy, I think. His grandfather's a judge. I already met his mother."

"Really? Small world."

"Har name Chevelle. Mi use to see har inna di support group meetings weh mi did get invite to," said Lucille as she sighed and lapsed into Patois. "She's a rape survivor just like many of the women."

Corey's eyes widened as he gasped. "For real?"

Lucille nodded. "That's how Delroy was born. And she was such an easy victim because she's autistic."

Corey reacted as though cold water was splashed in his face.

"Oh yes." Lucille nodded. "We don't and are not supposed to call people *retarded* anymore." She clenched her teeth and shut her eyes hard. "Ughhh. I shouldn't even have said that awful word. I'm sorry."

"Don't sweat it." Corey was reminded of the ticket stub. He reached into his wallet and took it out. "By any chance does Chevelle stay at the Seaview Group Home?"

"It's possible. How do you know about that place?"

Corey held out the ticket stub for Lucille to see. "This fell out of Delroy's pocket the last time I saw him."

She leaned forward as though to get a better look, then nodded. "Then I'm sure that's where she is. They give these to visitors, and they have to place it on top of the dashboard or else them car get towed."

Lucille sat back on the sofa as her hand went up to her temple. "What was I saying before?"

"You were telling me about…"

"Oh yes." Lucille's hand dropped. "Har own teacher did rape har. Him come out a prison but dem shoulda keep him lock up."

She pointed to the scars on her arms and face. "You see these marks? Over ten years ago I was coming home from work with my friend, Merlene. We used to work at the hospital. It was late, and we just finished our shift as we rushed to catch the last bus, when we were ambushed. I can't tell you how many they were because Merlene used her body to shield me from them. They dragged me on the concrete onto the side of the road in the bush where they beat and raped both of us, but I was the only one who lived to talk about it."

Corey's eyes widened again at hearing her say she was raped. He couldn't believe that she didn't flinch at saying it. But something changed in her face. It was as though she was struggling not to cry. But it was too late, she couldn't turn her head away fast enough for him to not notice a tear form in her left eye. "I'm sorry to hear that."

Lucille nodded slowly. "That's okay, son. I've learned to move on. That's why I show up often to these meetings. Many of them women broken, I just want to help as many as I can. But there was something I couldn't get out of my mind when it came to Chevelle."

"What's that?"

"I always felt as though Chevelle was holding back something."

"Like what?"

"I don't know, to tell the truth," said Lucille. "But something always bothered me about how Chevelle tell the story. But that caregiver of hers, Ann. She was always with her at the meetings."

"What about her?"

"I don't know. I just don't trust her." Lucille shook her head. "Something tell me that because of Ann, Chevelle won't open up to me."

The woman who greeted Corey came back carrying a tray with two glasses of ice and two soft drink cans.

"Thanks, Ira," said Lucille.

"You're welcome," Ira answered and turned to Corey. "Yuh ago stay fi dinner?"

"Thanks, but I can't stay."

"Nonsense," said Lucille. "When di lass time yuh eat? Yuh caan let yuhself go hungry."

"I don't want to impose."

"Oh, come on. Please stay, you're my guest."

Corey looked up at Ira, who raised an eyebrow while smiling. It was as though she silently agreed with Lucille. "How about I take something for the road?"

"Son, you need to slow down," said Lucille. "I know you want to find your friend, but you won't be able to think straight if you take off so quickly."

Corey thought for a moment and realized that she was right. He was too consumed with finding Eddie that he'd most likely make mistakes if he did not take a break. "I'll stay for a bit."

Lucille smiled. "Smart man."

Ira nodded and left them.

Lucille gestured to Ira as she walked away. "As you can see, Merlene's still taking care of me. Her life insurance is covering most of the bills."

"Did they catch whoever did this?"

"Just like Dwayne, no one saw or heard a thing—even though there were people close by."

"I guess you don't care much for the police."

"Please. They look down on women like me and Merlene. Young men like Dwayne get beat and killed, and all they say is 'a juss a fish a get fry ova deh-sah.' That's why I don't go out anymore. I was going to go to Dwayne's funeral but when I heard what happened after the service, I'm glad that I didn't go."

Corey was trying to be patient. This woman was too traumatized by Dwayne's killing, as it brought back terrible memories of her and Merlene, whom he assumed had been her partner. Eddie could take this, but Corey couldn't for much longer. "What did they say about women like Candace? Was she always there to help Dwayne?"

"Dwayne was able to take care of himself for the most part." Lucille smiled. "He make two dresses for one of mi nieces, except I had to tell she parents that it was Milly who was the one who make them."

"And when was the last time you saw Candace?" Corey hoped that this would bring her back to focus on why he was there.

"It was about two to three weeks ago, you know." She paused for a bit. "I know something wrong with her when I last saw her, next thing you know she disappear."

"Something wrong?" asked Corey. "Like what?"

"I believe a man touch har."

What the fuck? "Who? I mean, why did you think that?"

"I don't know." She raised both hands before dropping them. "That's just the feeling I get when I lass si har. I never told anybody this. I tried to ask her but she wouldn't open up to me. That's why I think a man touch har. Next thing I know, Dwayne got killed and Candace disappeared. And now you tell me that you and your friend are looking for her and now your friend disappeared too?"

"Yes, it happened this afternoon right after Dwayne's funeral."

She shook her head and sighed. "Oh no. Mi coulda call one a Dwayne frien to see if dem hear anything. Or—"

Corey leaned forward as she let her head fall back. Her sigh told him that she knew of something else but didn't like it. "Or?"

She raised her head up and looked at him. "I was going to say that you'll have to find a way to contact Candace's uncle."

"Who's her uncle?"

"You hear about Brutus?" Yeah, he just heard that name. "It was all over the news today how the military moving in on Guava Hill. He's her uncle."

"Candace's uncle is a don?"

Lucille nodded in response. "She's originally from Guava Hill. It looks like a normal town until you see men walking around with guns. The people who live there are used to it, so they're not scared because they know Brutus protects them. The police can't even get into the village without Brutus's permission. That's how powerful he is."

Lucille reached forward to grab the soft drink can, but Corey moved in faster.

"Let me get this for you," he said as he cracked open the can and filled her glass.

"Thank you, son," she said. "It's possible that Candace went there to hide, because she knows she'll be safe."

Corey handed the full glass to Lucille and rested the quarter-filled can on the tray before filling his own glass with the other can.

"If Candace is hiding anywhere, it's there. And if you and your friend have been asking questions to the wrong people, then I'm sure one of them would've told Brutus because he has people everywhere reporting to him."

"You think Brutus kidnapped Eddie? I was thinking that he was kidnapped by the same ones who snatched him the other night."

Lucille gasped. "Him get kidnapped before?"

"Two nights ago, but we don't know who they were because they drugged him."

"An him no mention Brutus neider Candace when him did si yuh?"

"No, he didn't," Corey answered. "You're saying that if Brutus had kidnapped him the other night, he would've let Eddie know it was him?"

Lucille nodded. "I'm sure."

"And there's a military strike that's supposed to happen at Guava Hill." Before he realized what he was doing, Corey was looking for the remote.

"What is it, son?"

"May I turn on the TV? There's something I need to check."

"Sure." She grabbed the remote off the couch beside her and turned on the Sony Bravia HDTV. "You want to see if Brutus is on the news? Hold on."

Corey nodded as he turned diagonally to watch the television, which was adjacent to them.

Lucille flipped through the channels until she came to a news station which appeared to be broadcasting live outside of Guava Hill. The only thing on the screen was Brutus's partially formed barricade being bulldozed by an army tank. Lucille's hands shot up to cover her mouth.

"Mi hope seh yuh frien nuh deh-bout." *I hope your friend is not there.*

"If Eddie's there," said Corey as he shook his head, "then he's never been in this much shit before."

Chapter 21

Guava Hill (present time)

"Move, bwoy!" yelled Brutus's henchman as Eddie raced to catch up. If there was anything that scared him more than the gunfire and explosions he heard outside, it was the haphazard way the henchman held onto his AR-15.

Candace had three armed guards accompanying her while the bulk of the armed men surrounded Brutus as though they were his personal Secret Service detail.

Another rocket-propelled object grew louder by the second. *Boom!*

The ground quaked under Eddie's feet as the lights flickered and glass shattered somewhere nearby. This was the fourth blast since they had left the gymnasium, and they seemed to be getting nearer.

They took a hard right into what Eddie soon realized was the locker room, where they rushed down an aisle that separated four rows of lockers on both sides. It ended in an unfinished area with bare concrete instead of a tiled surface, where it appeared a shower area was to be built to Eddie's right. Yet, to the left were four lockers by themselves against the wall.

Eddie turned to the sounds of heavy, rapid gunfire and a helicopter that appeared to be hovering close by. There was a *whoosh* followed by an earth-shaking blast. This time dust was expelled from above. There were screams from outside the building. Brutus's men must have been exchanging gunfire with the helicopter on the other side of the wall.

Eddie was shoved to the side as Brutus's men formed a barrier where they aimed toward the wall, as though they were expecting the next blast to breach their area. Eddie's stomach tightened as his breath shortened, wondering who he was safer with. Should he run away and yell to the army that he's a hostage and risk getting shot due to flawed intel, or should he take his chances with Brutus?

He turned to Brutus, who punched in a series of numbers on the button pad on the locker in front of him…wait, that wasn't a locker. The drug lord then pulled the locker door, and all four moved at once. The lockers were bolted to a steel door.

Eddie heard another *Whoosh!*

Oh shit!

Eddie felt a moment of weightlessness before rebounding off a light metal surface before his body hit the floor. There was an intense ringing in both ears along with head spinning. The only other sound he heard was himself coughing—except internally.

The room spun as he struggled to catch his bearing. He closed his eyes tightly for a second and reopened them with rapid blinks—hoping that the spinning would go away. No such luck.

What just happened? There was a blast, and he felt himself being thrown diagonally backward into…the lockers. Now he was in a coughing fit from having inhaled so much dust. That's when his hand fell on what felt like someone's leg. Getting up on his knees was a bit of a challenge as the room spun. There was an intense ringing that blocked out the sound. His hand touched something…no…*someone.* There were other bodies on the floor—Brutus's men.

Are they dead? No, this can't be happening. I'm still alive. They must be alive too. They were closer and must have gotten the brunt of the shockwave. There was movement to the side, one of the guards appeared to be in a coughing fit as he got up on hands and knees, feeling the area for his gun. There was movement from the others. Some tried to stand but stumbled. It then occurred to Eddie that the lights were all off, but they weren't in total darkness. Sunlight was pouring in from outside through a large hole in the wall that was big enough to drive a VW Beetle through. And although he couldn't hear the propeller blades, he could see their shadows against the wall where the sun shone.

They found us. But how did they know Brutus would be here?

Adrenaline must have been surging through him because he should've felt *some* pain after the way he was thrown into the locker.

There was a faint *rata-ta-ta-ta-ta-ta*.

Eddie turned to see that reinforcements had rushed into the locker from where they came and were exchanging gunfire against those who were outside, using the wall as a shield as they took turns shooting upward through the hole in the wall. He counted six, and two even ran outside.

Fuck the dizziness! He had to get up and take his chances with Brutus. No army or law enforcement would've used such lethal artillery against a building knowing that there may be innocent bystanders inside.

His attention turned back to the gunmen, just as he saw one of them flying backward. Another spun as pink mist sprayed from his head.

The five who had formed a wall were back on their feet to assist, but Eddie noticed that the ones near the breach were moving backward and away from it.

That's when Eddie saw an assailant jump through the hole into the locker room. He was dressed in black. He wore a helmet, and a plate carrier, and was armed with what appeared to be a large 1911 of some sort. He held it with both hands, firing away and emptying his cartridges into another one of Brutus's soldiers. The slide locked open, and the assailant pressed the mag-release with his thumb, dropping the magazine. With expert handling, he grabbed another from his plate carrier, popped it in, released the slide, aimed, and fired.

Brutus's men showered the assailant with bullets. He appeared to be hit once or twice, as he was knocked back. But he never went down.

What the hell? A single gunshot at such close range should've killed him. Yet he was still standing. How?

The assailant ditched the 1911 and pulled a sword from a sheath at his back. The saying that one should never bring a sword to a gunfight was debunked as the assailant moved very swiftly, chopping off the arm of one of Brutus's men and impaling another before the arm hit the floor in a combination of martial arts and swordplay. Blood and guts sprayed all over as Eddie scrambled on the floor, pushing himself backward as he watched in horror.

There was something familiar about the assailant's movements. And although there wasn't any physical contact, a strange sensation of five calloused fingertips grabbing his face resonated.

Holy shit. It's Hansel!

He had the same height and build. And was, no doubt, dressed in the latest body armor. Eddie read about battle armor that can stop close-range gunshots while being light enough for the wearer to move swiftly. However, he understood this type of equipment would've been in its experimental stages and most likely would be used by the Americans or the Russians.

They found him. But Hansel, Gretel, and Stepmother couldn't be part of the Jamaican military. Although they were Black, they definitely weren't Jamaican. He was sure of that. Perhaps they were working with the military in some capacity? But why would the military be involved with Dwayne's murder?

Someone grabbed Eddie's arm and yanked him to his feet. It was the same henchman he was with earlier. Before he knew it, he was shoved toward the hidden doorway. He caught his footing and stumbled through the doorway and into semi-darkness. Light from somewhere down a staircase below partially illuminated the stairway next to him.

He turned to see the henchman pulling the door slowly shut, then shifting a lever from right to left to lock it. The brotha then walked, or more like stumbled, toward him. Eddie caught him just as he was about to fall. He nearly tumbled too, as the man's weight combined with his own near loss of balance made Eddie lose control.

Something was wrong. "You okay?"

The man responded by grunting and then coughing. This wasn't good, the man becoming heavier as though he could no longer stand on his own. Eddie helped him sit down—there was no point in helping him walk—and propped him against the wall in a seated position.

"Go. Yuh can't save me."

It was the first time Eddie realized that his hearing had returned. There was a stickiness on Eddie's hands, and he didn't need light to know that it was blood. The man had been shot just before he closed and locked the door.

"Guh long. Run, bwoy!"

Eddie didn't want to leave him, even though he knew that he couldn't do anything to save his life. This was his fault. He had allowed himself to be petrified and he lost focus that there was an escape. The brotha in front of him snapped him out of it, saved Eddie's life, and lost his as a result.

"Barrow?" someone yelled from downstairs. "Yuh there?"

There was a pause. "I'm here."

"Get your ass down here."

Eddie shook his head as he was startled by the boom on the other side of the door. Judging from how slow the dying guard had pulled the door, it may be heavy enough to slow down the assassin too. But Eddie wasn't counting on it to stop him.

"Barrow!" came the yell from below.

Eddie turned to the sound as he got up. "I'm coming."

He ran down the concrete stairs to a landing where he rounded a corner to go down another flight. He did this for three more flights before he was caught off guard when he saw Candace and her three protectors.

The three of them rushed Eddie at the bottom of the stairs. "You and Candace, guh long."

There was the growing sound of gunfire and blood-curdling screams from above. No way should the gunfight upstairs be that audible.

Oh, shit! Hansel got through the steel door. He's coming.

"Eddie!" yelled Candace. "We have to go."

He understood. These men would hold off the assailant as long as they could—a suicidal move from what Eddie had seen earlier. He joined Candace, who had already begun running down the sloping tunnel. They were about fifty meters away when Eddie heard the rapid gunfire behind. The tunnel twisted and turned as the sound of the shots echoed, only to stop abruptly. That could only mean one thing, and he knew that he had to haul ass, no matter that he was already fatigued from running. If Hansel was in good shape, as Eddie thought, then he'd be able to close the distance between them like the T-1000 Terminator without breaking a sweat.

With Brutus having a construction company that served as a shell for his illegal businesses, having this escape tunnel built was a great idea. El Chapo would be impressed. Since more than ten minutes went by and he didn't hear any gunfire, Eddie knew that this tunnel only bought him and Candace some time.

Around a diagonal corner they came to a door that led outside onto a dirt path with two more of Brutus's soldiers standing there beckoning for them to hurry. But Eddie was almost out of breath. He couldn't remember the last time he had run so far and so fast. But he kept close behind Candace as he nearly slipped. The ground sank under his feet. It was all muddy from the hard rain that had fallen earlier. To his right was a steep incline. To his left was a hill that led down into the river. He wished he had brushed up on his local geography to know which river was closest to Guava Hill. At least he'd have an idea where he was. All he knew was that he was in the mountains.

When Eddie looked back over his shoulder, he noticed that the two soldiers had hung behind. Eddie couldn't afford to keep looking back. He saw Brutus and a few of his security detail not too far ahead. Brutus stopped to look back.

"Candace, hurry!"

Gunfire could be heard behind them as Eddie grabbed Candace's hand and pulled her with him, but she yanked her arm out of his grip as though she had been touched by hot coals. His foot suddenly sank into the ground, causing him to stumble and fall.

What the hell did I step into? It was then he noticed that Candace also stumbled and fell. Something wasn't right. It's when he heard flowing water beside him. It was runoff from above.

The ground was suddenly sloping downward toward the hill, which ran down into the river.

"Oh shit! Candace, get up now!" Eddie yelled.

The ground collapsed below them. Eddie tumbled onto his side before spinning onto his back. He heard Candace screaming while they were carried off in the landslide. Mud splashed into his face and mouth, causing him to close his eyes out of reflex as leaves and twigs stung him in his face and hands.

As fast as Eddie was sliding, if he were to be thrown into a tree he'd either be seriously injured or killed instantly. He picked up speed to the point that he could suffer serious injury if he bounced up and was thrown into an obstacle.

The ground then leveled off, and Eddie felt himself flying through the air. He opened his eyes and saw the treetops in the distance a second before he fell. Looking down, he saw the white raging water fast approaching before he plunged into its coldness, helpless to the power of the current. The priority was to get to the surface. There was no telling if an undercurrent would pull him under and drown him. He did not try to fight the current but instead swam with it and broke the surface.

Air.

It was brief but long enough for him to catch a breath as white water splashed into his face, disorienting him. He had to swim to shore where the current would be weaker, a difficult task since he was tossed underwater a few times.

After the sixth or seventh dousing, Eddie saw a pair of flailing arms.

Candace. She was still alive but a bit farther downstream.

"Canda—" he yelled before he inhaled water into his mouth and was blinded by bubbles. The force of the water gradually dissipated, giving Eddie a better chance of staying on the surface. It was then that he was able to see Candace swimming to the river's edge on the opposite side.

"Candace," Eddie called out as loud as he could between breaths. He swam after her.

She didn't answer as she crawled onto the shore, coughing.

Eddie was not too far behind as he felt the rocky surface digging into his knees and palms the shallower it got. He was too tired to stand and followed through with throwing up the water he had accidentally swallowed. Eddie didn't care that he lost both of his shoes and a sock, he was alive and that's all that mattered. When he was able to breathe normally, he fell to the side and rolled onto his back. From there he stared up into the blue sky, dotted with cirrocumulus clouds as the rays of the sun baked him.

He wanted something to dry himself off with as he began to shiver. His first instinct was to rest and probably go to sleep, then the thought that the assassin would catch up to him made him sit up. He ripped off the remaining sock he still wore and turned to Candace. She too was lying on her back with her knees raised, her forearm over her brow. He then glimpsed her breasts being completely visible through her soaked shirt, causing him to look away as he raised his hand to block his view.

"Are you okay?"

She groaned and then sat up slowly. "I'm fine." She stood and began to walk away. "You best catch up because I'm not waiting on you."

"Seriously?"

"What?"

"You don't need to be so rude."

"Stop being such a pussy. What did you expect when you came looking for me?"

"I can tell you what I didn't expect…being kidnapped by your uncle and brought to his place at a time when he was being targeted by your government."

"He didn't even know that the government was going to attack. Besides, you shouldn't have come looking for me." She put her hand on her hip and turned to Eddie, cocking her head to the side. "Why are you doing this? What do you have to gain by pretending to be a detective? Yuh wunnuh die quick?"

"I guess it comes from being unable to say no to Dwayne's sister. I'm sure she'd like to know what you and Wesley got yourselves into that got him killed and has you on the run. Both of us as a matter of fact."

Candace rolled her eyes with a sigh and walked upstream.

"Where are you going? Shouldn't we be heading the other way?"

"If you want to go that way I ain't stopping you."

"You know where you're going?"

"Mi grew up around here, of course mi know where to go."

That's right, he had already forgotten that. Eddie got up and ran after her, stopping after the first three steps as the sharp rocks poked the bottom of his feet.

"Wait up." Eddie skimped along, trying not to put too much weight on his feet.

Candace looked over her shoulder at Eddie. "You and your baby feet."

"Well excuse me for not making walking barefoot outside a habit." She had obviously developed hard feet from walking without shoes for quite some time. It would explain why she wasn't sensitive to the sharp rocks.

Eddie found a patch of soil farther from the water with fewer rocks to walk on, allowing him to catch up to Candace. "Can we talk for a bit?"

"No."

The shoreline slowly began to disappear, leaving them with no choice but to walk through the forest. Candace was in front of Eddie.

"You should know by now that someone's trying to kill us," said Eddie. "Ignoring me isn't the answer."

She still did not respond.

Enough of this! Eddie barely touched her before she spun around swinging at him. She got in a few blows to his shoulders and a stinging slap to the face before he raised his hands to fend off the rest.

"Don't touch me," she screamed.

"I'm sorry, I just want to talk."

"And you always talk by touching people?" she said as the slaps diminished. She was getting exhausted.

"What was I supposed to do? You were walking away from me."

"I tell you already that we need to keep moving. Are you deaf?" She stopped slapping him.

"Are you done?"

"One more thing. Never lay your hands on a woman without

her permission." She scowled and stormed off.

Eddie made a mental note of that last statement, and hoped that she truly did know where she was going. "Can you at least tell me if Brutus has a location where we can join him or other members of his posse?"

A few moments went by before Candace looked over her shoulder. "He has a few safehouses."

"Where's the *next* closest one?"

"Why do you ask?"

"Because I think it would be best if we don't go to the nearest one."

"And you think being out here in broad daylight where we could be easily spotted is better? Yuh a mad."

"Paranoid, yes. Mad? Far from it," said Eddie. "The army was only supposed to capture Brutus, yet they knew precisely where to locate us. I expected to see a large group. Instead, I only saw an individual who not only knew precisely where to find us, but single-handedly took out Brutus's men as though it was nothing. Doesn't that strike you as odd?"

"And your point is?"

"My point is that the guy who killed Brutus's men wasn't with the army. He's a hired assassin—one with the same height and build as the one that I walked in on at the hospital, seconds before he killed Wesley."

Candace stopped and turned to him, wide eyed with raised eyebrows.

"As I said," Eddie continued, "the assassin wasn't after Brutus. He was after you. And he wouldn't have hesitated to take me out, given the chance."

"But...but how did he know that I'd be at the rec center?"

"Isn't it obvious? Your uncle may have a mole. Perhaps the assassin and his partners used a thermal imaging device—one that was mounted on a drone." Eddie glanced upward. "These trees should provide us with some cover unless they use the same drone with thermal imaging. We may want to stay in the bush as long as possible."

"What difference will that make if they got a drone that could spot our body heat?"

"Drones run on batteries, and batteries need to be recharged." By the look in her eyes, Candace was surprised to hear him say that. It was as though she did not expect him to be that confident. Eddie gestured in the direction they'd been heading. Candace turned and led the way.

"Whoever's after you used the assault on Guava Hill as a cover to get to you," said Eddie. "We can only hope that they lost our trail."

They walked for several minutes without speaking. Even though the sun wasn't shining directly on them, Eddie's clothes began to dry. However, they were still stained dark brown from the mud. At least he did not have to be concerned about stepping on sharp river rocks, though the forest floor wasn't exactly danger free, at least he could see where he was stepping.

"I don't know how far we have to go, but I'd appreciate it if you'd tell me what happened that you're on the run," said Eddie. "Do you at least know why Dwayne was killed?"

"I'm not saying anything."

"And how's that going to help?"

Candace stopped to turn around. "How are *you* going to help?" She gave Eddie a once over. "What are you, like, five foot eight? Probably weigh less than one hundred and sixty pounds. Who gweh fraid a yuh? A ten-year-old boy in Trenchtown wouldn't even be scared of you."

Candace gave Eddie a dismissive head shake before she turned and continued walking.

"First of all, I'm one hundred and sixty-seven pounds and I think I've handled myself pretty well so far." Eddie caught a swinging branch Candace did not bother to hold for him. "And just because you don't think that I'm intimidating doesn't mean that I'm dumb."

"Okay, then, Mister Smarty Pants. What do you suggest we do?"

"Where are you planning to go?"

"To a safehouse my uncle told me to go to in case of emergency, the nearest one."

"Bad idea."

"And why's that?"

"Because we have to assume that the people who are after us gathered enough intel on you and your uncle to anticipate your next move." Eddie followed Candace as he stepped over a fallen palm tree trunk.

"Intel? You now sound like a wannabe spy instead of a pretend detective."

"I'm serious," said Eddie, momentarily gnashing his teeth. "You said the nearest one. I take it there are others. We should head to one that's farthest away, or not head to any of them at all."

"My uncle said that if ever we were to get separated, I should head to the nearest safehouse," said Candace. "There are many people who are loyal to him in these parts who'll protect me."

"Your uncle didn't anticipate being attacked today, did he?"

Candace did not answer.

"This is why I strongly suggest that we change strategies," said Eddie. "We're being chased by professional assassins."

"And what do you know about the people who are after us?"

"I was hoping you'd be able to tell me," said Eddie. "Why do they want you dead?"

"It doesn't matter. It's not like you could do anything," said Candace. "I thought that my uncle could protect me—one of the most powerful men in Jamaica. Now he's on the run just like us."

"It *does* matter! I'm just as deep in this as you are." Eddie pointed back to the direction from where they came. "I don't know if you forgot, but your uncle kidnapped me from *your* best friend's funeral and then interrogated me because he believes that I know something that could help him. Whatever it is he thinks that I know, I'm assuming that it's something that he could use to get you out of whatever mess you're in. The least you could do is tell me why I'm in this shit you're in."

Candace kept walking without answering.

Eddie sighed. "That's it? You're going to play the silent game again?"

"You're better off not knowing."

He walked closely behind her for several minutes without any verbal exchange. They had been walking for more than half an hour in the woods when they came to the border of a clearing.

"Are you still not going to talk to me?"

She looked over her shoulder. "Just save your breath and keep up."

"Now listen." Eddie raised his voice along with a finger, but immediately noticed how her body tensed. She stepped back as though in fear. A thought then came to him, and it was all making sense. Even though it was a short period, he noticed how the guards appeared to go out of their way to maintain a space between themselves and Candace when she was in the rec center—with the exception of when they assisted her in escaping. Right before they got caught in the mini-landslide, she pulled away from him when he went to grab her arm. Then again as they got out of the river several minutes ago. Now, just raising his finger in the air in front of her. She was exhibiting some form of posttraumatic stress syndrome.

Eddie lowered his hand and took a step back while looking her in the eyes. "Someone physically hurt you. Is that what this is about?"

He remained silent and waited for her response. He noticed her hands trembling, then her knees. He looked around him and saw that they were close to a guango tree.

He gestured to it. "How about we sit down over there. I could use the rest, what do you say?"

She ran toward the tree and then collapsed to her knees, inches away from the trunk. She reached above her head and placed a palm on the trunk. He didn't have to see her face to know that she was crying. From behind he could hear her cough and sniffle.

Eddie approached her but was careful not to make any sudden movements to startle her. "I didn't mean to upset you. It's just that there was a pattern to your behavior."

She shook her head and sat on her ankles as she remained in a kneeling position. "Dwayne always spoke about your attention to detail in your writing. He said it was as though the reader was standing next to the characters hearing, seeing, and smelling everything they did. You figured out what my uncle was hiding from you back in the rec center and now you came close to guessing right again." She turned to Eddie. "How do you do it?"

Eddie shrugged his shoulders. "I notice things, I can't say more than that. Again, I'm sorry for upsetting you."

"Don't trouble yourself," said Candace with a wave of her hand. "You would've found out eventually. I just didn't expect you to figure it out so quickly on your own."

"I can't figure out everything on my own." Eddie sat down adjacent her with his back to the tree. "I need you to help me fill in the blanks. I know you're stressed, even scared, but you must believe me when I tell you that I don't want to and will never do anything to hurt you. And even though we hardly know each other and you don't have any reason to trust me, you should know that Dwayne's sister, Jalissa, does. She expects me to find his killers."

"I guess it's because Dwayne couldn't stop talking about you." Candace got off her knees and sat. "He's read all your books, some of them more than once, and he always had to remind me that you were framed for murder and that you and your friends solved the case on your own. I guess that's where he got the motivation."

Eddie raised an eyebrow. "Motivation to do what?"

Candace breathed deeply, then exhaled. "To go after the man who raped me."

"What?" Just hearing her say the word "rape" felt like a punch to the gut.

"Yes," said Candace. "This is what it's all about."

Eddie didn't feel comfortable pushing her, but he felt at this point she was warmed up to him enough that he'd built a trust. "Who did that to you?"

"I don't even know who he really was. Everything I thought I knew about him was a lie." Candace hung her head, shaking it as though in shame. "I was so stupid thinking that I was pretty enough to be in a music video. It's always the lighter-skinned women who are favored."

"Ah." Eddie shook his head. "He told you he was a talent scout. Where and when did this happen?"

"It happened a little over a year ago at the bar where my girlfriends and I sometimes go for drinks after work." Candace held up her head. "That evening it was only supposed to be me and one of my friends. I was the first to arrive, and I waited on her. When I called, she told me that she would be late, so I waited. She then called back later to say that she had some family emergency and had to cancel."

"Where do you work that you finished so late?"

"I'm a receptionist at a resort," she answered. "So, there I was all alone at the bar. I was about to pay for my drink when the bartender told me that someone already paid for it. That's when he gestured to some foreigner at one of the tables."

"Was he alone or did he come with friends?"

"He was alone. I walked over to thank him, when he asked me to join him. As you guessed, he told me that he was a talent scout and gave me his business card. I didn't think it would hurt, so I sat down with him." Candace closed her eyes tightly and shook, then held her head. "Mi can't believe mi fall for this." She sniffed as she wiped away a tear with the back of her forearm.

"What happened next?"

She looked away. Eddie interpreted it as another sign of shame and admission of another error.

Eddie recognized the con before she said another word. How long did he struggle with his first manuscript when he had unknowingly contacted fake literary agents and agencies who told him that they were ready to represent him if he were to pay an upfront fee.

Candace turned to Eddie. "He was a smooth talker. He even showed me a selfie with him and Cardi B—or someone who looked like her. We had a drink and he offered to show me the location where his client wanted to shoot the music video, then drive me home."

She paused. Eddie noticed that her breathing intensified. Rather than speak and, resisting the urge to hold her hand to comfort her, he gave her time and space to recompose herself.

Candace rubbed the corner of her eye. "Part of me said it wasn't a good idea to go with him, but I ignored my gut and went with him." She let her head drop in her hands. "I can't believe that I was so stupid. I knew that something was wrong the moment that I was suddenly drowsy."

She paused again, as though she were trying to work up the courage to continue.

"I couldn't move, I just felt...so powerless," she continued. "Then I felt myself being carried, then lowered onto the sand. And I just felt his fingers...inside me...I was trying to tell him no, but just couldn't get any sound to come out of my mouth. He was kissing me all over. He then held a finger to my nose for a few moments."

Ah, so that's why she reacted when I raised my finger to her earlier.

"I remember feeling my legs being forced apart...and then... *pain!*"

She swallowed and then took a break. Eddie did not say a word, he just looked at her a few more seconds, when he suddenly began thinking that this was all a very bad idea. Then came the tears down Candace's face as her hands went to her mouth and nose—all to muffle the sounds. Why did he try being Dr. Phil? For he all he knew could've very well messed with her head.

Shit! He needed her to be on her A-game if she was going to help him keep ahead of the ones who were after her, and now most likely him as well. "That's enough, I mean it. You don't need to say anything else." Eddie was about to grab her shoulders but withdrew his hands nearly as quick. Maybe it was best for him to shut up and let her cry this out.

She recomposed herself about a minute later. She breathed in a slow breath. "I remember waking up, opening my eyes. I was lying on my back when I noticed something moving beside me. I turned my head and I saw a beach crab. It was less than a foot away. It startled me, and that's when I realized that my ankles were tangled in my panties. Bits and pieces of the night before flashed back to me."

She closed her eyes tightly. "I felt so filthy, so dirty, the first thing I did was run into the ocean and bathe. I don't know where that man went, but I still felt him all over me."

A natural reaction, Eddie thought. Unfortunately, doing so would've washed away DNA evidence that the rapist may have left behind.

"I was on foot, and I cried all the way home, where I locked myself in my room for the whole day."

Candace closed her eyes and let her head fall back. She sighed deeply, then swallowed. "My roommate knew that something was wrong and called Dwayne because she knew that he was the one friend that I confided in the most. He came over right away."

"Did you call the police?" He chose his words carefully, to not come across as someone who was trying to shame her.

Candace chuckled. "The police? Please. All they'll do is take a statement. I'd be lucky to hear from them again. And even if they get back to me, they'll just say that because *I* was drugged, they don't want to risk arresting the wrong man. And because he was a foreigner with a lot of money, he'd end up hiring a lawyer and sue them for false arrest. And even if the arrest was justified, he'd use the same lawyers to attack me in court, call me a liar, then make a fool out of me. And when he gets away with it, I'll be ridiculed. People will call me a whore. I'll lose my job and have little chance of getting another." Candace's voice began to crack. "All I could think was that monster's child might be growing inside me."

Eddie was about to rest a hand on her shoulder, then pulled back without saying a word.

"Fortunately, I wasn't pregnant," said Candace.

Eddie sighed. "That must've been a relief."

Candace nodded with her eyes closed. She opened them. "It was. As I was saying before, the police would've only made things worse. I thought it best to just work through this on my own and learn from it."

She was blaming herself for what happened. He wanted to ask her how this was connected to Dwayne but thought better than to interrupt her story. This wasn't *Law and Order: SVU*, where the rapist is caught 9 ½ times out of 10 and faces justice in a forty-three-minute-long episode. Real life situations are a lot more complex—especially in the Caribbean.

She looked away and paused as though in thought. "I don't know if it was fate or not, but I saw him on my way to work about three weeks ago. That's why everything feels so fresh to me now."

Eddie saw her clench both hands in fists. "What did you do next?"

"I don't remember what happened immediately after. All I recall is that I was on the bus, and he pulled up beside it at the traffic light in a convertible. I must've froze for several minutes because I missed my stop."

"I hope you took the day off."

"I had to. I called in sick, took the bus home and spent the day in bed. I was alone at the time, so I called Dwayne. I didn't know what else to do. He insisted on doing something to 'make things right,' as he said." She paused. She was on a roll, and Eddie couldn't afford for her to stop because she may not want to continue.

"And what did he have in mind?"

"He told me not to worry, that he'd fix things."

Yup, I saw that one coming.

"I did everything to talk him out of whatever he was going to do, because I didn't want him to get hurt." Candace sighed and looked away. "I didn't even know at the time what I was getting myself into. But Dwayne wouldn't listen to me. He was stubborn."

And...

"That's when Shenice came into play." She smiled. It was as though she had fond memories of Dwayne as Shenice. "He wore an outfit that he knew I liked, then put on the blond wig, and went to the same bar my attacker was at."

"Was it the same bar where you met the guy?"

Candace shook her head. "No, another one. Dwayne used his network of friends to track him down."

Candace paused for a moment.

"It wasn't too long before he got that man's attention. The man told Dwayne the same story he told me—how he'd make him a star and all, and Dwayne played along. The man bought him a drink, but Dwayne only pretended to drink it. To make a long story short, they went for a drive and Dwayne pretended that he didn't feel well, as I had described to him. They got to the beach where he carried Dwayne from his car to the sand. In the end, the man carried him and laid him down where he…made a move on him."

She paused again, as though what she was about to say would be more difficult.

"Dwayne told me that he pretended that he couldn't move but kept saying no. The man wouldn't stop. Once the man pulled down his panties and got the surprise of his life, Dwayne used the moment of hesitation to kick him in the balls. Once he was down, he struck him in the head with his purse—where he kept a rock and a knife. While he was down, Dwayne kicked him nonstop."

"Damn!"

"Yeah." Candace chuckled sadly. "Dwayne was fierce when he had to be. I know what he did was dumb, but all I can say is that with all Dwayne went through in life, he had no choice but to learn how to fight."

"He's lucky."

"He came prepared. He even surprised his would-be rapist with his cell phone recording," said Candace. "He had it all on video from the moment he got in the car."

A thought then came to Eddie, one that he wasn't too thrilled about. "When Dwayne said that he would *fix* things, he wasn't planning on blackmailing this guy, was he?"

Candace turned to him. "A few days later he called me, telling me to get dressed because we're going to see his lawyer, Owen Hines. I was wondering how he was able to afford an attorney on the salary he was being paid from Milly. So, Dwayne and I took a taxi to Falmouth to see Hines. That's when I learned that he was also representing me. Hines asked us to sign some documents, then handed both of us a check in the amount of one-hundred-thousand dollars each."

"One-hundred grand? US?"

Candace cleared her throat and nodded.

That made sense because one-hundred-thousand Jamaican dollars didn't sound reasonable, given the exchange rate which would put it close to around six hundred US. "It was an out-of-court settlement," said Eddie. "You were both paid off in exchange for keeping quiet."

Candace nodded once. "I appreciate what Dwayne did for me, even though it was dangerous."

"Did either you or Dwayne at least find out who he was?"

"Yeah," said Candace. "He's the vice president of some large company, Vincent Lee Weiss. That's how Dwayne knew that he would have money to settle out of court."

"And also hire a hit squat," said Eddie. "A VP facing sexual assault allegations would be bad PR for the employer."

Eddie balled up a fist and punched into his other palm. "I knew that this didn't have anything to do with a gay bashing."

"What?"

"Sorry, I was thinking about the night I ran into Dwayne."

Candace held her head in her hands. "I don't understand why that man would pay us off then try to kill us after. It doesn't make any sense."

Eddie shook his head. "It doesn't. Paying you off should've been the end of it. Unless Dwayne kept a second copy of the video. Do you think that he used it to blackmail Weiss for more money?"

Candace shook her head now too. "I doubt it. We all signed a non-disclosure agreement. Besides, Dwayne would've told me had he done so." She sighed. "The bastard could sue me if he found out what I just told you."

"This is between us two," said Eddie. He then raised his knees, where he rested his elbows and let his head drop.

"What's wrong?" asked Candace.

Eddie shook his head. "I can't help but think there's something missing. You're right. The NDA should've put an end to everything. Even if Dwayne had extra copies of the video, if they were leaked it would be a violation of the agreement. It doesn't make sense that Weiss would have you killed. He'd know that it's unlikely that he'd get his money back."

"Maybe he changed his mind."

"That's possible." Eddie crossed his legs and tapped a finger on his lips. "But still, I can't help but think that something else is going on."

"Like what?"

"I don't know. Maybe there's something on the video." Eddie stretched his arms out. "Did you see it?"

Candace shook her head. "I don't want to see that man's face again."

Eddie shrugged his shoulders. There were so many unanswered questions, it left him unnerved. The whole ordeal left him exhausted to the point that he was ready to take a nap. He would've done so had he not been concerned that Candace may use the opportunity to leave him behind. Then what? He had no idea where on the island he was. He also didn't have a phone, nor any money. All he had was a group of real pissed-off killers who were after them.

They were screwed.

He'd do almost anything for a large iced-coffee, or even a regular one right now to keep himself alert.

"I'm curious," asked Eddie. "How did both of you go about hiding the settlement money? A large sum like that would've made you targets."

"Our lawyer told us the same thing," said Candace. "We signed an agreement with him where he would hold onto the money and disburse smaller amounts to us whenever we needed it."

"Makes sense. Had you deposited that amount in the bank you'd be forced to disclose where you got it," said Eddie. "If you don't mind me asking. Did you have any plans with that money?"

Candace looked toward the sunset. "I was probably going to leave the country and start a new life elsewhere. I wanted Dwayne to come with me, but he wanted to stay."

"No offence, but Dwayne was a moving target every day he lived here," said Eddie. "His parents disowned him, and he had to work in secret. I thought he would've used the opportunity to go somewhere where he'd be safer."

"As I said before, Dwayne was stubborn. Once his mind was made up you couldn't change it."

"Speaking of which," asked Eddie. "Did Dwayne ever tell you why he went to Citrusville the other night? I can't shake the suspicion that he did so to prove that Pusey had stolen his designs."

Candace looked at Eddie in awe. "Really?"

"I was piecing things together," Eddie answered. "Did you know in advance what he was up to that evening."

She shook her head. "Not a thing. Had I known I would've done my best to talk him out of it. And look what happened."

"Don't blame yourself. I think we can both agree that Dwayne was a target well in advance."

Another dead end. But it was likely going to be nightfall soon, which for him was not the best time to be out. Plus, he was starving and was sure Candace was too. Not to mention Corey would be going out of his mind, worried about Eddie. Not that he could do anything about contacting Corey right now.

Eddie slowly got up and stretched both arms. "We should start moving before it gets dark. How far is one of your uncle's farther safehouses, one we could reach before nightfall?"

"If we can somehow catch a ride, then I'd say about an hour's drive from here."

"How well do you trust the person we're going to? Do you trust them?"

"I can say that I'm acquainted with him," she answered as she stood. "It's been a while, but I know that he's loyal to Brutus."

Eddie then gestured ahead. "Lead the way."

Chapter 22

Eddie sat opposite Candace in the back of a pick-up truck among a tall stack of bananas, clueless to his whereabouts on this rock. The only road signs he saw indicated that they were somewhere in Saint Elizabeth Parish. He saw a sign that said Parrotee and Fullerswood, but that did not tell him much. There were very few words exchanged between the two of them, mostly because the roaring of the engine combined with the whipping wind drowned out anything they said. The driver insisted that they help themselves to some of his stash. Not knowing when his next meal would be, Eddie took him up on his offer. So did Candace.

The driver dropped them off at the side of the road per the agreement, where they would hike the remaining two miles to a village that locals called The Drought. The driver gave them a wave and a nod before driving off. Even though he did not want to show it in front of Candace, the thought of what was ahead made Eddie apprehensive. They hadn't even reached The Drought, but he knew that they were close because the stench of weed was stronger than ever. There was no doubt in his mind that he'd have a contact high within the next few minutes.

The first set of chattel houses marked the entrance to the village, as they were on both sides of the road as they walked past them.

"What do you know about this guy?" asked Eddie.

"Do you want to know the short version or the long version?"

Eddie saw movement to his right and noticed two children, no older than five and six, in one of the chattel house windows staring back at them. Both, likely brother and sister, stared at them as though they knew that something bad must have happened for two strangers to just walk into the village. "Short is good."

"He inherited half a fortune from his father's business. The other half went to his brother. While the brother chose to keep running the family business, Lenny—whom we're going to see—decided that he wanted to live an honest life and make an honest living, unlike his father, and wanted nothing to do with the business. So, he got his MBA from the Indiana University Kelley School of Business in Bloomington, Indiana, moved to New York City to work on Wall Street, got even wealthier than he already was, bought a condo overlooking Central Park, found the love of his life—a self-proclaimed Christian. She was from Ethiopia, I think. Everything was getting better, he asked her to marry him, and she said yes. Then, one evening he came home, he walked in on her in the bedroom cheating on him—" Candace then stared at Eddie. "With a white woman."

Candace then looked in front. "He had a meltdown and kicked them both out instantly. A few days later, he found out that this so-called 'love of his life' took her own. Lenny became guilt-ridden, fell into a depression, lost his mojo, and kept making one bad stock speculation after another. He lost a lot of clients' money. They tried to sue him, except he had lost too much money of his own to cover his legal expenses. He sold the condo, then turned to drinking. His brother reached out to help, but Lenny was too proud to accept it. A few nights later he was attacked on his way home—stabbed, actually. They tried to make it look like a mugging, but he knew that it was a message from one of his," she raised both hands to mimic quotation marks, "clients."

"Were the suspects caught?"

"I'm getting to that part," said Candace. "That beating seemed to have—how do I put it?—*woken* him up. It was as though he was suddenly made aware that 'The Business' was in his DNA. He called up his brother, had him send some of his associates to New York, and they all paid the client a visit. The next morning the NYPD found the client somewhere in Queens—a victim of *necklacing*."

Eddie shuddered at hearing the term. He was familiar with it as he had read that *necklacing* was method of torture where the victim had a gasoline-filled tire wrapped around their chest and arms. Once set on fire, the victim would be screaming for the next twenty minutes as their skin melted away while spectators watched. It was commonly used in Apartheid-era South Africa by the Black majority against their own when one was outed as a police informant.

"Let me guess, the client-slash-victim was a Black South African," said Eddie.

Candace stopped and turned to Eddie with a hand on her waist as she leaned back on one leg while tilting her head. He too stopped and turned to her.

"You're smart."

In the window of the chattel house behind Candace, Eddie spotted an elderly woman leaning on the windowsill. Her gray hair was tied in two sets of cornrows, and the way she narrowed her eyes at him made him uncomfortable to the point that he gestured to Candace for them to keep moving.

"As for the thugs the client sent after Lenny," Candace said as she started walking, "they were found in their apartment with their throats slit. Lenny then left New York and, as you can see, this is where he settled."

Eddie felt as though he had walked into a wall, as he stopped abruptly. "What kind of *business* did Lenny's father run?"

Candace stopped and turned to Eddie. "Guess."

Eddie put a hand to his forehead as closed his eyes. "And Lenny's brother is Brutus, which makes him your uncle."

"Half-uncle, but I still call him uncle." Candace then smirked. "That's my family. Full of surprises, isn't it?"

"What about the NYPD's investigation? Didn't they suddenly notice that Lenny had disappeared. And what about Homeland Security or the Port Authority? Wouldn't, or shouldn't, they have picked up on the fact that associates of Brutus entered the country around the same time that Lenny's client was killed?"

"Didn't you want to hear the short version?"

"Well, yeah. But you can't tell a story while leaving in a bunch of plot holes."

Eddie noticed the sound of a skipping rope as it hit the ground intermittently. He turned to see two girls holding it while another girl was jumping. They were enjoying themselves, but the girl facing them suddenly noticed Eddie. The smile dropped from her face, followed by her hands. It was then that the other two turned toward Eddie and Candace.

Silence.

Walking in their direction was a Rasta with a joint. His locks hung so low that they bounced against the back of his knees. He eyed Eddie as he approached, then blew a cloud of weed smoke into his face as he passed.

Eddie instinctively waved his hand in front of his face, which he scrunched up out of disgust. "Didn't you say that this was a *safehouse* you're bringing us to?"

"Yeah, why?"

"Because I don't feel so safe."

"This was your idea."

"I expected the residents to be more welcoming. I didn't expect everyone to be suspicious of us."

"Us?" Candace pointed a finger back and forth between the two of them. "They aren't suspicious of *us*. They're suspicious of *you*."

"That's not the best way to make me feel better."

"I wasn't trying to. It's no secret to them that you're not from around here."

"And not a doubt that one of them would've called ahead and informed Lenny that some *foreigner brethren* was heading his way."

She turned to a house diagonally to their left. "Here we are."

It was obvious that they were at the right place. This home was a bit bigger compared to the other houses, with newer and higher-quality wrought-iron grills covering the windows. Behind the house was a TV satellite dish Eddie imagined could rip off during a hurricane and possibly cause more damage to the house and the neighbor's than the hurricane itself. On the front patio he saw two women, sitting in rocking chairs, staring at them as they approached.

The screen door opened as a middle-aged balding man dressed in his office clothes exited. Eddie figured that this place was the one stop he made between leaving work and heading home to his wife. The man was in such a hurry that he forgot to zip his fly as he shuffled past them.

"Lenny's a pimp?"

"Yup. That's Uncle Lenny."

It was then that he noticed one of the women on the veranda, a skinny little thing, most likely from undereating. She had her hair twisted in Bantu knots, wore a peach crop-top and skinny knee-length jeans.

The grill to the front yard was left open and they entered. As they walked up the three steps to the veranda, Eddie was closest to them. Bantu Knots reached out gracefully to touch Eddie's arm. "I'm sure you got a big cock to put in me."

Eddie yanked his arm away. To a woman that thin anything would've been big.

"Brutus sent us," Candace cut in. "Go and get my Uncle Lenny."

Bantu Knots scowled. It was as though she interpreted that Candace was telling her that Eddie was *her* man, and that she'd better watch herself. She then sighed as though in defeat, got up, and went inside.

"A who dat?" yelled a man's raspy voice from inside, as Bantu Knots exited and sat back down in the empty rocking chair.

Eddie watched as Candace caught the screen door and entered. He grabbed it while it was open and followed her inside. They were in the living room where Eddie saw who he assumed was Lenny—and he was not the business-suited Wall-Street-type-turned-mobster he had pictured earlier. The man had a thick beard with patches of gray, and long dreadlocks that practically hung down to his waist. Eddie barely had a moment to react before Lenny reached beside him and pointed a sawed-off shotgun at Eddie. By reflex, both of Eddie's hands flew up.

"A who dis bumboclaat yuh bring come a mi yaad?" *Who's this you brought in my house?*

Candace sidestepped in front of Eddie. "He's with me. Brutus sent for him."

The pimp lowered his gun and Candace stepped aside.

Eddie cautiously lowered his hands as he watched Lenny scan him from top to bottom. "Wah mek Brutus sen fi dis bwoy? He shot his bookkeeper again?"

"He's with me and that's all that matters," Candace said.

"Oh yeah?" Lenny glanced at Eddie's bare feet. "I don't know him and I don't trust people I don't know."

This was obviously getting nowhere. He was playing tough, possibly for his need to establish his dominance. "Brutus trusted me enough to ask my help."

Lenny snickered. "You? A foreigner? Help Brutus? Nonsense. Brutus no ask fi help from nubady."

"Then he must've been desperate," said Eddie. "The fact that he didn't harm me says a lot about how much he believes that I'm of value to him."

"How? You didn't stop the military."

"That attack had nothing to do with Brutus," said Eddie. "The public was misled, at least that's my theory."

Lenny's eyebrows raised.

Eddie nodded toward Candace. "This is all about her. Brutus couldn't protect her as well as he thought he could. So, he sent for me, hoping that I'd know something that could give him some form of leverage over the people who are after Candace."

"And were you?"

"I was trying to think of what I may have seen or heard which could help him, except we came under attack."

"Seen or heard?" asked Lenny.

Candace nodded to Eddie. "He was there when my friend Dwayne was murdered."

"Dwayne?" Lenny leaned his head to the side. "Yuh mean di bwoy deh weh get himself killed fi wearing a frock?" *You mean the boy who got himself killed for wearing a dress?*

Candace nodded. "His sister thought that Eddie could catch his killer." She eyed Eddie mockingly. "Obviously, he couldn't say no."

"Yuh a detective?"

Eddie shook his head. "Not exactly."

"And you couldn't say that to Dwayne's sister?"

"I did, but I made a promise to her. I just didn't expect to find out the things that I did, which led me here."

"So, yuh a nuh detective. Who yuh be?" Lenny narrowed his

eyes.

Eddie sighed. "I'm an author."

Lenny furrowed a brow. "What?"

"I write thrillers. I came here for a book signing."

"From where? Barbados?"

"No, Montreal."

"You sound Bajan."

"My family's originally from there."

"So, you're just a writer," said Lenny. "And that makes you think you can play detective?"

"No," said Eddie. "But after being kidnapped twice, drugged, nearly blown up, chased through a tunnel, and having to travel cross-country barefoot after nearly drowning, I'd like to know why. And the same people that are after us will surely be looking for my best friend that I came here with. Brutus kidnapped me because he was certain that I knew something of value, I only wish I knew what it was."

Eddie saw that he had Lenny's attention. As he looked into his eyes, what was once apprehension was now curiosity.

"Beebi?" Lenny shouted out the window to the veranda. "Bring out three Red Stripes."

Eddie turned to see Bantu Knots walk in and disappear down the hallway.

Lenny propped up the sawed-off against the wall beside him, leaned back in his chair, and looked at Eddie. "Yuh's a wicked smood-talker."

"I'm much more," said Eddie.

"Look," said Candace. "We're going to need a burner phone and a car."

"A car?" asked the pimp. "To go where?"

"We can't stay here," answered Eddie. "The people who are after us won't stop. It's only a matter of time before they come here."

"Nonsense," said the pimp. "No one will think of looking for you here."

"That's not a chance we're willing to take," said Eddie. "Brutus underestimated the reach of these people. What chance do you think you have?"

"And where will you go?"

"I have a few ideas."

"And how will you get there?" asked Lenny. "You know your way around?"

Eddie turned to Candace. "That's where she comes in."

Bantu Knots came back and handed the uncapped beer bottles to Eddie and Candace. She handed the last bottle to Lenny and then went back outside.

The pimp shook his head and stared at them as he took a swig, then rested the bottle on the floor next to his chair. He reached beside his chair on the opposite side and grabbed a phone that was plugged into the wall via a USB cord. Lenny unplugged it and dialed a number. He reached up beside him and turned on the lamp. It was at that moment that Eddie realized how dark it had gotten outside. Lenny then got up and disappeared down the hall, leaving Candace and Eddie alone.

Candace sat down on the sofa that was adjacent Lenny's chair as she looked at Eddie. "You may as well sit. It's not like we're going anywhere soon."

Eddie gestured to his clothes with both hands. "My pants and shirt have mud stains, and your uncle already threatened me with his shotgun. I'll stand."

"Suit yourself," said Candace.

The couch was tempting, as his legs were tired. So, he sat down next to her. "I don't like the idea of us hanging out here."

"If you're looking for a fancy hotel you ain't getting one. So just be happy that you're not out in the bush."

Eddie pointed to the window.

"What's the matter?" asked Candace.

"Everything."

"Will you relax?"

"Take a look outside." Eddie gestured to the window again. "In a few minutes it'll be pitch black. For all we know anyone could be hiding out there right now with guns pointed at this house."

"I wanted us to go to another place and you said we should go to the one that's farthest away."

"Yes, I know what I said. But I wasn't planning for us to stay."

"Then where should we go?" asked Candace. "My uncle invested heavily in these safe spots in the event of something like this. Do you think he and his security didn't think ahead?"

"He only bought us some time."

"So, where do you think would be safer for us to go?"

They were interrupted as Lenny walked back in the room. Eddie was about to stand, but Candace grabbed his arm and pulled him back down.

"I just spoke to Brutus."

"Where is he?" asked Eddie as Candace nudged him.

"You don't need to know," said Lenny. "He knows you're here and said that you're not to go anywhere unless he says so."

"Let me speak to him," said Eddie.

"He doesn't want to hear from you." Lenny sat back down in his chair.

"Seriously?"

Lenny grabbed the sawed-off shotgun and raised it slightly from the floor. "Do I need to repeat myself?"

Candace's hands shot out. "It's okay. Eddie's not from around here and doesn't know how things are done."

The pimp released his weapon. "Him betta watch himself."

Time for a different approach. "A question, sir," Eddie asked. "I need to get a message to my friend."

"What friend?"

"My best friend, the one I told you about earlier," Eddie answered. "He needs to know to stop looking for me or else he may end up leading the police right to us."

"And how will he know where to look for you?"

"He's very resourceful, trust me." That bluff sucked.

"Which is why I'm not letting you communicate with him."

"If I don't reach my friend, then the people who are after us and Brutus will certainly track his movements through his cell phone, unless he thought of dumping it."

"He'll have to take his chances."

"He knows almost as much, if not more than I do," said Eddie. "If he's captured and is forced to talk, who knows how much longer it'll take before he reveals something useful to them that could help them find us. Think about that. Brutus wanted me because he thought that I knew something. So, it's in his best interest that he protects my friend."

Lenny sighed and looked at Eddie as though he were contemplating what was just said. He then took out what Eddie assumed was a burner phone, dialed a number, and held the phone to his ear. "Mek mi chat to di one Brutus."

He waited, and then he conversed with someone Eddie assumed to be Brutus. The call did not last too long, and a minute later, he put the phone down.

"Where's your friend now?" asked Lenny.

"I don't know," answered Eddie. "The last place I saw him was at the funeral home. He could be anywhere."

"What's his number?" asked Lenny.

Eddie hesitated at first, then gave it to him. Lenny tapped in a text on his phone and then hit the *Send* button. "I just texted your friend the location to download a secure app. Once he does, he'll receive instructions to destroy his phone and buy a bangaz."

"A bangaz?" asked Eddie.

"Yeah, mon. We call burner phone a bangaz," said Lenny. "As I was saying, your friend can then download the app from a secure website onto that phone. It's an app like Signal or WhatsApp with end-to-end encryption which cannot be hacked. Once he's connected, I'll automatically receive a notification. You can talk to him then, you understand?"

"I understand," said Eddie.

"Good. You must be hungry."

Both Eddie and Candace nodded.

"Then come to the kitchen and get something," said Lenny as he got up from his chair. "Beebi?"

"What?" came her answer from the porch.

"Find my niece and the Bajan some clean clothes." Lenny turned to Eddie. "You need to bathe, because you stink."

Chapter 23

Why did I think I had a chance of rescuing Eddie? It was a question Corey kept asking himself. Brutus's men were armed, but he doubted that his men stood a chance against tanks and missiles being fired from military helicopters. The news footage freaked him out to the point that he had jumped off Lucille's couch and headed to his car while Lucille pleaded for him to stay. As much as it pained him to ignore her, he left, telling her that he wouldn't be back unless Eddie was with him.

Bros don't leave bros hanging.

But he barely made it halfway when heavy traffic formed on the one road leading to Guava Hill. He came to a dead stop. On the road's opposite side, a bald, shirtless man with an unkempt gray beard was passing, telling motorists to turn around because police blocked off the road.

Corey lowered his window and stuck his head out a bit. "Hey."

The man stopped and turned to him. "Waah gwaan? Yuh nuh si seh yuh caan pass. Police block off di road."

Of course the police would've blocked off the road. What was I thinking? "Is there another way into Guava Hill?"

"Why yuh waan guh deh so? Fi get shat?" The man laughed and continued walking.

Who the fuck am I kidding? He's right. Why would I try to get there unless I'm looking to get shot? Corey slammed his fists on top of the steering wheel. He then did what cars up ahead were doing and pulled a U-turn.

His phone rang. Corey hit the *Answer* button on the steering wheel. "Eddie?"

"No, it's me, Nancy. Where the hell is he? Denton's waiting on him."

Corey shook his head with a sigh. "I know. It's been a shitty day."

He then summarized the events following the funeral service. "I've been running all around town looking for him. I'm still driving."

"This trip's been a nightmare," said Bevins. "I can't believe this is happening."

"Are you sure he didn't call you?" Corey slowed down and drove in a zigzag on the shoulder to avoid a stretch of rough, uneven road. "Did you check all your text and voice messages? How about email? Did you check your spam?"

"Checking now…no…no text…voice…email…nothing…there's nothing from him."

"Fuck, man!"

"Corey, listen to me," she said calmly. "Go someplace where you can sit down. You shouldn't be driving in your present state."

"How can I find Eddie by sitting around and doing nothing?"

"Because you won't be of any use if you get into an accident. Please listen to what I'm saying."

Corey followed the path of the car ahead of him as he cleared the rough road and drove back onto a smoother surface.

"Are you there?" asked Bevins.

"I heard you," said Corey.

"Please do this for me. I'm going to hang up now so you can focus on the road. Okay?"

"Yes, Nancy."

"Call me as soon as you get any news."

"For sure." Corey's attention switched back to the road. It was only when he heard the disconnecting beep sound that he realized he forgot to end the call.

A red light flashed in the dashboard. He had been so distracted by everything that he didn't even notice the gas tank was practically empty. He drove to the first service station he came to and moved into a spot at the pump that a previous motorist just left. Corey lowered the window as the female attendant wearing a red shirt and blue pants approached him. "Full, regular."

The attendant nodded then went to fuel the car. Corey rested his arm on the windowsill for the time it took for her to finish. He gave her a five-thousand-dollar Jamaican bill and headed back to Lucille's.

He had driven roughly two clicks when his phone buzzed in its dash holder. A notice flashed on the dashboard monitor alerting him to the text message, and that it came from a private number. He reached forward to the screen but paused when his fingers were less than two inches from it. Sure, he usually ignored calls with blocked numbers because often it was a scammer. But his friend's life may be on the line. He tapped the dash monitor to voice play the message.

The car's digital lady voice read out loud the text message. "Go buy two burners now, cash only, and download the following app to it. Then dump your phone and call eight seven six, seven three one, one zero thirteen on the new phone. Important, do not activate the new phone until you're at least ten kilometers away from where you bought it. Do not give this number to anyone. Must do this asap, life or death. Eddie."

Corey swung the wheel to the side and stomped on the brakes, skidding to a stop at the side of the road. He grabbed the phone from the dash holder and read over the message again, just to make sure he heard correctly.

He grabbed a pen and the car rental agreement from the glove compartment and wrote down the name of the app and the phone number he was given. He then did a Google Maps search for the nearest Digicel store. Luckily, he was only eight clicks from one. Once he wrote the directions down on paper, he tossed his phone out the window into the path of an oncoming van, listened for the *crunch*, and headed there.

Once he got the burners—paid for with the cash Milly had given him earlier—Corey drove, not caring where he went, just that he had driven ten kilometers. Only then did he pull over and activate the burner, downloaded the app, and call the number he was given.

The phone rang once.

"A who dis?" It was a man's voice, one that sounded like those who had lost some of their home accent from being overseas for too long.

"Who's *this*?" Corey asked. "I got a message from my friend to call this number."

"Is this Corey Stephenson?"

"Who's asking?"

"I am. Ansa di question ar mi hang up."

Whoever this was held all the cards. "Yeah, it's me, Corey Stephenson. Now let me speak to Eddie."

"Yuh get di two bangaz?"

"What?"

"Di bangaz. Yuh get dem?"

Bangaz, bangaz, bangaz…he means burner phones. "Yeah, I got two of them."

There was some background noise as though the phone was being passed on to someone else.

"Corey?"

"Jesus Christ, Eddie! What happened to you?"

"Did you toss your other phone?"

"Of course I did. What's going on? Where did you run off to? Were you kidnapped?"

"I'm fine, relax."

Corey couldn't believe how calm his friend was, considering how lightheaded he got from shooting off all those questions at once.

"You there?" asked Eddie.

"I'm here." Corey took a deep breath and exhaled. "Do you have any idea what you put me through?"

"I know, and I'm sorry about that. It's been crazy since the funeral."

"Were you kidnapped by Brutus?"

There was a short pause. "How'd you know that? Actually, don't tell me."

"Why not? I thought this app was secure."

"It is, it's just that I get a bad feeling about you telling me too much."

"Anyhow, I found out that Candace is Brutus's niece."

"How'd you know—no, don't answer."

"Did his men beat you up or torture you for information about her whereabouts?"

"Relax, it wasn't like that." Eddie was still as calm. "I don't want to get into too much detail. But speaking of Candace, I found her."

"In Guava Hill?"

"Yeah, she's with me now."

"Where?"

"You're better off not knowing." There was an audible sigh on Eddie's end. "Jesus, this is much bigger than I thought."

"What did you find out?"

"Assassins were hired to kill Dwayne. And they did it in a way to make it look like a gay bashing."

"Hired by whom, Vanessa Pusey?"

"No, and I'm sure that it wasn't her. I found out that Dwayne was an important witness to a rape. The guy who did it is a company vice president named Vincent Lee Weiss."

Corey listened as Eddie summarized what happened to Candace and Dwayne's sting operation.

"Got it," said Corey. "Do you think Weiss has anything to do with the Essis file?"

"What Essis file?"

"Remember when we were at Wesley's place? We saw an empty file folder on Dwayne's laptop called Essis."

There was a pause, as though Eddie was in thought. "Shit, Corey. I completely forgot about that. When Brutus was interrogating me, he wanted to know if I saw anything unusual while we were there. I didn't even think about that."

There was another pause as Corey overheard Eddie telling someone to call Brutus and tell him to find out what he could about Essis.

"I hope this turns up something," said Eddie.

"Me too, for all our sakes," said Corey. "But what I don't get is that if Candace was hiding out with Brutus, given his reputation and resources, shouldn't he have dealt with this rapist on his own?"

"Under normal circumstances, yes. But Wesley's killer showed up during the attack."

"He's part of the Jamaican military? You sure it was him?"

"I'm pretty damn sure it was him. He had the same height and build. But I don't think he's with the Jamaica Defense Force, because while they were attacking other areas of Guava Hill, he knew exactly where to find us. And when he did, he singlehandedly took out Brutus's men like Deathstroke."

"Deathstroke?"

"You know, from the *Justice League* movie?"

"Holy shit!"

"Brutus's men didn't stand a chance," said Eddie. "The only reason I'm still alive is because they held him back long enough for the rest of us to get away."

"Weiss must have some damn good connections," said Corey.

"You think? For years the prime minister refused to honor the DEA's request to turn Brutus over to them, only to take action now," said Eddie. "Do you see where this is going?"

Corey sighed. "Yeah. You said that the assassin knew where to find you and Candace."

"Possibly," said Eddie. "With the help of the latest in wall-penetrating radar."

"You're talking about radar that could spot people behind solid objects?" asked Corey. "That exists?"

"It does," Eddie answered. "I read an article about researchers at MIT who created one."

"Do you think that there's a mole in Brutus's group?"

"It's possible."

"What's your next move?"

"Nothing. Brutus ordered Candace and me to stay here."

"Oh, before I forget, I found out a bit more about Delroy."

"Like what?"

"He was born from rape, and his mother lives in a group home for the mentally challenged."

"I believe you mean *intellectually disabled*."

Corey cringed. "Yeah, that's what I meant." Eddie was always the more politically correct between the two.

"That parking stub you showed me came from a group home.

That's where she must be."

"I was thinking the same. But I don't see how that's going to help us."

"What do you mean?" asked Eddie. "We know that Delroy visits his mother."

The sound of a honking truck flying past his car startled him. When he realized that it was nothing to worry about, he exhaled. "Sorry, I missed the last part. What were you saying?"

"I'm saying that just because Delroy and his mother don't live together, it doesn't mean that they aren't close. Who knows, maybe he told her what he saw the night Dwayne was killed."

"Possibly, but I doubt that he'd tell her because she may tell someone else and put both their lives in danger."

"Yeah, that's true too. But if you want my opinion, getting to Delroy means getting to him through his mother."

"And just how am I going to do that?"

"Be creative," said Eddie. "I'm sure you'll think of something. Who knows, maybe she can fill in a few gaps. Oh, before I forget, give me your numbers."

Corey gave both burner phone numbers to him as he heard the same man who spoke to him earlier bark orders to Eddie.

"I got to go," said Eddie. "Remember only call me when you absolutely need to and switch burners occasionally."

"Yeah, I'll do that. Just be careful," said Corey seconds before he heard the beep coming from Eddie ending the call.

Eddie was hiding with Candace somewhere with a don's allies, and now Corey was using a burner to communicate with his best friend while having to check over his shoulder to make sure he wasn't being followed. His first instinct was to call home, at least hear from his wife and son. They must be wondering why he hadn't called, or why he can't be reached. He thought of Bevins. It wouldn't be wise to call her at this time. Having tossed his regular phone, both she and his wife must be going insane trying to reach him.

This trip sucks ass!

Heading back to the Airbnb would be suicide. For all he knew, the people who were after Eddie would be waiting for him to show up. He started up the car and drove back to Lucille's. Hopefully she wasn't asleep. He parked around the corner from her house and walked the rest of the way. It occurred to him that he had his regular phone on him earlier when he came here. If his phone was being tracked earlier, there was a chance his followers may be waiting for him in the area. True, Corey could drive around and could recon the area for anyone suspicious who was sitting in their car outside of Lucille's place. However, if they were waiting for him, they'd be expecting him to be driving, not walking. While on foot, if his gut told him to bolt, that's just what he'd do.

From what he saw, there weren't any parked cars on Lucille's street. They were all in driveways. It did not take long for him to get to her place, and he walked to the door and knocked.

"Who it is?" came her voice from inside.

"It's me, Corey."

"Hold on, son," she answered. "I'll be right there."

It took about a minute, but soon enough the inner door opened before she unlocked the outer gate.

She moved to the side to give Corey room. "Come in."

"Thanks," Corey said as he entered. "I would've called before but I forgot to take your number. I don't know where else to go."

"Don't worry yourself." Lucille closed the door and locked it. She then turned her walker to him. "You can stay here as long as you like. Any news about your friend?" she asked.

Corey turned to her. "I spoke to him. You were right, Brutus kidnapped him but didn't harm him."

Lucille's jaw dropped. "He still in Guava Hill?"

"No, he escaped with Candace, but got separated from Brutus along the way."

"So, she was there all this time."

"You were right about that too." Corey showed her the burner phone. "I had to get this in order to talk to him."

"What's wrong with your phone?"

"Just a precaution. This phone's location can't be tracked, so no one knows I'm here."

"I see." Lucille nodded. "You must look at the bright side. He's not at Guava Hill and wasn't among those who were either arrested or shot. I watch the news after you gone, it was just pure madness what happened today."

"But he's not out of the woods yet. He can't even tell me where he is. All I know is that he and Candace are hiding out with Brutus's men."

"Oh dear." Lucille walked past him. "Come to the kitchen with me and have some cheesecake. Ira won't be back until tomorrow morning."

Corey let her lead the way. "There's something I want to check out tomorrow. I'm hoping that you could help."

Lucille turned to him. "Anything, son."

Chapter 24

Lenny's Safehouse. Wednesday 7:41 AM

The loud *bang* shook Eddie from his deep sleep, causing him to spring up from the mattress. He heard someone yelling something in Patois he couldn't understand. The person who ran past his room only added to the tension as he heard screams and cries from outside.

Where am I? What's going...the safehouse!

It all came back to him.

That had to have been a gunshot that startled him awake. He stood up from the mattress that was on the floor, dressed in nothing but his boxer briefs, and stepped into the hallway, only to be shoved back into the room.

"Guh put on yuh clothes," yelled a man he didn't recognize. But the AK-105 he carried was all it took for Eddie to guess what was happening.

They found us.

Another gunshot, one that rattled Eddie's bones.

Eddie ran to the closet, ripped the Champs cotton armhole shirt and polyester basketball shorts from the hanger and threw them on. He didn't expect to be given an older pair of Jordans—let alone a pair that fit him. Eddie was just happy to be wearing shoes again.

Despite what he was told, he stood at the threshold and peeked his head out in the hall, looking toward the front of the house where he was able to see through the front door, which was left open.

There were several armed men walking past on the road toward the end of the village from where he and Candace had arrived.

Eddie didn't have to see anything else to know that Lenny's men were taking defense positions—bracing for an attack. Yesterday it was the army with a lone assassin who hid among them to target him and Candace. Eddie did not have to see who showed up to know that Guava Hill 2.0 was about to happen.

Chapter 25

Lenny

Lenny had been woken from his sleep long before the gunshot woke the village. He had sentries posted miles away, ready to call in at the first sign of trouble. One of the two women he shared his king-sized bed with accidentally knocked over the electric fan as she scrambled to put something on in a hurry. But Lenny didn't have any patience and yelled at them both to get out, before sending a sentry to wake up Candace and the Bajan.

With his locks tied on top of his head and held in place with a stretch turban, he left his house lightly dressed in long jeans and a white sleeveless vest. As he walked past homes on either side, he was not surprised to see windows being slammed shut or to hear the locks on doors being bolted. As per protocol, two cars were horizontally parked on the road at the edge of the village—serving as both a barricade and shielding six other sentries who had their rifles aimed at their unwanted visitors. Lenny walked up to his sentries and stared ahead at the four black SUVs that blocked the road roughly sixty to seventy meters away. Brutus confirmed what the Bajan said, that it wasn't only the army who attacked Guava Hill. These visitors were clearly the *other* faction.

He recognized the routine. First, show off each other's muscle, then the two ambassadors would come to meet between them halfway. Then, the negotiations would begin, where they each present their demands. If there is an agreement within a reasonable time, no one gets shot at. If things dragged too long, then there would be a lot of bodies either being buried or burned before the end of the day—a week at least if his entire village was wiped out. The police, forensics experts, and other specialists would be combing the area for days. All Lenny could do was deny and keep denying that Candace and the Bajan were here. He knew that any chance they'd accept that story was practically non-existent, but he'd keep denying it long enough to buy him time. These people were pros because they chose the right time of the day to meet—early in the morning, where the sun shone from behind them, making it more difficult for his men to see their targets. Fuck, his backup better be on their way to trap the invaders. As long as they showed up within the half hour, Lenny's disadvantage would then be theirs.

Three doors of the SUV closest to the front of the pack swung open. The driver and the passenger—a brotha, and an older sista—got out, followed by a sista around the same age as the brotha who exited the back. The three walked a few feet and stood ahead of their SUV, with the older woman in the middle. There was something about the two who flanked the elder sister that told him they were professional killers. He didn't know if it was the way they walked or how they looked at him. There was a coldness in their stares that was unmatched by the South-African's henchmen who'd jacked him up near his Park Avenue condo. The elder one was clearly all business. The red pantsuit and designer shades she wore would fool the average person. But he'd bet his last dollar that the suit was lined with Kevlar. Anyone crazy enough to go after Brutus and nearly succeed by getting the military to back them is someone with true power—or works for someone who does. And he couldn't think of anyone who could match or outdo Brutus's resources who was at war with him.

It looked like she was waiting for him to come out front as a sign that the meeting would begin. He walked around one of the cars and was joined by one of the sentries as they walked together to meet the invaders halfway.

Lenny saw the leader gesture to the sista to stay behind as she and the brotha walked toward him.

The negotiation.

"I'm going to keep things simple," the elder sista said, stopping about four feet away with the brotha a few feet behind and diagonal to her left. "We know that Miss Coke and Mister Barrow are here. So why don't you hand them over and we'll spare your village."

"I don't know where you get your information from, and I don't know those people, and no stranger stay in my village without me knowing. Sah, move up ar get shat, pussyclaat."

"Now, now, there's no need for vulgarities. I know that you're loyal to Brutus, but you would've heard by now that he's on the run. Guava Hill has fallen, and Brutus's men are either detained, on the run, or dead. They can't help you."

"You're all bark and no bite."

"On the contrary." The woman raised an eyebrow. "You have soldiers positioned, or I should say, *had* soldiers positioned precisely zero-point-eight-seven kilometers from here. *I* know they were supposed to show up a few moments after we arrived to trap us between your men and themselves. That would put us at a disadvantage if we got into a shootout. *I* know that because I made sure that my men arranged for them to be *unavailable*."

"Yuh a lie."

The woman tilted her head with a half-smile. "If you don't believe me, call them."

Lenny knew that she wasn't bluffing. How else could she know about his backup, and precisely how far they were.

"Not so much to say, I see." The woman smirked. "*You're* not in control, Lenny. So, I'll ask you again, politely, to please turn over Candace Coke and Eddie Barrow. I don't want to have to burn down your village. But if I must, I won't spare a single man, woman, or *any* children—many of which I know to be yours."

"Those peeps aren't here." Lenny raised his finger to the woman's face. He didn't care where this sista was from. No one threatens his children. "Just keep my little ones out of this. Don't you dare—"

Lenny couldn't utter another syllable before the henchman snatched a 1911 from behind his waist and unloaded a headshot to his own sentry. Before he hit the ground, he saw a flash—milliseconds before he felt an object rip through his left eye and blow out the back of his head.

***

Eddie and Candace

That did not sound good.

The two gunshots were clearly the catalyst, as a barrage of gunfire was heard soon after.

The bedroom door burst open, and the same sentry who had seen him earlier motioned for Eddie to follow him. Eddie followed him to Lenny's bedroom, where Candace was already waiting. The sentry then pushed the bed to the side, then got down on one knee and dug his fingers into a groove in the floor to lift a trap door.

Eddie was about to follow Candace inside until he saw that this was not a simple exit leading to under the house but to a deep hole in the ground, possibly a tunnel. He got a flashback to the locker room at Guava Hill. "Wait."

"For what?" said the sentry. "Yuh wannah die?"

"Something's not right."

The sentry pointed his rifle at Eddie's head. "Go in, yuh bumboclaat!"

Eddie's hands shot up as his heart skipped a beat. "Hear me out."

***

Edge of the village

Bedlam!

Stepmother shot a glance at Hansel before gunfire erupted around them. Had it been anyone else she would've had a few unkind words to say to them once they were in the clear. But she trusted her asset's actions of shooting Lenny and his soldier. He had a sixth sense for telling if someone would comply or not—and he obviously sensed that Lenny wouldn't. She may have had some pull here in Jamaica, but if they didn't get their hands on

Candace and Eddie Barrow soon, the heavy gunfire would echo to the neighboring towns and villages, sparking a wave of curiosity from the residents.

She hurried back to the SUVs, and Hansel shielded her while being trigger happy with his 1911. Gretel led the assault with her AK-107 as staccato gunfire erupted all around them, but she distinctly heard the shots that came from Hansel's weapon as he popped off seven rounds—knowing that at least three shots hit their target.

Stepmother walked to the rear of the SUV, where she leaned her back against it. Her men had superior firepower as the buildings sustained more damage than her armored vehicles. Unless they had a rocket launcher, they'd give up soon.

The gunfire exchange continued for about another minute until one of her henchmen called out to her. She turned to see a fleeing Range Rover cutting across and away through the tall grass.

"So, *there* you are, Mister Barrow," she said, unable to contain her excitement. "You slippery sonofabitch." She had men positioned to wait next to a manhole outside the village. This is where she expected Eddie and Candace to emerge from after using the escape tunnel under Lenny's house. But they used an escape vehicle instead. *Eddie Barrow...that had to be his idea.* She called out to gunmen in two of the SUVs to go after the Range Rover. The men were inside their vehicles in under eight seconds and took off, burrowing through the tall grass after the Range Rover.

"Where are my eyes in the sky?" she yelled.

Immediately, Gretel was on the phone calling Team B who were half a kilometer away. They would launch the remote-controlled drone.

Moments later, Gretel walked to the back of the SUV and handed a tablet to Stepmother. Shortly after that she was watching the Ranger Rover from above and closing in on it. The driver of the Rover seemed to be aware of the drone as she saw muzzle flashes coming from inside it. At one point the vehicle made a sharp turn to shake its pursuers, and it almost appeared as though it would tip over. Somehow, the driver still managed to keep the vehicle under control.

The Rover would run out of field soon and end up on an open road unless they drove across onto the adjoining field.

Stepmother tapped the screen and a microphone icon appeared in the corner. "Get closer. I want to get a better look inside."

She didn't know why she was having doubts. But there was still a slight possibility that this may be a diversion, she couldn't leave things to chance.

The drone's pilot managed to get within forty meters from the Rover before she accessed the drone camera's controls via her tablet. She then zoomed in, but she wasn't viewing from the best angle.

She tapped the corner of the screen on the microphone icon to turn it on. "Stay on the side but get me in front of that vehicle."

The position of the drone changed and she spotted three occupants—and two of them weren't Eddie and Candace, but another man and woman with similar body shape. She saw a muzzle flash a split second before the camera signal was lost.

Shit. Decoys. She was immediately on her phone calling the pursuant SUV drivers simultaneously. "Turn around, Barrow and Candace are still in the village."

With a tap of the speed-dial, she was already in touch with Team C who waited outside the manhole where Barrow and Candace would escape.

***

Eddie and Candace

Eddie knew that their chances of success were slim, but he currently relied on Candace to make sure he did not misunderstand the sentry's directions. From what he had understood, he and Candace would run to the right of the tarp that camouflaged the Rover behind Lenny's house. They would run around the last home at the end of cul-de-sac, then run in a straight line until they reached the side road.

The first few minutes were terrifying. But the moment he

looked down the hole in Lenny's room, he couldn't help but think of the assassins knowing that Brutus would be in the recreation center the moment the army would strike at Guava Hill. There was no doubt that they would suspect another escape tunnel and recon the village before attacking. Eddie felt that Brutus would have had a plan B—and he did.

Eddie was fortunate to convince the sentry that the tunnel was a trap. The sentry had originally told them he would drive them in the Rover—camouflaged out back under a tarp—where they would hide in the cargo area. Eddie told him that there was likely a drone with thermal imaging overhead. And it would spot the Rover and its occupants the moment it left. That was when Eddie had the idea that they would run on foot and hopefully rendezvous with the Rover. It was the most unpredictable choice he came up with and hopefully would throw Stepmother, Hansel, and Gretel off their trail.

Eddie only hoped that it would be more than temporary.

These were professional assassins who prepared with data and intelligence. That type of access would've easily allowed them to recon Guava Hill and Brutus's numerous hideouts, including The Drought. However, gathering intelligence on Eddie would've been trickier. They would've obtained and studied his professional profile easily. But as for anticipating Eddie's movements, their best profiler, if they used one, would not likely predict that Eddie would've chosen what he and Candace were currently doing. And that was based on Eddie not even knowing that he would be hauling ass across a field in God knows where.

Eddie began to feel fatigued as the lactic acid in his quadriceps weighed his legs down. It was then that Candace overtook him.

"Don't stop now. We're almost there."

Eddie looked over his shoulder to see The Drought was just a spec in the distance. When he looked ahead, Candace was diagonally in front of him by roughly three feet.

Focus. Now isn't the time to run out of juice.

Eddie then had a flashback to the escape tunnel under Guava Hill, and how Hansel's running stamina allowed him to nearly catch them. The thought alone scared Eddie shitless, and he found a huge kick that allowed him to pick up the pace.

Adrenaline? Maybe.

Did he give a damn? Fuck no.

Moments later, Candace slowed down. Eddie soon saw that they had exited the tall grass onto a rough road where he stumbled to a stop.

Candace gestured to Eddie to follow her. "Come."

The lactic acid in his quads returned as he slowly trailed farther behind her. The road was in such bad need of repair that he watched where he ran. A twisted ankle was one of the worst things that could happen to either of them right now.

Roughly twenty minutes later they saw a vehicle in the distance. Eddie remembered the sentry's instructions that if they saw any vehicle then they should hide in the tall grass. Candace did not wait on Eddie as she was the first back in. He crawled on his hands and knees as he joined her. They did not have a clear view of the road, but it was clear enough for them to identify the Rover.

He waited as he heard the engine get louder. The vehicle was moving slowly. Eddie focused as he and Candace remembered what they had been told. The slightest movement would disturb the tall grass—giving away their position.

The engine noise remained constant as Eddie concentrated on slowing his breathing.

His chest still burned.

The first thing Eddie saw was the sun reflecting off the rims.

"Candace?" said one of the occupants. It was unmistakably the brotha who had accompanied the sentry, along with another sista.

Eddie felt some of the weight being lifted from his shoulders as he and Candace crawled out slowly.

"Here." Candace stood, waving.

The Rover stopped, and a skinny, bald brotha exited the front with his rifle, ran to the back and lifted the trunk, then pointed to Eddie.

"Get in and lie down." He then thumbed Candace to the back seat.

Eddie did not flinch seeing the brotha's gun, as he also saw a bullet hole in the lower half of the back passenger door as he ran to the cargo area. There was just enough room for Eddie to lie on his side with his knees slightly bent. He heard the trunk slam behind him just as the back door shut, followed by the front passenger door.

The Rover made a sharp semi-circle, reversed with a quick turn in the opposite side, then they bolted forward.

"Oh my God!" Eddie heard Candace's say. "Yuh bleeding."

"Mi get shat!" said the sentry.

"Weh part yuh get shat?" asked Candace.

"Inna mi foot," answered the sentry. "Mi can still drive."

"Quick, wi affi guh to di—"

That's when Eddie felt the Rover swerve, throwing him headfirst into the side of the vehicle.

"Mi sarry 'bout dat. Mi a hol on."

"Yuh betta whol on before yuh lose nuff blood and knockout," said the sista.

Eddie heard them quarrel with the sentry. All he understood so far was that he had been shot in the leg, and he still insisted on driving.

"Dem a tun roun," said the brotha.

"Yuh sure?" said Candace.

"Dem naw falla again."

"Mi shoot down de drone," said the woman.

The Rover violently bounced across a pothole—one that Eddie felt the most out of all of them. The Rover then sped up again. From what Eddie just heard, the assassins stopped following them. But he then heard them say something that made his stomach twist.

"Lenny's...dead?" said Eddie.

No one answered. He wondered if they even heard him. Either they did not or they were too upset to reply.

Eddie felt their vehicle slowing down, then it soon turned onto a much smoother road. It felt as though a half hour had passed before Eddie heard the engines of other vehicles close by. They must have been driving through traffic. There was more slowing down, stopping, and speeding up.

There were a series of turns, and then Eddie felt them come to a stop, followed by the engine being turned off. Two car doors opened and closed, and the trunk door was opened by the brotha.

"Back a di line."

Eddie assumed that this was Patois for *end of the line*. He breathed a sigh of relief as he shuffled on his side and slid out.

The first thing he saw was the bright sun reflecting off the Caribbean Sea. The shoreline was roughly eighty meters away. It was just beyond an old, partially mangled fence. There, just above it, was a white banner that read: 'Black River Welcome Center' written in blue. To his right was the entrance to a park with a yellow sign that read: Historic Town of Black River.

The name of the town didn't mean anything to Eddie. It did, however, give him some comfort that he knew where he was.

That's when he heard a long, agony-ridden cry from up front. The brotha dashed to the driver's door with Eddie close behind him. He tried to look inside, but he couldn't see around the brotha.

"How bad was he hit?" asked Eddie.

"Make sure those two get out of sight."

Eddie couldn't see the driver, but he heard the pain in his voice. It caught the attention of a few gawkers, who wouldn't have been able to see or ascertain what had happened.

"You need to get him to the hospital," said Eddie. "Candace and I will have to go on our own."

"He's right," said the sista in the passenger seat. "You're still bleeding." She unlocked his seatbelt, while the brotha in front of Eddie helped pull the driver out from his seat, where he then helped him limp into the back seat. Eddie was forced to back up to give them space. He caught a glimpse of the wound, and it looked deep. But from what he could see, the driver was made to lie horizontally with his injured leg stretched onto the seat.

After the brotha shut the back passenger door, he turned to Eddie. "He was supposed to protect you until Brutus came and got you."

"I'm sorry about Lenny," said Eddie. "You have my condolences."

The brotha sighed. "He's on his way to join the duppy dem." *He's on the way to join his ancestors.*

Eddie saw movement behind him and realized that it was

Candace.

"Tanks, bredgrin." The brotha nodded. "You remember where to go?"

"Don't worry about us." Candace nodded while turning her head away briefly to wipe a tear. "We'll be fine."

"I'm assuming there's another vehicle for us to switch to," said Eddie.

The brotha looked over his shoulder and gestured before leading them to a navy Honda Civic a few cars over. "Right deh so. Brutus set things up to have it waiting here when needed." The brotha then handed Eddie an envelope. "The keys are inside wid enough cash to get yuh through the next few days. Don't squander it, yuh hear?"

Eddie nodded.

"There's also a bangaz inside the dash and some chargers in the trunk wid some snacks. Whenever you need help, you know how to reach Brutus. But don't bother him unless it's absolutely necessary."

"You need to call him right now, and *only* speak to him," said Eddie. "He's got a leak."

"And you know this how?"

"Brutus has other safehouses where Candace and I would've been expected to go to. How many of them were hit?"

The brotha bit his lower lip and looked away for a moment before nodding at Eddie. "Yeh, mon." He nodded his head past Eddie. "Watch over Candace. Nuff respeck, bredgrin."

"Thanks," Eddie answered as he fist-bumped him. "Oh, one more thing."

"Wah dat?"

"How easy can you get a message out?"

"To where?"

"Boston."

"Who yuh waan link deh?"

"Someone who may have the connections to help all of us," said Eddie. "Find a way to get in touch with her and have her call me from a burner phone—or bangaz—as you call it."

"Then call her from the one in the car," said the brotha. "Dem can't trace di call."

"If you haven't noticed, this isn't your typical street gang who's after us. We can't assume that they haven't hacked the phones of all my friends and family—waiting for me to slip up."

"Brutus nuh have nobody ah wuk fi him a Boston."

"Then he needs to get someone up there, and quickly."

The brotha looked at Eddie as though he wasn't sure how to answer.

"You have a pen and paper?" asked Eddie.

The man went to the SUV, reached through the passenger window for a few seconds, then came back with a crumpled sheet and a pen.

Eddie wrote down the name and address of Nancy Bevins, then handed the pen and paper back to him. "How soon can you get instructions to her?"

"If I can reach Brutus, maybe by tomorrow."

"Good." Eddie nodded to the Rover as the sista stuck her head slightly through the lowered window space.

"Come on, we need to go," she said while slapping the side of the door.

"You better go," Eddie said to the brotha, who then ran back to the Rover.

Eddie and Candace got in their car, with Eddie taking the driver's seat. Candace grabbed the burner from inside the glove compartment and turned it on.

"Where are we supposed to go?"

"Clark's Town," Candace answered. "It's quite a distance."

"That concerns me. Pass me the phone." Candace gave him the burner, and Eddie read through the local news reports. Guava Hill still dominated the headlines he read through, then something else made the hairs on the back of his neck stand.

"What's wrong?" asked Candace.

"It's Pusey." Eddie held up the phone for her to see. "She's offering a US ten-thousand-dollar cash reward to anyone who gives the police information that will lead to my capture. Apparently, I'm wanted for a stabbing."

"What?" Candace grabbed the phone and stared at the news

item. "Who did you stab?"

"I didn't stab anyone. When the fight broke after Dwayne's funeral, one of the guys who assaulted him at Citrusville was about to stab my friend, but I jumped in and pushed him. He fell on his own knife."

"That's not what he's saying."

"And you expect him to admit that?"

"What does Pusey have against you?"

"I...kind of..." Eddie shrugged his shoulders, "...confronted her about stealing Dwayne's designs at her own fashion show in front of dozens of people."

"You're bold."

"I...may have also intimated that she had him killed."

Candace let her head fall in her hand. "Do you realize how much Jamaicans love this woman? Dwayne tried to fight her, and it didn't work. Now look what she's done to you? If you get caught, I'm going down with you. I'm going to have to let my uncle know."

"He probably already does by now. And he would've contacted us had he been able."

"I should at least try."

"Save it until we get to Clark's Town." Eddie pressed the *Start* button and turned on the engine. He turned to Candace. "By the way, what's the quickest way to Dwayne's previous home? The one where he stayed right after he was kicked out."

"Why would you want to go there?"

"I have a few questions for his former roommates."

"This ain't the time to do that. Besides, his roommates will turn on us to get the cash reward."

"I doubt it. Jalissa told me that they all looked out for each other, and they were at the funeral," said Eddie. "They don't sound like the kind of people who'd snitch on Dwayne's friends—especially if they believe that Pusey stole Dwayne's designs."

"You want to take that chance?"

"At this point, definitely."

Chapter 26

*Island Grill Restaurant, West Green Avenue,
   Montego Bay, Jamaica*

Four were shot dead, while five others were rushed to the hospital. No suspects were identified or in custody.

That was the morning's other news—not being sensational enough to bump the Guava Hill military strike off the top news spot. The only thing that crossed Corey's mind was Eddie being caught up in it. A military strike yesterday and then a gang-style shootout this morning? That can't be a coincidence. So far, no one had made a connection between the two events. But his gut told him that Eddie was there. Why else wouldn't he have called? Aside from the fact he had a hit squad chasing him, one which could've pulled off the attack this morning.

He sipped the water in his glass, letting one of the ice cubes slip past his lips. He swallowed the water while he sucked on the ice. Corey scanned the front entrance to the fast-food joint he was in.

No one suspicious looking. Those who were after Eddie could be after Corey too.

Eddie's warnings spooked him to the point that he found himself checking his rearview mirrors while taking several detours on his drive here—the same thing he had mocked Eddie for doing.

Earlier that morning, Lucille had made a few calls, to whom Corey didn't know. The next thing was her telling him that she set up a meeting between him and Chevelle—or rather, between Chevelle and a journalism student from University of the West Indies.

"Hi."

Corey turned and saw a squattish, plump woman whose face

was beaming with joy.

"Are you Michael?"

The level of enthusiasm in her voice told him that this was Chevelle.

"Yes, you're Chevelle, right?"

She nodded her head wildly with a beaming smile, showing off her teeth. "Yes, that's me." She then sat down across from him. "This is so exciting, no one ever interviewed me before."

"Really?" Corey answered as he placed his burner on the table and activated the recording app. "Why's that?"

"Well," she shrugged her shoulders, "I'm always at home. And when I'm not at home, I'm here working. I bus tables. So, I guess no one has time to come and see me."

"Do you live far from here?"

Chevelle shook her head. "I don't walk to work. It's too far. I was also told that it isn't safe."

"Do you ever walk anywhere from your home?"

"Not really. But when I do, I'm always accompanied by Ann, my caregiver."

"I meant to ask where do you live?"

"At the Seaview Group Home," she answered, much to Corey's satisfaction.

Corey sipped some of his water. "Does Ann usually drive you to work?"

Chevelle shook her head. "Not really. The bus driver comes and picks me up at the same time as my other friends, then drops us all off at work. She then comes to pick us all up when we're ready to go home."

"That's nice," said Corey. "How long have you lived at Seaview?"

"Hmmm." Chevelle's eyes rolled upward for a few moments. "Eight years. Before that, I lived in a boarding school."

You got her. Keep her talking about the school. "How'd you enjoy school?"

"Oh." She paused for a bit. "It was okay…I guess."

"Why, what happened?" asked Corey. "Wasn't everyone nice to you?"

She nodded enthusiastically. "Yes, they were very nice to me."

"So, wouldn't you say that things were great at school?"

She hesitated before nodding slowly. "Okay, things were good at school."

Corey noticed that she appeared to be uncomfortable. "Oh, I forgot, I should've told you before. I won't use your real name for my assignment. I can't do that unless you tell me that it's all right to do so."

"What assignment?"

"Oh, I forgot to remind you. I work for my school paper and we're doing a special on people who are living with autism."

Chevelle's face lit up with excitement. "Oh yes, I remember now."

"And as I mentioned earlier, I won't use your real name when I write my article unless you tell me that it's okay."

"You won't?"

"No," Corey answered with a shake of his head. "I was told to never give away the names of the people I interview unless they give me their written permission."

"You mean I have to write my name on a piece of paper to tell you that it's okay for you to use my name?"

"Yes. But I don't want you to feel pressured to do so. Just to be clear."

"Oh, okay."

She appeared to relax somewhat, but Corey could see that something still bothered her. "May I ask you a question?"

"Yeah."

"Does Ann know that you're talking to me?"

She briefly looked diagonally to the ceiling, raised both shoulders before she shook her head. "I don't think so."

He wanted to ask her about the sexual assault, but he held off, not wanting to take the chance of making Chevelle feel guilty. She may be his only link to her son. He couldn't afford to scare her off because he may never have another chance. And the way she fidgeted her fingers in front of her wasn't a good sign either.

"I'll make a promise to you," Corey began. "I promise not to tell anyone who you are or where you work. I can really use your help with this assignment. Would you help me?"

"You promise not to tell anyone my name?" The fidgeting slowed down.

Corey nodded. "I promise."

"Okay."

"That's great." Corey paused as he reminded himself of the importance of not diving into the subject about her rape. He did not need Chevelle throwing a tantrum and making a scene. "Tell me, what was it like going to boarding school?"

Chevelle began talking. She was so positive about everything she said that it was hard for Corey to believe that she was a rape survivor. He was relieved that she was relaxed, and that conversing with her was easier than expected. However, she did not mention anything about her sexual assault.

Roughly three minutes had passed, and Corey knew that if he was going to get her to talk about her assault, then he had to ease her into the subject soon before her break time was over.

"How were your teachers?" Corey asked. "Were they all nice to you?"

"Oh yes," Chevelle nodded. "I liked all of my teachers."

"And I'm sure they all liked you, didn't they?"

Chevelle tilted her head to the side, then scratched it.

Corey leaned over the table slightly, sensing that something was wrong. "Are you okay?"

Chevelle looked down at the table and grabbed her head with both hands, shaking it.

"No," she said to herself. "No, no, no, no, no!"

Shit! This is bad. "I'm stopping the interview." Corey paused the recorder app on his phone, swiped it off the table and put it beside him on the seat and out of Chevelle's sight. "You see? I'm not recording anything."

It seemed to be the best response, considering that she appeared to be trying to decide whether she wanted to continue with the interview or not. She looked back at Corey.

"I did a bad thing. I think people hate me."

"What?" Corey leaned back. "Why would you say that?"

"Because there's something I want to tell. I've always wanted to tell someone, but I'm afraid Ann would get upset if I did."

"What is it that Ann doesn't want you to tell anyone?" Corey saw an older man with short locks pass by as he mopped the floor.

Chevelle did not say anything but instead looked down at her hands clasped together on the table. Her fingers began to fidget again. "A very bad thing happened to me a long time ago. But Ann told me that no one would believe me if I told anyone."

Corey was all ears at this point. He could've used the digital recorder app right now but doing so might scare Chevelle off. "You can tell me."

She paused again as she looked down at her finger. It appeared that she had calmed a bit. "Take a deep breath," she said aloud to herself. And so she did.

"Two men took advantage of me—two very bad men." She shook her head quickly as though to shake off the disgust. "I didn't like that at all."

"Two?" *This isn't what I was told.*

"Ann keeps telling me that I'm confused because the police found only one person. And she told me that the police are always right."

Corey checked the entrance again. No red flags. He then scanned both sides from where they sat before lowering his voice. "Why are you so sure that it was two men who hurt you?"

"It just…felt like two different men attacked me. They blindfolded me. But I don't have to see to know that two men touched me."

"My friend, Lucille, who set up this meeting, you remember her, right?"

"Yes, she attended all of the support group meetings." Chevelle smiled. "She's a very nice and very brave lady. I think that she's the bravest person that I know."

"When you used to talk to her about what happened to you, did you tell her that there were two men?"

Chevelle hesitated as her fingers fidgeted again. *Why was she hesitating so much? Did I screw up somehow?*

She shook her head. "No, because Ann also accompanied me to the meetings. And I know that Ann would get very, very mad if

I told Lucille that there were two men."

Holy shit. Did Chevelle knowingly send the wrong man to prison? "The man they arrested. Did you know him by any chance?"

She nodded her head immediately. "Yes, that's Mister Mitchell. He was one of my teachers. He's always been nice to me. But he wouldn't have done that horrible thing to me."

"It wasn't him? Are you saying that the police put the wrong person in prison?"

She nodded. "I didn't want that to happen. I'm telling you the truth. I would never do anything to hurt Mister Mitchell." She looked over both shoulders and then behind Corey. It was as though she was worried someone was eavesdropping on their conversation. She then leaned closer to Corey.

"They made me say those nasty things about that nice man," Chevelle whispered.

"Who made you say those things?" Corey whispered back.

"They made me say those things because they told me that no one would believe me because they said that I was a retard," she continued. "But I know what I remember."

Corey instinctively reached out and took her hands to calm her down. It appeared to work. *I need her to focus.* "It's okay, you need to keep calm because we don't want other people hearing you. I kept my promise to keep your name a secret."

"Chevelle," called a woman from the kitchen. "Time to get back to work."

Damn it.

Chevelle looked over Corey's shoulder. "Okay, Missus Johnson."

I need an answer. Corey leaned closer to her. "Chevelle, please tell me. Who told you to lie? Does your son know this?"

"No, he doesn't know," she answered. She was visibly nervous.

"Take a deep breath," Corey insisted as he remembered it working for her earlier.

"Yes." She nodded. "Take a deep breath." She inhaled very deeply, paused, and let it out.

Corey waited anxiously.

"Okay," she said. "But you must not tell Ann, because she'll get very upset."

"Did Ann tell you to lie to the police?" Corey felt that he was jumping the gun, but he trusted his gut.

"She wasn't the only one."

"Who else told you to lie?" Corey asked again. "Who were the two men who did those bad things to you?"

"Chevelle!" It was a woman's voice, but not the same one as before as it came from across the room.

"Oh no!" said Chevelle as Corey saw that she recognized the person. "It's Ann."

"Who you talking to?" yelled Ann. "Nuh chat to nobody widout mi."

Someone must've tipped her off. The woman caught her purse as it slid from her shoulder, as she didn't take her eyes off Corey.

"Who are you?" she spat.

Corey extended a hand. "Good afternoon. My name is Michael Joseph , I'm a student at the University of the West Indies. I was referred to Miss—"

"I don't care who you are," Ann snapped. "Chevelle's very fragile and she cannot be talking to just any stranger." She looked down at Chevelle. "Isn't that right?"

Chevelle held her head down. "Yes, Ann."

"Good." Ann looked back at Corey. "Chevelle needs to get back to work, she doesn't have time for you."

"I'm sorry," said a near-tearful Chevelle as she shuffled out of the booth with her head held low and rushed back to the kitchen.

Ann called out to Chevelle. When Corey saw Ann walk after her, he used the opportunity to slip away. Talking to Ann would only stir up a hornet's nest. He exited the dining room and was in the hallway, where he walked as fast as he could.

"Psst!"

Corey looked over his shoulder to see a slender man with short locks, with his head bowed down. He still had the mop and stood beside a bucket on wheels. The man gestured with his hand for Corey to approach him. Getting away was a priority, but he was curious as to what the man wanted with him. As Corey got closer, the man reached into his pants and took out a folded piece of paper.

"I did hear you back there," the man whispered. "Mi wi tell yuh wha yuh want fi know. Just meet me a di spot at four thirty. Nuh badda late." *I overheard you back there. I'll tell you what you want to know. Meet me at this location at four thirty. Don't be late.*

Once he handed Corey the note, he immediately turned his back and resumed his mopping as though he hadn't stopped. But that wasn't important. Corey had to get out of there since Ann would most likely call the police once she learned that there isn't a Michael Joseph in attendance at UWI.

Chapter 27

Somewhere in the Blue Mountains, Jamaica

"Blue Mountain Coffee. Di bess ina di world," said Brutus as he stretched out and yawned while looking out at the breathtaking hilltops from the natural lookout point. He then turned to his security detail. "Nuh badda bumboclaat seh nuttin else cause mi wi shaat dat." He paused for a moment, then let out a deep chuckle that triggered the others to join in.

Brutus's soldiers knew when they should laugh and when they shouldn't. He looked at them and listened to their laughing. Although brief, he knew how loyal they were—so loyal that his laughter willfully triggered the others to join in and stop once he stopped, especially when he looked at them while doing so.

With all the shit that happened since Guava Hill was attacked, he needed to laugh to relieve the tension. His days as a free man were numbered, so he may as well make the best of it. Even though the problem he needed to deal with was nothing to laugh about.

He turned around to face his security detail. Brutus then popped a cigarette in his mouth and lit it with a lighter one of his men picked up for him the day before. He took a drag, then waved toward himself while eying one of his guards. "Larent, come walk with me."

Larent must've been forty-one or forty-two, but he had the face of a twenty-five-year-old. He was blacker than the coffee beans that grew in these mountains, so black one would think he just arrived here from Senegal—home to the Blackest people on Earth. He learned that from watching one of those science shows on NPR, from what he could remember. As Larent approached him, Brutus put an arm around his shoulders and walked with him.

"Yuh know seh mi love dis place," said Brutus as he looked at Larent, who nodded in agreement. "Twenty years since I took over Guava Hill after mi fadda dead, mi know seh mi can call on any a yuh for any protection when needed. Right?"

He did not have to look at Larent for him to know to nod in agreement. Just the way he said "Right" was his cue to do so.

"Because wi a family. Yuh tek care a mi and mi tek care a yuh. Undastan?"

His nod in agreement came on cue as they continued walking.

"But yuh know, mi niece, Candace, she a family to mi too. And mi mek a promise to mi bredda dat mi woulda tek care a har if nuttin happen to him ar di wife. But he didn't get along with me and didn't want me to come near har nor anyone in his family."

Brutus thought back to the moment and how he obeyed his brother out of respect, then one of his enemies, Mojo, had his soldiers shoot up his brother's car while both he and the wife were inside. Candace came home late from studying to find the police waiting for her. Mojo knew that they could've gone after her, but he chose to let her live.

"Remember Mojo?" asked Brutus.

"Yeah, mi memba him," said Larent.

"You remember what happened to him?"

"Yes, Mista President."

"Tell me what happened to him."

"Yuh did know seh he was in Miami. So yuh tell yuh soldier fi tamper wid di elevator controls in one a di tall buildings dungtown fi trap him when him guh in. Yuh did know weh him a guh deh, so yuh did know di exact moment he would enter di elevator. So, yuh mek dem stop di elevator in between floors."

"And what did I do next?"

"You called Mojo on his cell."

"And what did I say to him?"

Larent paused as he swallowed. "Yuh tell him dat yuh come a Miami just fi see him fall."

Brutus remembered the surprised look on Mojo's face as he

looked up at the security camera his men had hacked into right before the C4 on the roof of the elevator was detonated—sending over 5000lbs of steel plummeting to a crashing end. He swore he felt the ground shake while watching the entrance to the building from across the street. After he saw crowds of screaming people running outside he signaled his security detail to drive off.

"Good, you remember." Brutus began to squeeze Larent's shoulder. "Yuh know mi bredda, Lenny?"

Larent nodded. "Yes, sah."

"Did I tell you about the time when he lived in New York?"

"I think so."

"Wha yuh mean, yuh think?"

Larent began nodding rapidly. "Yes, Mista President, mi memba yuh tell mi, sah."

Brutus looked at the sweat that gathered on his forehead and noticed that Larent had barely looked him in the eye for the past few minutes.

"You remember when he was jumped by the South African's men."

"Yes, sah."

"And what did I do?"

"Yuh sent some of yuh soldiers to New York fi assist Lenny in burning di South African inside a few tires."

Brutus nodded. "So, yuh know mi always tek care a mi family. And yuh believe in di importance of family, right?"

"Yeah, mon."

"And mi tek care a yuh just like yuh tek care of mi, right?"

"Right, Mista President."

Brutus then grabbed both of Larent's shoulders and turned him to face him. Larent couldn't avoid looking him in the eye. "Then why did you tell those people that Candace was at the rec center?"

Larent looked like he didn't know what to say. Brutus stared him straight in the eyes as he saw his other security men close in behind slowly. No more Patois, just straight English to let Larent know that he wasn't fucking around anymore.

"Yeah, I know it was you," said Brutus and he took a drag from his cigarette while still holding Larent's shoulder with the other hand. "Don't deny it. And while you're thinking of an answer, you can also tell me why you told those people that Candace and the Bajan were hiding at Lenny's place. You were the closest one to me when he called to tell me that Candace was safe, so only *you* could've overheard me—especially when I called him by his name, Lenny, while I spoke to him. Next thing mi know, his place get shoot up. Because a yuh mi lose mi bredda."

Brutus didn't want to tell him that he found out that Candace and the Bajan got away again. He had a gut feeling that there was more to Eddie Barrow than he gave him credit for. He may very well be the reason why Candace was still alive.

"But that was my fault. I should've known that you're ungrateful, considering what I pay you." The security detail stopped about four feet away.

Larent's head hung forward. Brutus knew that Larent felt ashamed for what he did, and he held a hand to his ear to encourage the man to speak. "What's that I hear?"

"Mi sorry, Mista President."

"Really?"

Larent nodded as he clenched his eyes tightly. He knew that his time was coming to an end. Brutus felt that he may as well have some fun. He took a drag on the cigarette and puffed out the smoke that got carried off in the wind.

"Tell me. How sorry?"

"Very sorry, Presi."

"You're going to beg?"

"Mi beg yuh, sah."

"Do yuh beg?" he yelled.

"Yes, mi beg, mi beg." Larent couldn't control the tears as Brutus's voice still echoed through the mountains.

Brutus threw the cigarette away, then leaned closer to Larent's ear. "Beg mi seh dat mi mek dis end quick."

From a scabbard on the side of his pants, Brutus snatched the dagger and stabbed Larent three times, the last one being to his lower abdomen. Larent cried with each successive stab, then stumbled backward once Brutus let go of him, falling into the other four security men who had their daggers out and finished off what their president started. They then carried his bloodied, near-lifeless body to the cliff's edge and tossed him off.

Brutus walked to the precipice where his men were, looked down and spat. "You're welcome."

No wait till drum beat before you grine you axe

—Jamaican Proverb

Do not wait until the drum beats
before you grind your axe.

Chapter 28

Albion Community, Montego Bay

"How'd you know *not* to use the escape tunnel?" asked Candace as Eddie turned onto a cross street with more of the same type of homes with the same type of unfinished exterior, where the homes lacked outdoor painting. The sad truth was, though, that many of the homes he'd seen so far were in horrible states of neglect.

"Because that's what Brutus probably would've done had he been in the same situation," said Eddie. "At Guava Hill, the people who came after us knew exactly where to find you. I suspect that Brutus's mole would've tipped them off as to where you were."

"You really think that Brutus has a leak?"

"Were you at the rec center when I was brought there?"

"No, I only left Brutus's house when I found out that you were the 'prisoner' he brought in."

"Exactly," said Eddie. "How could the assassin have known that you'd be at the rec center unless he had someone on the inside tip him off?"

Eddie glanced briefly at Candace, who did the same to him.

"As I was saying, had they known that Brutus had an escape tunnel, or where it led to, then they would've had people waiting to intercept us the moment we exited. These don't look like the kind of people who make the same mistakes twice. So it's likely that they would've reconned Lenny's village before attacking."

Eddie slammed on the breaks as an old, stained soccer ball bounced in front of their car from out of nowhere. As expected, a little boy, who looked no older than eight, ran out onto the street without checking for traffic and caught up to the ball.

Candace stuck her head partially out of the window. "Yuh ah try to kill yourself?"

The boy, startled from being yelled at, froze, and turned to Candace. "Sorry."

Candace sighed and waved the boy off. "Gah-lang."

The boy tucked the ball under his arm and ran off in the same direction from which he came.

Eddie drove off slowly, while paying extra attention for other children in the area. "You all right?"

"What you mean?"

"You just yelled at a kid."

"You didn't see how he just ran out in the street?"

"You can teach children to look both ways before crossing the street, but a single distraction, such as a runaway soccer ball, can make anyone have a momentary lapse of judgement."

Candace was silent.

"I just thought that I'd put that out there," said Eddie.

Candace shook her head. "I'm just…I don't know."

"Scared? Stressed?"

"I just want to forget about it."

Eddie didn't say anything more.

They were silent for another half kilometer until Candace directed Eddie to turn onto a new road. "This is it." Candace pointed to the dilapidated building, one of many on this road.

Eddie was too slow to react and passed the building, but easily found a spot not too far away. There were other cars parked, but not in any organized way as they would back in Montreal. Eddie was aware of a group of men around their age across the street, speaking loudly among themselves—six or seven at most, either shirtless or dressed in plain white tank tops or NBA sports jerseys. His instincts told him not to make eye contact.

"What's the matter?" asked Candace.

"I'm trying not to draw attention to us."

Candace glanced at the brothas across the street. "You scared of them?"

"I'd rather not do anything that would make them talk about us," said Eddie. "Don't forget there's a bounty on our heads."

Candace sucked her teeth. "You don't need to worry. Anyone around here could tell that you're a foreigner, so they won't trouble you. However, if you looked like a bad boy, then that would be another story."

"Just my point," said Eddie as he resisted the urge to walk quickly. "The bounty is on a foreigner."

"Exactly," said Candace. "*Just* a foreigner. Not a foreigner *and* a local."

She was right. Her presence may be what was keeping Eddie out of trouble. "When did you last speak to Dwayne's friends?"

"Over a year ago, when I helped Dwayne move."

Dancehall music spilled out through the windows as Candace and Eddie approached the house. Candace banged on the grill while yelling, "Charlene. Shirley?"

A few moments went by and the music did not die down. She yelled even louder, enough that Eddie's chest tightened. Even though Candace told him that he wouldn't have to worry about the brothas close by, he did not have to be a genius to see that they wouldn't have been too friendly to Dwayne's friends. Another reason for them to have the grill locked.

He was relieved that the volume of the music dropped.

"Who dat?" came an effeminate man's voice from inside.

"Just come open up," Candace yelled.

There was continued silence for several seconds until the front door opened. A young man, early twenties, very thin, stood in the doorway for a bit, sighed, then slowly approached them. Aside from clearly showing his disgust at seeing them, Eddie noticed that something else was off about him.

"So *now* you wannah pass thru."

"Just let us in, Shirley," Candace answered. "You have no idea what we went through to get here."

"And why yuh come now?" Shirley answered. "Yuh tek Dwayne from wi—his only family. Now he dead."

"I never took Dwayne away from either of you," said Candace. "You know it wasn't like that."

"Who dat?" came another effeminate male voice from inside. "Jehovah's Witnesses?"

"It's nobody," said Shirley looking over a shoulder. "Guh weh. There's nothing for you here."

"Dwayne was my best friend. You know I would've done my best to stop him from going to Citrusville had I known before."

"If you're his so-called best friend, why yuh nuh come to di fineral?"

Eddie saw another brotha leave the house and approach, holding what appeared to be a bag of frozen vegetables on one temple. He was slightly taller and a bit more built than Shirley. "Candace?"

"She was just leaving," said Shirley.

Neither Candace nor Eddie could hide their concern for Charlene.

"Why you look surprised?" Charlene asked. "It's not like someone didn't try to kill me before."

"And I was also nearly killed at Guava Hill yesterday and survived a shootout this morning," Candace retorted.

Eddie saw both Shirley's and Charlene's eyebrows raised.

They were both barefoot, in old shorts and ragged halter tops. No doubt a result of being in abject poverty for months, if not years. Despite being dressed down, both still wore a full face of makeup.

"What were you doing in Guava Hill?" asked Charlene, giving Eddie a once-over. "Ah who yuh?"

"My name's Eddie Barrow."

"Eddie…Barrow?" Shirley turned to Charlene then back to Eddie. "Why does that name sound familiar?"

"You've probably seen Dwayne reading my books?"

Charlene gasped as though suddenly remembering where she heard his name, then looked at him with a squinted eye. "*You're* Eddie Barrow?"

Eddie nodded with a smile.

"Oh, I just didn't expect you to be so…short."

Eddie's smile dropped. "I'm two inches taller than Spike Lee. May we come in? We really need your help."

Charlene stepped back as Shirley took out a keychain and fit one into the padlock. Once removed she pulled the grill open to let them in.

Moments later, all four were inside. Eddie looked around the living room, which had a single couch that had seen better days, no carpeting, not even a coffee table. He didn't even see a television, only two small speakers connected to an iPod—making it unlikely that they knew of the reward that Pusey put out on him.

"We can't offer you anything to eat," said Charlene as she lowered the frozen bag, revealing a swollen purple bruise. "Up to now, wi nuh guh shop fi food."

"You don't need to worry yourselves over that," said Candace.

Shirley gestured to the couch. "Sit. I know it ain't much but at least make yourselves comfortable."

Eddie and Candace took a seat, while Charlene sat on the arm beside Eddie. Shirley stood across from them, leaning on the wall. Charlene still held the frozen bag to her head as she turned to Eddie.

"How you know Dwayne and Candace?"

"It's a long story," said Eddie, who then summarized how he met Dwayne and how it eventually led him to Candace.

Shirley turned to Candace. "Didn't Dwayne catch the man who raped you."

Candace nodded. "We thought that it was over. But he retaliated by putting a hit on Dwayne. The same people are still after both of us."

"Which comes to why we're here," said Eddie. "When did you last hear from Dwayne?"

"Him sen money fi help wi out," said Charlene. "It was not too long before he got killed. As mi seh before, we were Dwayne's family, even before his parents and the entire village try to kill him."

Shirley turned to Charlene. "How you mean, not too long before Dwayne got killed? It was two to three weeks since we last heard from him." She then turned to Eddie and Candace. "He made our clothes or stitched them so that we don't have to go to the store to buy them. Even though he didn't live with us anymore he never forgot us."

Eddie was afraid to ask what they did for money, and frankly did not want to know. He reached into his wallet and took out a few bills that he was given and held them out for Charlene. "This should help with the groceries."

Charlene took the bills with a smile. "Thank you."

"Don't mention it," Eddie answered. "By any chance, did Dwayne leave you anything?"

"Like what?" asked Shirley.

"Anything," Candace replied desperately as she looked at Shirley, then turned to Charlene. "He trusted both of you."

"What about special instructions?" asked Eddie. "Like, if something ever happened to him."

Eddie noticed that the two of them made eye contact. "I promise that we'll help you out if you can help us."

Shirley nodded. "Yuh know, he pass by about a month ago and left us an envelope. He made us promise never to open it."

"We were to drop it off at the post office if ever anything happened to him," said Charlene.

The tiny hairs rose at the back of Eddie's neck. "Please tell me you remember the address you mailed it to."

Charlene looked at Candace. "It was addressed to you."

"I never got anything," Candace answered. "It must have arrived after I left to hide at my uncle's place."

"Was there a return address?" asked Eddie without missing a beat.

"Mi believe so, yuh know." Shirley scratched her head. "I remember it being someplace in Greenwood."

"Amancia." Candace turned to Eddie. "Dwayne's aunt, that's where she lives."

"Of course," Eddie said. "The only family other than Jalissa who came to the funeral."

"I know where she lives," said Candace.

Eddie stood. "Then that's where we're going."

Chapter 29

Amancia's home. Greenwood, Jamaica

Amancia gasped once she saw Eddie and Candace on the other side of the grill entrance to her front yard. "Oh my goodness, Eddie!" She fumbled as she rushed to unlock the grill, yanked it open, and threw her arms around him. "You good, you had me so worried. I watched the news and they report that you were spotted in Guava Hill. What were you doing there?"

"It's a long story," said Eddie not wanting to waste any time as Amancia closed the grill behind them and locked it. She then appeared to notice Candace. "Hold on, Candace? I didn't even recognize you. Where've you been?"

She looked briefly at Eddie, then back at Amancia. "It's a long story."

"Long story this, long story that." Amancia waved dismissively. "Is that all you have to say?"

"A lot has happened since the funeral—" Eddie started.

"Oh, Lord." Amancia's hands shot up to the sides of her head and her voice became scratchy. "You had to bring that up? Oh, Jesus! Why couldn't they let Dwayne rest in peace? They don't care that *that* boy suffered enough?"

Eddie bit his lip. *Damn it, I shouldn't have brought up the funeral.* The slap to his arm from Candace was a reminder of how careless he was.

Amancia led them back to the veranda where they went inside. Her house was a one-story flat that was well decorated, with a floral garden and a few aloe plants. Once inside, Amancia ran down the hall and darted through the first doorway on her right as it was obvious that she was holding back tears.

Eddie realized that they were still too close to the door where a passerby may spot them. He removed his shoes and nodded to Candace to do the same. Eddie then walked in, gesturing to Candace to follow.

"Keep away from windows as much as possible," Eddie whispered.

Even though they still had on the same clothes since they escaped Lenny's village, Eddie felt that paranoia was the best defense.

Running water was heard pouring into a sink for a few moments before it stopped. Amancia emerged from the bathroom, her face dry. "I'm so sorry about that."

"That was my fault," said Eddie. "The last few days have been rough."

"But what happened to both of you?" She then turned to Candace. "I thought you would've been at the funer—"

"I've been in hiding," interrupted Candace. "I had no choice."

"And her uncle sent for me," said Eddie. "That's how we found each other."

Amancia turned to Candace, then to Eddie, then back to Candace. "Hold on, you're Brutus's niece?"

She didn't know.

Candace sighed with a nod. "It's not something I like to tell people. But you have to believe me that despite his...reputation, he's the reason why I'm still alive."

"Both of us," Eddie added. "May we sit down so we can bring you up to speed?" Eddie gestured to the dining room.

Amancia appeared to suddenly remember that they were guests. "Oh yes, where are my manners? Come through here."

Eddie and Candace followed her into the living room.

"Please, make yourselves comfortable."

Eddie went in, sat on the couch, and was joined by Candace.

"You must be hungry. It's a good thing I finished cooking." Amancia disappeared into the kitchen. "I have rice and peas, callaloo, snapper, mac and cheese, and some stewed pork. I also made some carrot juice. You want some?"

Candace's eyes lit up. "Mi hungry now!"

"Same here," said Eddie, thinking how Amancia must have prepared her meals several days in advance, unless she was expecting company.

There was the sound of ice clinking in glasses, and Amancia returned with a tray holding two glasses of ice-cold carrot juice. She settled the tray on the coffee table in front of them.

"I just need to put out the plates, it shouldn't take long," said Amancia as she sat down in the adjacent chair. "But you must tell me. What happened to both of you?"

Candace turned to her and told her everything from the moment she met Weiss, to him sexually assaulting her, to Dwayne getting involved.

"So, you see, even though I wasn't close to my uncle, he was the only person I could turn to."

"And didn't he do something?" asked Amancia.

"From what he told me, yes, at least at first," Candace answered. "But Weiss was better connected than my uncle had thought."

"That's who we're running from," said Eddie.

"My other uncle managed to shelter us for a night and helped us, but he's only bought us some time," said Candace.

"You heard about the mass shooting this morning?" asked Eddie.

Amancia's jaw dropped while she pointed to them. "You were there too?"

Eddie and Candace nodded.

"We're lucky we got away," said Candace.

"Don't worry," said Eddie. "They have no way of tracking us. But we didn't come here to hide. We need your help. Did you receive mail that was addressed to Candace?"

Amancia's eyebrows raised. "How did you know? A letter came this morning. Hold on a minute."

She got up and left them. Eddie heard her talking to herself somewhere else in the house—mostly about how she missed Dwayne and the memories she had of him as a youngster. About half a minute later she returned with a regular-sized envelope.

She turned to Candace. "The letter was addressed to you, but had my home listed as the return address. I was confused because

I don't remember mailing you this. It's not even my handwriting."

The envelope had already been opened. She reached in and took out a USB flash drive. "I don't even know what to do with this because I don't know what it is."

Eddie held out his hand and she gave it to him. "Do you have a computer?"

Amancia nodded. "Yes, but I hardly use it. I only recently learned how to send and receive emails. And I had to purchase something called wi-fi or whatever it's called so that I could read my messages. I also play games when I'm bored. Hold on while I get it."

Amancia left them, then came back a few moments later to the adjoining dining room. "Come to the table, there's more room."

Eddie and Candace joined her, and Eddie took a seat. Amancia slid the laptop in front of him already opened. Candace brought one of the chairs close to Eddie and sat too, leaning closer to not miss a beat.

"You may want to password protect the device," said Eddie as he noticed the absence of a prompt.

"Yes, I know," said Amancia. "But knowing me, I'd forget it and get locked out of my own computer."

Eddie inserted the flash drive, clicked on the folder icon. There were two MP4 files, along with an MP3 and some JPEGs. He double-clicked on the MP4 icon and a movie player window opened. It was Dwayne seated at a desk in front of his laptop and staring into the webcam. Eddie recognized the background as being his bedroom at Wesley's house.

"Hello, Candace, and or, Jalissa, or anyone who may be watching this. If you're seeing this, it's because I've gone to Heaven. But I'll always be with you in your heart. Aunt Amancia if you're watching this, I guess it's because someone taught you how to use the flash drive you got in the mail." Dwayne said the last sentence with a giggle.

Eddie smiled and noticed that Amancia and Candace were both on the verge of tears. He suspected that Amancia would be the first to break.

"Anyhow, Candace," Dwayne continued, "I hope that you're

okay. I kept these files initially for myself in case Weiss were to renege on our NDA. This is now *your* leverage against Weiss if ever he violates the terms of the NDA. The video and pictures I took are on a separate file. However, just to let you know, it's not perfectly clear as it gets scratchy at times. As you know, you are not supposed to show this to anyone unless you feel that there's an absolute need to do so."

Dwayne took a moment to exhale as he rested his head in his hands, then looked back up to the camera. "I could've sent this flash drive to Hines, but I don't think he would do anything because of the NDA I signed with Weiss. But something told me that it wouldn't be a good idea sending it to him, I guess I read too many Eddie Barrow novels. Men like Weiss know people who will find a way to intercept it. I may be paranoid, but there was something about that man the last time I saw him that seemed to be off. I don't trust him, and I get the feeling that he wasn't the right person anyway."

Amancia broke down crying and she ran from the room.

Eddie paused the video. "Hines. That's your lawyer, isn't it?"

Candace nodded.

Eddie tapped on the PLAY icon on the video app.

"Candace," said Dwayne. "I hope that you're watching this because I don't want to see you on the other side, not for at least one hundred years. And I know that you're an intelligent woman and you'll make something of yourself."

Eddie turned to the sound of Candace sniffling. He'd known that it would be just a matter of time.

"That's all I have to say. To Jalissa, you'll always be in my heart, lil' sister. To Milly, thank you so much for believing in me and for giving me the chance to do what I love. By the way, I'm not mad at you that you couldn't credit me for the help I did for your business behind the scenes. Hopefully, someday things will change, Jamaicans and the whole Caribbean will learn to love people like me, at which point you'll be able to come clean without any fear of repercussions."

For the next two minutes, Dwayne continued thanking everyone else in his life. "And, Candace, last but not least, I hope one day you'll be able to heal from what that nasty man did to you. You're beautiful inside and out and I love you to death...okay, that was a poor choice of words, but you know what I mean."

Dwayne smiled, blew a kiss, then waved. "Bye, everyone. Mi luv di whole ah-unuh."

The video ended.

Eddie felt a lump growing in his throat, but for Candace more tears covered her face, followed by sniffling as she wiped her face with the back of her arm.

He then clicked on the USB file folder and selected the second MP4 file. It was dark, but there was sound.

"Why can't we see anything, is it broken?" asked Candace.

"No," Eddie answered. "Don't forget Dwayne hid his phone."

Eddie leaned in closer to the laptop and raised the volume. Yes, Dwayne was clearly in a car. By the way the engine revved, it was probably a sports car. It went on the same way for a few minutes when Amancia came back in the room. He didn't like the idea of Amancia witnessing what was probably going to happen to Dwayne, so he turned to Candace.

"Maybe you can help Amancia with the meal while I listen to this."

"Oh, Lord," said Amancia. "I completely forgot. I hope I don't have to warm it over."

Candace nodded at Eddie and left him alone with the laptop.

As Eddie continued to watch, he heard a ringtone from a mobile phone.

"Yes," he heard a man say. Eddie assumed that it was Weiss speaking. "I can't talk now, I'm in the middle of something."

There was a moment's silence. "That's fine, just write three different checks with different dates instead of one...why are you asking me how my name is spelled, the payments aren't going to me, they're going to Plessis...Jesus, don't scare me like that. Just do what needs to be done, I have to go."

Plessis? What's Plessis?

Eddie tapped the *Left* arrow a few times to reverse the video, then let it play again.

"...just write three different checks with different dates instead of one…why are you asking me how my name is spelled, the payments aren't going to me, they're going to Plessis…Jesus, don't scare me like that."

Eddie paused the video.

Plessis…Essis. The file. Of course, Essis is actually Plessis.

Chapter 30

Turtle Grove Park 4:30PM

The drive through the hills was something ripped from the pages of a Stephen King novel: A long winding road with houses growing fewer and farther between as Corey drove. The only difference was that he was driving away from Mo-Bay and not from some small New England town. But it was enough to creep him out. What was he getting himself into?

Why did this place have to be so far away from the city? Corey didn't like the idea of traveling alone so far from civilization—especially since he knew nothing about the area. Had Eddie been with him, fine. He had to remind himself, though, that Eddie was the reason he was risking meeting a total stranger who may or may not be able to help him.

While those thoughts ran through his head, he realized he hadn't seen a house for at least the past half-kilometer. The mobile was attached to the dash via the grill of the air vent, and he reached over to wipe a smudge from the screen. The top of the Google Maps display indicated that there was still thirty-two minutes left before arriving at his destination.

One thought was running on a loop through Corey's mind. *This is a bad idea. This is a bad idea.* And it was. He didn't know where Eddie was. Was he safe? He'd been fine when they last spoke, but what if he wasn't now? He could be shackled to a chair in some rat-infested location being tortured—probably by the rats themselves, gnawing at his toes while the torturer took a break.

He had this graphic image of Eddie in a basement, the room pitch-black save for a lone lightbulb dangling by a thin cord above him, so slack it could've been swinging, except there were no windows, not even a vent or fan that could've given it a breeze to dance in.

Then he had a vision of the torturer—a shirtless, shredded brotha in knee-length shorts—in slow motion, smacking five firm knuckles so hard to the side of Eddie's face that it dislodged his lower jaw, ejecting four bottom teeth and an upper back molar from his mouth as the chair, and Eddie, toppled to the side from the blow, leaving him bloodied from the mouth and his left eye swollen shut.

No.

Corey had to shake that thought from his mind. He had already decided to go with Eddie's idea, and so far, it had led to this. There was no way Eddie would survive too long on the run, especially on this island, considering that he was all book-smarts with little to no street-smarts.

Damn trip. All Corey had wanted was to hang out with Eddie for moral support during his book signing. Instead, Eddie went and got his ass kidnapped—again. Now he was connected to two murders and a military raid.

With his mind adrift, time had flown by as Corey saw the sign for the turnoff to Turtle Grove. He veered off the two-lane parish highway and onto a dirt-and-gravel road that snaked for roughly a quarter of a kilometer before he saw an eight-foot wire fence blocking his path. He pulled over to the side, threw the gear to *Park,* and scanned the area. He was surrounded by dense woods, and with the fading light he couldn't tell if anyone or any*thing* was watching his every move.

"Corey, what did you get yourself into?" he said to himself with a sigh. He lowered the fan speed of the air conditioning as the inside of the car had become a bit too cool. He kept the windows up though, he didn't want any mosquito bites, especially out here in the woods.

A sudden *rat-tat-tat* on his driver's side caused Corey to throw his hands up, as he shot a glance to the window. He dropped his hands and relaxed his shoulders when he saw that it was the janitor sitting on a motor bike.

He lowered the window. "You nearly gave me a heart attack."

"Sorry. Come quick before the sun set."

Corey narrowed his eyes before nodding toward the fence. "What's in there?"

"Best to show you. Hurry, there's not much time."

"I'm not going anywhere until you tell me where we're going and what you want to show me."

The janitor looked away, muttering some colorful Jamaican slang under his breath, then turned back to Corey. "Yuh really waan know waah happen to Chevelle? I tell you the wrong man went to prison for har rape, and dem still control har."

Corey's eyes narrowed. "Who's controlling Chevelle?"

"Come," said the janitor as he revved the engine. "Wi nuh waan deh yah when it get dark." *I don't want us to be here when it gets dark.*

Corey watched as the janitor drove ahead to the side of the road, where he dismounted and pushed his bike a few meters into the woods to hide it behind a tree. The only other noises were the crickets and grasshoppers—sounds which he had grown used to hearing while growing up. The janitor was reluctant to talk, but Corey had no choice, as this guy may have some answers.

Corey switched off the engine, grabbed the burner from the dash and his hand towel from the passenger seat on his way out. He swung the towel over his right shoulder just as he watched the janitor scale the fence as though it was nothing. When he landed on the other side, he turned to Corey, who was hesitant, not knowing what was on the other side of the triple-padlocked barrier.

"Yuh coming ar not?"

Corey bit his lip, shoved the burner and an end of the hand towel into each back pocket as he walked to the fence. He scaled it and joined the janitor, who had already walked ahead. They were in an area which could've been used as a parking lot, considering that it was large enough to hold a few buses. To their left was what appeared to be an outdoor gathering spot. There were stone benches built to form a semicircle with a split down the middle to separate both sides of an audience. They appeared damaged from what could've been years of neglect. The same could be said about the main building ahead. It was a ground-level structure with a gable roof. Its windows were covered in cobwebs and there was more visible splintered wood than paint on the side of the building.

"What is this place?" Corey asked as he followed the janitor.

"I'm sure you have a lot of questions."

"What do you expect? You told me to meet you here without giving me any details. And I trusted you. I don't even know your name."

There was a silence while he kept walking, then, finally, "It's Nesta."

"Okay," said Corey. "Are you going to tell me why I'm here?"

A sudden rustling and beating of leaves in the branches above startled Corey into a defense stance.

Ambush!

"Relax," said Nesta, who did not even flinch. "Ah jus bat dem. Dem naw trubble yuh."

He should've expected that bats would be in the trees. And as Nesta said, they're harmless. They were all over Trinidad and Tobago, and he saw them regularly while growing up. Even though Nesta told him not to worry, Corey kept an eye on his surroundings. The tree cover blocked out a lot of the light from the setting sun. He grabbed his burner and activated the flashlight app. Nesta did the same with his phone soon after, then he stopped walking without explanation.

Corey scanned the area ahead, wondering why Nesta stopped. He then turned to him. "Are you going to tell me what this place is?"

Nesta did not return Corey's stare but looked ahead instead with a blank expression. "A nuff tings happen ya soh. Mi glad seh di lass two hurricane mash-up di place. It save me the trouble of burning it down myself."

He was glad that two hurricanes wrecked the place? "You asked me if I want to know what happened to Chevelle," said Corey. "This is where she was attacked, isn't it?"

Nesta gave two short nods. "Not just her alone, nuff girls and boys from twelve to fifteen. The people who did this say they want to correct the problem before it starts."

"Correct what kind of problem before it starts?"

Nesta closed his eyes and let his head drop. "You hear about Pastor Green?"

Corey sucked his teeth and sighed. "Yeah, I bumped into him and his peeps earlier today at a funeral."

"I hear about that. Him and his people don't give up when it come to harassing gay people," said Nesta. "Parents send their children to him for counselling when they think that they're gay or about to turn gay."

I knew it. "This is one of those gay-conversion camps."

Nesta nodded. "Pastor Green tell the children's parents that he's able to cast the *gay demons* out of them. And I'm sure most of them know how he goes about doing it too."

Corey's eyes widened. "As in…*rape* the gay away?"

"That's what you call it where you from?"

"It all means the same thing, any way you sugarcoat it," said Corey as he pinched the bridge of his nose. "Did Pastor Green ever participate?"

Nesta nodded as he curled his lips inward.

Corey saw that Nesta was staring at something. He shone his flashlight in that direction. "What's over there?"

Rather than answer, Nesta started walking again with Corey quickly following. From what Corey saw, it was obvious that this place deeply traumatized Nesta to the point that he had to work up the nerve to keep moving.

They came to a smaller box-shaped cabin that was no bigger than a regular-sized garage. Nesta was about to open the door, but as he grabbed the doorknob, he paused and glanced over his shoulder as he took out a kerchief from his back pocket. "You'll want to cover your nose."

The battered, splintered door had been left unlocked, and it creaked as Nesta opened it. He already covered his nose and mouth with the kerchief before entering.

Corey grabbed his hand towel as he followed him. He barely made it through the door before the rotten smell of mold and urine jumped out and bitch-slapped him. He pressed the towel hard against his nose and mouth, scrunching up his face that his lips curled inward to touch his teeth.

Corey raised his flashlight as his and Nesta's beams crossed. There was a loud series of clicks that made his body seize. A swarm of flying cockroaches—with wingspans almost as big as the average human hand—scurried away through cracks and holes in the floor, the walls, and in the ceiling. When the clicking stopped, Corey's flashlight fell onto two mice feeding on the rotting carcass of another.

Nesta saw them and stomped on the floor next to them—making them bolt. "Unuh guweh, shish!" *Go away, shoo!*

The room fell silent. Corey waved his flashlight around as he saw Nesta swatting away a few hanging spiderwebs. Corey aimed his flashlight where Nesta aimed his and saw a rusted bed frame in the corner adjacent where they stood. He paused his beam on the mattress, which was hanging halfway off, stained and floppy with age, rusty metal coils poking through its surface.

He then focused on the red stains, and he winced.

"Is that blood?" Corey looked away from the bed to Nesta—still covering his nose and mouth—and then back at the bed.

Corey's mind was assaulted with images of children being tied facedown onto that mattress, where a sadistic asshole held the cross in one hand and the Bible in the other before forcing himself on them. Completely helpless they would've accepted anything the abuser yelled at them—so long as the pain ended. He assumed that Nesta shared the same thoughts…his breathing had shortened to a quick staccato. Corey spotted Nesta stepping backward.

"Mi can't," said Nesta as he shook his head, then turned around and ran outside.

Corey ran after him, not being able to take the smell, nor the thought that he was standing inside an area that reeked of vermin and child rape.

"Nesta, wait."

Nesta slowed down and then stopped, allowing Corey to catch up and put a hand on his shoulder.

"It's okay."

Nesta shook his head as he grabbed his forehead with both hands. "No, sah."

Corey pulled his hand away to give Nesta some space.

After a few moments, Nesta dropped his hands to his sides and looked up to the sky. "Mi was collecting rubbish one evening," he said. "All mi hear a screaming coming from in deah. Where the children sleep, they can't hear what's going on because they're on the other side of the camp."

Nesta lowered his head and closed his eyes. "They hurt Chevelle the worst. They brought that girl in there at least three times to break har. Fi know dat dis a gwaan and mi caan do nuttin."

He felt powerless to do anything even though he knew what was happening to those children. "You didn't think anyone would believe you."

"It's more than that."

"Didn't any of the children speak out? Didn't they go to one of their teachers?"

Nesta shook his head. "The children all brainwashed into thinking that something wrong with them that need fixing. Only Chevelle spoke to someone."

Corey leaned in slightly. "Who?"

"One of her teachers, Tarone. He was the only one who believed her. He tried to help her, but it backfired."

"Did she accuse *him* of raping her?"

"That not how it happened," said Nesta. "I heard that after she told Tarone what happened to her, other people made her change her story because the police said that they found proof that Tarone did those things. Dem people lie, and that damn counselor is one of them. Tarone never did touch Chevelle."

"Are you talking about Ann?"

Nesta nodded. "She works at the group home Chevelle lives at. She controls everything Chevelle does. Yuh lucky yuh managed fi chat to har."

It was obvious that Nesta was convinced that whatever he did or could have done would not have changed the outcome. Pastor Green's influence was vast, and he probably had the police and those who worked at Chevelle's boarding school roped in. It was then that Corey realized that the sun had completely gone down.

"I want to know something else," Corey asked. "Why are you

telling *me* this?"

"Who do you think you fooling?" said Nesta. "I know that you ain't no student reporter."

"And who do you think I am?"

"At first, I thought that you were a reporter from overseas pretending to be a student. Then I see you didn't take any pictures of what I showed you, nor did you ask me my permission to record me with your phone."

Damn it, I blew my own cover.

"Whoever you are, I think that you're someone who cares," said Nesta as he looked away from Corey and downward with a sigh. "And who isn't a coward…like me."

"Don't say that. You're not a coward. You were cornered and didn't know how to help Chevelle or any of her classmates, especially when you saw what happened to Tarone."

"I want to see that monster fry for what he did to those children," said Nesta. "He hurt Chevelle so bad that from then mi affi mek sure dat mi keep mi eye pon har. She's a woman now, but I never forget the way she cried out in pain. Mi tink dat dem wudda kill har."

Corey paused in thought, looked away. This brotha was so traumatized that he felt it necessary to keep an eye on Chevelle. No wonder he worked at the same cafeteria she did. The way Nesta talked, Corey wondered if he had nightmares about what happened to Chevelle. Especially since, according to him, he thought they would kill her if she did not convert.

Corey turned to Nesta. "You really care for her that much?"

"Chevelle was an easy target for Pastor Green because he knew that no one would believe her if she talked. The same could be said for her classmates."

The jig was up several minutes ago. Nesta could've demanded that Corey tell him who he really was and why he was questioning Chevelle. Instead, he unburdened himself to a perfect stranger. Corey felt that perhaps now he ought to do the same.

"You're right," said Corey. "I'm not a reporter, and I *do* care. I also want to help."

"How?"

"I don't have any pull with the media. But I have a friend who does, except he's missing, and his life's in danger. I staged the meeting with Chevelle because I want her to put me in touch with her son, Delroy."

"What for?"

"You want to see Pastor Green brought to justice?" asked Corey. "Then her son needs to know the truth."

"And how are you going to go about doing that? By setting up Chevelle's son to meet Tarone?"

"That would be a start."

"Yuh mad? Chevelle's son don't want to have nothing to do with Tarone," said Nesta. "You put two of them in a room and they'll come to blows for sure."

"I'll take my chances," said Corey as they began to walk back toward the entrance.

"Why? What does this have to do with helping your friend?"

"The funeral I went to this morning was Dwayne Pottinger's. My friend and I witnessed his murder—in fact, we tried to save his life. Delroy's also a witness, except he won't talk. And seeing how Delroy doesn't want to have anything to do with Tarone proves that he doesn't know who his real father is. But if we can convince Chevelle to tell Delroy the truth about his father, perhaps she may be able to also convince him to reveal what he saw the night Dwayne was murdered. Hopefully, he'll be able to give us a clue which could identify Dwayne's killer. Once that's done, it may help my friend come out of hiding."

Nesta lowered his head and pinched his nose. He didn't appear to be convinced that this plan would work.

"If you want to bring down Pastor Green and get justice for Chevelle and for all of the children he raped," said Corey. "Then I'm going to need your help."

Two powerful flashlights exploded in their faces as two shadowy figures closed rapidly on their position.

"Police. Don't move unless you want to get shot, yuh bloodclaat!" was all Corey could decipher within the sudden barking of orders from both men. By reflex, his hands shot up seconds before he noticed that Nesta had bolted.

"One he a run," yelled one of the officers.

Before he could call out to Nesta, Corey was winded as a solid mass slammed into his torso, sending his phone flying from his hand. The force knocked him from his feet and crashing to the ground, where the back of his head scraped against solid dry dirt and grass.

"I'm not resisting," Corey wheezed.

"You think I care?" The officer's face was so close that Corey felt his breath and saliva splash over his face. "What are you two doing here?"

Corey could hardly breathe with the amount of weight crushing down on his chest. The guy had to be over two hundred and fifty pounds.

The officer got off him just long enough to flip Corey onto his stomach. Corey turned his head to the side as he seized the moment to inhale a deep breath but did so too fast, and he choked on some grass-scented dirt, sending him into a coughing fit. Seeing stars floating in front of him and being too weak to resist, the officer had no difficulty yanking his hands behind his back and slapping the metal bracelets on. He then felt himself being tugged by the back of his shirt collar so hard that he was forced to stand.

"You going to answer my question or what?"

Corey struggled, trying to catch his breath while shaking his head. "Nothing, I was—"

The punch he got to his solar plexus was so hard that he spat saliva and doubled over as he wailed, falling on one knee.

"You think you can lie to me? I'm going to ask you one more—"

A gunshot echoed through the trees from somewhere in the darkness, jolting Corey as his head swung in the direction from where it came. A massive beating of wings exploded above as dozens of bats took flight. Corey stared into the dark with his jaw hung open, where he saw a faint light from the other officer's flashlight.

He knew that he would never see Nesta again.

Chapter 31

Corey stumbled and bounced off the front end of the squad car with such an impact he swore he came close to dislocating his shoulder. When he fell to the ground, he instinctively curled up into a fetal position—anticipating that he would either be clubbed, kicked, or both.

"Yuh caan hear weh mi a say, weh yuh a do ya?" The pig who attacked him earlier was insisting that Corey tell him what he was doing here.

"And with a much older man too, and in the dark?" said the other. "Mi tink seh dis batty-bwoy came here fi him daddy."

"Wi nuh want no batty-bwoy ya, sah. All the reason to lock you up where you can get your backside fucked all yuh want."

"I swear..." Corey struggled to breathe. "I don't know that man."

"Oh yeah? You weren't seen with him earlier?"

How could they know that? "I don't know what you're talking about."

That's when he felt the kick to his ass which forced him to cry out.

"You." Another kick. "Want. To. Lie. To. Us." Each word was punctuated by another kick.

"Okay, I'll talk!" The pain from the repeated blows to his back and glutes was unbearable as he tried to form words with his lips.

"You're going to tell us what you two were meeting about and why you come here?"

Corey didn't answer. He didn't know what to do, considering they were asking questions they already knew the answer to. This was part of the torture.

He heard feet shuffling on the ground and was expecting to be kicked in the head, but instead, he was lifted and thrown back-first against the hood of the car.

"Help!" Corey bawled. "I'm unarmed. They're trying to kill me."

He only heard his voice echo.

"You think someone can hear you?"

He was right. They could kill him and get away with it. He walked right into a dead end, and these assholes sealed the only way out. They just killed Nesta, and now they were toying with him.

Before he could blink, he was grabbed by the front of the collar and had the business end of a Glock 17 jammed against his lips.

"You think anyone can hear you get shot all the way out here?" said the first pig. "I'll ask you one last time what were you two talking about, and why did you come here?"

Corey was afraid to open his mouth, knowing that the officer would jam the Glock inside.

He breathed hard through his nose and closed his eyes as a flashlight blinded him. He knew what was about to happen, and it made him forget about the pain in his back.

To his relief, the gun was yanked from his mouth. "Talk."

Corey's teeth clacked together as his jaw trembled. He swallowed hard as he breathed rapidly. "I'm looking for my friend. He went missing, I swear. I bumped into that guy who told me to meet him here because he said he could help. That's all. We didn't mess around, I swear."

"And why'd you think that you'd find your friend up here?" snapped the same pig. "Was he supposed to join you two in your nastiness?"

Corey was about to shake his head when he suddenly felt the tip of the Glock pressed against his lips so hard that they were squashed against his front teeth. A slip of the finger and the back of his skull would be splattered all over the hood of the car. The pig pulled the gun away far enough that Corey could stare below his nose and see the tip of the barrel.

"It's not like that. My friend was kidnapped. I don't know where he is."

"Now you're not making any sense," spat the second officer.

"Let me explain."

"Yuh had your chance," said the first pig as he nodded over his left shoulder. "What were you doing back there?"

He was afraid to answer with the business end of the gun pressed against his lips. They just killed Nesta out of pure hatred and would most likely argue self-defense. The pig in front of him would surely do the same. All the way up here in the middle of nowhere in a closed park. Who'd ever think of looking for his body up here?

Red and blue lights flashed all over before the pig suddenly yanked his weapon from Corey's face as tires rolled over gravel behind him. The sound of a few motors told him there was more than one car. Corey breathed a sigh of relief, releasing a load of tension that had built up in his chest, arms, stomach, and legs.

Corey didn't have to look to see who it was. All he knew was the pig in front of him was frustrated. In fact, it appeared that whatever backup just showed up seemed to have caught him off guard, interrupting what he was doing—or what he and his partner were planning.

"Bumboclaat!" Corey heard them both say. Someone messed things up for them, but who?

Several doors opened then slammed shut.

"What the hell is going on here?"

Corey recognized the voice as he heard the footsteps approaching. Detective Inspector Ellis came around the side of the vehicle. He looked at Corey with the same scowl from when they last crossed paths at the hospital. He then turned to Corey's assailants.

"Well. Is one of you going to explain what you two are doing here with Mister Stephenson?"

"Someone hinted that there was some funny stuff going on up here with two guys," said Nesta's killer.

"Really?" said Ellis. "So where's the other man?"

"Him roun deh, sah," said the first pig as he gestured in the direction where he had chased Nesta.

"Then why isn't he here?" asked Ellis.

"Him dead," the officer answered. "Neva had a choice."

Ellis's eyes jolted open, and he turned to the four other officers who approached from behind. "You three go and secure the area. You, call it in."

Ellis sighed, then turned to Corey without saying anything. He just stared at him for a bit then turned back to the officers. "What's the deal with him?"

"Him tried to fight," said the officer. "Mi did affi use pressure pon him."

Ellis walked up to Corey and helped him stand on his feet. He took out his flashlight and shone it in his face. "Where are you hurting?"

"Him tried to fight, mi tell yuh—"

"I wasn't talking to you," snapped Ellis as he turned and stared down at the officer.

Corey shook his head and whispered. "That's not true."

"What isn't?"

Corey snorted once to clear his nostrils, then whispered. "I wasn't resisting arrest."

Ellis paused as he stared Corey in the eyes for a few moments. As he continued to stare, Ellis reached into his own pocket, a set of keys jingling soon after. Ellis then turned Corey around to face the opposite way and tugged on his handcuffs.

"Don't say anything else." Ellis freed Corey's hands.

Something wasn't right. Moments ago, the two pigs were about to kill him, and now another appeared to be doing the opposite.

"Is there anything you need to get from your car? Can you walk on your own?" asked Ellis.

My second burner. "Yeah."

"Go get them, then wait inside of mi government car," said Ellis. "You can sit in front. The door should be unlocked."

Before Corey left, he searched for his phone in the area where he had been tackled. Even though there was very little light from the headlights behind him, he dropped down to his hands and knees and felt it among the dirt and pebbles. Getting back up proved to be a bit painful, as Corey was reminded where he had been kicked several times. The front gates were open when he arrived. He assumed that the pigs he heard Ellis arguing with had unlocked it earlier.

He grabbed the keyless lock, pressed one of the buttons, and the trunk of his car popped open before he got to it. Corey grabbed the second burner and slipped it in his other back pocket. He then closed the trunk and walked to Ellis's car—which he assumed was the one in front.

Corey climbed into the front passenger seat, where he watched as Ellis and the two pigs still went at it. Nesta's murderer gave his Glock to Ellis, then he and his partner headed toward Corey. He assumed they were heading back to their car. As they were about to pass, they made sure that Corey saw their menacing stares.

"Yuh lucky," muttered his assailant.

Ellis soon came back and got in. He sat behind the wheel and didn't say anything to Corey but let out a long sigh. He reversed in a semi-circle, then drove forward, heading back to the main road, the taillights of Corey's assailants' car not too far ahead.

"Why can't I drive my own car?" asked Corey.

"You can try if you want," said Ellis. "I don't know where you'll find two spare tires around here."

"They popped my tires?" He hadn't even noticed when he went to the vehicle to get his burner phone.

"They say they do it so no one can slip by them and get away," said Ellis. "Me, I'm not so sure of that."

Did he just admit that he knows his own men are dirty?

"So, are you going to tell me what the hell is going on?" Ellis asked while keeping his eyes on the road.

"What do you want to know?"

"Why's your friend Eddie the writer hanging around with a drug kingpin."

"Eddie doesn't hang around drug kingpins," Corey answered. "He was kidnapped, and I already spoke to you guys about that. But instead of rescuing him, you and the military rolled over the town where he was being held captive and shot it up."

"I didn't have any control over that."

"Really? You treated us like dirt rather than witnesses to Dwayne Pottinger's murder. You didn't seem to care about a gay man being killed—"

"Don't you dare say that," yelled Ellis. "We treat every victim the same."

"Really?" yelled Corey. "And you call every gay victim a *battyman*? Why don't you say his name, as you would with any victim?"

"Are you going to answer my question, or are we going to argue all night?"

"There you go, deflecting. Why should I be surprised?"

There was a pregnant pause as Ellis shook his head. "I'll be honest with you. If my best friend was kidnapped, the last thing I'd be doing is looking to court someone," said Ellis. "So, what *were* you doing here with that man? Do you even know him?"

Corey didn't answer. Ellis may have saved his life, but he still didn't trust him.

"Are you going to tell me?"

Corey looked away from him and out the window.

"Since you don't want to answer that, let's talk about your friend," said Ellis. "He was last seen in Guava Hill. Since you reported that he was kidnapped, I believe that he was taken by Brutus. Now, why do you think Brutus would want him?"

"I don't know. Maybe he's a fan."

Ellis shook his head. "Don't get smart with me."

"I don't know what he'd want with Eddie," Corey bluffed. "It could've been a mistake for all I know."

"With Brutus's resources, I doubt it."

"Then your guess is as good as mine."

"I didn't start this job yesterday." Ellis paused as though he was trying to remain calm. "Son, you can act tough all you want. I've come across many guys like you in my career. But many of you young people act that way because you're scared. And I know that you're worried about your friend."

The man sounded sincere. But this was the same person who had it in for Eddie and wanted to lock him up. For all Corey knew, he was trying to trick him into saying something which would give him cause to arrest him.

"You have a choice, son," said Ellis. "Let me help you. But I need you to tell me what's going on. Or else we're never going to find your friend. Or, if and when we do, you're not going to like what's left of him."

Corey turned to Ellis. "How did you know where to find me?"

Ellis nodded. "The officers who assaulted you and shot the guy you were with…I've had my eye on them for some time. Do you think only Black people in the States complain about police brutality? I can tell you some officers down here get carried away too."

Corey leaned slightly toward him. "Carried away? The guy shoved his gun into my face, and all you can say is that he got *carried away*?"

"Listen, a colleague informed me that they responded to a call about two men possibly heading to Camp Turtle Grove. The caller gave your description. The only problem was that they didn't notify me since this is my case. And given their reputation, I had to get there as soon as possible. But from what I saw, I was too late."

Corey looked ahead and saw that they had driven closer to the squad car ahead.

"I don't expect those two to tell the truth." Ellis nodded ahead. "So, for the last time, why don't you tell me what happened back there."

A part of Corey told him that Ellis was telling the truth. But then again, police always protect each other. This could be a variation of *Good Cop-Bad Cop* designed to manipulate him into setting himself up. "Let me out."

Ellis shot a glance at Corey as though in disbelief. "What?"

"I'm not under arrest, so let me out."

"Don't be silly. How will you get back to Montego Bay on foot in the dark?"

"Let me worry about that. Anywhere away from you guys is all I need." Corey looked ahead and saw that they were approaching one of the small towns he had driven past earlier.

"Don't be daft. You couldn't be any safer while I'm with you."

Corey's attention drifted to the opposite side of the road where the sweet, soothing voice of reggae superstar Lila Iké caught his attention. The crowd in the small roadside parking lot where the music came from didn't even seem to notice them drive by, nor did the four men who were on his side of the road, sitting at a small, square table slamming dominos. Her voice wasn't distorted, even with the volume of the speakers on full blast.

Corey pursed his lips as he still felt the Glock pushing on his lips and teeth from earlier. The most the two murdering pigs driving ahead of them would get is a slap on the wrist. They'd come back for him to finish what they started.

They approached an intersection where the road curved to the left, and a green "Welcome to Anchovy" road sign stood on the opposite side. Once around the bend, the road straightened.

Corey gasped as a garbage truck suddenly pulled out from the Cool Oasis gas station up ahead on his side of the road and smashed the pigs' car diagonally. There was an explosion of crunched metal and shattered glass as the car was sent spinning so hard that it flipped. Corey couldn't see where the vehicle landed since the garbage truck obstructed his view.

Ellis slammed on the breaks as he grabbed the two-way radio and yelled. "Officers down, I repeat, officers down in Anchovy."

What the fuck did I just see? And why did Ellis sound as though this was an ambush and not an accident?

Corey's head was spinning from what he just witnessed, but Ellis's panicked response was even more unsettling. Corey scrambled to unlock his seatbelt and shoved the door open.

"Corey! Wait!" Ellis yelled.

Corey's mind had already been made up. He bolted in the opposite direction. Two corrupt pigs had ambushed him and Nesta. Now this? This was not a coincidence.

Ellis's yelling was cut off abruptly by a series of rapid gunfire.

Chapter 32

Anchovy, Saint James Parish

Adrenaline must've fueled him. Corey hadn't realized how far he'd run. He certainly wasn't going to be slowed down by the injuries in his back, especially since bullets were probably being fired in his direction. The crowd he saw earlier, maybe they hadn't all dispersed yet. He could hide among them.

Then it came to him, his burner phone. Were they able to track him on it? Eddie told him that his location would be untraceable, and he got his instructions from Brutus, or someone working for him.

A pickup truck with a few men heading toward him slowed down to a stop. Some of the men in the payload were looking above the roof as to what was going on. When they appeared to hear the gunfire, one of the passengers slammed his hands a few times on the roof as he yelled something, assumingly to the driver. The truck flew into a U-turn.

"Hold up, brotha!" Corey yelled as more gunfire erupted.

The passengers saw Corey and alerted the driver, who stopped. Corey sprinted toward the truck as the brothas yelled at him to hurry up. When he was a few feet away, he jumped onto the bumper. There were three brothas in the back and they grabbed Corey to pull him in, just as the truck took off in the opposite direction.

As he lay on his back, Corey held his head with one hand as he caught his breath.

"Yuh get shat?" asked one of the brothas.

"No, they didn't get me."

"Dem after yuh?"

"No." Corey shook his head. "I...I don't know who they are."

It was probably the smartest lie he could tell them. It was either that or risk being thrown out. Who could blame them for not wanting to become targets?

Eddie had mentioned something about a company called Essis being connected to Dwayne's murder. From what he just saw, that ambush was likely organized by a very powerful group. Which was more of a reason for him to get his ass out of there as fast and as far as he could.

"We're heading back to town. You want us to drop you off somewhere?" asked one of the brothas as Corey heard other sirens growing louder by the second.

"That's fine," said Corey. "Just get me there."

Chapter 33

Greenwood, Saint James Parish, Jamaica, 4:30PM

Eddie did a Google search on Plessis. All he found was a post office box in the United States Virgin Islands. That was odd. All this time he thought that Plessis was a large corporation with enough assets to hire thugs, and it turned out to be only a post office box? Eddie shook his head and sighed. These were signs that Plessis was an anonymous shell company—one that Weiss was likely linked to.

Eddie's burner rang. Before answering, he noticed that the call came through the encrypted app. He tapped the screen to answer.

"Hello?"

"Eddie?"

"Nancy?"

"Damn right it is. What the hell did you get yourself into?"

Eddie was about to answer but she cut him off.

"I showed up at my office this morning and some stranger follows me into the elevator, slips me an envelope—telling me that I need to use the app on the burner phone to call the number inside."

"Your timing couldn't be better."

"Is it true what I've been hearing?"

Oooh boy.

"Your parents and Corey's wife have been calling me nonstop to find out if I've heard anything from either of you. And who was that guy in the elevator?"

"Are you alone right now?"

"Yes, I am."

"Did you follow the instructions that came with the phone?"

"Yes, I'm calling you from somewhere that's not my home nor my office, nor am I standing close to any windows. Are you going to tell me what this is all about?"

"I can't tell you everything right now," Eddie answered, trying to remain calm.

"Don't give me that bullshit! You and Corey have us all worried sick. Is he with you right now? Because I want some answers."

"He's not with me, but he's fine." Eddie took a slow, deep sigh. "I...I got roped back in on the Pottinger case. I found an important witness, was sort of kidnapped by the drug lord, Brutus, who, as it turns out, is the witness's uncle, escaped an attack by the army and some hired assassins. Now, I'm talking to you from a high-tech burner phone. That pretty much sums it up."

There was silence on the other end until it was broken with a heavy sigh. "Jesus Christ, Eddie! Do you have a death wish?"

"I know that it's a lot to absorb," Eddie said. "The man who delivered the phone works for Brutus."

"You made friends with a don?"

"I wouldn't go *that* far."

"Will I become a target because of you?"

"You're fine."

"For Christ's sake, from what I've heard, this guy chops his enemies up into pieces."

"Relax, no one's getting chopped up today." Eddie took a deep breath to calm himself. "You've probably heard about the attack on Guava Hill."

"You mean the *Massacre* of Guava Hill. That's what they're calling it. It's all over the news."

"You weren't getting the whole story."

"What do you mean?"

"The attack had nothing to do with capturing Brutus. The real targets were me and the witness."

"Why would the army want to capture you? And *who* is this witness you keep talking about?"

"Someone who may be able to identify Dwayne Pottinger's killer. He hired people who were able to convince the government to launch such a timely attack."

"Didn't you go to the police?"

"I wish I could, except I kind of burned that bridge a while back."

"Need I ask how?"

"It's a long story."

"Don't tell me this has something to do with your aliens and Jedi councils."

"It's more complicated than that. This is why I'm speaking to you and why you got those instructions because your home and office may be bugged."

"Who'd want to bug my home and office?"

"Have you ever heard of a company called Plessis?"

"No, why?"

"This company's somehow connected to the killer, who we believe is a man named Vincent Lee Weiss. He's the VP of PennSteel which is based in Pittsburgh."

"Why do you need to know this?"

"I think the key to solving Dwayne Pottinger's murder is to find out as much as we can about Plessis. I think it may be a shell company with Weiss as an anonymous owner. From what I've learned so far, Dwayne may have overheard a conversation where Weiss hinted that he may be the owner. Weiss must've found out and had him killed because his anonymity was threatened."

"And you have proof of this?"

"I just stumbled across a recording Dwayne made. But it doesn't reveal anything about what Plessis is. And from what I witnessed before I escaped Guava Hill, Weiss, or the people he hired, have a powerful influence over the government—and no doubt the police. This is why I can't simply walk into any precinct. I really need your help."

"And I really want to say that I can help you, but I don't know where to begin," said Bevins. "I've heard of police corruption. But gaining control over the Jamaican government? That's a stretch."

"Use your contacts. Don't you still have friends in the US government?" Surely, she would. Her late husband was the Governor of New Hampshire.

"Those were my husband's friends. I wasn't that close to

them."

"I don't know who else we can turn to." Eddie was startled by the sound of a speeding car. The thought that Weiss's men had found him came to mind, and he was about to bolt, when he saw that it was someone just showing off. He relaxed and his breathing returned to normal. "The people who are after us, I've seen what they're capable of. Are you sure there isn't someone you know who could help?"

Bevins sighed. "All right. I'll make some calls. I can't make any promises, but I'll do my best."

"I know you will."

"Just find somewhere safe where you can lay low. I can reach you at this number, right?"

"Yes, but I don't always have the phone turned on. Let me text you Corey's number, just in case." Eddie sent her the number. "Do you have it?"

"Got it."

"All right, I have to let you go," said Eddie. "And remember to watch your back. It's not farfetched to think that someone may be following you."

"Don't worry," said Nancy. "I still have Darwin."

That's right. Darwin's her Rottweiler.

Chapter 34

Law Office of Owen Hines, Rodney Street, Falmouth, Trelawny Parish

The black SUV was in sight once again. Eddie watched as it bobbed and weaved around cars until it was right behind them. It then sped up and rammed them, throwing their car forward.

Eddie woke up as the seatbelt gripped him across his chest as Candace slammed on the brakes.

"You okay?"

Eddie recognized Candace's voice, but he was too deeply hyperventilating to respond.

"Eddie?" yelled Candace.

Snapped out of his half-dreamy state, he turned to look at her. Then he checked out back.

No black SUV in sight. God, it was just a bad dream. He then closed his eyes as he rested a hand on his forehead. He looked in front and saw Amancia's grey SUV roughly three car lengths ahead. Thank goodness Candace was driving instead, seeing how quickly how matters could've gone sideways had he been behind the wheel.

"You all right?"

Eddie opened his eyes to see her looking at him as she leaned forward and waved, as though to catch his attention. She stopped when she saw that he was awake.

"I'm good," said Eddie.

"Sorry about that."

"No worries."

He glanced into the outer rearview mirror. How could he have gotten so sloppy over the day and not stayed in surveillance mode.

Just because their would-be killers missed their opportunity this morning didn't mean that they wouldn't have caught up to them.

He rubbed his left eye which began to itch. "How long was I out for?"

"I'd say around ten or twelve minutes. You passed out right after we left the office supply store." She referred to where they went after they left with Amancia from her home. "Why did you carry Amancia's computer inside?"

"I'll tell you later. By the way, were you able to reach your uncle to tell him about Plessis?"

"He's not answering." She suddenly braked to dodge a pothole. The left front tire caught the edge of it.

Eddie sucked his teeth. "What is it with these potholes?"

"Don't fret," said Candace. "They'll be gone right before the next election."

Candace sped up behind Amancia to shorten the distance to two car lengths. A few kilometers later the number of houses increased. There was a lot more shade, as the area was significantly denser with trees. A few kilometers after that and they reached the end of the road, where both vehicles turned into a single-lane driveway.

To Eddie's left was a stone wall, which separated them from the property next to them. Up ahead and to his right was a one-story residential building. It had a white exterior with a reddish-brown clay-shingled gable roof. Separating it from the street was roughly two hundred square meters of well-manicured lawn with a single palm tree, whose leaves hung above the clay-shingled roof. Lining the road was a six-and-a-half-foot-tall wrought-iron fence bordered by an evergreen hedge of the same height. The driveway wrapped around the back where there was a small parking area that could hold no more than four cars. There were already two, leaving enough space for them and Amancia.

Eddie had only opened his door halfway when the humidity hit him head on. He closed his door just as Candace got out. Amancia took a bit longer to climb from the SUV, not being as young and agile as he and Candace.

As he waited for Amancia to join them, Eddie noticed a wall at the back of the lot, with a thick set of caper hedges behind it that had grown to around eight feet, blocking all view to the house behind them. Eddie turned to Amancia as she joined them. They then walked to the side-door entrance, which was at the top of a small set of stairs. The door was unlocked and Amancia let herself in. There were two audible beeps, which sounded like it was part of an alarm system. Eddie was then greeted with a cool blast of air.

Eddie was surprised at how well Amancia had convinced Owen Hines's secretary to squeeze her in for one more appointment that evening. The plump, short, salt-and-pepper-haired woman in a sleeveless dress glanced up from behind her flat-screen monitor on her desk and smiled. "Good evening. You must be Amancia Pottinger."

"It is I."

"I'm Dominique, we spoke earlier," she said as she got up, standing at around four-and-a-half-feet. She gestured to the sofa adjacent her desk, between it and the front door. She then paused as she looked at Candace. "We've met before, haven't we?"

"We did, I'm Candace," she answered. "I was here with Dwayne."

Dominique's face lit up. "Ah, now I remember." She turned to Eddie.

"I'm just a friend," said Eddie. "You know, for moral support."

Dominique nodded. "I understand. Just give Mister Hines a few moments." She then grabbed a file folder from the corner of her desk and left.

Her sandaled feet clapped loudly across the tiles as she walked around a corner and disappeared down an adjacent hallway. The clapping stopped, to be replaced by a metal file drawer sliding open along its track.

While Dominique was in the back, Eddie's attention turned to his left toward the front door, where he saw the alarm-system control panel. It was a regular password activated button-control alarm.

He looked to the wall ahead. It had several photographs of the same person, whom Eddie assumed to be Hines, with several others. Two of them that stood out were the ones where he posed with the former Prime Minister, Portia Simpson-Miller. There was another with him and former President Barack Obama.

The cabinet door in the back slid shut, followed by Dominique's footsteps moments before she reentered the foyer. Leaning toward the ground near the computer tower at the foot of her desk, she appeared to press a button moments before Eddie heard the internal fan die down. She grabbed her handbag by its strap from the back of the chair where it hung.

"It was nice meeting you," said Dominique. "Mister Hines won't be much longer. He had a busy morning in court this morning and has been in meetings for most of the afternoon."

They all said their goodbyes as Dominique exited through the same door which they had entered. Her car must be one of the two that were parked in back before they arrived.

No sooner had the side door closed, Eddie turned to the sound of footsteps approaching from behind the closed door to Hines's office. The door opened inward with a slight creak, and a well-groomed, bearded man of around five ten, stepped through, wearing a beige golf shirt that highlighted well-defined arms and broad shoulders. He wore long pants and, instead of sandals, he wore expensive-looking leather dress shoes that Eddie wouldn't be surprised to learn were purchased or ordered from overseas.

Hines extended a hand as Amancia was the first to stand. "Good evening, Ms. Pottinger. I'm sorry for making you wait."

"That's fine. I'm just glad that you made room for me at the last minute." She turned to Candace and then to Eddie. "I brought along some friends—Dwayne's friends actually."

Eddie noticed Hines's eyebrows raise as he laid eyes on Candace. "Yes, Ms. Coke's a client of mine."

Candace grabbed his hand. "Hello."

"I wasn't expecting you."

"It's a long story."

Hines then turned to Eddie, who introduced himself.

Eddie scanned Hines's face. He appeared to be puzzled, as though he was expecting a surprise. He then gestured toward his office.

"Go in, have a seat."

"Actually," said Eddie. "May I use your restroom?"

"Sure. You passed it on your way in." Hines pointed toward where they had entered.

Eddie thanked him and headed there.

Five minutes later he walked into Hines's office. Judging from the small talk that was going on between them, Eddie assumed they hadn't begun the meeting without him.

"We know you've had a long day," said Amancia. "So we don't want to take up too much of your time."

There were only two mahogany high-back chairs to accommodate them, so Hines pointed to one against the wall while nodding to Eddie. "You can bring that extra chair over."

Once they were all seated, Hines leaned back in his executive high-backed leather office chair while he grabbed a pen, tapping it on the edge of the desk. "Now, what brings you here?"

It was agreed that it would be best that Amancia did all the talking. "It's actually about my nephew, Dwayne."

"Yes, I heard," said Hines. "You have my deepest sympathy. That was a horrible thing those people did to him."

Amancia nodded. "Thank you. I have something to show you that I'd like to discuss."

Hines gripped his pen and leaned forward with his forearms on the desk, looking anxious. "I'm listening."

She removed the laptop from her handbag and turned it on. "Just give me a minute."

Eddie handed her the flash drive just as the monitor turned on. She then turned to Eddie. "That's why I brought along Dwayne's friends because I don't know much about how these machines work."

Eddie got the video app up and running and fast-forwarded it to the part where Dwayne was in the car with Weiss. He then spun the laptop around for Hines and waited to see his reaction. Within moments, his body language spoke for itself: he let go of his pen as he sat back in his seat, arms crossed with one hand holding his chin. It was though he disapproved of what Dwayne had done. When Eddie recognized the moment where Weiss was carrying Dwayne out of his car, he slammed the laptop shut.

Amancia almost jumped in her seat. "What's wrong?"

Hines rolled his chair back and stood while pointing. "How'd you get this?"

Amancia gestured to the flash drive. "I received this gadget in the mail today."

"From whom?" He then looked at Eddie and Candace. "Did you have anything to do with this? Did you watch this video too?"

"What do you know about this video?" asked Eddie.

Hines looked away, cupping both hands over his mouth, then turning back. "I'm asking you a question. How much of this did you watch?"

"The whole thing."

Hines winced and then held onto his head as he shook it.

"Did you show this to anyone else? Did you make copies?"

Something was up. It was obvious that something on or about the video spooked him. "You didn't even watch the whole video, but you're concerned about what's on it," said Eddie. "Why's that?"

Hines sighed as he held his head. It was as though he was trying to avoid an outburst. "If you want my advice, forget what you saw and don't mention it to anyone."

"Even the police?" said Amancia. "What we just showed you could be a clue to why Dwayne was killed."

Hines chuckled as he sat back down.

"What's so funny?" asked Eddie.

"Listen," said Hines. "Dwayne was killed because he showed up at the wrong place wearing the wrong outfit."

"Why are you bringing that up?" Eddie could see that Hines was hiding something.

Hines pinched the bridge of his nose as he shook his head. "Why are you showing me this?"

"Because I don't know what to do with it," said Amancia. "I know that it's Dwayne on this video, but I didn't know about this. I only found out that the man in this video did the same to Candace a year before."

"We think that this guy, Weiss, reneged on the settlement," said Eddie.

"Candace," sighed Hines. "You're not supposed to divulge the details of your settlement with anyone. I told you that."

"He's trying to kill me."

Hines was silent. But Eddie failed to notice any emotional response. Not a gasp, nor a follow-up question. Was he aware of all of this?

"The people who killed Dwayne also killed another friend of mine," she continued. "I've been hiding with my Uncle Brutus. Then the killers came and nearly got me. I've been on the run ever since because of what's on that video." She nodded toward Eddie. "They're after him too because he's close to figuring out what's going on."

Hines let his head fall backward and he was staring at the ceiling. He then looked at them with a sigh. "Are you familiar with the term, *poisoned gift*?"

"Yeah," said Eddie. "It's an item one receives that could get its recipient into serious trouble the moment they are aware of its contents."

"Exactly. This is why I'm telling you to let this go."

"I don't think you weren't paying attention to the part where Candace told you that people are trying to kill us," said Eddie. "This video could give us leverage."

"Lord, you have no idea what you've gotten yourself into."

"Try us."

Hines snatched the flash drive from the laptop. Eddie reflexively went to grab his hand, and Candace cried out as she also lunged across the table toward Hines. However, the attorney had already snatched his hand away too fast for Eddie and Candace.

"What are you doing?"

"Trying to keep you out of trouble." He dropped the drive on the ground and stomped on it.

Candace rushed around the desk and dove to the floor. "What have you done?"

"A favor."

"Damn you." Candace sprung at Hines like a wildcat.

"Candace. No!" Eddie bolted around the desk and wrapped his arms around Candace's waist and pulled her off, then turned around, putting himself between Hines and Candace as she continued to kick and scream.

"Get your damn hands off of me," she screamed. "Don't touch me. I always told you not to touch me."

He immediately released her.

"I can't believe that Dwayne trusted you." A tear came to her eye. "I can't believe that *I* trusted you." She stormed out of the office.

Amancia got up and ran after her. "Candace, wait."

Eddie breathed deeply, then turned to Hines. "You just destroyed evidence that points to suspects in Dwayne's murder."

Hines stared at him without answering.

"They got to you, didn't they? What do they have on you? Or did they threaten you and your family?"

Hines pointed toward the door. "You need to go."

Eddie locked eyes with Hines. The stare was a way of letting him know that this wasn't over. Sure, he could've said it. But somehow, he felt that Hines would remember this hard stare more than simple words.

"Did you hear what I said?" said Hines.

It was time to retreat. Nothing good would come from staying here any longer. Eddie turned to walk away, and when he reached the doorway, he heard Hines.

"You're just like Dwayne, you know."

Eddie stopped and turned around.

"Both of you have a passion for justice, no matter the costs. Look where it got him. The same is waiting for you if you don't let this go."

Eddie left without closing the door to Hines's office. When he got outside, he saw Amancia consoling Candace, who was still visibly upset. It was almost nightfall, and a streetlamp just below the gutter by the roof turned on.

"What do we do now?" asked Amancia.

"I have an idea," Eddie answered.

"What can we do?" yelled Candace. "That man destroyed the evidence we needed to go after the men who are trying to kill us."

"That's what he thinks." Eddie reached into his pants pocket and took out a flash drive, holding it up for them to see before turning to Amancia. "I made a copy. That's why I went inside the office store with your computer."

"What are you going to do with that?" Amancia asked. "Go to the press?"

"We need something more solid," Eddie answered. "And I don't want to make any moves until I at least hear back from my contact."

"But where are you going to go now?" asked Amancia.

"For now, you're better off not knowing." He gave a nod to Candace to get in their car. He was about to take to the driver's seat when Amancia called out to them.

"You sure there's nothing else I can get you?"

Eddie turned around. "You've been more than helpful."

"Come back to my place," said Amancia. "You both need somewhere safe to stay."

"That might not be the best idea right now." Eddie walked up to her. "I don't want you to get any more involved in what we're in. You'll notice that there's no copy of that video on your computer."

"But where are you going to sleep? Let me call someone, you shouldn't be running around like this."

Eddie looked at Candace, hoping that she would say something, but didn't. "I don't think that would be a good idea. But now that you brought it up, do you have a friend *you* can stay with for a few days?"

Amancia gasped. "Why?"

Candace jumped in. "We don't want to leave anything to chance. Just to be on the safe side."

"We're sorry," said Eddie. "We never meant for any of this to happen. I hope you understand. Promise me you'll take my advice."

Eddie then walked back toward his car where he sat on the driver's side. Candace had just shut her door when he heard Amancia call out from behind him.

"Hold on."

Eddie turned as he saw her reach into her handbag as though

she was searching for something. She then walked up to Eddie's window.

"I know it's not much." Amancia handed Eddie several bills. "It should at least get you two nights at a motel somewhere."

Eddie stared at the cash without saying a word. He already felt bad for getting Amancia involved. Now she was offering him cash. "I...I don't—"

Amancia reached inside, grabbed his closest wrist, and shoved the bills in his hand, then wrapped her fingers on top of his tightly. "Take it and don't argue. Lord knows I won't sleep knowing that I didn't do everything I could to help."

After Amancia released his hand, Eddie thanked her and shoved the bills in his pocket.

They both left the driveway and headed opposite directions. There was a cross street where Rodney Street ended. Eddie turned onto it, then did a U-turn. He drove back and stopped before Rodney Street where he watched the driveway entrance to Hines's office.

"What are we doing here?"

"I want to keep an eye on Hines."

"Why? That man was a waste of our time."

"Not really."

There was a brief pause. "Are you planning on following him?"

"No, I'm just waiting for him to leave."

"To leave? What for?"

"I didn't come here for nothing," said Eddie just as Hines's car pulled onto the street and drove off in the opposite direction. He waited for the taillights to vanish out of sight before he started the engine.

"Are you going to tell me what you're planning to do?"

"I needed Amancia to set up the meeting. I knew that next to you, she was the only one Hines would've likely made an exception for. And he took the bait."

"Bait? Why didn't you let *me* make the appointment?"

"Lawyers run a business. And businesses thrive on getting new clients. Because of that, I figured that Amancia would've been stronger bait that he would less likely be able to pass up."

"And it was a waste of time."

"Not quite," said Eddie. "I didn't tell you this before, but I had a feeling that Hines wouldn't help us."

Candace's eyes widened and her head tilted as she looked at Eddie. "What made you think that?"

"Back at Amancia's place when I watched Dwayne's video I noticed that there were gaps—as though the recording accidentally paused, then Dwayne restarted it. I also didn't clearly hear Dwayne say no to Weiss before he attempted to rape him. That could've seriously weakened his rape allegation had it gone to court, and Hines would've known that."

"I don't understand," said Candace. "If Hines knew that the evidence was weak, why did he represent us? Unless he already knew something about Plessis."

Eddie grinned. "You're close. I doubt that he would've known about Plessis. However, let's say that after watching the video, he researched Plessis, discovered what I did, and reached a similar conclusion. He'd know with that kind of leverage he could get Weiss to cough up the sums that he did."

Candace let her head fall onto the headrest while she sighed. "Hines took extra money for himself. He took advantage of me and Dwayne. No wonder he was so evasive. I can't believe I was so dumb not to have seen this."

"You're not dumb, Candace. And I wouldn't jump the gun that Hines pocketed extra cash either because we don't have proof of it. Which brings us to why I'm waiting here for him to leave his office."

"Why?"

"You remember when I left to go to the bathroom?"

Candace narrowed her eyes as she turned to Eddie. "Uhhh... yeah..."

Eddie smirked. "I didn't have to go. I just wanted Hines to think that so that I could case the building."

"And you didn't tell me this before?"

"From what I read about Hines, he's been practicing law for over thirty years. I didn't want to take a chance that he'd suspect that you or Amancia weren't being completely transparent with him. So, keeping both of you in the dark allowed you to put on a convincing show."

Candace sighed and held her head in her hand. "I'm sorry, but I have to ask. Have you *ever* broken into an office or a house before? No offence, but you don't look like someone who would even steal mangoes from someone's tree."

Eddie cocked his head from side to side. "We all have to start sometime."

"Oh, Lord. Are you serious?" Candace shook her head. "Didn't you notice that there's an alarm system?"

"I have the code."

There was a moment's pause as Candace shook her head in disbelief. "How?"

Eddie got out of the car. "Come, I'll show you."

Chapter 35

Albion Community, Montego Bay

"We know they were here." The sista got down on one knee, grabbed Shirley by her hair, lifted her head off the floor, then spoke directly into her ear. "Where did they go?"

The woman loosened the gag that was tied around Shirley's mouth. She coughed up blood and a tooth and spat it out on the floor. Tears mixed with blood poured down her face as the sista's knee weighed down on her lower spine.

"I didn't hear you," said the sista as she pulled harder on Shirley's hair while applying more pressure with her knee. "Where did Eddie and Candace go?"

Charlene's gagged scream was heard behind them.

"Do you hear your friend?" asked the sista. "Why are you letting her suffer?" She then looked over her shoulder at Charlene, who was sitting on the floor with her hands and feet tied. Both of her eyes were swollen, one of them even shut amid dark discolorations. Her partner stood beside her, calm as usual, massaging his knuckles.

"Take her into the bathroom and run some scalding hot water over her face until she talks. I don't care if her skin peels off."

The brotha grabbed Charlene by her foot bindings and dragged her across the floor. She kicked and screamed and tried to flail herself out of his grip, to no avail.

Shirley began wailing, but the woman grabbed her head with both hands and slammed it onto the floor.

"What did I tell you about screaming? Huh?"

The sound of heavy water running was heard, mixed with gagged screams.

"You hear that?" asked the sista. "You're going to be next unless you answer my question."

There were some muffles under the gag.

"What was that?"

There was a long pause, then Shirley said something under the gag.

The woman loosened it. "Say that again."

There was some heavy breathing and then a hard swallow. "Mi wi tell yuh. Just nuh hurt Charlene. Please, mi a beg yuh."

"Aah, a beg." The sista then turned toward the hallway and yelled, "She's going to talk."

The water stopped running a few seconds later.

Shirley kept breathing hard.

The woman grabbed Shirley's shoulder and flipped her onto her back. "Talk."

Shirley swallowed hard again. "They...they talk about seeing one of Dwayne's people."

"Where?"

"Greenwood, but I don't know the address. That's all I know. Please, Miss."

"Why did they say they were going there?"

Shirley began to choke, and she rolled over onto her side and coughed up more blood. Those punches to the stomach the brotha gave her earlier were taking their toll. "They...they said they were after the envelope we mailed."

"An envelope? What was in it?"

"I don't know. Dwayne left it with us and tell us to drop it in the mailbox if anything bad happened to him. I swear I'm telling you the truth."

That crossdressing bastard was smart. He wasn't going to carry his secret to the grave. The sista patted Shirley on the shoulder. "I believe you."

The sista then yelled to her partner. "We got what we need."

She stood, took out her mobile, and tapped a few digits then hit the green phone icon. "I need an address in Greenwood. Focus on any of Dwayne Pottinger's relatives or close friends."

She hung up just as her partner dragged Charlene back into

the room and dropped her. The left side of her face was badly scalded, a white patch on her right cheek marking the spot where the water hit.

"Charlene," Shirley cried. "Charlene, please answer me."

The sista looked at Charlene, whose eyes were both swollen shut. "Your friend should've spoken sooner, it would've saved you a bath."

The sista then grabbed her HK VP9 and pointed it at Charlene's head while she looked at Shirley. "But I'm glad that you're still alive because I want to watch you watch your friend die."

There was a bang as she squeezed the trigger. The body hit the floor as she watched the terror in Shirley's frozen eyes. It made it easier for the sista to get a clean shot right between them.

Chapter 36

Law office of Owen Hines, Falmouth, Trelawny Parish

The first sign that Hines's office was a potential target for burglary was that the front and back were obscured with decorative hedges. These helped with the esthetics of the property, but when ornamental trees are too tall it presents a problem. A burglar could kick down the front door or remove it with the correct equipment—all while being unseen.

Eddie did not plan on kicking down any doors, nor did he have the tools to remove them. Instead, he'd left the bathroom window unlocked while he was there earlier.

Furthermore, Eddie had not spotted any closed-circuit video cameras. The wrought-iron gate was easy for him and Candace to scale. It was also dark out, which made it easy for them to gain access to the property unseen.

The bathroom window, which faced the lot, was slightly out of reach for him. Corey would've had an easier time grabbing the ledge than Eddie did, which is why he needed Candace's help.

"Lucky for us, Hines, being the type of person who relies on technology to protect his office, neglected the simple things any thief could exploit."

Candace looked up to the window. "Like not putting a grill on the window."

"There's that," said Eddie as he estimated its height to be at least nine feet above the ground. "Not only is Hines careless, but he's also cheap."

Eddie pointed to the window. "If you're wondering, I unlocked it earlier. I can jump and grab the edge, but I'll need you to give me a boost."

"I'm not lifting you."

"I'm not asking you to lift me, just hold me long enough so that I can pull myself in."

"Wouldn't it be easier to let me go instead?"

"So you want me to lift you?"

"Why not?"

"Even though you're against anyone touching you."

"Get down and I'll climb onto your back."

"You can lift your own bodyweight?"

"That's why you'll lift me."

"Which would involve me touching you."

Candace sighed, then lined herself under the window with her back to the wall while cupping her hands. "Make it quick."

Eddie stood under the window while looking up at it. He then lifted one leg into her cupped hands, then jumped up while she boosted him. It was clumsily done, but he managed to grab the edge of the windowsill.

"Some help would be good about now," panted Eddie while his legs dangled. He felt Candace lifting him from under his feet. She wasn't physically strong enough to lift his weight, and Eddie had to slide his fingers under the windowpane quickly to get a better grip or else he'd fall. His feet were no longer being held, but instead, he felt himself standing.

"I can't hold on much longer," said Candace.

Eddie then realized that he must be standing on her shoulders because those extra three seconds, along with the slight boost, was all he needed to quickly push the window up and then pull himself through. Eventually he no longer felt Candace's hands on his feet as he clumsily fell forward into the bathroom, landing and then rolling onto his back. He felt the coldness of the tiles under his hands.

"Eddie. Yuh dead?" came Candace's loud whisper from outside. Of course, it was a local figure of speech.

He struggled to calm his breathing as he got up and leaned slightly out the window. "I'm good. Go meet me at the side."

Eddie took out the burner and tapped the flashlight app to turn it on. He already knew where the motion sensors were, and they weren't anywhere near the bathroom nor in the hall leading to it, but there was one in the foyer where he and the others waited on Hines earlier. He walked to the alarm panel near the front door, flipped it open, and dialed the numbers he had memorized. There was a beep, followed by the red light switching to green, indicating the alarm was deactivated.

He then walked to the side entrance and let Candace in.

"You never told me how you found out what the alarm code was," said Candace from behind as she followed him to Hines's office. He went to Dominique's desk, picked up the desk lamp and shone the flashlight underneath. Stuck to the bottom of it was a yellow *Post-It* note with two sets of numbers.

"It's not unusual for someone who changes passwords or other codes often to write them down somewhere within reach. Just in case they forget."

"You sure you haven't done this before?"

"One of my books had a burglary scene," said Eddie. "While researching it, I had a chance to consult with a reformed burglar who taught me a thing or two."

He replaced the lamp exactly as he'd found it and walked down the adjacent hall to the room he heard Dominique go into earlier. As expected, there was a row of file cabinets that were just below shoulder height.

Eddie shone his flashlight on the labels of the cabinets until he came to the letter P. "We should consider ourselves lucky that Hines hasn't digitized all his files."

He handed the burner to Candace while he pulled open the drawer and fingered through the files. He found Dwayne's, took it out, and placed it on top of the file cabinet.

"One thing that stuck from what you told me earlier was that both you and Dwayne left your settlement money in Hines's business account."

"Of course, I don't want anyone getting suspicious that I have all that money."

Eddie took his burner and began snapping pictures of each document. He paused as he came to a copy of a check. "What's this?"

Candace leaned in to look. "What's what?"

Eddie held up the document. "This is a check that's written out to Hines's office. It's not directly from Weiss, but from…what do you know…it's Plessis Marketing Inc. With Weiss's signature on it."

He pointed to a corner of the check. "The bank account is based in the US Virgin Islands, the same location this so-called company is based."

"This check is for two hundred and seven thousand US. That's seven thousand more than it was supposed to be," said Candace as she pointed to the amount.

"It's normal that Weiss agreed to pay your legal fees in addition to paying you off in order to release him from any liability," said Eddie. "While we're here, go get your file."

While Candace searched the file cabinets for the letter C, Eddie flipped through two more pages and paused when he stopped at one which outlined the fees. "Here's Hines's rates. You can see that he charges twenty-five thousand Jamaican dollars per hour. He detailed every expense to justify the seven thousand US he charged Weiss."

Candace handed her file folder to Eddie, who placed it to the side on top of the cabinet. He snapped photos of the last set of Dwayne's documents before moving onto the ones in Candace's file folder. He did not see anything extraordinary except a copy of the same check he saw earlier.

When he was done, he was about to tap the upload icon to send them to Bevins via the encrypted app but paused to think.

"What's wrong?" asked Candace.

Eddie lowered the phone. "I was thinking of forwarding these documents to a friend. But I don't think that's a good idea."

"I thought that you'd send them to the police."

"After what we went through, they're the last people I'd send these files to," said Eddie. "We've just broken into a lawyer's office. A certain detective I've been trying to avoid will certainly use this as an excuse to lock us up. I doubt that he'll even pay attention to what we have to say about the documents."

"Do you think that this detective is working for Weiss?"

"If he isn't, then I wouldn't be surprised that at least one of his colleagues is," said Eddie. "If we go to prison, we'll be dead within twenty-four hours."

"What can your friend do?"

"She may be able to do something," said Eddie. "But she's overseas. What worries me is that these documents were obtained illegally. She may get into trouble if she were to show them to the proper authorities."

Eddie handed Candace back her folder while he returned Dwayne's to its drawer in the exact same spot where he took it. Once Candace returned her file to its drawer and closed it, they left the storage room.

After Eddie reset the alarm, they exited through the side door and were back to their car within minutes.

As he closed the car door, he paused to think.

Candace turned to Eddie. "I'd feel a lot more comfortable if we were moving rather than sitting here in the dark."

Eddie was too lost in thought to notice Candace trying to get his attention, until she slapped his forearm.

"What's wrong?" she asked.

"Yesterday, you said that you didn't know why Weiss would pay you off then try to kill you."

"And?"

Eddie placed the burner in the center tray, started the car, and made a U-turn, following the directions on the phone's GPS. "On Dwayne's video, Weiss was talking to someone about payments being made to Plessis. He was even freaked when the other guy suggested making checks out in his name instead of the company."

"Is Weiss married?"

"I don't know."

"If so, he probably wouldn't want his wife asking why he withdrew two hundred thousand dollars."

"That's true, but that's not what I was thinking." Eddie made a right turn at the intersection. "Let's say that Weiss is using Plessis to hide dirty money. Then whomever he got the money from could also be involved with whatever criminal activity he's involved in."

"Any guesses who his business partner is?" asked Candace.

Eddie exhaled. "None at the moment. Did you ever overhear your uncle talking about who's after you?"

"No, he was discreet."

"Did you ask?"

"Yes, but he didn't want to say." Candace looked out her window. "He said that it was for my own good."

"I hope he knows what he's doing."

Candace turned to Eddie. "Do you think that Weiss's business partner found out about us, didn't like the idea of the out-of-court settlement, and hired people to kill me and Dwayne?"

"And Wesley," said Eddie. "It's possible."

"But they attacked my uncle to get to me," said Candace. "Anyone here can tell you that's suicide."

"Which comes back to my theory that someone just as powerful, or even more powerful than your uncle is behind this," said Eddie as he and Candace were jostled when they bounced over a pothole.

"Did you spot any other names in the files we looked at back at Hines's office?"

"Not that I can remember. That's why I took pictures so that I could study them later." Eddie swerved to avoid a stray dog that appeared out of nowhere on the side of the road. "What is it with these stray dogs? They're always running in front of me."

"There must be something about you," said Candace. "Because I rarely see them."

"Or you've seen them so often that you barely notice them." Eddie glanced at Candace. "Call your uncle."

Candance tilted her head as she turned to him. "What for?"

"Because he has connections."

"He won't be able to do much now. Have you forgotten that he's also on the run?"

"Trust me. Just do it."

Candace shrugged her shoulders and grabbed the burner, as Eddie glimpsed her typing a message through the encrypted app.

"It's sent."

Not even ten seconds went by before the burner rang.

Candace checked the call display before answering. "Yes?"

Eddie glanced at Candace as he heard what sounded like Brutus's henchman's voice.

"I don't know, maybe you should talk to him," said Candace.

"What the hell are you doing?" The anger-fueled response blasted through the car's speaker via its Bluetooth connection. "You trying to get yourself killed?"

"Getting the answers that Brutus wants."

"You're supposed to be laying low, not gallivanting all over the place."

"I want to speak to Brutus."

"He can't talk to you."

"Then I guess he's not interested in knowing what I found out."

Eddie pressed the *Disconnect* button on the steering wheel to hang up.

Candace's jaw dropped. "Why did you do that?"

Eddie glanced at her briefly with a smirk. "Three…two…one…"

The phone rang, it was a blocked number. Candace tapped the phone icon on the screen.

"Barrow," came a growl. It was unmistakably Brutus.

"Speaking."

"Candace, you there?"

"I am," she replied.

"What are you doing in Falmouth?"

Eddie instinctively looked around him as though he were being watched.

"By the way," said Brutus. "I have the means to track your whereabouts. So, I'll ask you again. What the hell are you doing in Falmouth."

"We just left Owen Hines's office."

"What were you doing there?"

"Getting some answers. Have you ever heard of a company called Plessis?"

"No, who are they?"

"I believe it's a shell company owned by Vincent Lee Weiss—the man who attacked Candace. I also believe that he's using it for criminal activities."

Eddie then told him about the USB flash drive and the video.

"Dwayne was going to blackmail him?"

"We don't think so," answered Candace. "It's possible he kept it just in case Weiss didn't honor the settlement."

Eddie braked as the driver of the car ahead switched on their turn signal. "I don't think he realized it at the time, but I believe the real reason why he was killed is because Weiss suspected that Dwayne overheard him mention Plessis. It would explain why Candace and Wesley became targets because they're close to Dwayne."

"How are you so sure about this?"

"It's a hunch."

"And how is your hunch going to change anything?"

"*You* were the one who interrogated me because *you* thought that I knew something that could help you. Candace and I broke into Hines's office to get you this info."

"Bwoy, you've got balls speaking to me with that tone."

Shit! I just lost my cool with someone capable of ordering a hit on me. Eddie closed his eyes, then exhaled. "Listen. If you want to stop Weiss, then you need to find out everything you can about Plessis and whom they're doing business with."

There was a short pause on the other end. "Is that all?"

"It's not much, but it's a start."

There was another pause, one that was longer than the previous one. "Good. You'll receive an address in a few minutes. Go there and don't move until I tell you it's safe."

Eddie let his head fall back into the headrest as he sighed with relief.

"Weren't all those places raided already?" asked Eddie. "We barely got out of the last one alive."

"Not this place," said Brutus. "Do as I say."

"Okay, but I need a favor."

"What's that?"

"Do you have any contacts, like a lawyer or a police officer you could put me in touch with?"

Eddie heard a click.

"Hello?"

"Don't tell me that you really expected him to share that info with you," said Candace.

"It was worth a try," Eddie answered. "The more people we can get on our side the better."

The phone buzzed in Candace's hand. It was Brutus's text with the address. She gave Eddie directions.

Eddie turned to Candace. "Call this number."

Candace dialed as Eddie called out the number. They heard four rings through the speakers before the call was answered.

"Eddie?" It was Bevins.

"I'm here."

"Is everything all right?"

"We're fine. Did you find out anything?"

"I made some calls. But I have to be honest with you, I'm not too optimistic."

I can't tell her this. Oh, what the hell. "Candace and I stumbled onto some documents. They're related to a meeting she and Dwayne Pottinger had with their lawyer."

"What documents?"

"The name Plessis came up again. This time it was on a check, signed by Weiss."

"A check? What kind of documents are these?"

"I'd rather not say."

"I'm not going to ask you how you obtained a check that wasn't made out to either yourself, Candace, or to Dwayne Pottinger. But you should know that any document could only be used as evidence on the condition that it was obtained legally."

"Actually," said Candace. "The laws here in Jamaica are different. Any document could be used as evidence no matter how it were obtained. Many foreigners don't know that."

"Is this Candace?" asked Bevins.

"Yes, it is."

"I'm Nancy Bevins, Eddie's agent and friend. It's nice to finally talk to you. I just wish that it was under better circumstances."

"Likewise," said Candace.

"If I understood you correctly, why don't you turn over those documents to the police?"

"Uh...I was already arrested for lewd conduct and accused of harassing an Olympian. Not to mention that people are saying that I was seen with Brutus," said Eddie. "I don't think that showing up at a police station with documents that were not so legally obtained is such a good idea."

"What are you doing now?" asked Bevins.

"We're on our way to another safehouse," said Eddie.

"A safehouse?" said Bevins. "Let me guess, Candace's uncle set you up with this, right."

"He's given us instructions," said Eddie. "It's our best option for now."

There was a sigh on the other end. "God knows I won't be able to sleep tonight. By the way, have you heard from Corey? Is he all right?"

"I spoke to him earlier, he's fine."

"That's a relief. Whatever you do, just trust your gut. If you feel that it's not safe, then find somewhere else."

Eddie nodded. "Will do. I better let you go, just call me when you find out anything."

"I will. Please be careful." Bevins hung up.

Eddie turned to Candace. "What do you know about this place in Clark's Town we're being sent to?"

Candace shook her head. "Nothing."

Eddie briefly glanced at her. "That's what worries me."

Chapter 37

Williams Street taxi stand, Montego Bay

Over forty minutes had passed since Corey's *rescuers* dropped him off in the city center. As much as he wanted to, he resisted the urge to call Eddie to find out where he was.

Two brushes with death in one evening and he still wasn't that much closer to finding out what the hell was going on. It was highly unlikely that Eddie would be able to give him answers. Besides, Corey didn't need Eddie to tell him that Tarone was the next best person to talk to. Reaching out to Chevelle would be too risky.

His rescuers told him that there were two taxi stands that were close to the Scotiabank on Market Street. One was located on Williams and the other on Creek Street. After asking them, hypothetically, which taxi stand he'd be heading to had he taken the same route that Tarone took after he crossed paths with him at the bank, they told him that he would've been walking toward the Williams Street stand.

They dropped Corey off at the corner of Orange and William Street which was not only a stone's throw away from about a dozen cabs, but several food, drink, ice cream, and snow cone street vendors. Even though Corey had dumped his old phone, he still remembered what Tarone looked like. So far after having walked by several cabs, he did not spot him.

"You need a ride?"

Corey turned to see that it was a cab driver's head sticking out the window and looking back at him.

"I'm good," Corey answered. He looked away, then turned to

him. "Do you know Tarone?"

"Yeah, I see him around."

"Does he come to this stand often?"

"He was here earlier. He should be back. Don't know when, though."

Corey nodded. "Okay, thanks."

"Why you need to see him? I can give you a ride to anywhere you want to go."

"I lost his number, but I need to get a message to him."

The driver nodded to him, then popped his head back inside his car.

Shit! I just blew my chance on asking him what kind of car Tarone drives.

At least he knew that he was at the right taxi stand, and he'd wait at least another hour for Tarone to return.

Cabs left while others arrived, and Corey was getting frustrated checking each one.

"Yo."

Corey turned to see a skinny brotha around his age, sporting a two-inch afro, and wearing a netted tank top that hung below his waist, covering the top of his jeans. Like many brothas he'd seen while here, he wore them low enough that his drawers were exposed.

"I see you checking each taxi for the past half hour." The brotha reached into his cooler and took out a 1.5-liter bottle of water. "Come get some."

Corey nodded. "I'm good."

"You sure?" The brotha held up the bottle. "I know you must be thirsty from all that running back and forth."

Corey sighed. *I might as well.* He walked over to the brotha who handed him the bottle.

"That'll be one-fifty, unless you have American cash, that'll be a dollar."

Corey handed him three Jamaican fifties. "Why did you think I had American cash on me?"

"Because you sound Trini." The brotha rested an elbow on top of the cooler. "So, I know that you're not from around here. I hear you just now that you're looking for Tarone, but I haven't seen you around him before."

"You know him?" Corey took a few gulps, only now realizing how thirsty he was.

"Yah, mon. He's always around here."

"Do you have a number I can reach him at?"

"Yeah." The brotha nodded as he narrowed his eyes. He then leaned closer to Corey while gesturing to him to get closer. "You know about Tarone…right?"

That he's an accused pedophile? Of course I do. "How you mean?"

The brotha continued to stare at him, as though he was trying to probe him. He then backed away and pointed past Corey's shoulder. "Never mind. He's over there."

Corey looked over his shoulder and saw the white Yaris slow down at the back of the taxi line. "Thanks, bruh." Corey nodded before he ran slowly to the car.

Tarone had just turned off the engine as Corey jumped into the back seat.

"Mek mi grab something fi eat, nuh?" snapped Tarone. "I also need to top up my phone."

"Just drive," said Corey as he held out three bills totaling twenty-five-hundred Jamaican dollars. "We can grab something to eat along the way, and I'll even throw in a few more hundred dollars to top up your phone."

Tarone looked at the money, paused, then held up his hand and reached for the bills. He then crumpled them and slid them in his top pocket. "Yuh lucky I'm in a good mood. Where to?"

"Just drive."

"You need to give me a destination. I can't just drive anywhere."

Corey slipped him another five hundred. "Now will you go?"

Tarone sucked his teeth, snatched the bill, and drove off.

"You better have money to pay if you're going to have me driving all night."

Corey scanned the area, especially behind. Had Eddie been there Corey would've taken back what he told him about being overly paranoid. "You probably don't recognize me, Tarone, but I saw you at the bank last Monday."

Tarone made a quick side glance at Corey. "How you know mi name? Who are you?"

"My name's Corey and I need your help."

Tarone paused, as though he was wondering what was going on. "With what?"

"I spoke to Chevelle and Nesta." Corey saw his eyes widen through the center rearview mirror. "I know that you were framed."

"Who is yuh an mek yuh bring dat up?" snapped Tarone.

"You were wrongfully imprisoned." Corey leaned forward and grabbed the headrest of the seat in front. "And the ones who set you up are still out there."

"Listen, foreigner. Mi done wid dat. I did my time and now I'm out," said Tarone with a dismissive wave. "Who are you, a journalist? Because I don't have anything to say to you."

"I'm not a journalist—"

"Then why you bring up—"

"Nesta's dead!" Corey yelled.

There was a pause as Tarone's jaw hung open.

Corey sighed while shaking his head. "I'm sorry to break the news to you like this."

"What?" Tarone's voice squeaked.

"He was murdered this evening after he told me about Chevelle's rape. The cops who killed him nearly killed me too." Corey fell back into his seat, holding his head. He sighed and looked at Tarone, who had glanced away from the rearview mirror and stared ahead.

"Nesta." Tarone whispered. "Him…dead?"

Corey leaned forward and held the headrest in front. "You should pull over."

Tarone did not appear to have heard him and kept driving. Just as Corey was about to call him by his name, Tarone pulled over to the side of the road and parked. Traffic shot by in both directions as Tarone paused for a few moments before killing the engine. Corey saw he was still in shock, making him just as dangerous on the road as a drunk driver.

"How did you know about Chevelle and Nesta?" asked Tarone.

Corey heard how his voice cracked, it was as though he was fighting back tears.

"I bumped into Nesta earlier this afternoon after I met Chevelle at work. He intercepted me as I was leaving and told me to meet him at Turtle Grove Park."

"But *why* were you talking to Chevelle?"

"It's about Dwayne Pottinger. He was murdered last weekend."

Tarone shook his head and sighed. "Yeah, I hear about that. What does that girl-boy have to do with Chevelle and Nesta?"

"As far as I know, nothing," said Corey. "But Chevelle's son, Delroy, was there and I believe that he saw what happened."

"You shouldn't go talk to Chevelle. Why you get yourself linked up in that bwoy's death?" Tarone then sighed while shaking his head. "Him shoulda neva wear a dress and go whine-up pon nu man."

"There's a lot more to the story," said Corey.

"How yuh know?"

"Because I was there with my friend. We tried to save Dwayne's life, but we were too late."

Corey then summarized the events with him and Eddie from then until now. "As I said earlier, Delroy showed up to the club with his friends. And I think he may have witnessed something that Eddie and I didn't."

Tarone watched him through the center rearview mirror.

"All I want is for Delroy to tell me or the proper authorities what he saw that night. And I thought that the best way to get him to talk would be through his mother."

"What are you? A detective?"

Corey shook his head. "I just want some answers so that Eddie can come out of hiding so we can both go home. And yes, we tried the police, but they weren't any help."

"No one trust the police around here," said Tarone. "I don't even trust them, and never will."

"I can't blame you."

"But even if you reach Delroy, he won't talk."

"If he learns the truth, then maybe he'll stop hating you, and hate the system that punished you and let his mother's rapists get away instead. Hopefully by then he'll be more open-minded in coming forward."

Tarone was losing his temper. "I used to be a teacher." Tarone gripped the steering wheel and let his head fall on top of it. "I was making a decent salary to provide for me and my girlfriend." He lifted his head then waved one arm. "Look pon mi now, have to start all over from scratch. Woman gone, and I'm hardly getting by. What's done is done, just gone bad. The best thing for you and your friend is to get out of Jamaica as soon as you can."

"I'm not leaving my friend behind," Corey said loudly. He took a deep breath and raised a hand to his forehead. "Look, from what Nesta told me, you cared for Chevelle. Nesta also went out of his way to keep an eye on her—even up to earlier this evening when he showed me where she was attacked."

"I'm not going anywhere near Delroy because he has a restraining order against me. I'm not going back to prison over that."

"Which is why we need to get Chevelle to talk to him," said Corey. "Is she mad at you as much as he is?"

"I don't know, and I don't care to find out. Her father's a judge, did you know?"

"I've heard."

"There you go. What chance do you think you have?" Tarone sighed. "You can either get out of the car now or I'll just drop you off anywhere. Just don't bother me again. I hope you find your friend and get off the island. There's no difference between the police and the thieves."

"I'm not arguing with you." Corey shook his head. "Eddie and I once had problems with the police back home—and we were nearly killed, just because we were in the wrong place at the wrong time."

"And how did you survive?"

"We ran for our lives," Corey answered. "And we kept going until we ran into the right people who were in a position to help us clear our names."

Corey paused as he expected Tarone to respond, but he did not. "There's something Nesta didn't explain to me."

"What's that?"

"He never told me why you gave up so easily and went to prison for Chevelle's rape."

"I told you before I didn't want to talk about it."

"Nesta said you were innocent. So, why'd you confess to something you never did?"

Tarone sighed. "They were going to find me guilty anyway. That's just how things are."

"But why *you*?"

"They needed a fall guy."

Tarone's hiding something. "Of all the boarding school's staff, the police targeted you? Who did you piss off?"

"Yuh just nuh understand," said Tarone. "You don't have to do nothing to no one. When the police want fi get somebody, dem just do that. Planting evidence is what they do."

"And what evidence *did* they plant?"

"What's with all of these questions?" yelled Tarone. "You know what? Get out of my taxi."

"Nesta, for some reason, brought me to the location where Chevelle and others were raped," said Corey. "But you didn't confess to those rapes too, did you?"

Tarone didn't answer.

"This was a *so-called* Bible camp where those rapes took place. Nesta told me that Pastor Green—who was in charge—not only knew what was happening but that he joined in. Nesta knew what was going on, but he was too scared to come forward."

Tarone looked away from Corey. "You don't think I know that?"

"Then what were both of you scared of? Nesta spoke highly of you. It was as though you two were tight."

Tarone sighed. "It was more than that…I mean…I see him around because he the janitor where I used to work. But that's it."

Something's not right. He's holding back. The way he said, "But that's it," raised some red flags. It was though he was in a rush to say it.

"Nesta also told me that you were Chevelle's favorite teacher. Which is why I don't understand why she accused you of raping her. Nesta wanted the truth to get out, he just didn't know *how* without becoming a target. Guess what, I'm already a target, and so is my friend, Eddie. And from my past experience, running without gathering ammunition will surely get you killed. If I didn't think that there was something you could do to help end this, I wouldn't have wasted my time talking to you."

"There's nothing I can say that could help you."

"Try me," rebutted Corey. "How about going back to the moment you found out that Chevelle was raped."

"Look." Tarone shook his head and took a deep breath. "Back when I was teaching, every year Pastor Green's church organized a weeklong field trip so that the children could get some Bible instruction. Chevelle was in her first year at the school, and she was always a pleasant girl. To tell the truth, they were *all* good students. When they went away to the camp, everything was fine. It was after they came back, everyone else was fine except for Chevelle."

"What did you notice?"

"She wasn't smiling as often, and she always seemed to be somewhere else. She was even more aggressive than usual," said Tarone. "One evening after class, I sat down with her to find out what was wrong. She didn't want to tell me, but I knew something wasn't right. I reassured her that I wanted to help."

Tarone paused. The roar of a diesel engine grew as it approached. When the truck passed, he sighed before continuing. "She didn't want to talk. This went on for a few days until one afternoon—a few days later—she came to see me. We met in private, and she told me everything. I was shocked and couldn't believe what she said."

Tarone held a hand to his forehead as though to collect his thoughts, then let it drop beside him. "I mean, the details she gave—from being woken up at night, made to walk to the cabin on the outer part of the camp, to being blindfolded and tied down to a bed with her nighty pulled up and her panties being pulled down, while two different men took turns penetrating her."

Corey sat quietly. Tarone gave more explicit details than what Nesta had told him, while corroborating his version of what had happened.

"I was still new to teaching at that time—and the youngest at that school. I didn't have to be a psychologist or detective to know that's not the kind of lie a child makes up."

"Was she able to identify her attackers?" asked Corey.

"She told me that Pastor Green was one of them, but she didn't know who the other man was."

"Did you tell anyone?"

"I spoke to the principal, and he didn't take my concerns seriously. I couldn't believe that he said that Chevelle must have made up the whole thing because Pastor Green would never do that to anyone. It would be *unchristian* of him."

"You didn't stop there, did you?"

Tarone shook his head. "No, I went to the police. They say they can't open an investigation unless the victim comes forward. I tried to convince Chevelle to file a report and that I would accompany her, but she told me that she didn't want anyone to get in trouble. Soon after, I noticed how my colleagues' behavior toward me changed. I became an outcast."

"Did you suspect someone had gotten to her?"

"Isn't it obvious?" Tarone answered. "When I tried to approach Chevelle again, she kept avoiding me. The next thing I knew, she didn't want to talk to me. I could tell that she wasn't the same. Several weeks later she was always at the nurse's office because she was always sick. That's when I heard rumors that she was pregnant."

Tarone paused again and let his head fall back onto the headrest. "The next thing I know is that the police showed up at my house, asking me questions. I told them exactly what I told you. A few days later they were searching my classroom and my house. Then they arrested me—claiming that they can prove that I raped Chevelle."

"But that's stupid," Corey said. "How could they prove that you were at Turtle Grove?"

"They claimed that I raped her in the school. They found some drug called Quaaludes in my desk drawer in my classroom. I told them that I never saw those drugs in my life and that someone must have put them there."

"Didn't your lawyer argue those facts?" asked Corey. "I mean, wouldn't the authorities find it crazy that you would drug and rape Chevelle, then risk exposing yourself by encouraging her to report it? You said it yourself that when you saw the school principal that he didn't take you seriously."

"I know," said Tarone. "But they had me trapped. The ones who set me up, set me up good. There was no getting out of it."

"What do you mean there was no getting out of it?" Corey leaned forward. "If you're saying that they planted Quaaludes in your classroom desk, then what's stopping them from tampering with DNA results to frame you? It doesn't make sense."

"I confessed because I just wanted this all to end."

Corey was at a loss for words. "You could've been killed in prison. Why did you take that chance?"

Tarone didn't answer, but just let his head fall back on the headrest again. Corey sensed that he was still holding back something. To take the fall and spend twelve years behind bars, why would anyone do that? He didn't owe anything to Pastor Green...unless...

"They had something else on you, didn't they?"

Tarone didn't answer, except for the quick shaking of his head and then holding his forehead with one hand. Tarone's body language told Corey that he was getting closer to learning what Tarone was keeping secret.

"I don't want to be a pain in the ass," said Corey. "But I'm getting the feeling that these guys blackmailed you into confessing. Am I right?"

Tarone unbuckled his seatbelt, swung open the car door, and exited without even checking for traffic.

"Hey!" Corey got out as fast as he could and ran after Tarone, who wandered carelessly across the street.

"Tarone," Corey screamed as an SUV blasted its horn, but Tarone didn't seem to be paying attention, or to even care.

"Shit!" Corey muttered to himself as he sprinted behind Tarone and tackled him—throwing them both onto the sidewalk where they rolled over twice as a horn blasted and tires screeched across the asphalt behind them.

Corey's chest was tight as his heart pounded. More than relief, he felt a rush come over him and it went straight to his brain. Was this an adrenaline high? He nearly got himself killed trying to save someone he'd only met less than a half hour ago.

"Are you fucking kidding me?" screamed Corey as he rolled off Tarone's back. "Why'd you do that?" Corey wasn't expecting an answer, since he knew that it had everything to do with why Tarone allowed his life to get destroyed. It was then that Corey saw the tears rolling down Tarone's face as he buried it in his hands.

"Nesta dead," he sobbed. "What chance do I have?"

"What?" Again, he was talking about Nesta. Why's he so obsessed with someone he claimed was only the janitor he would see around the school…unless…hold on…how did he *not* see it?

Corey looked around as a few pedestrians gathered. He didn't want to say another word to Tarone. He didn't want any of the eavesdroppers to be gossiping. Corey grabbed Tarone's arm. "Come on, get up. Let me drive, you need some rest."

Tarone didn't get up on his own, and someone from the small crowd lent a hand in helping Corey make Tarone stand.

"Help me bring him to his car," Corey said as they walked back across the street. Corey did not lock the back door, which made it easier for him and the Samaritan to get Tarone inside.

Corey thanked the Samaritan and sat down in the driver's seat. The keys were still in the ignition, but Corey didn't start the car. He was a bit taller than Tarone so he had no choice but to adjust the seat to accommodate his height. Corey leaned to the side so that he could grab his burner from his back pocket. He logged online to check the local news, and almost immediately found a report of the shootout in Anchovy from which he barely escaped. The report verified that two of the officers were confirmed dead while the others—including Detective Inspector Ellis—survived the attack. He saw the names of the two officers along with their pictures. Sure enough, they were the ones who beat him up and killed Nesta.

He turned to Tarone and held up the phone. "Do you recognize these two?"

Tarone's eyes narrowed and he inhaled deeply.

"Let me guess," said Corey. "They were among the officers who searched your classroom, weren't they?"

Tarone swallowed, then nodded.

"Just so you know, we could've continued this conversation outside. But I didn't want anyone overhearing us." Corey paused because he knew he was venturing into sensitive territory. "I know that we just met. Whatever you're thinking, I want you to know that I'm on your side."

Corey let a few seconds go by before getting straight to the point. "There was something those two officers said to me that I didn't think too much of but is only now starting to make sense. They falsely accused me of trying to hook up with Nesta."

Corey stared into the rearview mirror and, as expected, Tarone slowly looked back at him. *That* got his attention.

"I thought that they were just looking for any reason to arrest me. But right now, I don't think that it was a coincidence."

Corey took a deep breath. He knew Eddie would chastise him for rushing into this too bluntly. "You were asked about your whereabouts the week that Chevelle would've been raped, weren't you?"

Tarone hesitated, then he gave a short nod. It was discreet, but still noticeable.

"I'm guessing that you didn't know anyone who could verify your whereabouts, at least, that's what you said, right?"

Again, there was a moment's pause before Tarone nodded.

"But you couldn't tell them that Nesta could corroborate your story that you weren't anywhere near the school the night Chevelle was allegedly raped." He glanced at the rearview mirror. Tarone was looking at him for a fraction of a second before he glanced away. The way he did it only further cemented Corey's suspicions. It was time to stop beating around the bush. "You didn't want Nesta to provide an alibi for you because you were with him that night."

More tears streamed down Tarone's face as his crying was more audible. Corey looked ahead, the cars passing by in either direction in his peripheral vision. He exhaled loudly. He couldn't believe it. Eddie probably would've figured out Tarone's secret a lot sooner. The brotha who sold him the water had asked him in a hushed voice, "You know about Tarone…right?" This is what he must have meant. He was probably on the 'down low' just like Tarone. The brotha may have been trying to guess if Corey was also—only to back off when he was convinced that he wasn't.

"Somehow, the police found out about you and Nesta. You couldn't tell the truth, because if you did, you'd be living on borrowed time. Word would've gotten out and you'd both be killed. Or both of you would've been thrown in prison where you'd then be killed."

Corey had heard stories of men and women being in heterosexual relationships as a cover for their homosexuality. He never imagined that he'd ever meet such a person—and at this moment, of all times.

"As I said before," Corey turned around to look Tarone in the eye, "I'm on your side. I don't care if you're gay, same-gender loving, or bi. I have gay friends, and I know that being gay in the Caribbean could be a death sentence. But I need your help, so outing you is the last thing I'd do. Since you care a lot for Chevelle, then she needs to know the truth. She has a right to a proper closure, and Delroy has the right to know who his real father is."

Corey checked the fuel gauge and saw that it was at half a tank. He started the car and drove off. "Are you going to be all right?"

Tarone nodded. "Where are we going?"

"To see someone who can help both of us."

Chapter 38

Amancia's house, Greenwood, Saint James Parish, Jamaica

Hansel and Gretel sat at the same dining room table. The two placemats adjacent from each other indicated that Eddie and Candace had likely eaten here earlier. There was some light from the kitchen.

The wrought-iron grill would've deterred most burglars from breaking into this home. However, both had broken into more secure places with more sophisticated locks. Getting through the back door of this home was child's play.

They'd been waiting patiently for over a half hour when they saw a car slow down and turn into the driveway. The headlights shone bright through the window as Hansel got up from the table and walked closer to the front door to hide in the coat closet. The goal was to wait until Amancia walked by and then block her escape while Gretel blocked her access to the kitchen.

The headlights were still on when Gretel's mobile rang. "Yes."

"Abort. I repeat. Abort." It was their boss.

"Yes, ma'am," Gretel replied then tapped the *Off* button as she turned toward Hansel. "We need to go."

She nodded toward the kitchen. "Through the back."

Without asking any questions, Hansel followed her into the kitchen where they exited, just as Amancia entered through the front.

Chapter 39

Route B11, outside Clark's Town

The idea of spending a night or two in an Airbnb that doubled as one of Brutus's safehouses did not sit well with Eddie. The last place was compromised, so why should he expect this place to be any different? Given that he did not have another location in mind, the address Brutus gave them was the only safe spot to go to. Eddie only hoped that Brutus had taken care of the mole.

Candace turned on the radio and went through the stations, then stopped in the middle of a reggae song. This was a welcome change that Eddie needed, and he wondered why he did not think of this before. He recognized the song "Pressure" by Koffee, having heard it several times on the reggae playlist Corey had made for him.

He glanced at Candace and saw that she was bobbing her head to the beat before she sang along. "'Under the pressure, under the pressure, yeah. Under the pressure, under the pressure. If yuh poor, trouble tek you. When yuh rich it nuh settle. Cuh we all under the pressure my friend.'"

It was the first time he'd heard Candace sing, and she wasn't bad. Before he knew it, he began tapping his fingers on the steering wheel while nodding his head to the rhythm.

"'Sometimes you feel it you cry on. Hurt yuh heart enuh. But do not stress it, yessah. 'Cause it haffi fi better. Cause you have to live ina the ghetto...'"

Eddie noticed that the volume was turned down and that Candace was no longer singing along. He shrugged his shoulders. "What?"

"Where did you learn those lyrics?" asked Candace.

"I hear them all the time."

Candace shook her head while she made a face. "No, sah. Yuh never hear Koffee sing it like that. She never sing: 'But do not stress it, *yessah.*'"

"I'm pretty sure that's what she sang."

"No, sah. You don't even know the words."

"Jesus, you're just as bad as Corey," Eddie mumbled.

"What?"

"Nothing."

Candance rolled her eyes. "Whatever."

Eddie saw a set of taillights that were not moving. He honked to signal to the driver that he was about to overtake him—a common practice among motorists in the Caribbean—until he saw that there was a traffic backup of at least six cars. He hit the brakes and came to an abrupt stop, missing the car's bumper by about a foot. There was a construction crew ahead who appeared to be working on the road, reducing the two-laned road to one. A road worker was up ahead with his flags, waving oncoming traffic through.

They were a stone's throw from a gas station on their side of the road where Eddie saw four brothas talking among themselves. One of them had a cigarette. His attention was then drawn to the sound of Candace unbuckling her seatbelt. "What are you doing?"

"Just making a quick stop."

"Where?" Eddie nodded to the gas station. "There? To do what?"

Candace opened the door. "I just want something to drink. You want something?"

"I'll pass, and so should you because you're just putting yourself on display for the station's CCTV cameras," said Eddie. "Next thing you know Weiss's hitmen will have the town surrounded."

"I'm sure their cameras are just there for show."

"You want to take that chance? Besides, I'm sure there are drinks where we're going. And if they don't have any, then I bet they'll get some for us."

Eddie was interrupted by loud laughter coming from the brothas up ahead. He looked toward them to see two of them jumping up and down, another hunched over slapping his thigh, while the other two ran around. He cringed at the thought of what may happen if they spotted Candace. By the time Eddie turned to her she was already standing outside the car about to close the door.

Eddie's hand shot out in her direction. "Wait."

Candace lowered her head to look inside. "What now?"

"I have a bad feeling."

Candace shook her head. "Just pull over and wait."

"Since we've met, how many times have I been wrong?"

Eddie looked toward the brothas to see that one of them was staring in their direction. No, there was no way the brotha could see him, it was too dark and they weren't close enough to the gas station's lights. It was then Eddie realized that the brotha was checking out Candace.

"Yo," the brotha said.

Eddie turned to Candace. "Get in."

Candace glanced at the brothas. By then they were all staring at her.

"Candace, get your ass in the car now!" Eddie looked back at the brothas to see that they were walking toward them. He then fixed his gaze on Candace, who hurried to get back inside while they continued to call out to her.

"Yuh nuh hear mi a call yuh?" the same brotha said as they got closer.

Eddie blasted the horn, but that did not get the traffic to move, nor did it deter the man from approaching.

"Is there another way to the Airbnb?"

Candace shook her head as she rolled up her window.

The car shook as the brotha slammed the hood of the car with his palm, twice, startling them.

"Mek yuh nuh ansa mi when mi a talk to yuh?"

Something changed in the brotha's facial expression as he looked at Eddie. From where he stood, he could get a clearer view of Eddie's face. His stomach tightened when he saw the brotha grab his mobile, tap the screen a few times and stare at it before looking back at him.

"A him, yuh know," the brotha yelled anxiously. "Who bloodclaat Vanessa Pusey a pay out the reward fah."

Eddie grabbed the stick and threw it into reverse then stomped down on the accelerator, scaring the brothas into jumping away from the car. The car rocketed backward for a second until Eddie stomped on the brakes the moment he saw headlights in the rearview mirror.

Eddie spun the wheel violently to the right before throwing the gear into drive and stomping on the gas, launching their vehicle into a U-turn. An oncoming car blasted its horn as it screeched to a halt. Again, he threw the gear into drive and floored the gas. He wasn't successful and had to reverse once before completing the hairpin turn before speeding off.

Chapter 40

Eddie could not remember the last time he drove so recklessly. One error and he'd throw the car into a barrel roll.

"Eddie."

He heard Candace's voice, but it did not register. He maintained pressure on the gas as the car increased in speed down the straight and narrow road. Headlights shone brightly in his eyes from the opposite direction. Eddie blasted the horn as they got closer, and the other motorist blasted his horn in return.

"Eddie."

He slammed on the breaks as he approached the curve, the car screeched across the pavement as the rear swiveled from left to right.

"Eddie!" Candace screamed.

"What?" Eddie yelled back.

"Slow down before you kill us," she yelled. "Nobody's following us."

Eddie eased off the gas and pressed down gently on the brakes, slowing them down as he negotiated the curve. *She's right. What came over me?* He didn't want to admit it in front of Candace, but he'd lost control of himself.

"I'm going to call my uncle and let him know what happened."

Eddie snatched the phone from its dash mount.

Candace shot him a glance. "What's wrong with you?"

"Haven't you noticed that everywhere your uncle sends us we get into trouble?"

"You can't blame my uncle for us being spotted back there."

"It's just too much of a coincidence."

"You're being paranoid."

"Am I?"

"I think you need to relax and give me the phone."

"Not going to happen. I don't trust your uncle anymore."

"Really? Then who are you going to trust to get us out of this mess?"

There was a crossroad less than one hundred meters away. Eddie slowed down and turned onto it. He had driven over two hundred meters and not another vehicle in sight. He swung the wheel, taking the car to the side of the road where he then parked.

Eddie switched off the engine and sighed. "I don't know. Everyone's out to get us. I didn't ask for this. I only came here for a fucking book promo, not to witness a murder and get so nosey that I have a fucking death squad chasing me all over the country before pissing off one of your former Olympians who now wants to get back at me by putting a bounty on my head. Why? All because a young woman asked me for help and I just couldn't just say…"

Eddie stopped short of completing his sentence. He inhaled deeply and let his frustration out with a big exhale.

"You couldn't say no to Jalissa," said Candace. "You could've given up and walked away at any time, but you didn't. Why?"

Eddie shook his head. "I wish I knew."

"I think you do," Candace answered. "It's the same reason why you didn't let me go off on my own or do the same. You wanted to help both me and Jalissa. You had to have known how risky it would be, but you still did so. That was very selfless of you."

Although he knew she was right, he was upset that she was. "I don't know how much longer we can keep running."

"You didn't know that a hitman would target me at Guava Hill, but you and I got away."

"That was a fluke."

"You didn't know that the hit squad would show up at Uncle Lenny's village," said Candace. "Yet it was your idea *not* to use the escape tunnel. We got away. That wasn't a fluke, was it?"

"At what cost? Lenny's dead."

"Are you blaming yourself for that? Shouldn't you be blaming the mole you suspect is among my uncle's group?" said Candace. "And I would've never thought of going to see Shirley and

Charlene. And because of you, now we know why Dwayne may have been killed and why the same people also want me dead. You can't keep flogging yourself, everything you've done hasn't been for nothing."

Eddie shook his head. "I just don't like being helpless."

"Why don't you call your friend, Ms. Bevins?"

"Not now," said Eddie as he looked at the phone's battery power indicator on the monitor. "Besides, I doubt she'd be able to help us out. I already asked her a favor. We should wait until she calls back."

"By the way, have you heard from your friend, Corey?"

Eddie shook his head. "Naw. Now that you mention him, it would be nice to be in his shoes. I don't see how his day could've been worse than ours."

"What do we do now?" asked Candace.

Eddie unbuckled his seatbelt then reclined his chair. "Get some rest. I can't think clearly when I'm tired."

A few moments went by as Candace looked out her window. Eddie did not know what she was staring at, since there wasn't anything but cane fields on either side. She then reclined her chair and lay back in it.

Eddie sat up to push the car *Starter* button to turn it on so that he could lower the windows. Once that was done, he pushed it again to turn off the car, reached up to slide open the moonroof, then laid back down.

Several minutes passed without a word being said between them, where Eddie stared through the moonroof at the stars. The only sounds came from tree frogs, grasshoppers, and crickets chirping their late-night symphony. Eddie looked at Candace and noticed that she had dozed off.

Eddie's mind drifted back to the time that he, Corey, and Corey's then-girlfriend, Jordyn, were on the run from the police after Eddie was framed for murder. It was one of the coldest winters on record, and he and his friends only had themselves to rely on. He and Corey didn't have a penny to their names, and Jordyn was the one person who came to their rescue. Now with the trouble he was in, he only imagined how Jordyn was lying in bed, sleepless and worried sick about them. And Eddie knew that he only had himself to blame for getting his best friend into this mess. He had blamed Jordyn and Corey for the mess he was in last time, which he soon came to regret.

Before he knew it, Eddie was asleep.

Chapter 41

Coral Gardens, Montego Bay, Jamaica

Delroy let his car coast as he looked out the window to see the house numbers, which wasn't easy in the dark. He'd normally be home right now but his mother said that she desperately needed to see him. When he had asked why, she told him that he'd find out when he saw her. He slowed down at the house with all the lights on outside, making the number visible. He found a spot easily and parked.

He never met his mother while she was working, which raised more questions. The person who hired her wouldn't normally allow her to have her own friends over. These issues swirled in his head as he walked up to the grill and rang the bell.

"Who dat?" came the voice of an elderly woman, whom he assumed was the homeowner, from inside the house.

"It's Delroy. My mum told me to come here, that it was an emergency."

"Yuh get here fast. Hol on, son."

A moment later, Delroy saw his mother exit the house. She came to the grill, unlocked it, and hugged him.

"Hello, thanks for coming," she said.

Delroy hugged her back. "What happened? What's so important that you had to see me at this hour?"

"Just come with me inside."

Without asking any further questions, Delroy closed and locked the grill, then followed his mother inside.

The first person he saw was an elderly woman with a walker.

"This is Lucille," said his mother. "She's a very, very nice lady. She wanted to meet you."

"Good evening, son." Lucille held out a hand. "I've heard so much about you. My goodness, Chevelle never said that you were so handsome."

"Thanks, nice to meet you." Delroy blushed as he shook her hand, then turned to his mother. "What's so urgent?"

"We can go into the living room." His mother led him inside and showed him a tray with a glass with ice and a champagne cola. "You see, I already brought a drink you like, and there's some coco bread."

"I baked that coco bread this afternoon," said Lucille as she followed them inside the living room and sat. "Tell me how you like it."

Delroy sat on the couch beside his mother. He wiped a bit of sweat from his forehead with the back of his arm. "What's the emergency?"

He saw his mother fiddling with her hands before looking away. She then turned to Lucille, who rested her walker in front of the recliner she sat in.

"It's okay, we already discussed this. I'm right here, don't worry," said Lucille.

"Worry about what?" asked Delroy.

His mother held her head in her hands, looking down. "I did something very bad. A very bad thing."

Delroy waited as she paused.

"No you didn't, dear," said Lucille. "You must not blame yourself."

"Blame yourself for what?" Delroy turned to Lucille. "What did my mother do?"

His mother turned to Lucille. "I can't do this. I can't."

"Yes, you can, Chevelle." Lucille said this calmly. "Don't forget. I'm a survivor, just like you."

"Survivor?" Delroy took his mother's hand. "Did someone touch you? Who hurt you?"

His mother shook her head. "No one hurt me, and no one touched me. No, no, it's not like that."

"Mummy, look at me," said Delroy.

His mother wiped a tear from her cheek with the back of her hand, then looked at him. "You won't get mad at me for what I have to say?"

"I won't."

"You promise?"

Delroy held her hands firmly in his palms. "I promise."

His mother wiped away another tear. "Earlier today, I met someone and he asked me some questions. The conversation changed and I spoke about what happened before you were born."

"What? Who asked you such questions?"

"No, don't get mad. You promised that you wouldn't get mad."

She was right. "Sorry, it's my fault."

"The man's name was Corey." His mother gestured to Lucille. "Lucille sent him to see me because he needed my help. I didn't get a chance to talk to him for too long because Ann showed up and scared him off."

She turned to Lucille.

"You're doing fine, my dear," Lucille said. "Take your time. Your son needs to hear this."

His mother looked at him. "After Corey left, Ann demanded to know what he wanted. I was so ashamed for agreeing to talk to him, that I confessed I told Corey about me being raped."

Delroy shook his head. "Why do you do this to yourself? If I was Ann, I would've done the same. In fact, I would've jacked him up for not minding his business."

Delroy then turned to Lucille. "How do you know this man? Why would you put my mother through this?"

"No, don't get mad at Lucille," said his mother. "There's more. I found out that Corey talked to Nesta. You remember him? He works with me at the cafeteria."

"Yes, I think I do."

"Nesta brought the man with him to Turtle Grove Park."

"Why?"

"Because Nesta wanted to tell him the truth, and he wanted to show it to him where it happened."

"What truth? How do you know this?"

"Ann must've seen Nesta talking to Corey because I saw her calling someone right after." She paused as she wiped even more tears. "The police went to the park and now Nesta's dead."

"What?" Delroy gasped as he let go of his mother's hands. "How did this happen? You never told me who this Corey person was."

"I'm Corey."

Delroy looked past his mother to the sound of the familiar voice behind the wall of the adjoining hallway. When he stepped out in the open, Delroy froze.

It's the guy from the bar who played dominos with me, Jucee, and Scuba.

A deep rage took over Delroy as he jumped off the couch and rocketed, both hands out, to tackle Corey. There were screams from Lucille and his mother as Corey caught his hands but was unable to stop the momentum, which sent them both slamming into the wall. They fell to the floor as he lost ground to Corey, who gained the upper hand and pinned his back to the carpet with both hands and a knee to his abdomen.

"Why are you bothering my mother?" Delroy yelled.

"Delroy! Stop it, stop it, stop it!" screamed his mother.

"I'm not here to fight," Corey yelled.

"Okay, that's enough, you two. Break it up."

Delroy turned to the sound of the voice. He recognized it and it made his chest tighten. It was then that he saw his mother's rapist approaching them from the kitchen.

"You!"

"Delroy, please," came his mother's cries. "You promised not to get mad. You promised."

"This is the *emergency*?" Delroy struggled to force Corey off him, but he was pinned down in a way that made it impossible for him to move. "What are they doing here?"

"They only want to help," said his mother as she grabbed her head with both hands. "No, no, no, no. This was a bad idea. A very bad idea."

"Look at me, Chevelle," said Lucille. "You didn't do anything wrong. Don't get upset."

Delroy wanted to hit Corey in the jaw so bad, but seeing his mother about to throw a tantrum worried him. He couldn't let that happen.

"Delroy, these men aren't here to hurt you or your mother," said Lucille. "You have to listen to what they have to say. If you're not going to do it for them, then please do it for your mother."

Delroy closed his eyes, sighed, and stopped trying to fight Corey. Everywhere around him was quiet except for the sound of his heavy breathing.

"I know they're the last people you want to see right now," said Lucille. "But believe me when I say that you need to give them a chance."

"Listen," said Corey as he removed his knee from Delroy's chest. "Your mother and Tarone have something to say to you. You have no idea what I went through to get all of you to come together. But you need to listen. Do you understand?"

Delroy looked into Corey's eyes, as Corey held his stare. He didn't sound as though he was being deceptive. As much as Delroy wanted to punch this guy out, he didn't see himself winning the fight. He closed his eyes and nodded.

Corey got off him and extended his arm in what appeared to be a truce. Delroy grabbed his hand and was hoisted up onto his feet. He turned and saw Tarone picking up a picture in its frame that had fallen to the floor during the brawl. He hung it back on the nail in the wall.

"Now that you boys have settled down, please come in and sit," said Lucille. "I don't have time to be calling the insurance company to make a damage claim."

Delroy sat in the same spot beside his mother. He looked at Lucille, then to his mother. "I'm sorry."

"That's all right, son," said Lucille. "Now that you got that out of your system, you should let your mother continue saying what she needs to say."

Delroy held his mother's hand. "Go on, I'm listening."

"As I said, Ann was very, very angry with me for talking to Corey without telling her."

Delroy turned to Corey. "You and Nesta went to Turtle Grove Park. Why?"

"Because..." his mother paused as she swallowed. "Because that's where it happened."

Delroy looked his mother in the eyes as his mouth hung open, not knowing what to say.

"Yes." She nodded. "That's where they did those bad things to me."

Delroy looked away from his mother to the coco bread. Some slices spilled off the plate and onto the coffee table, likely shaken from the plate after he bumped the table attacking Corey.

"You just said *they*. I thought there was only one man who did this to you." He thumbed in Tarone's direction. "Him."

His mother shook her head. "No, no, no, no, noooo! It wasn't him. He never did anything bad to me. He can't be your father because he wasn't even there. It was two men, two very bad men."

Delroy looked at Tarone and bit his lip, then looked away and stood. He walked to the window, holding his head.

"Then everything I was told…it was all a lie?"

His mother went over to join him. "Please don't be mad at me. I wanted to tell you the truth. I always did."

Delroy closed his eyes and breathed. He had promised not to get angry with his mother, but it was becoming increasingly difficult. "Why didn't you? I'm your son. How could you let me grow up believing a lie?"

"They told me that I was wrong." His mother scrunched up her face as she rubbed her eyes with both hands. She turned to Lucille, shaking her head. "This was a mistake. I shouldn't have done this. Everyone's going to be mad at me."

Lucille waved her hand toward her with her palm down. "Listen. I'm not mad at you. Neither is Corey nor Tarone." She then turned to Delroy. "You're not mad at your mother because she was manipulated. Are you?"

Delroy closed his eyes hard as his head was still in a whirlwind of thoughts. To think that he was misled into believing that the man standing less than five feet away was his father—his mother's rapist—for over twenty-two years. He didn't know if he could ever get over it.

"Delroy?"

It was Lucille. He didn't know the woman, but it was obvious that his mother trusted her and was well acquainted with her. He shook his head and turned to his mother. "I'm not mad at you." Delroy then turned to the others. "But I need answers."

"And you're going to get them," said Lucille, turning to his mother. "You see? None of us are mad at you. Delroy's your son, and we're your friends, and we're going to always stand with you. The only people who are going to be mad at you are the ones who want to hurt you. And *those* people aren't your friends. If they were, then they would've listened to you a long time ago—just like when Tarone tried to help you. You shouldn't feel ashamed for telling your son the truth, because what happened to you that awful night was not your fault."

It took a few moments before his mother got her composure.

"They made me believe that I was too confused to know what happened to me. They also said that if I told anyone that I was attacked at the Bible camp, many people would get mad at me and hate me because I'll get many people in trouble. They then told me that the police found out that Tarone drugged me and did those bad things to me. The drugs were supposed to confuse me."

Delroy lowered his head and shook it slowly with a sigh. He formed a fist and squeezed as hard as he could. He just wanted to pick up something and throw it against the wall. Delroy turned to his mother. "I can't blame you for being gaslit."

He saw his mother looking over his shoulder toward Tarone.

"I'm so sorry for what I did to you. I should've said something. I never wanted you to go to prison. You have to believe me."

"If I may say something?" Lucille looked at Tarone, then at Delroy. "I followed that story very closely in the news as it happened. "Chevelle was only twelve years old at the time. She never testified in court because both the detectives and her parents did not want to subject her to reliving the trauma by having her in a courtroom."

His mother turned to him. "I wanted to tell you the truth, I really did. But I wasn't sure what the truth was, or if you would hate me."

Delroy held onto his mother's hands firmly. "I believe you, and I will never hate you. But I want to know. Who were the ones that hurt you?"

His mother turned to Lucille, who nodded. She then looked back at him. "Pastor Green was one of them. I know this because he was praying out loud as he…as he forced himself on me. The other man I don't know."

"You don't know because you didn't recognize him?"

"No, I was blindfolded."

"Nesta knew," said Corey. "He was about to tell me, but the police showed up. He ran but couldn't get away fast enough before they shot him."

Corey turned to Delroy. "Do you want to know what they did next?"

Delroy stared at him without answering. He didn't feel like he wanted to know.

"They hurled me to the ground, handcuffed, and kicked me. Then they threw me against the hood of their car, where one of them shoved his gun into my face." Corey paused as his breathing intensified and his eyes narrowed. He shook his head gently and sighed. "I thought that I was going to die. I have a wife and a son, and I thought I'd never see them again. That cop was just looking for an excuse to kill me, and I'm sure he would've had it not been for their superior showing up."

"What happened after?" asked Delroy.

Corey told him the rest, from when he was driven by Detective Inspector Ellis, to the ambush, to meeting Tarone.

Delroy looked at Tarone, who appeared to be somber. Who could blame him? Delroy had spent his whole life hating this man, thinking that he was the one who had stolen his mother's innocence. All these years he'd hoped that he'd either be killed in prison or that it would happen to him once he got out. All these years of hatred and anger toward this man—his father, or so he'd thought—only to now learn that it had been aimed at the wrong person.

"Why did you tell the police you hurt my mum if you didn't do it?" Delroy shifted in his seat to face Tarone. "Pastor Green and one of his friends got away with it, and you let them. Why?"

"It's complicated," said Corey as Tarone was about to speak.

"Complicated?" asked Delroy. "How?"

"There's more to it—"

Tarone patted Corey on the shoulder. "It's okay. I'll tell him."

Corey turned to him and whispered. "You sure?" The rest of what he said was inaudible to Delroy.

"Tell me what?" asked Delroy.

"I don't know how else to say this." Tarone stepped back toward the wall and sat down with his knees bent where he rested his forearms, then let his head drop in between. "The night that they claim I was with your mother, I was with Nesta."

That's all? "What's wrong with that? So you hang out with Nesta, he could've told the police the same thing."

"Because I told mi girlfriend that mi was at school correcting students' homework for the whole week. She and I were having problems at that time and I would deliberately avoid going home after work because we were always fighting."

Delroy watched him sigh. Tarone was holding back on something.

"In fact, some nights I didn't even go home. I would just hang out with Nesta."

"So, you and Nesta were friends. It's normal that friends help each other out."

Corey caught Delroy's attention when he cleared his throat, put his hands in his pockets, and lowered his head while turning away.

Delroy connected the dots. "You and Nesta were…"

Tarone nodded, then bowed his head as though he was ashamed to admit this. He then looked back up and told Delroy how he had realized that something was wrong with his mother and that he'd reported everything to the principal, only for the whole thing to backfire on him.

"Nesta and I were trapped," Tarone continued. "The police somehow found out about us and pressured me to admit to raping your mother or else they would tell everyone our secret. We would've both lost our jobs, and if they were able to prove that Nesta and I messed around, we'd both have gone to prison."

Tarone paused as he took a deep breath. "Every day, and every night, for fifteen whole years, I prayed that no one in the jail would ever find out the truth about me and Nesta. I went to bed wondering if I would be alive to see the next day. I was scared thinking that if someone were to find out then they'd kill mi madda and bredda."

Tarone rubbed his forehead above his left eye, then closed his eyes as he looked away.

"You see?" said his mother. "Tarone is not a bad man. He did not want anyone to hurt Nesta, his mother, or his brother. I hope that you're not mad at him anymore." She threw her arms around him.

Delroy couldn't help but do the same in return. He loved his mother, and now he loved her more than ever.

After he let go, Delroy turned to Tarone. "Sir, I…I…"

Tarone stood and walked over to him as Delroy stood too. Before he could utter another syllable, Tarone's arms were already wrapped around and pulling him in. Delroy couldn't help himself but do the same. It was then that he realized that tears were streaming down both cheeks.

"It's okay. It's not your fault," said Tarone.

"No, sir. Mi did mek a mistake."

"I'm not mad at you."

Their embrace seemed to go on with no appearance of an end. Delroy could not let go of this man, and he didn't want Tarone to let go of him. He needed this hug, and he needed it bad. Every second that passed was an ounce of hatred and anger that was released from his body. The tears that poured from his eyes, the sweat he suddenly felt all over, every drop that left his body contained pain that had accumulated over time. This was the catharsis he needed.

"Now that we get the truth out and everyone's getting along," said Lucille more jubilant than ever. "We need to have a drink, a strong one. Corey, reach back there in the bar and grab the Wray & Nephew."

"That's overproof rum," Corey said. "Delroy won't be able to drive home."

"Nonsense, it won't kill him. And if it does, he can always sleep it off here," Lucille answered. "In fact, I'm going to have some myself."

Tarone loosened his hug and patted Delroy on the shoulder. He then sat opposite them, while Delroy returned to sitting beside his mother, just as Corey put the rum on the table beside the glasses.

As Delroy poured a drink for himself, his mother turned to him.

"You've heard me tell you the whole truth about what happened to me. You've also heard from Tarone, and from Corey. You heard us all tell you the truth."

Delroy felt that something important was about to come.

"But we haven't heard from you."

"Me? I don't have anything to say."

"You sure about that?" asked Corey. "The other night when we were playing dominos, something was bothering you."

Damn it, why did Corey have to go there? Don't look at him, if you do, you're finished. He took a sip of his drink.

"Your friends bragged about what went on that evening, but you were quiet. Why is that?"

Delroy put down his glass, perhaps a bit too hard, on the tray. "I didn't see nor do anything."

"We didn't ask you if you saw or did anything," said Corey.

"Then why are you asking me these questions?"

"Because a friend of mine is in danger. He needs your help."

"I don't know your friend, so how can I help him?"

"You saw him in the parking lot. In fact, you almost ran him over, remember?" Delroy had a flashback to the moment. How could he forget?

"My friends were hurt, that's why I was hurrying to get them to safety."

"Was that the only reason you were in a hurry?" asked Corey. "You didn't see something else that freaked you out?"

"What do want me to say? Why do you think I can help your friend?"

"Because the people who killed Dwayne Pottinger are after him," said Corey. "He didn't ask for this, nor did I ask for what nearly happened to me earlier this evening."

"And you think I know what happened to Dwayne? I don't. I

was gone long before someone kill him. Mi only learn 'bout it di next morning."

"How about what happened before?"

No, don't say anything. This could make all of us targets, even my grandparents. Delroy got up. "I need to go."

Just as Delroy took a step, his mother grabbed his arm. "No, don't."

He turned to his mother. "Mi sorry, Mummy. But mi can't."

"We are here for you, son," said Lucille. "Please don't let this secret wear down your conscience. It will consume you."

"Please don't be angry," said his mother. "We don't want you to be angry."

Delroy shook his head as he broke away from his mother's grasp. "I'm sorry, but I really can't do this."

He rushed to the front door, put on his shoes, then hurried back to his car. He heard the front door and the grill opening behind him.

"Delroy." It was Corey.

He heard the running from behind him.

"Leave me alone," he said. But that didn't stop Corey, who caught up to him and grabbed his shoulder.

"Wait."

Delroy pulled out of Corey's hold. "Mi said leave mi alone. Yuh can't understand?"

"I know that you're scared because of what you saw."

"I already told you that I didn't see anything."

"Bullshit! I saw the way you reacted when we were playing dominos. Your friends were bragging about attacking Dwayne, and how he deserved it, while you stayed quiet the whole time. Even from your body language, I could see that you didn't like the way your so-called *friends* were talking about Dwayne." Corey took a deep breath and shook his head. "You weren't involved in what they did, were you?"

"What do you want from me?" said Delroy. Corey was beginning to push his luck and Delroy didn't know how much longer he could tolerate it before he did something that he'd later regret.

"I want you to tell the authorities what you know about Dwayne's killing."

"I never saw who kill him."

"But you saw something else, didn't you?"

Jesus! He isn't giving up.

"My best friend was kidnapped by Brutus and barely survived the military strike. Now, both him and a witness are in hiding. You're holding back something that could possibly save their lives."

"You want me to snitch," snapped Delroy. "That probably happen in Canada where you from. But we don't do that here in Jamaica."

"Even if it means saving a life?"

"And you don't think people won't retaliate? They'll come for my mum, my grandparents, and even me. I just now learn that the man I thought was my father, isn't. Do you know how fucked up that is?"

Delroy unlocked the door to his car and got in. He gunned the engine, did a U-turn in three steps due to the narrowness of the road, and sped off, leaving Corey standing at the side of the road.

His breathing was heavy, squeezing the steering wheel as he gnashed his teeth. He kept this up for as long as a half kilometer before he violently pulled off to the side of the road and stomped on the breaks. He carelessly threw the gear into park then slammed his fists multiple times on top of the steering wheel. He found himself out of breath and let his head drop, his forehead resting on the wheel.

This was not fair. He never asked for this, none of it. From Pastor Green or some other asshole being his father, to Dwayne coming to the party dressed like a girl. His grandfather already told him not to say anything that could get his friends in trouble. Imagine, he was a judge and he was telling Delroy to withhold information. His grandfather never hid his contempt toward gays and lesbians. And the man often chastised Delroy for *not* hating them. Delroy didn't know anything about Dwayne, except that he was beaten and set on fire after he got away from Delroy's friends. Coming forward and telling the truth was all he wanted to do, but he couldn't. Delroy wished he did not see what he saw that night. Just thinking about it made him want to look over his shoulder all the time.

It took him roughly twelve minutes to get home. As he pulled into the driveway, he saw a Maserati.

Bloodclaat! Pastor Green's here.

He parked beside the Maserati, and got out. Delroy balled up both fists as he walked to the side entrance and let himself in. The television was the first thing he heard, and when he glanced toward the living room, he saw his grandmother relaxing on the couch with her legs stretched out.

"Where were you?" she asked. "Your grandfather's been wondering why you never answered your phone."

"I forgot to turn it back on because the battery was low." Which wasn't true. "I went to see Mummy."

"At this hour?"

"We were playing Scrabble."

"Oh, I see."

Delroy heard voices coming from inside his grandfather's study. Seconds later the sliding doors to the office opened. His grandfather appeared in the middle.

"I've been calling you all evening, why you don't pick up?"

"I'm sorry, it was the—"

He froze as a knot tightened in his stomach.

Exiting the office behind his grandfather was Pastor Green, dressed in black and shamelessly wearing his clerical white collar.

That man. My mother's rapist. Why is he here talking to my grandfather?

"It was because of what?" His grandfather wasn't fooling around, as he was visibly agitated.

But Delroy couldn't take his eyes off Pastor Green. "I…I'm… it, I mean, my phone was off because the battery was weak."

Pastor Green approached Delroy and extended a hand. "How are you, son?"

Delroy didn't acknowledge his hand, reflexively backing away from him. "Mi good."

I ought to smash your face in right now, knock you to the floor, and bash your head on the tiles, you fucking pussyclaat.

But his body stiffened, his breathing quickened, and he felt himself wandering toward the stairs. "I'm going to bed. It's been a long day."

"Delroy?" called out his grandfather behind him as he rushed up the stairs. He bolted to his bedroom and shut the door so quick that it slammed unintentionally. He dropped his bag on the floor as he paced back and forth holding his head. Pastor Green hadn't done anything to him personally, yet, he felt as though he had been violated. He didn't even want to breathe the same air as that monster, knowing that his filth would contaminate his surroundings.

He should've kicked his ass right there and called him out for the hypocrite that he was. So why did he freeze? Didn't his grandparents know what that man did and what he allowed to happen to his mother—their daughter? Were they aware and just in denial? And if so, why?

His back was to the door when the knocking from the other side startled him away from it. He turned around and didn't get a chance to respond before the door flew open.

"What was that all about?" snapped the judge. "Why were you so rude to Pastor Green?"

Fuck, I don't even know if I should tell him the truth. "I wasn't in a good mood."

"Why's this? Your grandmother told me that you were playing boardgames with your mother."

"Yes, sir. That's what we were doing."

His grandfather raised an eyebrow as he crossed his arms and leaned his back against the door. "And where was this?"

Why would you ask me a question like that? "At Seaview."

"The whole time?"

This wasn't looking good. He knew something, but shit, Delroy was already in knee deep. "For the most part, yes."

"So, you weren't there the whole night. Is that what you're now saying?"

"Why are you interested in my whereabouts all of a sudden?"

"I'm the one asking the asking the questions, young man,"

snapped his grandfather. The last time he spoke to the judge that way got him a set of hard slaps across his face. "Where did you go afterward?"

"I just drove around."

"Why?"

"I needed to clear my head."

His grandfather didn't look convinced. In fact, the way his eyes narrowed, he clearly didn't believe him. "Who do you take me for, an idiot?"

Delroy hesitated briefly before the words "No, sir," slipped through his lips.

"You think I'm an idiot?" his grandfather yelled, rattling him. "All these years sitting behind the bench looking down at ruffians and other troublemakers and you don't think I can tell when someone's lying to me?"

"I never said…" The slap to his face came hard and swift, knocking him so hard off balance that he fell into the wall before dropping to the floor. The room spun so quickly that he couldn't keep his balance, his only instinct was to push himself backward across the floor and away from the judge until he backed up into the wall.

"I called your mother's home when I couldn't reach you," said his grandfather. "They told me that she was with a client. So, I'm going to ask you again. Where were you tonight?"

With the dizziness subsiding, Delroy used the wall to help himself to his feet.

"Answer me," yelled his grandfather. "Are you taking drugs? Or are you sleeping around with some battybwoy?"

Where did that come from? Delroy hung his head and shook it. "So, that's what you and Pastor Green were talking about."

"Excuse me?"

"Pastor Green thinks that I'm sleeping with other men. So he come all the way here to snitch on me?"

"Are you a battybwoy?"

"That's it, isn't it?" Delroy swallowed. "Pastor Green wants to start a rumor about me because he doesn't want anyone to know that he like to fuck children."

His grandfather's gasp was audible, followed by his shaking of the head, and eyes that narrowed as he pointed a finger at Delroy. "You watch your mouth."

"You didn't know that, did you?" Delroy threw in a callous chuckle. "You just told me that you could spot a liar. Yet the biggest liar you've ever known was standing right in front of you."

The judge lunged at him. "You sick battybwoy."

Delroy anticipated the move, and both hands went up and absorbed the fist he got, just below the back of his wrist. The impact was powerful enough to knock him back into the wall. The next thing was his grandfather's tight grip on both his wrists as he wrestled them apart. Delroy pushed back, momentarily knocking his grandfather off balance long enough to swing at him. His fist crunched into the left side of his grandfather's mouth, knocking him onto the bed before he fell to the floor.

He watched as the judge held onto the front of the bed with one hand while he covered his mouth with the next. "Did you know that Pastor Green was the one who raped my mother?" yelled Delroy. "Did you know that he's my father?"

"What's going on in there?" came Delroy's grandmother's voice from the door.

She noticed her husband on the floor, as he was getting up. "What the…" she cried as she rushed to assist him. She turned to Delroy. "What is wrong with you?"

Delroy gnashed his teeth as he looked at his grandmother. "Did you know too?"

"Know what?"

"Don't mind him," said the judge. "He's just being stupid."

"I found out this evening that Pastor Green raped my mum and that he's my father," said Delroy. "But I guess you knew that too."

His grandmother squinted as her jaw dropped. "Son, what foolishness are you talking? They caught the teacher who did that to your mother. And he even confessed."

"The confession was forced out of him. Besides, did my mother tell you that Tarone raped her?"

"Your mother was young," said his grandmother. "And given

her condition, she wouldn't have been able to process what she went through and be able to assist investigators."

"That's a bunch of shite and you know it."

"You watch your mouth in this house," growled his grandfather.

"Why don't you tell her what you and Pastor were discussing?" said Delroy. "Why don't you tell her about the police killing the only witness to see the pastor raping my mother and other children at that Bible camp you send she too."

He saw the way his grandmother looked at him. Her head slightly tilted to the side, looking back and forth between Delroy and his grandfather. Something told him that she was hearing this for the first time.

"This is the most ridiculous thing I've ever heard you say in my life," she said. "I don't know who you've been talking to, but I know Pastor Green is a good Christian. No, he's a *great* Christian. He would never do anything so horrible."

"Then you don't know Pastor Green."

"Watch your mouth," snapped the judge.

Delroy sucked his teeth. These two were hopeless.

His grandfather got up and blocked Delroy's path as he tried to leave. "Where are you going?"

"I'm going to confront that bastard right now since neither of you want to."

"You're not going anywhere," said the judge.

"Move out of my way."

His grandfather gave him a hard shove, to which Delroy pushed back. His grandfather didn't yield too easily, while they both struggled as he heard his grandmother screaming in the background. They smashed into the wall, the chest of drawers, then shattered a mirror, and wound up on the floor with Delroy on his back, his grandfather's hands around his throat.

Shit. He's really trying to kill me. The amount of hatred in his grandfather's eyes as he stared at him was more painful than his fingers digging into Delroy's neck, as though he were trying to puncture his skin. Delroy grabbed his grandfather by the wrists, trying to pry his hands off, as Delroy struggled to breathe. He tried to turn his head from one side to the next to break free. It was then that he saw a bottle of cologne lying on the floor, almost within reach. It must've fallen when they crashed into the chest of drawers. Delroy reached out for it, but only his middle fingertip grazed it. His arm snapped back to grabbing his grandfather's wrist. He squirmed the best he could, but his grandfather had placed his weight onto his right leg, limiting Delroy's movement.

His grandmother suddenly came out of nowhere and tugged at his grandfather. "Stop it, you're going to kill him."

Delroy felt the tug as his grandfather's weight was lessened briefly, as well as the grip around his neck. It was enough for him to stretch out, grab the cologne bottle, swing his arm around as hard as he could and smash it into the side of his grandfather's head.

There was an audible pop, as the judge fell onto his side with a hand to his temple where he was struck. He heard his grandmother scream but didn't pay attention to whether he had severely injured the man. All that was on his mind was getting away.

He made it to the hallway where he had to stop. He held the wall as he coughed violently, gasping for air. He stumbled ahead, holding the wall for support as he approached the curved staircase ahead. A set of heavy footsteps were fast approaching from behind. He turned around just in time to see the judge lunge at him, both palms striking him in the chest and shoving Delroy backward.

The last thing Delroy remembered was the house flipping upside down several times as he fell onto his back, struck his head and shoulders, and tumbled down the ceramic-tiled staircase.

Chapter 42

Near Pastor Green's Home, Spring Farm, Montego Bay

"I don't think he's coming," said Tarone. "Delroy had a few minutes' head start. He should've been here by now."

"I didn't know Pastor Green's home was this… secure." Corey stared at the front gate, which was the only entrance to the gated community. "Delroy could already be inside for all we know."

"Call his number again."

Corey knew that this was a longshot but dialed Delroy's number. The call went straight to voicemail. "He's not answering."

Watching how Delroy refused to reveal what he had witnessed the night Dwayne was killed only made Corey more anxious to know what was on Dwayne's phone—if he had recorded anything.

For now they had to wait for Delroy. Fortunately for them, there was a turn off opposite the country club that led to a sugar mill—a relic of the plantation period. Tarone had reversed in and parked, allowing them to see every car that entered or left.

A pair of headlights shone at them head on as a vehicle approached. Once it drove past, both Corey and Tarone were able to see that it was a Maserati.

Tarone pointed to it. "That's Pastor Green."

It was too dark for Corey to properly identify the person inside, but he took Tarone's word for it that it was Green. Corey suddenly felt the vibration of the revving motor, then looked down to see Tarone's hand on the gear. Instinctively, Corey grabbed Tarone's hand.

"Weh yuh a do?" yelled Tarone.

"What are *you* doing?" Corey answered as he forced the gear back into park, resisting Tarone.

"That man send crooked cops to kill Nesta. He's got to answer for that."

The two fought over the gear, when Tarone punched Corey in the arm with his free hand, causing him to release his grip.

"Let go!" spat Tarone.

Tarone switched the gear back into drive. He was about to floor the accelerator only to see that Pastor Green had already driven inside and that the gates were already closing.

"Yuh bumboclaat idiot. Yuh mek mi miss mi chance fi get him!" He threw the gear back into park and slapped the top of the steering wheel.

"And what would you have done? Rammed his car?" Corey yelled back as he held his arm, rubbing the spot where he was hit. "Had you attacked him right here, the security guard at the front gates would've called the cops. Then what? How far do you think we'd get with a busted-up taxi?"

Tarone stared ahead as Corey heard him fuming through his nostrils.

"You seem to forget that Nesta's killers were going to kill me too." Corey pointed toward the front gate. "You don't think I want to get my hands on that sonofabitch?"

Tarone still didn't look at Corey, as though he no longer acknowledged his presence. Corey wasn't sure how much of what he'd said Tarone had actually absorbed.

"Don't forget why we came here. We came to stop Delroy from making the same mistake that you were about to. It's obvious that Delroy didn't come, at least I'm not sure he would've been let in if he had."

Tarone sighed. Corey noticed the relaxed composure as a sign that he was listening.

"Oh rass!" Tarone palmed his face. "I was supposed to pick up mi madda this evening and mi figet. Pass me your phone."

Corey unlocked the burner with his thumbprint before handing it to him, remembering that Tarone's pay-as-you-go had run out of credits.

Tarone dialed a number and put the phone to his ear. "Yeah, a mi. Something came up and...what...what you mean Garfield went looking for me?"

Corey looked at Tarone. His mouth hung open and his face froze. Corey's chest tightened, knowing that the news would be bad.

"What? They...did what?"

Corey leaned closer. "What happened?"

"No, no, no, no, no." Tarone tossed the phone to the floor, striking Corey's feet.

"What's going on?"

Tarone closed his eyes hard and did not answer him.

Corey grabbed his arm. "Tarone, what's the matter?"

Tarone turned his head slowly toward Corey until he saw the tears in Tarone's eyes.

"Mi bredda, Garfield. Him get shot."

Corey gasped. "No."

Tarone swallowed then wiped his eyes with the back of his hand. "Him dead before di ambulance reach di hospital."

Corey's throat suddenly became dry as he looked away. He swallowed and turned to Tarone. "I'm so sorry. I...I can't believe that this is happening."

"I was supposed to pick up mi madda from Bible study this evening and when I didn't show, she called but couldn't reach me. So, a mi bredda she called fi come fi har. After him dropped her off, him passed by mi place fi check pon mi. Him surprised a robber and got shot."

Corey didn't know what else to say and didn't even know if he *could* say anything else. In one evening, Tarone lost a former lover and now his brother.

He was caught off guard when Tarone started up the engine, threw the gear into drive, and stomped down on the gas. The wheels spun and screeched violently against the asphalt as the car shot forward—accelerating so fast that Corey felt himself thrown back against the seat.

"Tarone."

He wasn't listening. He was in his own world.

"Tarone," Corey said louder. Tarone still ignored him as he slammed on the breaks and swerved onto the highway so violently that Corey gripped the door handle to prevent himself from flying into Tarone. Once they were on the straightaway, Corey fumbled for the seatbelt and pulled it across his chest. Tarone was going to get them both killed.

"Tarone! Stop the car."

Tarone ignored him as he ran a stoplight. He was afraid to look away from the road ahead, knowing that any second someone or another vehicle could pass in front.

"Will you stop the damn car!"

"Shut up!" Tarone snapped.

Corey felt his heart racing. Tarone had completely lost it. Even the way that he answered, just the tone in his voice.

Moments later without warning, Tarone slammed on the breaks—throwing them forward as the car skidded for several meters, the rear end fishtailing, tossing them against their doors and into each other until the car came to a dead stop nearly fifty meters ahead on the shoulder.

With the smell of burned rubber filling the inside of the car, Corey grabbed the dashboard in front to catch himself. He then felt an arm reach across in front of him, fumbling with the door handle.

"Out."

"What?"

Tarone couldn't get a proper grip on the handle. "I said get out."

"I'm sorry about your brother, but you have to—"

"Shut yuh bumboclaat mouth and get the fuck out a mi car." He finally managed to release the latch and push the door open. "This is all your fault. First Nesta, now my bredda. All because of you."

"You want to blame me? Fine. Blame me," Corey spat as he matched Tarone's scowl. "Did you stop to think that *you* were the target? Wake the fuck up! This isn't a coincidence."

There was a momentary glitch in Tarone's scowl, as though he did not consider Corey's point of view beforehand.

"Think." Corey maintained the same aggressive tone. "They killed Nesta because of what he knew. Then, they were about to kill me. How much you want to bet that they weren't waiting on you to come home to take you out too?"

"Yuh lie."

"Your phone's out of credit and is turned off, so they couldn't track you. What's left is to wait for you to come home. Does that sound like a lie to you?"

Tarone looked away from Corey, breathing loudly as he shook his head. "Jesus Christ."

"I don't know what else to say to convince you. Whether you go to your house or to your mother's I guarantee they'll be waiting for you." Corey then raised a thumb and pointed behind. "Everything points to Pastor Green having the police officers on his payroll to help him tie up loose ends. He's obviously desperate. My friend Eddie told me that desperate people make mistakes. They've just made a big one. I'm just glad that I was able to stop you from making one a few minutes ago. You abandon me now, and you're guaranteed to get us both killed. Is that what you want?"

Tarone still breathed hard and loud, then slammed his fists on top of the steering wheel. "Why can't they just leave me alone? I went to prison, now I'm out and they still want to kill me."

Corey let out a slow deep breath. "We're in the same boat. I don't like this any more than you."

Tarone took a few moments to compose himself. "What now?"

"For starters, you should let me drive. You've been through too much already."

Tarone let his head fall onto the steering wheel. It only then occurred to Corey that Tarone wasn't wearing his seatbelt when he went berserk behind the wheel. He opened his door, sighed, then got out. Corey's door was still open, so he did the same. Once they'd switched places, Corey's phone rang.

It was still on the floor on the passenger side where Tarone had thrown it earlier. Tarone reached down and handed it to Corey.

"Yeah?"

"It's Lucille." The tone of her voice told Corey that there was trouble.

"What's wrong?"

"It's Delroy," she said. "He's been in an accident."

Chapter 43

North of Clark's Town, Trelawny Parish

Eddie jumped up from lying in his seat as he was startled awake by a roaring sound that shook the car. He was hit with the stench of diesel fuel which made him look out his window. A dump truck had passed, and the roar died down. He turned to Candace, wondering how she could've slept through the noise, but there was nothing but an empty seat. He spun around to check the back. Nothing. He fumbled with the window before he got it open and stuck his head out. The dust was still settling as he looked around. Candace was nowhere to be seen.

"Candace?" Eddie shouted.

The fuck? I should've known not to go to sleep. Now she's abandoned me. Eddie shoved the door open and jumped out in the street without closing the door.

"Candace?" Eddie ran a few dozen meters in front of the car and yelled her name a second time. He then rushed back toward the car and past it. "Candace."

"Eddie?"

He turned to the sound of her voice as she emerged from the cane field beside the car. "Where were you? You had me scared shitless."

"Calm down," she said dismissively. "I just had to relieve myself."

"And you couldn't tell me?"

"You were sleeping. Why would I wake you to tell you that I need to pee."

Eddie was about to counter her argument, but he realized that he couldn't. "Come to think of it, I better go myself." Eddie walked toward the cane field. "I just hope there aren't any snakes."

Candace nodded. "Oh yes, the moment you drop your pants they may confuse you for competition and attack."

"You're funny."

"I'm just teasing you," said Candace. "Venomous snakes were eradicated when the colonizers brought over the mongoose."

A few minutes later, Eddie emerged from the bush and joined Candace, who was already inside the car.

He glanced at the clock on his burner and saw that it was five minutes past midnight. He'd been asleep for a little over two and a half hours, but he wasn't alert enough to drive. And even if he was, he didn't know where to go. The phone buzzed, followed by a notification that the battery level was below five percent.

"Just what we need. The phone's almost dead," said Eddie.

"Hold on," said Candace as she unbuckled her seatbelt, hopped out and walked to the back. "Open up."

Eddie reached to the right of the steering wheel and pressed the button to unlock the trunk. He heard it being opened, followed by Candace unzipping and then zipping the bag, followed by the trunk closing several seconds later. Candace got back in and handed him a palm-sized rectangular battery with a USB cord.

"Your uncle thinks of everything." Eddie plugged in the phone then rested it in the glove compartment.

He laid back down in his reclined seat and stared out the moonroof.

Minutes went by without either of them saying a word. He then heard Candace moving around in her seat, as though to make herself more comfortable.

"Eddie?"

"Yeah?"

"I never asked, but how did you get into writing?"

Eddie stared at the stars through the moonroof as he reminisced on how it all began. "It's just one of those things that just happened. Story ideas keep coming to me, so one day I felt the need to write them down."

"Where do your ideas come from?"

"Practically everywhere. From the news, conversations I'm in or that I overhear. Sometimes I hear a soundbite on the news and

Bam, a plot for a suspense novel comes to mind."

"Really? Just like that?"

"Sometimes it works against me. I was in between novels and was driving while listening to the radio. An idea came to mind from something the news anchor said. I was so distracted that I ran a red light and nearly got hit by another car."

Candace gasped. "Oh my gosh."

"Yeah. That was a close one."

A few moments of silence went by. "I always wondered why Dwayne was so into your books," said Candace. "He was always excited for the next one to come out. He had just bought your latest…"

Eddie could tell that she was choking up.

"I don't think that he had a chance to finish it." Candace's hands went to cover her face as she couldn't avoid the tears.

The moment was especially difficult for Eddie, as he was apprehensive of hugging her—considering that she did not want to be touched. In an interesting twist, Candace turned to him and buried her head into his shoulder.

Oh my gosh! Has she broken free of her trauma, or did she decide that she can trust me?

Eddie slid his arm from under her head and pulled her closer to him while holding her head with his other. "It's okay," he whispered. She did not cry loudly, but he could still hear her trying to hold it in.

There was more sniffling than crying, and Eddie still held onto her. This was the first sign that Candace was comfortable around him to the point that she showed how vulnerable she was. Should he bring it up? No, why spoil the moment.

There was a glow inside the car which caught Eddie's attention as he looked up. At first, he thought that a vehicle was approaching, but then he realized that the car beams would've had a broader shine. Eddie then saw what it was, and he followed the tiny little light as it flew above him and Candace in a circle, then drifted toward his window before exiting.

It was a firefly.

At that moment, Eddie saw intermittent lights floating above the moonroof. From where he lay, he had a clear view through Candace's window where he saw dozens more hovering above the cane field like tiny UFOs.

"You know," said Candace as she swallowed, "Dwayne told me that he hoped your books would become movies."

The movies. Wait a minute. Eddie sat up so fast that he unintentionally pushed Candace off him. *Holy shit, why didn't I think of this before?* He pulled the lever beside his chair and the seat popped back up. He hit the *Start* button and turned on the engine.

Candace caught herself and wiped her face with one hand. "What is it?"

Eddie unlocked the burner and called Corey. He then did a U-turn and sped back up to the intersection as the phone rang once before going to voicemail. "You just gave me an idea for a safehouse. It's a longshot, but it's worth a try."

Chapter 44

Cornwall Regional Hospital, Montego Bay

This was the last place Corey wanted to be. At least, he wasn't the one in the ICU on life support, which he could've been, considering what happened to him earlier. He and Tarone agreed that it would be best if he checked up on Delroy while Tarone waited in the taxi as the lookout. Corey had given Tarone his second burner phone to call him if he spotted anything of concern.

Corey made it to the Emergency Room area where he looked around for Lucille or Chevelle.

"Corey."

He turned to Chevelle's voice as she rushed to him with tears in her eyes.

"How is he?"

"The doctor said that he was hurt very, very bad." Chevelle wiped her eyes with the back of her hand. "He fell down the stairs and bumped his head many times."

"Where?" Corey asked.

"At home," Chevelle answered.

Corey immediately hugged her while shaking his head. "Delroy's strong. I'm sure that he's going to pull through."

It was then Corey noticed an older couple staring at him from a row of chairs. The gray-bearded gentleman held what appeared to be an ice pack to his temple. However, Corey was more nervous about the way that the man stared at him. It was as though he had some form of contempt for him. The woman—whom Corey assumed was the wife—stood and approached them.

Chevelle saw the woman walking toward them then gestured to her. "This is my mother."

"Hello," said Chevelle's mother, who extended her hand. "I'm Henrietta. Are you a friend of Delroy's?"

"Yes." Corey shook her hand. "Nice to meet you. How did this happen?"

"Like Chevelle said. Delroy tripped and fell down the stairs," said Henrietta. "It was a terrible accident."

Corey glanced at her husband, who still stared at him through narrowed eyes. He then looked back at Chevelle's mother. "Yeah...sorry to hear about that."

Delroy's grandfather just happens to have a fresh bruise on his head while Delroy's fighting for his life? Tripped and fell down the stairs, my ass. Those two were fighting.

Corey noticed how Chevelle fidgeted with her fingers. She obviously didn't believe what her mother was saying either.

"That's the man." Corey looked behind him to the yelling from the person he had hoped not to run into. "That's the imposter."

"Ann?" said Henrietta as she glanced at Corey and then back at the caretaker. "What are you talking about?"

"Get away from her, you ruffian," yelled Ann, barreling down the hall toward them, not caring whom she bumped into while making heads turn.

"No, you shouldn't call him that. That's not nice," defended Chevelle.

"That's okay, Chevelle," Corey said as Ann shoved him to the side to stand between them. "I'm sure she's wondering how I'm still alive. Aren't you?"

"What are you talking about?" she snapped.

"I'm talking about how you called the police on me. What did you say to convince them to beat me up and kill Nesta? Or was it Pastor Green who did that?"

Corey waited for Ann to answer, but she remained tight-lipped.

"They were going to kill me too. But you were hoping for that, weren't you?"

Ann waved a hand in front of Corey's face while shaking her head. "No, no, no. You don't show up here making false accusations."

"I just mentioned that someone was killed, and you didn't even react," said Corey calmly. "Why is that?"

Henrietta turned back and forth from Corey to Ann. "What is he talking about? Who's Nesta?"

"He's just someone who works at the same place as Chevelle," answered Ann with a dismissive wave as she turned to Corey. "And if he got shot and you got roughed up, then both of you must have done something to deserve it."

At that moment, Corey saw Chevelle's father stand, holding the ice pack to his head.

"What is going on here?" asked Chevelle's father loudly as he approached, not taking his eyes off Corey. "Who are you?"

"Someone who was pretending to be the student so that he could talk to Chevelle," said Ann.

"I thought you were Delroy's friend," said Henrietta.

"You were with my son this evening, weren't you?" asked the judge.

Chevelle turned to him. "Daddy, don't—"

"Stay out of this," growled the judge. He waved off everyone. "You can go. I'll handle this."

"Corey didn't do anything wrong," said Chevelle.

"Didn't you hear what I said?" snapped the judge.

Corey could not help but notice the apprehension on Chevelle's face. Henrietta quickly consoled her by walking her back to where they sat.

Ann hung around for a second longer, as though to be sure that Corey saw her scowl at him. She then stormed away.

The judge turned to Corey. "I know who you are, Corey Stephenson. I also know about your friend, Eddie Barrow. It's a miracle that you're both still alive."

"Sorry to disappoint you," Corey said as he smirked. "Too bad the cops who shot Nesta and roughed me up won't be around to be interrogated. But I get the feeling that you're fine with that."

The judge smiled. "I have no idea what you're talking about. You were lucky this evening, but luck tends to run out eventually."

"Is that a threat?"

"Consider it free legal advice."

Corey chuckled as he lowered his head and pinched the bridge of his nose. "So that's what you guys call it." He then dropped his hand and looked the judge in the eye. "Did you give the same legal advice to Nesta?"

"I don't know who that is."

"How about Delroy?" Corey nodded to the judge's bruise. "Did he give you that before he had his so-called *accident*?"

"Are you accusing me of attempted murder?" asked the judge. "Where's your evidence? In all my years behind the bench and as a prosecutor, I've never heard of a case that was ever won purely on speculation."

"Hopefully Delroy recovers. Then we'll know what really happened."

"Yes, I'm hoping so," said the judge. "He was terribly upset this evening when he came home. I imagine that you had something to do with that."

"I don't know what you're talking about."

The judge smiled. "Well played." The smile slowly dropped. "I'm warning you, Mister Stephenson. Stay away from my family. If I learn that you've been speaking to either Chevelle or Delroy, or if you even try to contact them, you have no idea how far I'll go."

He walked past Corey, deliberately bumping his shoulder as he passed.

Corey turned to him. "Oh, Judge?"

The judge paused to look back.

"You ever raise chickens when you were younger?"

"Why yuh waan know?"

"Then you ought to know that they eventually come home to roost." Corey looked at Chevelle, who had witnessed the exchange, and nodded. She did not respond, but he could tell that she was upset. Ann still had her scowl, while Henrietta did not even look at him.

Less than a minute later, Corey was roughly forty meters from the entrance when his phone rang. He grabbed it and hit the green phone icon without checking the number.

"Yeah?"

"Get out!" It was Tarone, the trepidation in his voice made

Corey pause and look away from the entrance.

"I'm about to exit, don't worry."

"Don't use the main entrance," Tarone shouted. "That's where they are."

The back of Corey's throat went dry as he glanced at the entrance and froze—two Jamaican Constabulary Force Officers just entered.

Oh Shit.

Corey pivoted around and walked in the opposite direction as he tucked his phone in his back pants pocket. *Okay, they didn't see me. Just keep cool and they won't notice me. Why didn't Tarone call sooner?*

He turned a corner and picked up the pace, thinking that the hospital was large enough for there to be another exit close by. Corey checked his six, no JCF in sight. He breathed a sigh of relief. Perhaps they did not spot him after all.

It was then that he saw both appear in the intersecting hallways and walk toward him—their pace quickening.

He'd been made.

Corey walked rapidly as he passed hospital staff and patients—some of which were laying in hospital beds in the hall.

"Corey Stephenson!" someone he assumed was one of the officers yelled behind him. "Stop where you are!"

Corey blasted off into a sprint. Another intersecting hallway was ahead to which he skidded around. His chest suddenly seized up on him, as Detective Inspector Ellis was in front of him, blocking his path. He skidded so suddenly that he slipped and fell. He didn't have time to get up before he was grabbed and pinned to the floor.

"Listen to me," said Ellis whispering loudly. "I'm on your side. Go hide in that room, quick!"

Corey felt himself being pulled to his feet and shoved toward the room to his left. The door was open as he stumbled in and scrambled to the floor where he hid beside the patient's bed that was farthest from the entrance. He was in a semi-private room, where both patients were separated by a curtain. Corey didn't get a chance to see them. All he heard were the sounds of the monitoring equipment and heavy snoring from the patient he was next to.

From where he crouched, Corey heard the commotion outside in the hall.

"Don't mind me, I'm not hurt," said Ellis. "He ran that way."

Corey's burner suddenly rang, causing him to fumble for it before it rang again.

Shit, Tarone! Now's not the time.

He grabbed it from his back pants pocket and hit the red icon to hang up. But he glimpsed the number and saw that the call wasn't from Tarone, but from Eddie. Corey then immediately turned it off. There's no way that the police did not hear that. That's it. He was screwed. But still, Corey did not budge. Not only did he feel a tightness in his chest, but also in the pit of his stomach. Sweat dripped from his forehead onto his eyelashes as he tried to control his breathing. He wiped away the sweat with the back of his wrist while staring down at the few droplets on the floor, not even wanting to look up.

"Stephenson," came a whisper from the door. "Stephenson? Come out quickly."

Corey raised his head above the bed and was hit by the smell of the patient's feet which weren't fully covered by the sheet. Ellis stood halfway in the doorway making a series of short, quick hand gestures for him to hurry.

He got up but was still hesitant on approaching Ellis.

Ellis cocked his head to the side. It was clear that he guessed what was on Corey's mind. "I could've arrested you if I wanted you. Why would I help you hide if I wasn't on your side?"

He had a point.

Corey joined Ellis in the hallway, checking both directions to make sure there weren't any other officers, before turning to him.

"Go that way and you'll find an exit out back." Ellis pointed. "Meet me there, but don't go outside until you see me."

"I'm not here alone."

"You'll have to leave him—"

"No can do. His name's Tarone, his brother was killed earlier this evening."

"What?" The way his eyebrows raised showed alarm. "Where is he?"

Corey gave Ellis a description of the vehicle and which section of the parking lot he could find him.

Ellis inhaled through his teeth. "Jesus Christ!"

He then closed his eyes as though he were thinking quickly on how he'd rescue both. He gave Corey a light but panicked shove. "Just go. I'll find Tarone, and don't forget what I said about not waiting outside. And turn off your phone, you nearly gave yourself away."

"Already done," said Corey as he took off.

Corey followed the directions posted throughout the halls until he arrived at the exit almost half a minute later. He kept a safe distance from the exit, being mindful of cops who may drive by and look in.

He leaned against the wall, staring at the entrance, wondering how many cops were on Pastor Green's payroll. The last words Chevelle's father told him did not sit well with him either—it was obvious the man may have been involved to some extent with what happened to Corey and Nesta earlier. As for Ellis, this was the second time this evening he saved Corey's life. Ellis had already acknowledged that he was aware of crooked officers on the force, but how much did he know?

Corey kept nervously checking up and down the hall, trying not to appear too suspicious to anyone who walked by. All he wanted was for Ellis to hurry up.

Five minutes went by, no sign of him. Maybe those two pigs found Tarone, forcing him to flee. What if those pigs were involved in killing Tarone's brother, and then made it look like a burglary gone wrong? If they caught Tarone, then they'd drive him somewhere outside of the city where they'd kill him. If either of those scenarios occurred, Ellis would never find him.

Roughly two minutes later Corey saw a squad car stop outside. There was a quick flash of the lights on the roof of the vehicle, telling him that it was Ellis's car.

Still nervous that he was being followed, Corey intermittently looked over his shoulder as he went outside.

"Get in the back and lie down," said Ellis through a lowered window.

Corey did not waste time as he yanked the door and slammed it shut behind him, curling up so that he could fit as he laid down. He felt the car swerve as it sped up, then slow to a quick stop that jolted him into the back of the seats in front.

"Where's Tarone?"

"I back here."

Corey turned to the sound of Tarone's muffled voice from behind the car seat.

"I made him get in the trunk," said Ellis. His voice was still loud and commanding.

"Where are we going?" Corey asked.

"Somewhere safe," answered Ellis. "You know, you're lucky I found you."

"How'd you know I was at the hospital?"

"I'll tell you that when we get to where we're going," said Ellis. "We have a lot to talk about. I know you don't have any reason to trust me, but you have no choice at this point. You understand? You and Mister Barrow should've listened to me from the beginning. I told you both not to get involved in this investigation. You see what nearly happened?"

"You should've listened to *us* from the beginning," rebutted Corey. "Maybe my friend and I wouldn't be in the shit we're in right now."

"Look, we can't go back in the past," said Ellis. "I'm putting my life on the line for all of you right now. It's only a matter of time before those crooked officers figure out what I did back there. So, if you want to help you and your friend, then you'll have to help me fill in the many gaps by telling me what the hell is going on."

Chapter 45

Somewhere in Saint James Parish

Corey heard the gravel crunching under the tires as Ellis drove slowly on the narrow road with thick bushes on either side. From the front passenger seat he saw what appeared to be moths flitting in front of the high beams. Tarone was so quiet that Corey checked over his shoulder to see he was okay. He was glad he didn't have to come here on his own because he'd be wondering who might be hiding on either side waiting to jump him the moment he stepped out of his car.

The car dipped as Ellis took extra care driving around small potholes, but there were so many that avoiding one still resulted in the other front tire hitting a different one.

Corey overheard Ellis muttering something along the lines of him losing the front end of his car in one of the potholes. Despite that, Ellis clearly knew the road well enough that he knew when to slow down and when to accelerate.

In the last hour, Corey checked his voicemail and listened to the message that Eddie had left him. It was brief, only giving an address he and Candace were heading to and what he had discovered about Weiss's connection to Plessis—all without going into detail on how he found out. Corey told Ellis what had happened since the funeral. With regards to what happened at Turtle Grove, Ellis confirmed Corey's suspicions about the two officers who assaulted him and killed Nesta. When Corey told him about Pastor Green, Ellis did not dismiss what Corey had learned from Nesta before he was shot.

Tarone only spoke when Ellis spoke to him. Without going into specifics, Tarone confessed that Nesta was his alibi for the night that Chevelle was raped. Corey noticed Ellis's facial expressions—specifically when his mouth opened without him speaking and then he nodded as though to say he had figured out Tarone's secret. Unlike what other cops would've done, Ellis did not ask any specific questions which would lead Tarone to say anything that would incriminate himself—considering that Jamaica still had their Buggery Law, a relic from the colonial period that criminalized gay sex.

Just from that alone, Corey's gut told him that Ellis may not have been the enemy he thought he was. However, he did not want to get too cozy to the point of letting his guard down around him. Given his past experiences with police officers he would never fully trust one.

As they drove, the bushes disappeared and the full moon was visible. Soon after, Ellis turned into a driveway to a two-story house that appeared to date back to the plantation era.

"Who lives here?" asked Corey.

"An old friend," said Ellis as an automatic outdoor light came on to illuminate the space. He parked behind a black SUV. "He retired ten years ago from police work."

"Whoa! Another police officer?"

"What's your problem with police officers?" asked Ellis.

"I was nearly killed by two of them before you arrived," Corey answered. "And I'm sure the ones who showed up at the hospital were there to finish the job."

"And dem shaat mi bredda too," Tarone continued.

"We won't know that until we catch them," said Ellis.

"Mi know a dem sed one," said Tarone. "Dem a probably di same ones weh showed up a di hospital."

"Look." Ellis shook his head. "I'm risking my life for you. And from what you both told me, possibly my career. The least you could do is show some gratitude."

Ellis then got out of the car and slammed the door.

"I ain't disrespecting you," said Corey as he got out. "But when it comes to the police, me and Eddie go way back. And I'm not talking about random street checks for *Driving While Black*."

"Would you rather I drop you off anywhere so that you can

fend for yourselves?" asked Ellis. "Do you think you'd still be standing here had I not shown up at Turtle Grove when I did? What about at the hospital?"

Corey sighed. "I just want some reassurance that your friend can be trusted."

"Mister Stephenson." It was a raspy, bass voice which came from the balcony.

Corey turned to the man's voice but all he saw was darkness. There was a creaking noise that sounded like wood rolling on wood, like a rocking chair. As they got closer, the man leaned into the light.

He was bald, medium build, wearing an old pair of slacks with his shirt unbuttoned, and rocking back and forth in a rocking chair. He looked battered, not physically, but more emotionally as though he had a few decades worth of trauma that he was trying to keep buried underneath. The bags under his eyes made him look as though he was in a state of perpetual sleepiness. Perhaps on and off depression. Why else would anyone isolate themselves so far from civilization—and hidden behind the bushes on top of that. Looking up at the old house, it may as well be a part of him.

"Come forward, young man. I ain't going to attack you," said the man who then looked at Tarone. "You too."

Ellis gestured for the two of them to walk ahead. Corey did not know what to think of the stranger. Someone sitting on his balcony all alone in the dark in the middle of nowhere must have some serious issues. He walked up to the front steps, which were only three. Tarone followed him, and then Ellis.

The man coughed into the crook of his arm a few times, drawing Corey's attention to the ashtray full of cigarette butts on the small stand beside him—along with a bottle of liquor, which he then held in his hand. "Yuh both look like shit. Have a glass to calm your nerves."

"No thanks, I'm good." Corey shook his head. A former police officer meeting him for the first time and expecting him to sit down and have a drink with him? Hell no.

Ellis's friend nodded as he put the bottle on the floor on the other side of him and out of Corey's sight. "That's right. I forget you used to have a drinking problem. I'm sorry about that."

How the hell?

"If you're wondering how I know this, I read your friend's book."

He was obviously talking about Eddie's second published novel, where he gave a fictionalized version of a previous incident where Eddie was framed for murder after a publicity stunt that Corey and Jordyn came up with in order to help Eddie get a book deal—which backfired horribly. Now here they were, minus Jordyn, on the run again. Boy, he was a heavy drinker back then. A life that he did not want to return to. Part of him wished he did not give Eddie permission to make his fictionalized character an alcoholic.

"It's not that," said Corey.

"Then what? You think I put poison in it?"

On any other day, Corey would've snickered at the stranger's raw sense of humor.

The man closed his eyes and nodded. "I get it. You don't trust police after what you and your friend went through."

"What do you know about my friend's books?"

"I read too, you know," he answered. "We just met and you're already insulting me."

The stranger then turned to Tarone. "As for you. I followed the court case involving you and that young girl—the student you were accused of raping."

The man shook his head as he grabbed the glass from the stand and took a swallow. "I was telling Ellis back then that something wasn't right about that case, that your *confession* didn't sound genuine. That poor victim, she had no chance of being taken seriously and they didn't want to force her to testify because she's retarded."

"And you wonder why we don't trust police," said Tarone. "My life got completely destroyed because the police didn't want to do their job. They just want to pretend that they are, to please the public."

"I get why you're angry," said man as he grabbed both armrests to help himself stand. "I lost sleep over the outcome of that case.

I've always wondered if there was something else I could've done. The biggest problem was that I couldn't get that poor girl to talk."

Tarone's eyes widened. "It was you? You were the one who interviewed me."

The man nodded. "You telling me that I aged *that* much? Now you're the one insulting me."

He then walked slowly to the door and waved his hand toward himself. "My name's Karlos, by the way. Come in." He pulled open the spring-activated wooden screen door. "We have a lot to talk about."

Corey watched Karlos walk inside, then glanced over at Tarone, who returned the look.

"Well, go in!" came Ellis's booming command, startling them. "I'm not going to carry you."

Corey entered, followed by Tarone when Ellis called him.

"Oh, I almost forgot."

Corey turned around with Tarone to see Ellis as he took out a plastic vial from his jacket pocket and handed it to Tarone. "Remove the cap and swab inside of your cheeks with the tip."

Tarone stepped back defensively. "What for?"

"I'm doing some cleaning up. Proving that you're not Delroy's father is how we start." Ellis held up the vial to Tarone. "Here."

Tarone glanced at the vial for a moment, then took it. He uncapped the swab, stuck it in his mouth, capped it back, and gave it to Ellis.

"Why you think the results are going to be different this time?"

"Because I'm going to oversee the procedure myself," Ellis answered. "You both should be safe as long as you don't leave here."

Ellis started walking back to his car. "Hopefully Delroy's regained consciousness by now and can answer some questions. Oh, and do me a favor."

"What's that?"

"Don't lie to Karlos. He no longer has a badge, so you won't like what happens next if you do."

Ellis was then back in his car and sped off.

Chapter 46

Dennis Denton's cliffside villa, Negril, Westmoreland Parish

Eddie ended up leaving a message on Corey's voicemail and gave him the address to where he and Candace were going to, along with a brief update of what they'd learned so far.

The drive was a little under two and a half hours before they reached the resort city of Negril on the island's western tip. Eddie knew that it was a longshot from the beginning. But given his past and that Denton admitted that he was a fan, hopefully he would provide temporary shelter for him and Candace. Eddie did not doubt that he could've used one of the known apps with end-to-end encryption to call Denton's cell, but since Brutus warned him against doing so, he decided not to take the chance.

An eight-foot-high wall bordered the side of the road, and it curved inward at the entrance, which was blocked by a wrought-iron gate of the same height.

Eddie pulled up close to the intercom, reached out, pressed the button below the speaker, and waited. Concerned that someone may be watching them, Eddie pressed the button again. It was then that he noticed there was a camera lens embedded in the intercom. Made sense, Denton would be able to see who's visiting, possibly via an app on his smartphone. Eddie wouldn't be surprised if there were other hidden cameras that focused on the license plate and the vehicle's model.

"Are you sure he didn't go back to Hollywood?" asked Candace.

"He's supposed to be here at least for the next few days," Eddie answered. "By the way, not all movie directors and actors *live* in Hollywood."

There was some static through the intercom followed by someone clearing their throat. "Eddie Barrow?"

"It's me."

"What the hell did you get yourself involved in?"

"I'm really sorry to bother you so early in the morning," said Eddie. "But I really don't know who else I can turn to."

"Who's that with you?"

"An important witness," Eddie answered. "Listen. Whatever you heard on the news about Guava Hill isn't the full story, and we can prove it. But we really need your help."

"I really don't know if it's a good idea to let you—"

"Excuse me, sir," Candace interrupted. "I don't expect you to understand what's going on because we never had a chance to make our side of the story known. All we're asking for is that you hear us out before deciding. If you don't believe us, we'll leave you alone."

There was a pause from Denton. Eddie wished that Candace had not interrupted him, only because Denton did not know her personally. Eddie kept his eyes on the intercom, hoping that Denton was a good face-reader and would trust he was telling the truth.

A buzzing sound caught their attention, and Eddie looked ahead to see the gates swing slowly inward. Eddie breathed a sigh of relief and stepped on the gas.

Chapter 47

Karlos's House, Saint James Parish

There was a staircase to their right once they entered, with a hallway to the left of it.

"Don't bother taking off your shoes because I haven't mopped the floor," said Karlos.

Something was odd about the walls, and Corey had to reach out and touch it. He realized that there was a covering on it…then it hit him.

"What's wrong?" asked Tarone. "You never seen wallpaper before?"

"Yeah, at my grandmother's house back in Trinidad when I was about five," Corey answered. "I didn't know that this was still 'a thing' down here."

"It isn't," Tarone answered.

They followed Karlos to a room which Corey assumed was an office, except it was highly unkempt. There were stacks of old newspapers on the floor, which most likely contributed to the musty, old smell. He looked up to a clicking sound. He expected to see a ceiling fan, but it was a beetle which kept flying into the glass lampshade. Just above it was a small green lizard on the ceiling, waiting patiently for the beetle to fly close enough to become a meal.

"I don't get company too often, which is why there aren't more chairs, so you'll have to stand," Karlos said as he sat down on the swivel chair in front of his desk that was propped against the wall. He pulled out what appeared to be a scrapbook from one of the desk drawers and placed it on the surface. He opened it, releasing a plume of dust as Corey and Tarone stood on opposite sides of him. From where he stood, Corey saw that the scrapbook had bristol board pages with an adhesive that held pictures and newspaper clippings in place under a sheet of plastic.

Karlos then grabbed a pair of glasses from the desktop and put them on as he flipped the pages. "The moment I heard about the shooting at Turtle Grove Park, I got flashbacks to a case I investigated years ago about a young girl, ten years old, and disabled mentally. The rapist tied her down on a bed. I'm sure you can guess what he did next. And this happened during one of Pastor Green's Bible Camps. The case never went anywhere because the girl changed her story and recanted. The parents never allowed me to talk to the girl."

Karlos stopped on a page where he pointed to the paper with notes written on it. The date at the bottom was from twenty-five years before. He turned the next few pages, which contained newspaper clippings and investigative notes about Chevelle. "Unlike the previous case, *this* one made the papers. When I heard that the pregnant victim was the same kind of victim—mentally disabled, around ten to fourteen years old, my gut told me that those cases were related. I knew this wasn't a coincidence. But even though I couldn't get any proof, I was convinced that either Pastor Green or someone working for him was the culprit."

Karlos then glanced briefly at Tarone. "All of that went down the toilet when you confessed to raping Chevelle, along with your DNA identifying you as the father. I interviewed several people—at the school, the church, and none of them wanted to talk. The only person I felt wanted to say something was a groundskeeper who worked at Turtle Grove. He was also the janitor at Chevelle's school. Except when I tried to get him to talk, he kept denying that he knew or saw anything."

Karlos turned to Corey. "Ellis called me this evening because he found out that two officers were heading to Turtle Grove because they got word that the same janitor was meeting you there. He called me while heading there because he remembered that first case, the one where the victim recanted. Ellis couldn't have been on the force for more than ten years when that happened. He also knew that those two officers were known for being rough with people and would probably end up killing both you and the janitor and then claim self-defense."

Karlos then turned back to the scrapbook where he slammed his palm on the page in front of him. "I told him that he needed to get there quickly before anything happened to either of you. I followed the news about your friend Eddie Barrow and I told Ellis that he must be trying to find out who killed Dwayne Pottinger." He turned to Corey. "Now he's rumored to have been at Guava Hill, and you just happened to be meeting a witness at Turtle Grove of all places. How could those officers have known that both of you were there unless someone suspected that you were heading there and tipped the police off? You're lucky Ellis got there in time."

"But too late to save Nesta," mumbled Tarone.

"Nesta. I couldn't remember his name." Karlos spun his chair around. "Ellis didn't go into details, so why don't you fill in the gaps as to what happened after."

Corey recounted everything that happened from the night he and Eddie were at Citrusville up until this moment. When he got to the part about meeting Tarone, Tarone added a few things, as he and Corey reciprocated. Corey saw that it wasn't easy for Tarone, but he came clean about his relationship with Nesta.

Corey waited for Karlos to react, as his facial expression remained the same throughout. However, to his surprise, Karlos grinned. He then shook his head and chuckled as he slammed a palm on the scrapbook.

"So *that* was it. Nesta kept quiet because Pastor Green most likely knew about the secret and must've threatened him with exposure if he talked." Karlos sighed as he turned to Tarone. "I tell you both the truth. I ain't into no religion, so I don't care what you do on your own time." He spun his chair back around so that he could look at the scrapbook and pointed to Pastor Green's picture. "If you ask me, if there was a God, then he wouldn't let monsters like him become multi-millionaires by swindling people who are so stupid that they give away their hard-earned money to him every week with the promise that Jesus would make their lives better. And while he preached hatred, and about the sins of others, he was raping young girls."

"The police officers who arrested me," Tarone answered. "They were the same ones I heard killed Nesta. Now they're both dead in that ambush. Serves them right."

Karlos turned to Tarone. "Them getting killed may be retribution for you, but it'll be more difficult to prove that Pastor Green paid them off."

"Isn't it obvious that it was Pastor?" said Corey. "He has the money and a secret to cover up."

"I'm sure that he's involved in some capacity. But we can't prove it," said Karlos. "Assuming that it was Pastor, he would've paid them in cash and used a middleman to make the delivery, making it more difficult to trace everything back to him. And don't forget that there were at least two others who were after you at the hospital."

Karlos then turned to Tarone. "And if they turn out to be the same ones who killed your brother, as you suspect, imagine what would've happened had they found you."

"So, basically, anyone could be working for Pastor," said Corey.

"Assuming that it's him who paid them off." Karlos flipped a few pages in his scrapbook and removed a thick sheet of paper that had been folded several times over. After Karlos unfolded it, it was large enough to cover the desk's surface. As Corey looked at it, he saw that it was a map of the Caribbean. There were stickers next to each island nation with different hyphenated numbers.

"What's this?" asked Tarone.

"These are all the countries where Pastor and his Bible Camp visited."

"What do the numbered stickers mean?" asked Corey.

Karlos turned to Corey. "Take a guess."

Corey leaned in and glanced at the numbers. He saw 2-0-0, 3-1-0, 1-0-0, 5-2-0, and it went on. "The number of times that Pastor visited each place versus the number of times a rape was reported?"

"You're close." Karlos turned to the map and pointed at the island nation of Saint Lucia. "Here, it's six-two-zero. Pastor Green visited there six times in the last twenty years. There were two rape complaints which were later recanted, resulting in nothing."

Corey ran his finger over each mark on the map and counted them. "I'm counting nine complaints with no arrests," said Corey. "And you're saying this map represents the last twenty years?"

"It may be longer," said Karlos. "These are only complaints. It doesn't mean there weren't more victims who were either too scared or ashamed to come forward."

"How could something this big be kept a secret?" asked Corey.

"Because they could never build a case. All the victims are mentally retarded, which makes it very difficult to build a case because from the time they're little they're taught to obey and respect their elders. And since most of them can't speak or express themselves too well, they're often ignored."

"Today we use the term *intellectually disabled* or *developmental disability*," said Tarone. "Mi waan yuh fi know dat."

"Anyhow," said Karlos, "as I was saying, with all these barriers, prosecutors were reluctant to take on these rape cases. They tell me that children who suffer from menta...sorry, *intellectual disabilities* often have difficulty recalling the details of the crimes perpetrated against them."

"In other words," said Tarone, "they knew that Pastor Green's high-priced lawyers would exploit that to their advantage and tear them apart on the witness stand if it ever went to court."

"No wonder they all retracted their complaints," said Corey.

"Now you're beginning to understand." Karlos nodded once. "These victims are extremely easy targets for sexual predators. And I'm sure that many of them children that attended Pastor Green's Bible Camp got raped more than once."

Karlos turned and nodded toward a glass cabinet. "You see that bottle of rum?"

Corey and Tarone simultaneously looked and nodded.

"That bottle I save for a special occasion," said Karlos. "I never touched it, and don't want to until I see Pastor Green face justice."

Corey's phone rang. He checked it and did not recognize the number. He excused himself and turned away. "Hello?"

"Corey, thank God, I reached you."

"Ms. Bevins?"

"Yes, I've been trying to reach Eddie but he's not answering his phone."

"Why, what's going on?"

"He asked me to find out as much as I could about a company called Plessis."

"Yeah, he mentioned that name on my voicemail."

"I found out a few things that he needs to know. Where did he say he was going?" Corey heard the anxiety in her voice.

"He said that he was going to see Dennis Denton. He was hoping he could hide out there."

"Oh no."

The tone of her voice made Corey tense. "What's wrong?"

"We need to stop him. Denton isn't the person Eddie thinks he is."

Chapter 48

Dennis Denton's cliffside villa, Negril, Westmoreland Parish

The driveway snaked up a slant hill, ending in a circle with a water fountain as a centerpiece. The cliffside villa was well lit from the outside, with spotlights shining from above and below the sides of the villa. Looking at it as they approached, Eddie was reminded of Tony Stark's cliffside mansion in the Iron Man movies, except this one was a lot less extravagant and was limited to being on the ground floor.

Eddie saw Denton exit through the front door, his hair in a tussle, and looking like he threw on the first pair of shorts and t-shirt he could get his hands on.

He waved Eddie toward the garage, which had two doors. "Park inside."

He drove around the water fountain so that he was facing away from the villa, then waited for the garage door to flip open before he reversed inside—parking next to a white Mercedes-Benz GLS-Class SUV. At a $160k price tag, it was obvious chump change for someone like Denton.

Eddie unplugged the burner from the charger and took it with him as they got out of the car. He turned it back on and glanced back at the Honda. Parked next to the Mercedes-Benz, he couldn't help but feel how out of place it looked. The garage alone put his entire apartment back home to shame. They left the garage and saw Denton stretch his arm out toward it, holding a keychain. The door closed soon after.

"Mister Denton, you're a lifesaver for giving us a chance," said Eddie as he shook Denton's hand on entering the foyer.

"Don't mention it, and you can call me Dennis." Denton motioned Eddie and Candace forward to the living room. "Make yourselves at home, we're pretty much isolated out here so you don't have to worry about anyone seeing you. I hope I'm doing the right thing."

"You're giving us a chance to tell our version of the events," said Eddie. "So, you're off to a good start."

"Let me get you both something to drink," said Denton as he left them in the living room. "Champagne cola, pineapple, cream soda?"

Eddie gestured to Candace to answer.

"Champagne cola."

"I'll have pineapple," Eddie answered as they shared a sofa and he gawked at the spacious design of the home, which allowed a breeze to flow through. Not a fan in sight, not that one was needed. He heard what sounded like a fridge door open and shut, and the tinkling of ice filling two glasses. Denton returned roughly a minute later with the glasses on a tray.

"So, what do you think of the villa?"

"Roomy," said Candace.

"Yeah, lots of space," said Eddie.

"You should see it from the ocean," said Denton. "Breathtaking view of the forested hills, and there's even a rooftop deck where you can catch the sunset. The villa is on roughly two acres of land, which is great for hosting parties."

Denton then took a seat on an adjacent couch. "But enough about my place. Tell me, how did this all start?"

Eddie allowed Candace to go first. She started from the beginning, from the moment that she met Weiss to the moment she escaped to Guava Hill. Eddie drank from his glass while she spoke, and then spoke to give Candace a break—it clearly wasn't easy for her to talk about how Weiss sexually assaulted her. Eddie did not leave out a single detail, except the moment where they broke into Hines's office.

Denton leaned forward in his chair with both elbows on his knees as he listened. His eyes were narrowed as though concentrating on each word they said, in order to absorb everything the first time so they wouldn't have to repeat themselves. When they were done, he inhaled deeply and let out a long, exhaustive exhale.

"I never would've imagined that both of you would've gone through what you described." Denton turned to Candace. "If you'd been in Hollywood as long as I have, then you'd know when someone's telling the truth about being raped. Besides, what you've said about Plessis isn't something anyone just makes up."

"Does this mean that you're going to help us?" asked Candace.

Denton nodded. "You bet. I know a few people."

Eddie and Candace breathed a double sigh of relief, even though Eddie knew that they weren't out of the woods yet.

"I hope that you don't mind, but I already told Corey to come over," said Eddie.

"That's fine," said Denton as Eddie grabbed his phone.

"May I use the bathroom?"

"Sure," Denton answered as he pointed away. "Just down the hall, second door on your left. I don't think you're going to get a signal because the reception hasn't been too good today. Damn cell phone companies can never get it right around here. You can use the landline."

Eddie nodded as he looked at the burner's monitor. Sure enough, no bars. He put it away and went to the bathroom to relieve himself. Coming here was simply on the hope that Weiss's mercenaries never learned of him having already met Denton. As easy as it was for them to get into Guava Hill, Denton's home would be a piece of cake to them. After relieving himself, he flushed the toilet, washed his hands, and walked back in the hall. As he headed to the living room, he felt a breeze coming from behind him. Out of curiosity he walked the other way and came to a door which led into the back yard. Just a quick peek, no harm in that.

The lawn was professionally manicured, and even though all he saw was blackness while staring out at the ocean, he heard the waves crashing against the side of the cliff close by. He followed a stone path around the back of the villa and saw a swimming pool which had stairs leading inside. This was way too much luxury for him. He recalled when Nancy Bevins invited him and Corey to a dinner party in Manhattan once, where she introduced Eddie to some of the top executives in the literary industry. Saying that it did not go smoothly was an understatement—especially when Corey asked if they had any crackers to put in his soup. Being here reminded him of that moment, and he felt that it was time for him to head back.

Eddie came to an entrance and walked in, only to realize that he didn't enter through the same door which he had exited earlier. He was inside what he assumed to be Denton's office. It was lavishly furnished with a desk with an open laptop on the surface, framed photographs on one wall and framed movie posters and box-office results on another, there was also a full bookcase.

No, he couldn't allow himself to be caught in here by Denton, he'd risk blowing his trust immediately. He backed away then turned to head out when a softcover book on Denton's desk gave him reason to pause. In bold print it read: Fermont Scrap Metal Suppliers, Inc.

Even though he was tired, Eddie could not ignore the red flag that flapped inside his head. He did not know why this seemed off, he debated whether he should leave it alone and go back to join the others.

Oh, a quick peek won't hurt—especially if Denton doesn't catch me.

Eddie walked to the desk and flipped open the first few pages. Fermont was based out of West Palm Beach, Florida, and the book contained a report for sales figures, profits, and losses. This copy was prepared specifically for someone named Marian Walters. *Who's she and what would Denton be doing with a copy that's addressed to her?* Eddie flipped through a few more pages, nothing interesting so far that jumped out at him. *Why am I even looking through thi—what the? Holy Shit!*

Eddie's stomach tightened into a knot. Written on the page in front of him were details of an $833,000 payment made to Plessis Marketing, Inc.

Eddie shook his head and backed away from the desk. Plessis, a company linked to Weiss, with Fermont Inc. paying for their services? Earlier he had mentioned Plessis and Denton acted as though he had never heard of the company before. In fact, he'd told him that what he'd said about Plessis wasn't something anyone just makes up.

Eddie's thoughts were interrupted when he backed up into the wall. He felt that he had bumped a picture frame, and instinctively spun around to catch it. What he saw before him was a framed newspaper clipping with a photograph of a woman next to a much younger man. The man was Denton from a few years before, and he and the woman were standing in front of what appeared to be stacks of metal. Below the photo was a caption that mentioned the woman's name was Marian Walters, the president of Fermont Inc. However, the caption identified Denton as Bilbo Dennis Walters. Marian Walters must've been Denton's mother.

Eddie backed away from the picture. *The cell phone signal was out, just like at the Citrusville Bar the night Dwayne was murdered. What if Denton had a similar jamming device somewhere in the house. What if...Hansel, Gretel, and Stepmother were close by?*

Eddie's only thought was getting Candace away from here.

Stupid, stupid, stupid, stupid, stupid!

Why didn't he call Brutus and ask him to find another hideout? Never mind that, he needed a weapon. He turned to the desk and found a letter opener in the top drawer. This would have to do.

The drink. What if...?

Eddie ran back out into the yard, dropped to his knees, bent over, and jabbed a finger deep down his throat. His gag reflex caused him to project a stream of vomit, which left him momentarily dizzy and slightly weakened. Denton served them drinks that were already poured into the glass. A perfect way to drop in chloral hydrate or something similar, which was odorless and tasteless, and could take fifteen to thirty minutes to take effect. He didn't feel groggy or confused yet, maybe he managed to get most of it out of his system if he had ingested any. He ran back into the house through Denton's office.

Eddie found his way back to the living room where he literally screeched to a stop, startling both Candace and Denton who were chatting.

"Eddie," chuckled Denton. "Where were you? You got lost?"

Eddie did not answer him immediately as he turned to Candace.

"I was at first." Eddie took two short breaths and turned to

Denton, whose smile dropped from his face when he noticed Eddie holding the letter opener. "Not anymore."

Candace tilted her head slightly at him. "Eddie? What—"

"How are you feeling?" Without taking his eyes off Denton, Eddie slowly approached Candace.

There was a moment's hesitation before she answered. "I'm fine, but why are you asking me this?"

Eddie kept his eyes on Denton. "We have to go. Now."

"What? We just got here."

"We made a mistake. *I* made a mistake."

Denton grabbed the armrests of his chair as he was about to stand. "What's gotten into you? Put that down."

Eddie raised the letter opener, pointing it toward Denton, who stumbled and fell back onto the sofa.

"Whoa, what the hell?" yelled Denton with his palms up.

"Don't move, you sonofabitch!" growled Eddie.

"Eddie, what's gotten into you?" yelled Candace.

Eddie still did not take his eyes off Denton. "You set us up."

"What?" said Candace.

"No time to explain," said Eddie as he approached Denton with the blade. "Garage door and the front gate opener, throw them to Candace."

Denton still had his palms raised. "What is wrong with y—"

"Do it!" Eddie rushed Denton with the blade.

"Okay, okay. You win." Denton reached into his pocket with one hand while keeping the other raised, grabbed the keychain, and slid it across the floor toward Candace.

"Are you sure you're okay?" asked Eddie without taking his eyes off Denton. "Because you're going to start the car and meet me out front."

"Eddie...I..."

Eddie heard the sofa's legs scraping on the floor where Candace was.

"Candace?" He turned just in time to see Candace hit the floor. Eddie looked back at Denton, who went from being tense to lowering his palms and relaxing his shoulders. He then sighed with a smirk.

"It's a good thing she passed out now, because that could've been a very bad car accident."

Eddie ran over to Candace, while keeping his eye on Denton. "Candace, say something."

All he heard was a moan. It was over. They were fucked.

Denton got up and stood with his hands in his pockets. "Let me guess. You were riffling through my office, weren't you?"

Eddie raised the blade as he stood. "It was you all along. You were the one who had Dwayne killed. Then ordered a hit on Wesley, Candace, and me."

Eddie stepped away from Candace. He knew there wasn't anything he could do for her. Even if he were to neutralize Denton by stabbing him, he'd still have to contend with carrying or dragging Candace into the car. And seeing how relaxed Denton was, he clearly wasn't afraid of anything.

"Your mother's the president of Fermont and you're the owner. Your real name is Bilbo Dennis Walters. Let me guess, you knew that you'd never be taken seriously in Hollywood with a name such as Bilbo. So, you used the name Dennis Denton instead. The eight hundred grand your company paid Plessis didn't have anything to do with marketing services, did it? It was a kickback paid to Weiss—one that was disguised as a legitimate business transaction. Film production business often involves large infusions of capital, which makes it likely that the kickbacks you paid Weiss were to guarantee PennSteel's business—and I'll bet that you even overcharged them. And with Weiss being the vice-president, he'd be the only person in a position to approve a deal that could be so financially harmful to PennSteel. How am I doing so far?"

Denton's smirk grew into a grin as he nodded his head from side to side.

"The recording that Dwayne made the night when Weiss thought that he had drugged him, he knew that it could be used to connect him to Plessis. This would explain why he tried to make the problem disappear on his own by settling with Dwayne and Candace out of court with an NDA. But I imagine that you didn't share the same optimism when he disclosed his secret to you. You probably feared that Dwayne made other copies of that recording. If it were ever released and the proper authorities were to connect Fermont to Weiss and Plessis, you'd all be exposed."

Eddie felt a weakness start to creep into his legs, and his focus began to waver. He shook his head violently to fight it. The drug. It had already been partially absorbed into his bloodstream before he induced vomiting. It was the only explanation as to why he outlasted Candace.

"You look tired," mocked Denton. "How about I pour you another drink?"

Eddie raised the blade. He was ready to stab Denton, but he was losing strength.

"I think he's had enough," came a woman's voice from behind him.

That voice. He recognized it. Eddie looked over his shoulder toward the entrance and saw Stepmother. He didn't even hear her enter. It was the first time he saw her since the night he was kidnapped from the hospital, when she and her henchmen wore masks. Movement on the side caught his attention and he turned to see Hansel and Gretel, they must have entered from the back or from another entrance.

Eddie pointed the blade to one, then the other, but he was surrounded. Fighting them off would be impossible—even had he not been drugged, knowing what Hansel was capable of.

"How much does he know?" asked Stepmother.

Denton chuckled. "The little shit knows everything. He only figured it out a few minutes ago."

Stepmother turned to Eddie. "How unfortunate."

"Are you kidding?" said Denton. "He's brilliant. The way he pieced it all together and risked his life going about it? I could write a movie script with everything they've told me."

Stepmother raised a hand. "Let's not get carried away."

Eddie turned to Stepmother as he felt his legs getting weaker. "I don't know everything. I don't know what dirt you have on the prime minister that he'd suddenly authorize a military strike on Brutus, allowing you guys to infiltrate them so they could get to Candace."

Stepmother raised an eyebrow and slipped a hand in one of the pockets of her pantsuit.

Eddie shook his head. "That's not a coincidence. Besides, to pull that off you'd have to have access to a high level of intelligence. Who are you? Former CIA? MI-Six?"

"You have a very vivid imagination, young man," chuckled Stepmother. "I can see why Denton speaks so highly of you."

"Trust me," said Eddie as he turned to the movements of Hansel and Gretel circling him while maintaining their radial distance. "My hunches, they haven't been…wrong…so far."

Eddie anticipated Hansel moving in on him and swung the blade in his direction. Eddie was so clumsy with the blade that Hansel had no trouble catching his wrist. With a twist, Eddie cried out as he released the blade, which clanged on the floor. Hansel then shoved him in the chest, causing him to stumble and fall. He tried to sit up, but the room spun. Whatever he was drugged with overwhelmed him. He was too weak to even clench a fist. He took deep breaths, as though that would somehow help him fight the effects of the drug.

The last thing Eddie saw were the faces of Denton, Stepmother, Hansel, and Gretel as they looked down at him.

Chapter 49

Karlos's House, Saint James Parish

Corey tapped the red phone icon on his mobile to hang up. This was the tenth time he called Eddie within the last two minutes.

Why aren't you picking up? Corey turned to the Karlos. "Did you reach Ellis yet?"

"Him nuh answer," he said as he put down the phone.

"Goddammit!" Corey stormed off. "Isn't there anyone else you can call?"

"Yuh tink mi nuh try dat?"

Tarone stepped in between the two of them while lowering both arms with open palms, as though to deescalate the tension in the room. "We're not going to come closer to reaching Eddie by arguing nor by waiting here."

"You're supposed to stay here for your own safety," said Karlos.

"My best friend's life's in danger," said Corey. "Don't you get it?"

Tarone held up a palm to Corey, then turned back to the old man. "What Corey's saying is that we can't do anything by staying here."

"Let's say you go to that man Denton's house," said Karlos. "Even if we find him, what are we going to do? Arrest him? Mi annuh police officer again."

"Arrest him?" said Corey. "I'm going to kick his ass."

"You forget that assassins work fi him an him fren?" said Karlos. "You go there and dem a wait fi yuh."

"He won't be alone," said Tarone while looking at Corey.

"They may be expecting Corey but they won't be expecting me."

Karlos shook his head. "This is suicide."

"And you have a better idea?" asked Corey. "Look at you. Do you even go out? You sit here in this old plantation house all by yourself unless you need to refill on booze and cigarettes. What happened to the detective who hunted sex predators?"

"Corey," said Tarone.

"Is this what you did when you knew someone's life was in danger? Drown your sorrows?"

"Corey!" Tarone yelled.

Corey sighed. "I guess you did all of that just so you can sit in this house like a fossil."

"That's enough!" Karlos slammed his palm on the desk. "You dare lecture me and say that I don't care? I did everything I could to save those girls. Mi try an try again, and mi could neva save de whole a dem. You want to know why I quit? I quit after one victim killed herself. So don't say that I don't care. I care enough to let some of the younger people take over."

Karlos got up and stormed past Corey and Tarone and headed to the front door. However, he paused once he pulled the door open.

Tarone followed him halfway, with Corey behind him.

"We're sorry about what you went through," said Tarone. "I know that's nothing to have on one's conscience. But it doesn't help that you keep punishing yourself like this. I mean, you convinced Ellis to listen to Corey, and it worked. Obviously, your instincts are still sharp, and you still have a desire to help."

Corey walked toward Tarone and stood next to him. "What are your instincts telling you now? It's not only Eddie whose life is in danger, but another young woman—a rape victim. And my friend's been able to keep her alive for this long ever since the attack on Guava Hill. Now her rapist and his associates are out to kill them both. Those so-called *younger people* aren't around. What will *you* do to save her?"

Karlos still did not move. From where Corey stood, he saw Karlos drop his head and shake it. He then pounded a fist into the side of the threshold, turned around, and walked toward them.

Both Corey and Tarone saw that he wasn't stopping and stood with their backs to the walls to let him pass. He stopped in front of a door, pulled it open, and reached upward. He stepped back holding a box and turned to Tarone. "Here."

Tarone took the box. "What's this?"

"Open it," said Karlos.

Corey watched Tarone unlock the latches and flip the lid open. He nearly gasped when he saw that it was a Glock 17. It looked like it had some history behind it, given that there were scratches on the slide and the grip was worn down in a couple spots. But make no mistake, the gun was well loved and obviously still in fine working condition. They both turned to Karlos.

"You still know how to use this?"

"Of course," said Tarone. "I practice enough times."

"Good," answered Karlos. "If we're going to give Mister Barrow and that girl a fighting chance, we're going to do it my way."

Quatti buy chubble, hunjed poun' cyaan pay farri

—Jamaican Proverb

*A penny-halfpenny (1 1/2d) buys trouble,
one hundred pounds (£100) cannot pay for it.*

Chapter 50

Dennis Denton's cliffside villa, Negril, Westmoreland Parish

"Is he awake yet?" asked Stepmother.

"He's coming around," answered Gretel.

"Can we get things going now?" asked Denton. "I don't like the idea of these two being in my house."

"Had you listened and followed my instructions and not drugged them both so heavily, we wouldn't have had to wait so long for him to wake up," snapped Stepmother.

"Then why is she still asleep?"

"Maybe because you didn't drug their drinks equally."

"Hey, I poured the same amount into each glass," said Denton. "Maybe he has a higher tolerance. Besides, why didn't you just check the call history on his phone. You guys should be able to find out who he spoke to?"

"That's no ordinary burner," answered Stepmother. "It's programmed to delete every phone number once they're dialed."

Eddie only heard the voices, but he didn't know where he was nor what was going on. He opened his eyes and saw Stepmother and Gretel looking down at him, but his eyelids were so heavy that he couldn't keep them open more than a few seconds. He felt the presence of Gretel being closer to him, or practically face to face with him.

"His breath," she said. "It smells like vomit."

"So, the young amateur detective figured things out, and induced vomiting," said Stepmother. "Now we know why he's not as drugged as the girl."

"Can't you pump him with something else to wake him up?" asked Denton.

"You don't know anything about drugs, do you?" said Stepmother. "We'll end up making your mistake even worse."

"Mister Barrow?" It was Stepmother, and he felt her slapping both of his cheeks. "Can you hear me?"

Is she talking to me? Eddie opened his eyes and saw her briefly, but his eyelids were so heavy that all he wanted to do was go back to sleep.

"Hey, Eddie. Answer the goddamn question. Can you hear us or not?" said Denton loudly.

"Will you shut up and let us do the questioning?" said Gretel.

"Go sit down somewhere and be quiet, unless you want us to sit you down somewhere," said Stepmother.

There were a few moments of silence, and then he heard Stepmother speaking to him. "Eddie, can you speak?"

Eddie heard what she said, but his mind was all over the place as he drifted in and out of slumber. "Back…back to…life…back…back…to when I was three."

"What?"

"Back…to…life…back to when…I was three…back to the… hills and light of day."

"Hills? Which hills?" asked Stepmother calmly. "You learned some new facts about Denton, Weiss, and Plessis. Who else did you talk to?"

Eddie only heard an empty sentence. "However do you want me, just…tell me how you need me. Back…to life…back to when I was three."

"What is so special about three? Or did you mean to say there?"

"Yeah…there…you gonna go back to life…and give me presents this time."

"Presents?" Stepmother paused. "Eddie, this isn't a game. I need you to focus."

"Game…we need to end this foolish game."

"Hold on," said Gretel.

"What is it?" asked Stepmother.

"There's something familiar about what he's saying," said Gretel.

"How so? Like a code?" asked Stepmother.

"I don't think so. I just don't why I feel I should know what he's saying, but I can't figure it out."

"Tell me how do you want me," repeated Eddie as he slurred his words. "How do you need me...just take me back to the hills and light of day."

"What are you saying, Eddie?" asked Stepmother. "What hills and what light? Did you hide something in the hills about Plessis that we should know about?"

"How do you want me? How do you need me?"

"What I *want* from you is for you to tell me who you told about Plessis?"

Eddie heard the anger in her voice, but he was too disoriented to even care.

"Oh for fuck's sake," Gretel yelled as she slapped both hands to her sides. "Back to life? Back to when I was three? He meant to say, 'Back to life, back to reality.'"

"What are you talking about?" asked Stepmother.

"He's rambling the lyrics from some old song from the early nineties before he was even born," said Gretel. "He doesn't even know the words."

"Are you serious?" Stepmother then waved her hand in front of Eddie's face. "Oh my God, he's been talking in his sleep. All my years in the business and I've never seen anything like this."

"What do we do?" asked Gretel.

"We wait until the drugs Denton gave him wear off."

Eddie rambled something else that did not even make sense to him, then the room fell silent. All went black.

***

His nostrils...no air...Eddie was inhaling liquid...can't breathe...he was underwater...no he wasn't...it was black... as though a bag had been pulled over his head. A pause...liquid was being poured on his face again, causing him to spasm and accidentally inhaling more fluid into both nostrils. It was water. He wasn't only drowning he was being smothered without any means to move—both arms and legs tied down to the hard surface he lay on.

"Who did you talk to about Plessis?"

That voice, it was Stepmother.

The water stopped and he snorted and coughed it out, but it was difficult to breath, as he ended up inhaling more water from the soaked face covering.

"It's been over an hour, we know the drugs have worn off," said Stepmother. "Are you going to tell us?"

Eddie tried desperately to speak but it was next to impossible to get any air. He would die any second now. *Please, just let me up.*

Eddie felt the straps across his chest, waist, and legs being loosened, and a cloth being removed. He was helped to sit up, the black bag yanked off, then was turned on his side as the water shot out of his nostrils and mouth. The coughing impeded his effort to breathe, making his lungs burn. Eddie stared at the concrete floor below. He realized he was sitting on a wooden table being held by both Hansel and Gretel as Stepmother leaned forward and grabbed his chin to hold up his head. He saw Denton standing in the background with his arms crossed. His fingers were fidgeting, he was nervous.

"What do you know about Plessis and who did you share the details with?" Stepmother asked.

"Plessis…" Eddie took his time to breathe. His thoughts were racing in his head, but his gut told him not to tell them anything. "I don't know anything about Plessis."

Stepmother released Eddie's chin as he was pulled back up, the head covering yanked back on, and he was roughly slammed onto his back. A set of strong hands—most likely Hansel's—held his chest down even as Eddie kicked violently and tried to break lose. But the straps went back across his chest—crushing him to the table. His legs were soon bound.

"No, noooo, I don't know anything," Eddie pleaded as he felt the water-soaked cloth being slapped over the head covering.

"Too late," said Stepmother.

Water splashed his face on and off. Eddie took a deep breath hoping to defeat the torture. But instead of inhaling air he inhaled the water that weighed down the cloth and the black bag, which made things worst.

Splash, a second, two seconds, slow pour, no air, slower pour, one second, two seconds, slow pour.

My mind, I can't think. I'm drowning, no air, lungs burning up, can't move. I'm dying. I'm dying. Stop. Stop!

The washcloth and mask were yanked off and the straps loosened some more before he was helped up.

This time Eddie took deeper breaths after coughing out more water from his nostrils and mouth. But the tears also flowed from his eyes as he shook his head and raised a hand in surrender. "Okay, okay, you win. I'll talk."

"Who did you talk to?"

"Brutus," Eddie gasped. "I told Brutus. He has contacts all over the place who are helping him. He would've figured everything out by now. If he didn't, then one of his contacts would've."

Eddie heard a groan from somewhere behind him.

"I think she's awake," said Denton.

"Finally," said Stepmother before turning to Eddie. "Who else did you tell about Plessis?"

Eddie shook his head. *Please let them believe me.*

"Put him under again," said Stepmother.

"I swear there's no one else I spoke to." But that didn't matter, the hood was back on, he was pinned down, straps dug into his chest, arms, waist, and legs, and the water was forced into his mouth and nostrils again.

No air.

More water.

No air.

This time, they held him under for a lot longer than they did the two previous times. When he was unleashed and helped back up, Stepmother grabbed the front part of Eddie's hair and snapped his head up. "I want to know who else you told. You think I was born yesterday? You're not the only person I've waterboarded. You couldn't even begin to imagine what else I've done to make people talk. I know when someone isn't telling me the whole truth."

It was then that Eddie heard Candace screaming, but it wasn't too long before Gretel walked toward her and the screaming stopped.

"Don't hurt her, please," Eddie sobbed as he shook his head. "It's not her fault."

"Oh, you're such a gentleman," said Stepmother. "But you'll still be responsible for what happens to her if you don't answer my question."

"Bevins, it was Nancy Bevins." Eddie stared into Stepmother's slanted eyes. There was an icy coldness in them that told him that she was ready to waterboard Candace. But there was something else, it was as though she was looking past his eyes to probe his brain. She let go of his hair, and Eddie's head dropped to his chest as he breathed in deeply.

"Phone?" Stepmother said as she stretched her hand out to Hansel. In an instant she dialed a number and turned around as she spoke to someone briefly, before turning back with the phone at her side.

Eddie stared at the floor. *What have I done?*

Eddie turned to Denton, who still stood against the wall with arms crossed. "If anything happens to her, they'll know it was you. You don't think someone will figure things out if anything happens to the both of us."

"I wouldn't be so sure of that," Stepmother said. "Accidents happen, and evidence disappears. As for your friend Corey, you no doubt spoke to him with your burner. Even if you told him anything, I'm sure he'll keep quiet once we inform him that his wife and son, Jordyn and Malcolm, already have targets on their backs."

"Shouldn't you be saying something like…*Bumboclaat* right around now?" chuckled Denton. "Oh right, you people from Barbados don't use that word."

Eddie wanted to rush and strangle this woman so badly, but he felt Hansel grab his shoulder with a firm grip. Eddie turned to see him return the stare with slanted eyes, it was as though he read his thoughts, which freaked Eddie out. He looked over to where Candace was. She was sitting on the floor with Gretel standing next to her.

"We know everything about you and your best friend, Corey," said Stepmother. "With the exception of where he currently is. Fill us in and tell us where to find him."

Eddie looked toward the floor to avoid staring her in the eyes.

"That's okay, we'll get to him soon. You and Candace, on the other hand, we don't have any further use." Stepmother leaned closer to Eddie. "It's time for us to go for a ride."

Chapter 51

TriniJam Metals scrapyard, Cascade, Hanover Parish

Eddie was bounced back and forth, along with Candace, as they sat on the floor of the Toyota HiAce panel van, both gagged with wrists zip-tied behind them. He couldn't bear to look at Candace, considering how he failed her. Going to Denton's place before checking with Brutus on any other possible safehouses for them to hide was not only a serious tactical error, but it was also just flat-out stupid. For the whole ride, all Eddie could think of was how he hadn't seen that Denton was the one who masterminded everything. Him showing up at his book signing and throwing the movie ideas in his face. From that moment he should've seen the red flag. Added to the fact that he just happened to still be here in Jamaica. The only reason why Denton hung around was because he was betting on Eddie calling him for help. And Eddie took the bait. Now he and Candace were prisoners—with Stepmother up front, and Hansel driving. Since Gretel wasn't with them, he assumed that she was following them in their car.

The ride was slow and uncomfortable. Eddie wished that it continued, though, because as long as he was tied up and on the floor of this van, he and Candace were still alive. Hopefully, Brutus had figured out by now that something was wrong and had gone looking for them—using Eddie's burner's last known location. However, that hope faded, considering that the phone's signal had been blocked.

They came to an abrupt stop, causing Eddie and Candace to fall over on their sides. The driver's side door opened, the engine still running, and Hansel exited. Roughly twenty seconds later he was back behind the wheel and the van drove again. By the way they bumped around, it was clear they were no longer driving on a paved surface. Not too long after, they came to a stop and Eddie felt the vibrating and humming of the engine cease.

End of the line.

Both front doors opened and shut, the back doors flew open seconds later. Then a pair of strong hands grabbed Eddie's ankles and tugged him across the floor until his legs dangled out. He was then yanked by his shirt collar to force him to stand so he came face-to-face with Hansel. Eddie felt his breath on his face as he stared into his eyes. He recalled how Brutus's men had intimidated him, but they had signs of being human even though they were tough. This wasn't the case with Hansel, whose stare was void of any warmth or humanity, the signs of a true psychopath. It's what most likely made it easy for him to slaughter Brutus's men one after the other during the raid.

"I wouldn't cross him, Mister Barrow," said Stepmother, glancing at Hansel. "He doesn't need a gun, a knife, or any blunt object to kill you. His fingers alone are deadly weapons."

Hansel nodded his head once to his left. It was all Eddie needed to see for him to know where he was to stand. Hansel then pulled Candace out and directed her to stand beside Eddie, just as Gretel drove past them in their car and parked.

From where he stood, Eddie saw that the car was parked diagonally and a few feet ahead of the van, and that they were in a wide space, surrounded by several mounds of scrap metal, a propane tank to his right, and a crane with a claw to his left. Roughly fifty meters ahead was a red vehicle in the shape of a box on caterpillar treads, with the name *Red Giant* and *VB 750 DK* in white letters printed on the side. Its dimensions were large enough to contain a small truck. Attached to it from the bottom and pointing upward at a thirty-five- to forty-degree angle appeared to be a conveyer belt. It ended above a mound of crushed metal parts over fifteen meters high.

Hansel shoved Eddie and Candace from behind to make them walk to their car just as Gretel got out and stood beside it.

"Remove the gags and free their hands. They won't be needing them anymore," said Stepmother as they got to their car. "Scream all you want, no one will hear you."

Hansel took out a bowie knife, grabbed Eddie's wrist, and sliced through his bonds. He then did the same for Candace.

"I'd be lying if I said I wasn't impressed with the way you've been able to evade us for as long as you did. This chase you led us on across Jamaica—your *Jam Run* —is over." Stepmother then walked up to Eddie and placed a hand on his shoulder while pointing to the car shredder with the other. "You *do* know what that is, don't you, Mister Barrow?"

Eddie didn't answer her. Instead, he turned to Candace. "I'm sorry."

She held his hand. "It's okay." Candace began to choke up. "It's not your fault."

Gretel opened the back passenger door and held it like that as Stepmother gestured toward it. "We don't have all day. In you go."

Hansel was walking toward the crane, as Eddie turned to Gretel, who was tapping the top edge of the door.

Eddie was the first one in and Candace followed. Just as Gretel was about to close the door, she bent over to better see them and smiled.

"Just in case you were both wondering," she said as the shredder roared to life, "Dwayne hid in the bushes beside the road, right where I waited. He actually believed me when I told him that it was safe for him to come out. Bashing his head in with the rock was my favorite part."

She then nodded toward Hansel as he climbed into the crane's cockpit. "He splashed the accelerant on him and I lit the match. You know the rest."

Her smirk was singed into Eddie's brain as she shut the door and backed away, snatching her gun, and pointing it at them. "Stay in the middle, away from the doors."

"Eddie." Candace grabbed his hand again as she cried into his shoulder. "I'm scared."

Eddie held onto her tightly. "So am I."

The back of his throat went dry. Eddie swallowed just as he saw the neck of the crane swing toward them and the claw opening.

Chapter 52

Dennis Denton's residence, Negril, Jamaica

"Is it finally over?" Denton heard Weiss's voice through the speakerphone as he packed the last of his documents into his carry-on.

"It's over. Barrow and the little bitch are good as dead, and it'll only be a matter of time before Brutus is caught. You can relax."

"Are you sure?" asked Weiss as Denton pulled open his desk drawer for his passport, exactly where he had left it.

"I'm positive," Denton answered. "I was guaranteed a professional cleanup crew, and I got 'em."

"Are you referring to those three who paid me a visit?" asked Weiss.

"Who else?"

"I don't want to know how you found them, but I don't want to ever see them again. They give me the creeps."

"Neither do I." Denton tucked his passport into one of his carry-on pockets. "You nearly fucked us both over with your part-time activities. Just don't let it happen again. When is it you leave?"

"The conference finishes tomorrow. I'll be on the three-PM flight back to Pittsburgh."

"Good, we'll talk later. We'll have to find another way to conduct business now that Congress has banned anonymous shell companies. Give it a few months for this to blow over."

He tapped the red icon on the phone's screen to hang up. He then dialed another number. "Is my jet ready?"

"We'll be ready by the time you arrive, sir."

"Great. I'll see you in a bit."

Moments later he was behind the wheel of his Mercedes-Benz heading down the driveway. Although Eddie Barrow and

Candace Coke were finally out of his hair, all he thought of was getting off this island. This whole experience left such a bad taste in his mouth. He didn't know when he would come back—if he'd ever come back. Putting the villa up for sale even came to mind.

Why the hell did Barrow have to get involved? The cleaners had the perfect setup. They knew Pottinger would show up to the straight party in drag. A little tip-off to a few people and let the homophobic mob take care of the rest. But Barrow just *had* to be there to screw things. It was a shame because he'd been looking forward to working with him. With Barrow's creativity, he could only imagine the blockbusters he'd help make. For now, he'd have to write this off as another loss, just like his earlier films before he partnered with Weiss.

He pressed the gate opener attached to the car's visor and slowed down. The gates opened inward, and when they were fully open, he accelerated slightly. The black SUV came out of nowhere and barreled through the entrance, racing toward him as though they were in a game of chicken.

"Jesus!"

Denton's chest tightened as he stomped on the breaks, causing the Mercedes-Benz to fishtail.

The black SUV skidded to a stop a few feet away, and two men—one older and one younger—jumped out of the front seats brandishing their guns at him.

Holy shit! I'm being robbed.

Denton switched the gear into park and raised both hands. "Whatever you want, money, whatever, you can have it. Just don't hurt me."

The older one approached him on his side. "Where are they?"

Denton shook his head. "I don't know who you're talking about."

"Nuh lie to me!" the man yelled as he yanked the door open, shoved the business end of his gun into Denton's sternum, while grabbing him by the collar to pull him out. He then slammed Denton, back-first, onto the side of the vehicle, pinning him with the gun. "I'm going to ask you one more time. Where are Eddie Barrow and Candace Coke?"

Holy shit! Denton felt the beads of sweat dripping down his forehead as his breath shortened. It was then that he spotted someone familiar—the other gunman appeared with Eddie's friend Corey. Where did he...? How did he...?

His assailant removed the business end of the pistol from his chest and pressed it hard into his penis.

"Nooooo!" Denton screamed as he lost control of his bowels and shit himself. "I'll tell you, I swear. Oh God, please!"

"Talk."

"They went to a scrapyard. The one in Cascade. I swear I'm telling you the truth. Please you have to believe me."

"How long ago was this?"

"Not even ten minutes ago, you just missed them."

The old man turned to the other two. "You know where that is?"

The other gunman nodded as Denton saw Corey run back to the SUV.

"Go, quick!" said the older man. "Don't worry about me."

Denton felt the sweat and tears streaming down his face as he watched the other gunman jump back in with Corey and reverse out. This man was going to blow his dick off, he just knew it. *Please, don't let it come to this.*

"One more thing," said the older man as he pulled the pistol away from Denton's gonads. "Welcome to Jamaica!"

Denton's brain could not process the rock-hard knuckles smashing into his nose at warp speed before everything went black.

Chapter 53

TriniJam Scrapyard, Cascade, Hanover Parish

Eddie held onto Candace as the claw was above their car. Moments later its jagged edges crunched through metal. Eddie closed his eyes and lowered his head while shielding Candace, who screamed into his chest as glass exploded around them. The roof caved in enough to force them to lean slightly sideways, just as the car being was lifted.

Eddie was not confident that the claw held the car properly. One slip would send them crashing to the ground below. Candace did not stop screaming as they were lifted in the air, and Eddie couldn't blame her. The crane stopped rotating and they were being lowered. They were dropped gently onto a surface, which Eddie saw was the loading bay. The claw detached as Eddie felt a vibration below.

Everything went silent.

Eddie checked around him. The roof was so badly crushed that it was impossible for either of them to crawl through the window space.

Eddie unlocked the door closest to him and tried opening it.

Jammed.

He leaned across Candace to the other door.

Same thing, but it moved a little.

He reached over the front seats and tried the two other doors.

Jammed shut.

He then pushed Candace toward the floor. "Lie down and start kicking."

Eddie brought his feet up on the seats and started kicking the back passenger door with both legs, just as the loading platform rose diagonally. As the steel shredders roared to life, Eddie felt the car slowly being lifted from the rear.

The car was at about a fifteen-degree angle, then twenty, twenty-five…then…it did not tilt anymore.

"Don't stop kicking, whatever you do," screamed Eddie over the sound of the shredders.

There was a point he could not hear his and Candace's feet smashing against the car door, however that changed a few moments later when Eddie realized that the shredders grew quieter. Then they stopped.

What happened? Eddie did not care, he just had to get this door open if they hoped to avoid being crushed to death. He then heard a voice, one that he recognized well enough that he stopped kicking. He sat up in what little space he had below the mangled roof to peek out the window. Someone was yelling below.

Corey?

Chapter 54

Corey didn't have time to argue with Tarone. It was a suicidal plan as far as he was concerned. Then again, they didn't have the time to think of an alternative. Tarone told him that this scrapyard was closed due to too many unpaid fines—there were multiple, frequent explosions. Residents of the nearby town complained to the point that the government authorities had no choice but to step in. It made sense that Denton's cleaners would choose this spot to get rid of Eddie and Candace.

Tarone stopped a few hundred meters away from the scrapyard and got out, instructing Corey to continue and head inside the yard. Corey did as he was told and was on time to see a moving crane as it lowered a car onto a car crusher. He knew that his best friend and Candace were inside and he immediately blasted his horn nonstop, hoping that they were still alive.

An older Black woman turned to him and pointed a gun, holding it with both hands. He gasped as his stomach tightened and he immediately stomped down on the brake pedal, causing the SUV to skid to a stop. He raised his hands high enough for her to see.

"Don't shoot!" Corey yelled. "I'm not armed."

Judging from the way she stood with her feet planted firmly on the ground and her shoulders squared up directly at him, this woman was a professional.

The woman called out to someone else without taking her eyes from Corey, who then realized she was talking to a sista who operated the car crusher. He saw the sista punch what may have been a button on a control board, being too far to see exactly. It was then that the roaring of the spinning blades died down.

Corey's attention then switched to the crane, where a military-type brotha in a black tank top with glistening biceps and shoulders jumped from the cockpit and walked toward the older woman. The sista did the same, as they converged on Corey.

The woman, who still had the gun trained on Corey, approached the SUV from the driver's side.

"Mister Corey Stephenson." The woman smiled as she stopped a little under ten meters from him. "Step out of the vehicle slowly and keep your hands where I can see them."

There wasn't any messing around with this woman. Corey knew that she would drop him in a second if he did anything to panic her. He got out with his hands held to the height of his ears—leaving the door open.

"How did you find us?" asked the woman.

"I went to Denton's place to meet Eddie as planned," said Corey. "Except when I got there, he was on his way out and told me that he didn't see Eddie. I knew he was lying so I made him talk."

The woman raised an eyebrow as she lowered her weapon. "Is that so?"

"Corey," yelled a familiar voice that made him look toward the partially mangled car that sat on top of the Red Giant.

"Eddie!"

"Help!" It was Eddie and whom Corey assumed to be Candace.

Corey turned to the woman as he shook his head. "Please, don't do this. They don't have to die."

"Oh, but they do." The woman let one hand drop as she held onto the gun with the other. "And I'm glad you're here to join them. You've saved me the trouble of coming to find you."

"I know about Plessis."

The woman raised an eyebrow. "Do you?"

"I know how it's connected to Weiss and Denton," said Corey as he saw the brotha and sista out of the corner of his eye begin to circle him like sharks going in for the kill. "It's a shell company owned by Weiss, and he's been taking kickbacks from Denton's company, using Plessis to hide the money. Do I need to tell you about how Dwayne Pottinger and Candace fit into the picture?"

There was no change in the woman's facial expression. Either what he said did not phase her or she had an excellent poker face.

Time to change tactics.

"And there are others who know this too," continued Corey. "I have to call them every hour, if they don't hear from me they're going to call the proper authorities."

"And would that happen to be Barrow's agent, Nancy Bevins?"

Corey's eyebrows raised.

"Ha!" the woman chuckled. "You weren't expecting me to know that, were you?"

"What did you do to her?"

"I only sent someone to pay her a visit," said the woman as she holstered her weapon. By the way, have you been following the news in your hometown lately?"

Corey tilted his head, wondering why she'd ask such a question.

"Your cozy little business, the one you share with Eddie and... what's your wife's name...ah, Jordyn."

Corey lowered his hands as they slowly clenched into fists. "What did you do? If you did anything..."

"There was a fire, very terrible. Total loss from what I've heard." The woman smiled. "The cause was electrical. At least, that's the official story."

Corey was about to charge her when both the brotha and sista whipped out their sidearms faster than any cowboy he had seen in a western. His hands shot up halfway as he stopped dead in his tracks.

"Relax, she's fine. The fire broke out after closing hours," said the woman. "Your wife, and baby, Malcolm, are okay...for now. Whatever happens to them next depends on you."

The woman then turned to the sista. "Turn on the shredder. Show Mister Stephenson that he's not in control."

The sista smirked as she holstered her weapon and walked back to the shredder.

"No, no, no," Corey pleaded. "You don't have to do this."

The woman chuckled. "Watch me."

The sound of a small metallic object falling caught everyone's attention. It was Tarone climbing a mound of scrap, trying to gain the high ground.

The brotha turned and spotted him, opening fire, forcing Tarone to take cover. He then returned fire.

Corey dashed back to the driver's side of the SUV to take cover as bullets flew all around him.

Chapter 55

Eddie and Candace

Eddie couldn't listen to what was being said below. But if he couldn't hear them, then it stood to reason that they wouldn't be able to hear him or Candace either. He and Candace resumed taking turns slamming the soles of their feet into the passenger door. It gave way to the point that only their fingers could fit through.

"Come on!" yelled Eddie. "Come on!"

They furiously kicked for over a minute before Eddie felt the seat vibrating. The platform then continued rising on an angle as the shredders roared to life.

Chapter 56

Corey

Corey heard the gunshots and knew that as long as they continued then Tarone was still alive. But it was three against one, and Tarone's ammunition would run out first. Making a run to the Red Giant wasn't an option, a single bullet would take Corey out long before he got there. That's when he noticed a steel rod a few feet away from where he was. He thought of the steering-wheel lock that had been beside him in the back seat as he, Tarone, and Karlos drove to Denton's place. Corey would never make it over to the shredder, but he may still be able to disable it.

Corey crawled over to the steel rod, grabbed it, then crawled back to the SUV, pulled open the driver's door and climbed in. He snatched the steering wheel lock from the back seat, grabbed the car keys from the ignition to find the right key to unlock it, once done, he fitted it on the steering wheel. Fortunately, the vehicle was already pointing at the shredder, so all that was left was to jam the steel rod between the gas pedal and the edge of the car seat. Corey adjusted the seat until it floored the gas pedal. He then fired up the SUV, which roared to life, showing off its true horsepower. With one hand pressed down on the brake pedal, he threw the gear shaft into drive, then jumped out quickly while the front tires spun violently, spitting up dirt and gravel.

Corey would lose his cover any moment, and sprinted for the nearest stack of compressed, cubed scrap metal.

He peeked above the scrap-metal cube and saw both women brandishing their guns, unloading them toward the SUV. They managed to shoot out one of the front and back tires, causing the vehicle to swerve violently as shredded rubber flew, leaving nothing but heavy steel mags bouncing on the uneven surface toward the propane tank. The steering wheel lock was useless at this point as the SUV swerved violently and flipped over onto its side—the propane tank being the only object in its way.

Corey ducked behind the cubes as he braced himself for the worst. He did not hear an explosion, see any flying debris, or feel a blast of heat. He stood and turned toward the vehicle. It had bent the fence inward toward the propane tank. However, the fence was sturdy enough that it looked like a net wrapped around the front end of the SUV—stopping it less than a meter away from the propane tank to prevent a collision.

Something moved in his peripheral vision. Just as he turned the other way, he saw the sista, her well-groomed eyebrows slanted downward and what appeared to be gnashing teeth behind closed lips. Corey felt the full force of the sole of her boot to his solar plexus, throwing him back as he stumbled to regain his balance. The impact disrupted his breathing and disoriented him as a roundhouse kick to his shoulder threw him into the row of stacked cubes where he bounced off. Seconds later Corey was inhaling dirt.

Corey coughed and sputtered as he saw stars. *No, I can't let this stop me.* Corey rolled onto his side and saw the sista walking away and disappearing around the stacked cubes. Corey thought she could only be heading toward the Red Giant. She could've shot and killed him, meaning that she possibly used up her ammunition shooting out the SUV's tires.

Using the side of the cubed stack for support, he stood. He let go and stumbled forward initially but forced himself to break out into a sprint—charging the sista from behind. She did not appear to hear him, but just as Corey was about to tackle her, she surprised him by ducking low and to the side while effortlessly doing a foot sweep—hooking his lower shins and sending him crashing to the ground.

Enough of this shit!

Come on, Tarone. Why don't you shoot her? It was then that Corey noticed that there weren't any more gunshots.

Corey heard her approaching. *Okay, think fast. She likes using* her feet. *If I roll to the side, she'll aim to kick me in my lower extremities—that's when I'll catch her leg, twist, and throw her on her back.*

Corey turned to his side and his arms formed an X-block, as her foot came toward him as anticipated, however, he didn't expect to actually catch her foot. She struggled to pull her leg away.

Got you now.

Corey twisted in a jolt—the woman could only turn where Corey turned—and flipped her over to the side. However, he got too caught up in the moment to notice her shoe shooting up to his head, until the blow snapped his head back. Corey saw red and black flashing as he felt an explosion of pain. He yelled as he rolled onto his back and his hands shot up to his face.

"Stay there," she casually said as she got up. "The view should be better from where you are, or actually you can back up a little."

The view for what? Corey squinted as he opened his eyes. His mind came together as he saw the bright red container—and the purple, shiny back of the sista's outfit standing next to it. She turned to look at him with a smile, as she pressed a button on the control pad.

Oh, hell naw!

Adrenaline must have been the only thing fueling Corey's muscles as he got up. He watched as she held both hands out to the side as though to invite him to take his best shot. Corey didn't care if he hurt this woman by going all out, she's a goddamn sociopath. *Think fast.* She'd go for the legs again.

Corey let his anger take over as he charged her. When he was less than eight feet away, he jumped into a forward slide as though he were gliding into first base. But she didn't do a floor sweep, instead she did a jumping split. It didn't matter, he got past her and that's what really mattered. Corey scrambled back to his feet and threw his hands out in front and wide, stopping him from crashing into the side of the Red Giant.

The controls! Where are they? Where are they? He saw the button clearly identified as *OFF* and he punched it.

Corey's intuition screamed that the sista was charging him—maybe even in some sort of flying kick. He guessed right by jumping to the side as she crashed into the side of the Red Giant. But her recovery was instant, fueled by the anger that spilled from her eyes and gnashing teeth while she paced toward him.

Look into her eyes. She made a brief glance at his torso. Corey anticipated the fist before she threw it and was able to twist and dodge it. That's when he side-blocked it, but it was the side kick that caught him off guard. The tip of her shoe struck him in the temple, sending him smashing into the side of the Red Giant. The world spun and his head hit the ground with a thud.

Lying on his side, Corey—through a blurry view—saw the sista walk back to the control panel where she made a fist with her left hand and hammered the *ON* button. He felt the ground begin to vibrate under his head as he heard the shredder scream back to life. That...that sounded like steel being crumpled. The car, it was being sucked into the shredder. And although the sound was faint behind the noise from the shredders, he knew that it was Eddie and Candace he heard screaming.

Corey cried a long drawn out "Noooooo!" He was back on his feet and charged the sista, forgetting to anticipate her move. She sidestepped, ducked, and swung a wide fist which connected right to his balls.

An explosion of pain simultaneously shot straight through to his toes and rattled his brain as Corey crashed to the ground, curled up into a fetal position, with both hands clutching his manhood.

With one foot, the woman flipped Corey onto his back and then pinned him down by applying pressure to his chest. The pain he felt in his gonads was not enough to block out the pain to his chest. The best he could do was squint as he looked up at her, to see her staring down at him—he swore that he was feeling his ribcage begin to buckle.

"I didn't want to kill you yet," she said. "I just want to watch you, as you watch your friends d—"

A ground shaking explosion sent a shockwave of heat that Corey felt from the top of his head as an object simultaneously flew over him. The pressure and pain to his chest was suddenly gone as he turned to see his attacker stumbling backward until she stopped and stood still. Something wasn't right, and it was all about her stare. That's when Corey noticed blood squirting from her right hand...*wait...she ain't got no right hand. Shit!* The lower part of her right arm was missing. The sista's torso then separated from the rest of her body, as it slid downward diagonally to the left as her legs buckled.

What. In. The. Actual. Fuck. Just. Happened? Corey gasped at the gory mess of bloody intestines and other internal organs he could not name that spilled out of what was left of the assassin. He forced his feet into the ground to push himself backward. He looked away, freaked out to the point that he ignored the pain in his groin. That's when he saw the blazing plume of fire and black smoke emanating from what was left of the SUV.

Shit! The crash ignited the propane...or was the gas tank damaged in the collision? He looked to where the woman once stood and saw the crane, but something was embedded in the side of the cab. It was one of the mags from Karlos's SUV. The explosion turned it into a projectile. What were the chances of that? Suddenly, it then hit him.

The shredder!

Corey scrambled to his feet, ran, and threw himself at the control panel, punching the *Off* button. His hands fell to his knees as he took deep breaths. But the only thought in his head was that he was already too late.

Chapter 57

Stepmother

An ambush. Goddammit, Corey came with an ally and she did not anticipate it. Everything they knew about Stephenson didn't indicate that he knew anyone who owned a firearm. She wasn't close enough to see who the gunman was. But Hansel wouldn't fail her. A drug lord's damn army couldn't stop him. This hooligan should be child's play.

But it was Corey she was fed up with, and she wished that her other asset would quit toying with him. Obviously, the woman was not going to back away from an opportunity to satisfy her sick fetish of making Corey watch his friend die. Yes, she had serious issues, but she always got the job done.

Hansel just engaged the hooligan at the top of the scrap mount. Corey must've only come with one ally because, had there been others, they would've attacked by now. But if Corey could bring one, then he could very well have brought others. God forbid some of them turn out to be Brutus and his crew.

She took out her mobile and dialed a number. "It's me. I need you to tell me if there's been any reports on Brutus…Are you sure? I'll take your word for it." She switched off the call. Things were going to come to fruition. And not a moment too soon. Candace Coke, Eddie Barrow, and then Corey Stephenson would be no more. God, she didn't want to hear of them, Denton, or his company for that matter. He would be indebted for the next several decades to those she worked for. After all, they'd own almost half the shares of his company per their agreement. Help fix his dilemma, and, as payment, he gives up 52% of the shares of Fermont. That's why this mission was so important. The poor bastard had no idea that he was being used all along. Come to think of it, if what Corey said was true, then Denton could be lying unconscious somewhere in his home. If the police were called and they were to show up at his place, God help them.

She dialed Denton's number and put the phone to her ear. The phone rang while she watched Corey make an impressive attack to the other asset Eddie Barrow had nicknamed Gretel. But she would still kick his ass in the end. An elite fighter and assassin versus gutter trash, the victor was obvious.

Why isn't Denton answering? It went to voicemail. She dialed his number again and once again heard the ringing on the other end. The sound of the third ring was overpowered by the explosion as a blast of heat hit her so hard that she nearly dropped her phone. She turned in time to see a fireball erupt dozens of feet into the air. But it was what happened in her peripheral vision that caught her attention even more—and her disgust. Gretel stumbled backward and…*fell apart? Did I see that right?*

She then watched Corey looking first at the explosion and then back to where Gretel stood, as though he were trying to process what he just saw. He then scrambled clumsily to his feet.

She pointed her MP-443 Grach at him, it was time to end this. She watched as Corey ran to the Red Giant and slammed his hand on the control panel, stopping the shredder just as the car was flipped upward, halfway eaten. There was no way Barrow and Coke were still alive. Sure, she could have shot them before sending them to the shredder. But there would not have been any suffering or fun in that. Any moment now, yes, why not wait and then watch Corey break down once it hit him that he could not save his best friend. And then he would die, one bullet to his head. Or she could let him live—the memory of his friends dying in front of him would kill him psychologically. His wife would eventually leave him and take his son away. Pity, he'd fall back to hitting the bottle and be too drunk to see little Malcolm grow up to be a man.

She remembered that she'd emptied her magazine into the runaway SUV. There were more in the van. She walked back to it and climbed into the passenger seat where she'd left her handbag. From where she sat, the shredder was to her left. She ejected the mag, grabbed a fresh one from her purse, then popped it in.

As Stepmother was about to jump out, her attention was caught by a roaring engine that got louder by the second. She turned to the driver's side to see Denton's Mercedes-Benz speeding toward her. Out of reflex, she grabbed the passenger door handle and pulled it shut just as there was an explosion of crunched metal. The impact threw her into the passenger door a split second before the world spun upside down.

Chapter 58

Tarone

Whoever this guy was, he was a maniac. Who the hell rushes a gunman while being shot at? As Tarone sprinted up the mount with little to no effort, he took aim and pulled the trigger. Nothing. A jam, a fucking jam! Tarone couldn't react before he saw a flying kick that knocked the gun out of his hand. The maniac then followed through with a second kick while he was still in midair, striking Tarone in the shoulder, sending him toppling down the mound. He managed to get control and get to his feet quickly just as the soldier slid down the mound, flawlessly upright. The last position to be in was on your back—especially when facing off against an obviously specially trained soldier.

The space between rows of cars in this vehicular graveyard limited their attack space. This meant that this guy could only score points by doing forward attacks. The maniac would've come to the same conclusion, and he wasted no time rushing Tarone. The attacker's jabs were quick—like a cobra's strike—but so were Tarone's blocks, as he matched his speed. All those sparring moments he had with Garfield as a teenager and in his early twenties inadvertently prepared him for prison. But it was his preparation from being incarcerated with some of the most dangerous ruffians that would be tested.

And this guy wasn't like anyone he'd fought in prison. Tarone didn't even see the fierceness in his eyes, as he darted toward, then leaped sideways and rebounded off the side of a scrapped car. What Tarone saw next was the maniac's solid thighs being wrapped around his neck and twisting, forcing Tarone's body to turn in the same direction the attacker flew, throwing him over, where they both crashed into the side of another scrapped car. Tarone fell on his back, while the maniac landed on one knee.

Shit. Not on my back.

Tarone planted his palms beside his head with his fingers pointed toward his shoulders. He then swung both legs above his head, forming a bridge, then swung them forward, executing a flawless kick-up. Just as Tarone landed on both feet, his opponent charged him, leaped in the air, and executed a Triple Ap Chagi. It was the same move Neo did as he sparred against Morpheus in *The Matrix,* where he did three consecutive front kicks while in midair. Tarone could not ignore the alertness of his opponent—most likely achieved with drug use. He had read about Captagon, the drug of choice in war-torn Syria as it was known to stimulate the nervous system, making soldiers more alert and taking away their fear.

Was that an explosion?

Tarone's focus was on the powerhouse in front of him as he nearly landed the last of his air kicks, followed by him staving off a series of punches.

Time to go on the offensive.

Tarone returned his set of punches, but the maniac dodged and blocked each one, effortlessly, as though Tarone was moving in slow motion. The way he feigned to a side or pivoted was unbelievable. This dude was a brotha, yet Tarone wondered if he was raised in Japan in one of those martial arts schools. This brotha could take on both Bruce Lee and Jet Li. Yes, that's how unnatural this man looked when he moved. Tarone was at least making him walk back toward the mound. But his opponent grabbed an empty window space on the nearest car to him and thrust both legs out simultaneously into a sidekick. Tarone needed his gun if he was going to stand a chance against this animal. He was beginning to feel fatigued, while his opponent appeared to only be warming up.

Tarone ran around the trunk of another car as he circled back toward the mound. A fence surrounded this scrapyard, and he could get cornered if he made a wrong turn, which would be fatal for him. Instead of following Tarone around the car, the killer ran back the way he came to cut him off in front of the mound. But Tarone was just fast enough to beat him to the spot and was able to run around the base of the pile.

What happened next was something he could never have prepared for. Karlos appeared out of nowhere, pointing a gun at him…no…he was aiming above him.

There was a loud *bang,* and the maniac cried out, but it came from above. Tarone looked up behind him to see his assailant fall from the sky and crash to the ground, ending up on his back as what appeared to be a bowie knife fell a few feet away from him. Tarone figured that the attacker had run up the side of the scrap mound to do an aerial assault. Lord knows what would've happened to Tarone had Karlos not shown up when he did.

Tarone turned back to Karlos. "When did you get here?"

He shook his head. "Not soon enough."

Chapter 59

Eddie and Candace

The door had opened a few more inches. Despite being tossed around, Eddie did not lose focus. They were going to get this door open. They had to. Adrenaline was keeping him going.

"Come on. Open," he screamed.

The car paused for a moment, then they were reversing. Wait, now they were being pulled forward again. The shredders, they hit a piece that wasn't succumbing to the force of the massive steel pressure. A little extra time, but he knew it wouldn't be long. This kick seemed to make a difference, as the door flew open almost halfway.

"Candace, you need to kick because your fucking life depends on it," yelled Eddie. Candace had all but given up, but he couldn't let her when the door was almost open.

The car still jerked back and forward, and they kept on kicking. The door flew open more. Finally, enough for them to fit through.

He grabbed Candace. "Go, go, go."

She twisted out of the floor space and pushed herself forward as the car was momentarily jammed. Even though they were still at a slight angle, she made it through. But it wasn't over yet—if the car swung violently in her direction it would squish her against the side of the loading bay.

"Jump," Eddie screamed as he grabbed the side of the door to pull himself through as hard as he could. He just needed to clear this bay and jump. He'd fall several feet. At most he'd break both legs and arms. Hell, he may fracture a spine and never be able to walk again. But that was way better than—

Eddie was spinning around with the car and struck his head.

He felt himself falling onto the back of the front seats as metal succumbed to the screaming shredders. Then there was complete blackness.

Chapter 60

Corey

"Eddie!" Corey yelled as he looked upward to the top of the Red Giant while backing away for a better view. "Candace?"

He limped on one leg as best he could toward the back of the Red Giant while looking upward toward the loading deck. He paused. From where he stood all he could see was the tail end of the car, as it stood upright. Corey's heart sank.

"Eddie…no…" he whispered, breathless.

The voice was faint, but Corey still heard it on the other side of the Red Giant. He circled from the back to the other side where he saw a young woman sitting on her ankles, screaming his best friend's name.

"Where's Eddie?"

The young woman shook her head as the tears flew on either side. "I don't know. He was right behind me. He was supposed to jump."

Corey looked to the top of the *Red Giant.* "Eddie!"

No answer.

Corey didn't care if there wasn't a ladder. He was going to get to the top of this machine. He limped to the front where the conveyer was diagonally attached and pulled himself on top of it. He then scaled the front side of the machine, finding a few indentations that simplified things, and climbed into the loading bay from the front. The front end of the car was gone and all that was left was the front passenger section and up. The windshield was gone, the dashboard partially mangled.

"Eddie!" Corey held onto the edge of the loading bay as he inched along the side of the vehicle. The passenger door hung open as it touched the edge of the wall. He felt the jagged edges of the shredder under the soles of his shoes. God help him if they were to be turned on.

He leaned over the top of the passenger door and looked inside where his chest tightened. He saw the soles of a pair of Nike Air Max's. There Eddie lay on the back of the front car seats.

"Eddie." Corey grabbed Eddie's leg and shook him. "Come on, bruh. Answer me. Please."

Tears flowed down Corey's face as he grabbed Eddie's ankles and pulled. He got his legs out, then turned him diagonally so that his legs hung off the edge of the car door, when he saw bloodstains on the back of the front car seats. He gasped and screamed, "Eddie!"

The side of Eddie's head that lay on the back of the car seat was bleeding. He may have a concussion. Was it safe to move him? He certainly couldn't leave him here where they were so close to the shredders. The thought of the shredders suddenly turning back on was something that he could not shake.

The loading bay.

It was horizontal again, obviously due to the machine being turned off.

He would not take any chances. Corey finished pulling Eddie out until his back was on the car door. He then climbed over Eddie to the other side of the door, where he continued pulling below the armpits until they were on top of the loading bay. There, Corey fell on his ass as he cradled his best friend's head on his lap.

Corey's chest was still tight as he looked down into Eddie's seemingly lifeless face. He did not care that blood was on his left hand. He felt for a pulse on Eddie's neck, but barely felt anything. Maybe he was touching the wrong spot. What did he know? He wasn't a doctor. He tapped the side of Eddie's cheeks gently. "Come on, bruh. Don't do this to me, man."

A lump in his throat had grown to the size of a golf ball, as more tears fell and landed on Eddie's face.

Corey closed his eyes tightly as he shook his head and bawled. "Don't do this to me, man. It can't end like this, bruh. Come on, wake up, please!"

Corey opened his eyes, as another tear dropped. The moment that it hit Eddie's face, it appeared to revive him as his eyes opened partially.

You're alive! "Bruh, it's me, Corey."

Eddie began to blink slowly, but then squinted as though he was in pain. His hand slowly went up to touch his head in the spot where it was bleeding.

"Bruh," choked Corey. "Say something…please."

There was a pregnant pause as Eddie closed his eyes again and appeared to swallow. He then opened them without letting go of the spot where he was wounded. This time he was staring back at Corey, appearing more cognizant of whom he was with.

"How about that." His words were slurred as he still appeared to be in agony. "I've got another head wound to complement the one I got the other night."

Corey began to chuckle as he wiped the back of his forearm across his face to clear away the tears. "Stay with me, man."

He bent over and gave Eddie a partial upside-down hug. His best friend didn't appear to have the strength to hug him back.

"Look, we got to get off this thing," said Corey just as he heard what sounded like a gunshot, startling him, causing him to turn in the direction it came from.

No, please don't let it be Tarone. The assassins would be coming for them, and there was no way he could get Eddie down from this machine. This was it. This was how it was going to end for them.

Corey stared down at Eddie. "I just want you to know that I'm not mad at you. I'm sorry that I let you down."

"Corey, Eddie, Candace!"

Corey turned to the voice. Was that Karlos? The loading bay was somewhat of an open container, preventing Corey from seeing over the side.

"Any one of you, say something."

That was Tarone. Both relief and excitement hit Corey at once.

"We're here. We need an ambulance," Corey yelled back. "I don't want to move Eddie. He has a head injury.

"Don't move him, I'm coming up," said Tarone.

Corey didn't care how Karlos and Tarone took care of the assassins, or if they had escaped. All he cared about was that he, Eddie, and Candace were safe.

"Corey?" whispered Eddie.

Corey turned to his friend. "Don't worry, bruh. Help's coming. Just hang on."

"I was going to say…" Eddie took a deep breath. "You can never let me down." Eddie managed to smile as he looked at Corey.

Corey wiped away another tear as it rolled down his cheek. He sniffled. "Thanks, bruh."

"There's something else."

"What is it?"

"This metal's scorching my ass through my pants. Can you help me get me off this thing?"

Shit, Eddie was right. Corey had not even realized how hot the surface was under this hot sun. There was movement to his right, and Corey turned to see Tarone holding onto the top of the loading bay. The hot surface either did not bother him or he had a higher tolerance.

Corey dragged Eddie slowly over to Tarone and helped him to sit up. When he looked over the edge, he noticed that Tarone was standing on the roof of what appeared to be Denton's Mercedes-Benz SUV.

"I got him." Tarone helped Corey lift Eddie over the edge, then took Eddie from Corey and laid him down on the roof of the SUV, while Corey climbed over the side of the loading bay. From this point it was easier as Corey jumped down from the roof to assist Karlos as they helped Tarone lower Eddie to the ground. Candace stood next to them, as she wiped away tears of joy with the back of her forearm.

Eddie looked at Karlos, Tarone, then him. "Who are these guys?"

"A few friends I met along the way," said Corey.

"I don't think the ambulance is coming fast enough," said Karlos. "Let's get you into the car."

"What happened to the sista?" asked Tarone.

Corey nodded his head in her direction, and Tarone looked. A second later he turned his head away in disgust. "Bumboclaat."

"What about her male partner?" Corey asked.

"Mi shoot him," said Karlos as he looked toward the flipped-over van. Corey then saw him reach for his gun. "Hold on."

Corey glanced at the van and saw what Karlos saw—there was movement inside. He and Tarone joined Karlos as they walked together toward the van. The back door closest to the ground fell open. Crawling out was the older woman, bruised, her wig crooked, and clearly in pain. She struggled to hold the side of the van to help herself to her feet. Even then it was clear that she could not stand on her own—the attempt left her winded.

Karlos raised his gun. "Don't move."

She looked at him and shook her head as she breathed in large puffs. "Don't be silly. Do I look like I'm going anywhere?"

"Just keep your hands where I can see them," Karlos answered. "One sudden move and I'll blow your head off."

The woman then glanced toward Eddie and Candace. "So, they both survived," she sighed as she looked away. "And from the looks of things both my associates didn't."

There was a growing sound of sirens in the vicinity, and soon, screeching tires—a JCF squad car leading two ambulances, which led several more JCF squad cars.

The lead car drove around the van and skidded to a halt as the ambulances drove past before stopping. Detective Inspector Ellis jumped out of the driver's side of the JCF car. He nodded to the trio, then looked at the woman, who raised her head slowly to look back.

Dozens of policemen and policewomen were fast approaching on foot as Ellis called out to the first two, motioning them toward the injured woman.

"You'll find another around the mound there." Karlos pointed to where he shot the brotha.

Corey turned to the three paramedics who exited the first ambulance and led them toward Eddie and Candace. "My friend's over here. He's badly injured."

Corey then joined Eddie as Candace sat and cradled his head

on her lap.

"By the way, I'm Corey. You must be Candace."

Candace nodded as she couldn't help but smile. "Nice to finally meet you. Eddie told me so much about you."

Corey and Candace backed away as the paramedics helped lift Eddie onto the stretcher. One of them asked Corey a few questions on what happened, while the others consoled Eddie.

"Don't worry, we're going to get you in the ambulance and give you something for the pain," said the female paramedic to Eddie as they strapped him in, after Corey answered the last question.

"Let me ride with him," said Corey.

"Patients only, sorry."

Corey pointed to Candace. "Then let her go with him. She's still shaken up."

"I'm fine, you know," Candace answered.

"It would be safer if you ride with us," the paramedic said.

Candace nodded. "Okay, I'll come."

Soon after, she followed Eddie as she was handed over to the paramedics in the second ambulance.

Corey ran behind Eddie and watched him being lifted into the belly of the ambulance. Both paramedics joined him inside, as the third jumped behind the wheel. Moments later the siren was screaming. The ambulance Candace was in was right behind Eddie's as they turned around and drove out.

Ellis pointed to four officers. "Go escort the ambulances. I don't want anything to delay the patients' rides to the hospital, and you stand guard at all times. If anything happens to Mister Barrow or Miss Coke, I'll be coming after you personally."

Ellis then turned to Corey as he joined Tarone and Karlos. "You three can ride with me."

"Don't tell me that we're in trouble," said Corey.

"No, sah," said Ellis. "I want you to tell me what happened. I want to know all the details."

"Detective Inspector," said Corey.

Ellis turned to him. "Yes, sah."

"I never thought that I'd hear myself saying this. But I'm so glad to see you."

Ellis reached over and patted Corey on the shoulder as he nodded. "So am I, son."

Good frien betta dan packet money

—Jamaican Proverb

A good friend is better than money in the pocket.

Chapter 61

Cornwall Regional Hospital, Montego Bay, Jamaica

Eddie opened his eyes, yawned, and stretched as he noticed that he wasn't in familiar surroundings, nor an ordinary bed. He felt a sharp pain in the crook of his left arm when he extended it—it was an IV tube. The head injury, he was knocked unconscious before nearly being crushed alive. It was coming back to him.

He then noticed he had company. Corey was fast asleep on the chair beside him. He was slouched with his head hanging on one side. He was obviously catching up on lost sleep. Eddie looked for his phone. He just wanted to know what time it was. That's when he realized that he had no idea what day it was. Then it came to him that he'd had a burner which was taken from him by the people he did not even want to think of at this moment.

Eddie saw a remote control sitting on a small table well within reaching distance. It was hooked to the bed by a cord. He looked at the buttons and saw one with the icon of a person. Eddie pressed it and heard the beep of an intercom. About fifteen seconds went by before a middle-aged Asian in baby blue scrubs showed up holding a Styrofoam cup and a pill cup.

"Ah, you're awake." Her velvety Jamaican accent caught Eddie off guard. She smiled as she placed both cups on the table and dragged it closer to where Eddie could reach it. "How are you feeling, Mister Barrow? My name's Vera, and I'll be looking after you during my shift. Here's some Tylenol. Are you feeling any pain?"

Eddie shook his head. "I'm okay for now."

"That's good. You can take it if you begin to feel pain again." Vera raised a finger. "Hold on, I'll be right back."

She returned less than thirty seconds later with a tablet and handed it to Eddie.

"What's this for?"

"Take a look," Vera answered. "So far, it's just rumors that you and your friends were involved to some capacity with what happened this morning. Since you arrived, the hospital's been bombarded with phone calls from the press wanting to know if you're a patient. Every hospital in the Cornwall County was instructed to neither confirm nor deny your presence."

That's a relief. He didn't need that kind of attention right now.

"I'll leave you two alone," said Vera as she left. "You know how to reach me if you need anything."

Eddie turned to the sound of Corey's yawn. His arms were stretched out until Corey noticed Eddie staring back at him. He couldn't help but smile at seeing Corey's face light up.

"Bruh." Corey dragged his chair closer. "How are you feeling?"

Eddie shrugged his shoulders. "Like crap."

"At least you'll finally be able to rest." He leaned closer to watch a video from the Canadian Broadcasting Corporation's website. "What's going on?"

"That's what I'm looking to see." There was a caption at the bottom of the video which said: *Developing Story*. On it he saw Denton in handcuffs being escorted out the front door of his villa by two officers. Something was wrong with Denton's face, and after holding the tablet closer, Eddie noticed the injuries."

"What happened to his face?"

"He pissed off Karlos."

"*He* did that?"

"I wouldn't have believed it had I not seen it with my own eyes," said Corey. "Tarone and I were warned not to lie to him, and that's what Denton did."

The video then switched to Weiss as he was being escorted by the police, also in handcuffs, through the resort. His audience, unlike Denton's, was a lot larger. He, just like Denton, went calmly as he got in the police cruiser. Just before the car drove off Eddie saw him in the back seat first look away, and then slightly toward the camera. Weiss appeared to sigh heavily, which told

Eddie that even Weiss knew that he was done. The Jamaicans would go after Weiss and Denton first, then the Americans would pick up where they left off.

Eddie rested the tablet on his lap and turned to Corey. "How long you've been here?"

"I never left," said Corey, who then used this moment to tell Eddie everything that happened to him since they last spoke, which was when Eddie and Candace were at her Uncle Lenny's.

"Anyhow," Corey continued, "after you spoke to Nancy about the check you found with Weiss's signature, she made a few phone calls. A few hours later she got a call from a financial investigator in Chicago who told her that Weiss and Denton had been under investigation a few years ago because they were both suspected of fraud. Except they couldn't find any hard evidence which could link Weiss to Plessis Marketing. So, they had to drop their case. She didn't want to tell them about the Plessis check you and Candace found because she didn't want you to be stuck explaining how you found it. But after what you told her about Weiss, and now learning that both he and Denton were suspected of criminal activity, she put two and two together and was afraid that you were walking into a trap."

Eddie continued staring at Corey as he summarized how he and Tarone convinced Karlos to help them out, and how after they confronted Denton, he stayed behind to restrain him and lock him in a closet before coming to join them. As Eddie listened, the back of his throat ached to the point that even drinking his water wasn't enough. His best friend had been nearly killed trying to help Eddie out. Their coffee shop could always be rebuilt, but he would never be able to forgive himself if he had lost Corey. He looked away and sniffled.

"What's wrong?" Corey asked.

Eddie didn't know how to answer as both hands went to cover his eyes. His mind flashed back to when he was trapped with Candace inside the car, seconds from being crushed. He'd made Candace go first, and when he tried to get out, everything went wrong. Only for him to regain consciousness and see Corey.

"Remember how we met?" Eddie asked.

"Sure, how can I forget," answered Corey. "Those skinheads were going to kill you."

"Until you showed up. Then there was the time I was framed for murder. You were there too."

Eddie took a moment to clear his nostrils by inhaling deeply, then exhaling. "When we were at Citrusville Bar, I went out to the parking lot. Why was it so important for you to come looking for me when the phone signal was interrupted? I mean, I didn't argue or piss off someone that they'd ambush me."

Corey sat with his legs open and his elbows resting on his quadriceps, shaking his head. "I really don't know. I know you wouldn't have gone out dancing had I not dragged you out of the Airbnb. When I didn't hear back from you and I couldn't reach you, I guess my gut told me to look for you. I mean, this is our first time in Jamaica. We don't know the place nor anyone here."

"Then we got separated after the funeral," continued Eddie. "We were apart for two days, and you still found me when I—and Candace—needed you the most."

Two tears streamed down his face. He wiped them away with the back of his arm, but he knew that it wouldn't be enough. Corey leaned forward and placed a hand on Eddie's shoulder.

Eddie then reached across his chest with his other hand and placed it on top of Corey's. "I don't think I realized until now how much you truly are my best friend."

Corey got up and wrapped his arms around Eddie and gave him a tight embrace. All Eddie wanted to do was hold on as the tears flowed.

***

An hour had passed when an orderly showed up to take Eddie to get a CAT scan. Corey told him that he'd wait in the visitor's area until he came back.

Eddie did not have to get out of bed until he was about to get the scan, which was when the orderly and two other male nurses lifted him off his bed and onto the motorized platform. When that was done, he was transferred back to the bed, and the same orderly brought him back to his room.

"Thanks," said Eddie.

"No problem," the orderly answered as he propped up Eddie's pillow before he left. Roughly a minute later Corey, Candace, and Tarone walked into the room.

"Hey," Eddie said, barely capable of containing his excitement. They all answered him simultaneously with their own greetings, pats on the leg and shoulder as Corey and Tarone stood on one side while Candace came on the other and hugged him.

"You had me so worried," she said. "What did the doctor's say?"

"I still have to wait for the CAT scan results. But so far, I'm okay, I guess. Or else I'd be in the ICU. But what about you? What did the doctors say?"

"Nothing serious, but they recommended me to a psychologist," Candace answered.

"I think we'll all need to see one," said Tarone.

There was movement near the door that caught Eddie's attention. It was Ellis, and he looked more battered than ever.

"Good afternoon, everyone."

They all replied with their individual greetings.

"You come to arrest me again?" asked Eddie.

"Since you weren't running around naked in the street, you're good," Ellis said with a smirk.

"I never got around to asking," said Corey, "but what happened to you last night that we couldn't reach you?"

"I'll tell you eventually. But as of now, I have some good news and some bad news. The good news is that both Denton and Weiss were apprehended. As expected, they got their lawyers but the Crown Prosecutor's gathering more evidence as we speak. She was also contacted by a forensic accounting firm from somewhere in the States—Chicago, I believe. Two of their investigators arrived here in MoBay a few hours ago. It has something to do with Weiss being suspected of owning some shell company that was involved in holding kickback money from Denton's company."

"Did the Crown speak to Hines?" asked Eddie.

Ellis raised an eyebrow. "As a matter of fact, we've been trying to contact him. But it turns out that he, his wife, and little girl left the country."

More like, fled the country, Eddie thought. And he wouldn't be surprised to learn that Stepmother, Hansel, and Gretel paid him a visit after he learned about Plessis.

"Why you ask about him?" asked Ellis.

Eddie's head rolled from side to side. "It was just a thought, considering that Candace told me that's who she and Dwayne hired to settle with Weiss. I figured, oh I don't know, maybe Weiss would've paid with money which came out of the Plessis account with a check—one which would have *his* signature on it."

"Right…because…" Candace jumped in, slowly catching on to Eddie's lead. "Because such large amounts being paid out from his personal bank account would've certainly caught his wife's attention."

Ellis narrowed his eyes and held his head steady while looking suspiciously at Eddie and Candace. "It just so happens that the Crown Prosecutor's office received an anonymous tip that she should search Hines's office if she wants to find the motive behind Dwayne Pottinger's murder. You wouldn't happen to know anything about that, would you?"

"Don't look at us." Eddie nodded toward Candace. "We were on the run. And as you can see, I've been stuck here. I don't have a phone."

"Really?" Ellis nodded toward the one beside his bed.

"I'm talking about my own smartphone. Besides, I don't even know the Crown's phone number."

"I swear, it wasn't us," said Candace.

Ellis then glanced at Corey and Tarone with the same suspicious gaze.

Corey raised his hands showing his palms as though in surrender. "Don't look at me."

"I don't even know who Hines is," said Tarone.

"Anyhow," Ellis turned to Eddie, "we obtained a warrant to search his law office in Falmouth. The police are over there as we speak."

Brutus. The anonymous tip had to have come from him. Eddie smiled. The documents he sent Bevins would not be admissible. But now that this had become a murder investigation, the copies of those checks he and Candace saw would now be admissible. The Chicago investigators will have the proof they need to go after Weiss. With this, along with their testimonies, the Crown may have enough to go after both Weiss and Denton for murder—maybe even an additional charge against Weiss for sexual assault.

"You also said that there was bad news," said Eddie.

Ellis shook his head. "Yes, about that. Back at the scrapyard, I was told that there were three assailants. We have one dead body, and the older woman—whom I assume was the one in charge, is in custody. Karlos said that he shot another out of self-defense."

"He was hit, I saw him go down," said Tarone. "What about him?"

"My men searched the entire area and couldn't find him."

"What?" said Corey and Tarone simultaneously.

"There was blood found at the spot where Karlos claimed he shot him, so there's no doubt that he was hit," said Ellis.

"I knew there was something not normal about him," said Tarone. "I see some vicious men while I was in prison. But that one I fight at the scrapyard, he was a different kind of wicked I never see in my life."

"I'm not surprised," said Eddie. "I saw him in action. He took out Brutus's men like it was nothing."

"Do you think he's going to come looking for us, like for revenge?" asked Corey.

"There's more," said Ellis.

Eddie listened to Ellis as he spoke. What he said made his chest tighten.

Chapter 62

An Hour Earlier

As the prisoner transport truck crossed the city limits out of MoBay, Stepmother sat on the bench with her back flat against the wall, her wrists and ankles chained together. She should take it as a complement that the police considered her to be such a dangerous person. All she wanted was to get off this island and get as far away as possible. Under the current circumstances, that would not be the case. She'd never been in a Jamaican prison before, but she didn't have to see the inside of one to know that they weren't too exotic.

How could it have gone so wrong? By all accounts she should be on her private jet flying off to wherever she was instructed to go.

The truck was slowing down, it was the first time she looked away from the wall and toward the front. Something told her that this wasn't a traffic light. The truck came to a full stop, followed by the humming of the engine dying down.

Where are we? What's happening? She sighed as she shook her head. Who was she kidding? This was a setup, one no doubt orchestrated by Brutus. Payback for targeting his niece.

The two gunshots from up front startled her. Why would Brutus pay two police officers to bring her to this spot and then have them executed? She turned to the sound of the door being unlocked. Her chest and stomach tightened—she was completely defenseless being shackled the way she was.

The back door flung open. Her first instinct was to backslide down the bench away from it, only for her movements to be restricted. Hansel stood, weapon in hand, an apparent gunshot wound to his shoulder. It seemed that the bullet had passed right through. He hadn't wasted any time patching himself up as best he could. As for the Glock he held, he most likely disarmed one of the police officers before shooting them both.

She relaxed as she sighed with relief.

Hansel had survived. She did not need to know how he pulled it off. All that mattered was that he did. As for her other subordinate, the local authorities will never find out who she was. She'll just be another Jane Doe.

Stepmother raised her hands to Hansel to show off her chains. "Are you going to stand there, or will you take these off?"

He tucked the Glock away in the back of his pants, hopped inside, taking out a set of keys. Seconds later, she moved freely and followed him out of the truck. It appeared that her superiors still had some pull in these parts, convincing the prison transport officers to drive off course. They were probably expecting to get paid. Pour souls.

She still had pain in her left leg, which hurt every step she took. Her left arm was not much better, and she walked with a slight limp until Hansel assisted her. Imagine that. Three of them came here on a mission. One was dead, while the two of them were left battered and bruised. She had no idea where she was, except on the top of a hill on the island's interior. She saw the Atlantic Ocean in the distance. By the position of the sun, she guessed that she was staring at the north shore. The red hatchback parked a few feet away wasn't her usual mode of transportation, but it would have to do.

"Let's hurry," she said as she walked to the passenger side. "It won't take long before the authorities come looking for their truck."

Hansel got behind the wheel, while she sat beside him. He gunned the engine, and within moments they were gone.

A little over an hour later, they arrived on an airstrip somewhere in Saint Elizabeth Parish, where a private jet waited for them. As Hansel assisted Stepmother in walking toward the jet, the pilot greeted them outside the plane and handed them a phone.

"It's for you," he said.

Stepmother took it as she turned away from Hansel for privacy.

"Yes?"

"Hello," said a woman's voice. "There isn't much time, so I'll be brief."

"I understand," Stepmother answered. "I'm sure that you've heard by now that we lost Denton and one of my assets. There's no chance that we can salvage that venture. But everything's secure. Aside from our personal meetings, Denton doesn't know anything about us. We don't have to worry about getting exposed."

"Are you sure?"

"I'm positive."

"Unfortunately, I don't share your optimism."

"Ma'am?"

"Your mission failed because you allowed a civilian to interfere."

"I appreciate your concern," said Stepmother as she took a step farther away from Hansel and the pilot. "But Eddie Barrow's no longer a problem. After what he's gone through, he and his friend will be too traumatized to play detective."

"That may be true," the woman answered. "But your failure to dispose of Mister Barrow has also attracted the attention of the local police. There's only so much we can do on our end to make sure this blows over. As a result, I was left with no choice but to intervene and call off the hit you put on Mister Barrow's agent."

"I see," she answered. Canceling the hit was a tactical move since Denton and Weiss were already exposed. It was pointless to proceed.

"Mister Barrow's emerged from this mess bigger than ever."

"I commend you for canceling the hit on Barrow's agent. Fewer questions will be asked, allowing us to move forward."

"Oh, but there won't be an *us*."

Her throat went dry. "I beg your pardon?"

"Your failure wasn't only costly. It's an embarrassment," said the woman. "As of now, your services will no longer be needed."

Stepmother felt her stomach drop.

"I want to speak to the asset," said the woman.

Stepmother swallowed to soothe her dry throat and closed her eyes as she suddenly felt short of breath. She lowered her head slightly and took a slow, deep breath. "Yes…Ma'am."

Stepmother held out her hand slowly. Hansel walked over and took the phone from her. She let her arm drop to her side without even looking at him. There was no denying what was going to happen next—especially since she knew that she could no longer refer to him as *her* asset.

"I…I can't believe that I'm no longer in control."

Hansel handed the phone back to the pilot before he raised the Glock to her temple. The bullet shot through her brain and exited before she even heard the bang.

Chapter 63

Cornwall Regional Hospital, Montego Bay

"No one knows where the plane flew to?" asked Eddie.

"We'll find out eventually," said Ellis. "But with their head start, the plane will land in another place, where her henchman will switch planes or travel by boat to his next destination. We may get lucky, but there's a good chance that he'll get away."

"Any idea who their leader was?" asked Corey.

"We'll find out eventually," said Ellis.

"My money's still on her being former CIA, MI-Six, or some other foreign intelligence agency," said Eddie. "But whomever she worked for is even more ruthless."

"Will that make it more difficult to convict Weiss and Denton?" asked Candace.

"I believe there's enough evidence to send them to prison," said Ellis. "And the investigation isn't over."

"The people who killed the leader were cleaning up." Tarone turned to Ellis. "Speaking of which, did you find the man who killed my brother?"

Ellis shook his head. "We don't have a suspect yet. But trust me, you'll be the first to know when we have one in custody. I have my most trusted investigators working on this case, taking into account everything that both you and Corey disclosed about last night's events. And given the situation, INDECOM is also investigating."

"What's INDECOM?" asked Corey.

"It's the Independent Commission of Investigations," Eddie answered. "They investigate Jamaica's police and security forces."

Ellis shot Eddie a glance. "How yuh fi know dat?"

Eddie shrugged his shoulders. "I read."

They were interrupted by Ellis's ringing phone. He answered it and turned around, having a very brief exchange with the person who called him. He put it in his pocket while he turned around to pat Eddie on the leg, considering that Candace was in between them. "Sir, you get well. I need to go. But I'll see you soon to get your full account of everything that happened."

They all exchanged their goodbyes, and Ellis was gone.

Corey then turned to Eddie. "I almost forgot. You could use some of your personal items. I should go back to the Airbnb and get them. Besides, I could do with a change of clothes too."

"Yeah, hoping that it wasn't robbed while we were away," Eddie said. "Another thing. Bring me Dwayne's scrapbook."

"Bruh, you should be resting," said Corey.

"He's right," said Candace. "You *should* be getting as much rest as possible."

"I'm going to get bored very quickly. At least this will give me something to do."

"Then you should read a book, or watch TV," said Corey.

"I don't have either. Besides, I just suffered a head injury. How else am I going to recover unless I use my brain to keep it active?" said Eddie. "Just bring me Dwayne's scrapbook. Please?"

Corey sighed. "All right. I'll bring you Dwayne's scrapbook."

"I'll drive you," said Tarone. "My taxi should still be in the parking lot where I left it."

After they left, Candace dragged a chair over and sat next to Eddie. "You solved Dwayne's murder. We're safe now. Why don't you rest?"

"I made a promise to Jalissa," said Eddie.

"And you kept it. His killers are in custody. I'm sure Jalissa will be grateful."

Eddie tilted his head as he shook it once. "I don't know what it is. But I still feel as though I've overlooked something. Now with all this time on my hands and no stress, maybe I'll be able to focus more."

"You're talking about proving that Dwayne's designs were stolen?" asked Candace. "You're not going to let that go, are you?"

Eddie shook his head and smiled at her. "Not yet."

Chapter 64

Microlabs, Ltd., 15 Humber Avenue, Montego Bay

Ellis was happy that he found a place to park on the premises. The parking lot to the three-story blue building could barely fit five cars, and he wasn't in the mood to park on the road or a few blocks away and then walk. The only thing stopping him from taking a half-hour powernap was getting the DNA results. If the outcome from the tests proved that Tarone was not Chevelle's father, then it would confirm another theory of his that he'd had for some time.

His presence had drawn stares from those who were waiting outside on the wheelchair access ramp, as well as from those who were inside. With this many people, he was glad that not all of them drove. He was also glad that he did not have to take a number and wait to be served. Once the secretary behind the counter saw him, she was on the phone to inform the doctor of his arrival. Once she was done, she looked up at Ellis.

"Doctor Sweeney will be with you in a moment."

Ellis nodded as he stood to the side and leaned his back against the wall. When he got the phone call from Doctor Nordia Sweeney back at the hospital, he immediately picked up on the anxiety in her voice. He turned to the clapping sound of low-heeled woman's shoes approaching from the adjoining hallway. When she entered the waiting room, the first thing he noticed was how red the doctor's eyes were. He had not yet thought of how he would make it up to her for doing him this special favor. She didn't appear to have had the time to properly freshen up. She only did what was important, tie her hair in a bun, then throw on the lab jacket.

"Doctor Sweeney," said Ellis.

She turned to him. "Detective Inspector Ellis. You can come."

He followed her down the hall to her office where she gestured to a chair in front of her desk.

"Thanks for coming so quickly," said Sweeney.

"I was only at di hospital up di road," said Ellis. "And thanks again for seeing me late last night and for doing this rush job."

"You owe me big for this because I was up until the early hours of the morning and got no more than an hour's sleep." She smirked as she opened a folder on her desk and picked up a document. "As for the results, I don't know what you were expecting. I was… well…I ran the test a second time, just to be sure there wasn't an error."

Ellis raised both eyebrows. "An error? About what?"

"To begin, the DNA results prove that your subject A is not the father of subject B."

I knew it, thought Ellis as he nodded once. "So why did you have to do the test again?"

"As I already mentioned, I didn't know what you were expecting. So, here's what the results also show."

Ellis listened as Doctor Sweeney explained what she discovered. What she told him made him lean closer as his eyes widened. "Seh dat again?"

"I repeated the test, and the results came back the same." Doctor Sweeney handed the document to Ellis. "Science doesn't lie."

He turned the document around so that it would be right side up, then read it. With each line he read his jaw dropped even more.

"Oh rass!"

Chapter 65

Cornwall Regional Hospital, Montego Bay

Corey stood in front of the elevator with Tarone and pressed the *Down* button.

"Why don't we go check on Delroy." Tarone hit the *Up* button.

Corey nodded. "Sure, why not. I just hope his grandparents aren't there. For both our sakes."

"We nearly got killed, both this morning and last night," said Tarone. "What can they do to us?"

Corey admired his courage. It then came to mind that Ellis was supposed to get a paternity test done on Tarone. He wondered what became of it.

The elevator arrived and the passengers confirmed that it was going up before Corey and Tarone got in. When they got to the Intensive Care Unit, Delroy was asleep. It was a sad sight to see him in this state, hooked up to monitors, the top of his head wrapped in bandages, and he had a ventilator in his mouth. Chevelle was sitting beside him with Lucille. When Corey and Tarone arrived, Chevelle was the first to spot them. Her face lit up as she jumped from her chair and ran over to hug them both.

"You came back," said Chevelle.

"Of course. It's always nice to see you," said Corey as he returned the embrace just as he saw Lucille smile with a tear in her eye. She waved them both toward her.

"My sweet boys." Lucille stretched out her arms. "Come over here and give me a hug."

Corey was the first to hug her, followed by Tarone.

"Mek yuh neva call last night after yuh left?" said Lucille as she turned to Tarone. "I watched the news and saw that there was a shooting. They then showed a picture of the victim and he looked just like you. Mi couldn't sleep, yuh knuh."

Tarone shook his head. "He was my bredda."

Lucille's hands shot up to cover her mouth and stifle her gasp. "I'm so sorry. You have my deepest sympathy. Oh Lord, this is not right." She pulled Tarone down to her as she hugged him hard.

Corey saw the sadness on Chevelle's face as she approached Tarone.

"I'm sorry for your loss," she said. "Did you see your parents yet?"

Tarone shook his head. "It's just me and my mother now. My father passed away when I was young."

Chevelle gasped. "I'm so sorry. I didn't know."

"No worries."

Both Corey and Tarone took turns explaining what happened to them after they left Lucille's home.

"So the two white men we see getting arrested on the news this morning, they were responsible for everything you, Eddie, and Candace went through?" asked Lucille.

Corey nodded. "Everything."

"How's Eddie and Candace?" asked Chevelle.

"We just came from seeing them," said Corey. "Eddie's recovering from his injuries, while Candace is keeping him company. We were just on our way to get Eddie's things."

Corey then turned to Tarone and held onto his shoulder. "And also give *him* a chance to see his mother."

Tarone responded by patting Corey's hand in approval. He then turned to Chevelle and Lucille. "How's Delroy?"

"They operated on him last night," said Chevelle. "The doctors said that they stopped the swelling in his brain, but right now he needs a lot of rest. The nurses back there are watching him very closely to make sure nothing bad happens to him."

"What are you two doing here?" The man's voice was loud and hostile.

Aw shit! Corey recognized the voice and turned to see the judge and his wife, Henrietta, standing in the hall just outside.

"And you?" Judge Stewart pointed to Tarone as he walked

toward him. "The nerve of you showing up here around my grandson and my daughter. You really are looking for a reason to go back to prison, aren't you?"

Corey saw Henrietta go to the nurse's station on the other side of the hallway facing the ICU. He figured she was telling them to call security.

"Come on, Tarone. Let's go," said Corey.

Corey was about to be joined by Tarone when he felt someone tugging his arm.

"No."

Corey turned to see that it was Chevelle.

"You stay here." Chevelle then turned to Tarone. "You too, Mister Mitchell."

The judge's eyes narrowed. "What?"

Chevelle passed between Corey and Tarone and stood between them and her father. "Corey and Mister Mitchell are my friends. They are also Delroy's friends. They're staying because I want them to stay. And I also know that Delroy would want them to stay too."

"Don't be silly," said the judge as he pointed to Corey and then to Tarone. "This ruffian and this pedophile aren't your friends."

Chevelle shook her head and stomped the floor once. "No. You don't get to call Corey and Mister Mitchell bad names because they're not bad people."

"What nonsense are you talking about?" asked Judge Stewart. "This man drugged you before he raped you, that's why you don't remember. He even said that he did it."

"That's because he was scared. If he did not lie, some very bad people would've hurt the people he loves. And I know that Mister Mitchell didn't hurt me because he wasn't even there when it happened."

"Listen to me," said the judge. "He drugged you and raped you in your bed at the boarding school. That's what happened."

"No," said Chevelle. "That's not how it happened. I was at Camp Turtle Grove with the Bible Camp. I was carried to a cabin where I was blindfolded and tied down to a bed. Two very wicked men hurt me very bad. One of those men was Pastor Green. He told me that what he and another saint were going to do to me was to help me get rid of my lesbian demon."

"Don't you dare say that about Pastor."

"Yes, I will say that about Pastor because he's a very evil man," yelled Chevelle, causing heads everywhere to turn. She then wiped the back of her forearm across her face. "He did very bad things to me. I did not want him and that other man to do those things, but they never listened to me. They never wanted to stop. Why won't you believe me?"

"I'm not going to tolerate this a second longer. I told you to get away from them, and you're going to do as I say." Stewart grabbed Chevelle violently by the back of her neck. Corey didn't think, but reacted and grabbed the judge by his wrists, Tarone was about to join in until Chevelle began coughing as though she had problems breathing. The judge released her with palms up as she backed away from him, outside the unit and in front of the nurse's station.

"Stop. Get away. Don't hurt me," Chevelle screamed. "Don't grab me like that again, please."

Corey glanced quickly at Tarone who returned the look: *Did she just say, "Don't grab me like that again?"*

Henrietta rushed to console her, but it only made Chevelle lash out.

Judge Stewart slowly waved his palms downward. "Chevelle, be calm, it's okay. I'm sorry. No one's going to hurt you."

Corey saw that a few orderlies and other nurses had crowded into the area.

"Yuh lie," Chevelle snapped at the judge. "You're a liar. The way you just grabbed me. The way your thumb pushed into my neck. Your thumb nail. I remember now. I felt that thumbnail dig into my neck a very long time ago. That's exactly the way my rapist attacked me inside the cabin."

Tears flowed as Chevelle scrunched up her face and shook her head. "But now I know it was you. You were the other man who helped Pastor Green hurt me."

Gasps erupted all over.

Chevelle collapsed onto her knees and bawled her eyes out. "I was only a little girl. How could you do that to me?"

A few orderlies were about to move in and grab Chevelle, but her mother waved them off. The orderlies paused, then took a few steps backward. Henrietta then walked toward Chevelle and slowly extended a hand but hesitated when Chevelle curled into a fetal position on the floor. It was as though she was unsure whether it was the right thing to do or not. She then lowered her hand and turned to her husband just as Chevelle's bawling diminished. A tear fell from her eye.

"Is...is this true?" she asked.

The judge hesitated as he looked around and saw the gathering crowd staring back at him. "Of course not. This is preposterous."

"Why would she say something like that?"

"She doesn't remember, she's traumatized. She doesn't know what she's talking about." The judge pointed to Corey and Tarone. "Don't you see what's happening? They did this to her."

Henrietta continued staring at her husband. Corey didn't know how to interpret her expression. It was as though she wanted to believe her husband, however, deep down she knew that her daughter was telling the truth.

"Corey. Tarone," came a loud whisper from behind.

Corey and Tarone turned to see Lucille shaking her finger at Delroy.

I'll be damned.

Delroy was awake. And by the look in his eyes, he was fully conscious as to what had just happened. Corey wondered how much of it he saw and heard. But from the look in Delroy's eyes, it was clear that he was staring right back at him. He looked at Tarone, who returned a similar look of astonishment.

Corey turned to the judge. "Why don't you tell that to Delroy."

Stewart shot him an angry glance, revealing a damp, shiny forehead under the light. Then his eyes met Delroy's. The anger flushed from his face only be replaced by what Corey saw was anxiety.

"Now that he's awake," said Corey, "why don't you give him some peace of mind and tell him who his real father is. Is it Pastor Green or is it you?"

The judge looked back and forth between Delroy and Chevelle—who was still on the floor.

"Nesta knew what happened at Turtle Grove. He knew that Pastor Green was using his Bible Camps as a front so that he could prey on intellectually disabled children. That's why you had him killed."

Judge Stewart wagged his finger hard at Corey. "Watch it."

"Or what?" asked Corey as he gestured to everyone in the room. "You're going to kill me right here in front of all these people? Or will you get the police to do it, just like you had them kill Nesta?"

"I'm warning you."

Corey lifted his shirt. There was another collective gasp as everyone saw the bruises on his stomach and his back. "The same officers gave me these after Nesta showed me where Chevelle was attacked. One of them shoved their gun in my face. I'm sure he was ready to blow my head off before he was interrupted."

The judge lowered his hand as Corey heard his breathing grow more intense.

Corey lowered his shirt and took a step toward the judge as he pointed to Tarone. "You even tried to have him killed last night because you were worried that he'd start talking the moment he found out Nesta was murdered. The only problem is that your goons messed up when they shot his brother instead."

Corey noticed that Tarone began to fume as he took a step toward the judge, but Corey held up a hand with his palm facing him. Things were too hot right now for Tarone to screw it up by rushing the judge and pummeling his ass in front of over a dozen witnesses.

"You know Chevelle's telling the truth." Corey nodded toward Chevelle, who was still lying on the floor in a fetal position. "When you and Pastor Green learned she was pregnant, you framed Tarone and gaslit her." Corey then pointed a thumb over his shoulder to Delroy. "Aren't you going to give Delroy some peace of mind and tell him the truth?"

Stewart's breathing was audible—huffing and puffing as though his lungs weren't functioning.

There was a bit of shuffling in one section of the crowd and Corey saw two police officers pushing through.

Judge Stewart turned to them with a sigh of relief. "It's about damn time." He then gestured toward Corey and Tarone. "Arrest those two men. They won't stop harassing and intimidating me and my family."

Both officers were about to take a step forward when a strong baritone voice broke the silence.

"Stand down, Officers."

Corey watched as everyone turned to the sound of Ellis's voice. The crowd parted as he walked through, holding a legal-sized brown envelope.

"What's going on here?" asked Judge Stewart, who then turned to the officers. "I just gave you an order. Arrest those men."

"Hold on." Ellis held up a palm toward the officers. He then turned to the judge. "A call was made about a disturbance here so I came as fast as I could. I overheard some of what was just said."

Ellis then gestured to Corey. "Your Honor, Mister Stephenson asked you a fair and reasonable question."

"I don't have to answer to them," snapped the judge. "I'm sick of this rapist and his ruffian friend poisoning my daughter's mind."

"Tarone Mitchell *did not* rape your daughter," said Ellis. "And I can guarantee that he's *not* Delroy's father."

"You're walking on thin ice—"

"I had a paternity test done." Ellis held up the envelope to eye level. "The results show that Mister Mitchell's DNA doesn't match Delroy's. I immediately faxed a copy of these results to INDECOM to help them with their investigation."

"What investigation?" asked Stewart. "And you went behind my back to obtain my grandson's DNA? You're way out of line."

"I called you last night, hoping that you'd sign off on a warrant for Delroy's DNA, but you didn't answer your phone. I figured that you were here with him and most likely wouldn't be in the mood to sign anything. So, I went to another judge," said Ellis. "As for the identity of Delroy's father, the DNA results revealed that he's a relative. In fact, the technician who conducted the tests told me that she was able to conclude, with certainty, that both parents are *first-degree* relations."

Mumbling and whispers were heard around the room.

"In case you're not familiar with the term, *Your Honor*," said Ellis, "it means Delroy's parents were either siblings or parent and child. We already know that Chevelle is his mother. So, unless Chevelle has an older brother we don't know of, it pretty much narrows it down to one person. Doesn't it?" Ellis then handed the envelope to the judge. "Do you care to comment, *Your Honor*?"

Rather than take the envelope, the judge backed away while shaking his head. "That doesn't prove anything. It'll never stand up in court."

"That'll be for *another* judge to decide. In the meantime, another warrant was just issued to search your property and your bank accounts. It's standard procedure, I'm sure you understand." Ellis then looked at Corey and Tarone, who met his gaze. "This time, I want to make sure the investigation is done properly."

Ellis winked at them.

Judge Stewart was perspiring heavily—he couldn't wipe his bald spot enough times to keep it dry. He turned to Henrietta, but she responded by shaking her head and her palms raised outward, backing away from him as though she did not want him to touch her. She then turned and stormed off crying, pushing her way through the crowd.

Ellis then knelt on one knee beside Chevelle, who had not moved from where she lay. "Miss Chevelle, isn't it? I know that you've been through a lot. But would you like to come with me down to the station so that we can talk. I promise you this time that my colleagues and I are going to listen to *everything* you have to say. Would you like to do that?"

A few moments went by before Chevelle clenched her eyes shut and gave short, quick nods.

"Let me help you." Ellis held out his hand. Chevelle did not react immediately, but she eventually extended a trembling hand. Ellis took it gently and helped her to stand. "Is there anything you want to bring?"

Chevelle shook her head. Ellis then walked with her to the

elevator with his arm around her shoulder. The hospital staff parted to the side to let them pass. They were a few feet away from the elevator when Ellis stopped and turned around to the judge, wagging an index finger in front of him. "You know something, *Mister Stewart* ...I almost forgot." He stopped wagging his finger and sighed. "You're under arrest. The charge is incest and grievous sexual assault on a child under the age of sixteen. Since you're a judge, you ought to know that you don't have to say anything because it'll be used against you in court." He then nodded to the two officers.

The judge didn't even resist as one of the officers pulled his hands behind him and slapped the metal bracelets around his wrists. Stewart gave one last look at Delroy before the officers marched him off. Ellis and Chevelle stepped aside to let them pass.

Corey watched as Tarone took a few steps forward while giving the judge a hard stare. Corey joined him just as the elevator pinged. Stewart glanced at them briefly before turning his head away, just as the elevator doors opened.

Once the judge and the officers were gone, the crowd dispersed as they talked among themselves. Corey did not have to overhear them to know that they'd be talking about this moment for days, if not weeks.

Tarone sighed while shaking his head. "Mi know seh a dat man kill mi bredda."

"Think about it this way," said Corey, "your brother's killers are part of the snake's body and Judge Stewart may be the head. Once you cut the head off, the rest of the body won't survive."

They both joined Delroy, as they watched Lucille console him.

"It's okay, young man. It's okay," she said as she dabbed his eyes with a tissue. Even though the head injuries would eventually heal, he may never recover from the injury he just sustained to his soul.

Chapter 66

Tarone's car was right where he had left it. The bill was sky high, to no one's surprise, considering that the car had been parked there for more than twelve hours. When they got to the Airbnb, there was a sticky note on the front door from a postal company, showing that there was a delivery attempt.

Corey grabbed the note. "What do you know? The Colorado guy sent back Dwayne's smartphone."

"Whose phone?" asked Tarone.

"Dwayne Pottinger," answered Corey as he unlocked the front door. "Eddie and I found it at the crime scene." Corey brought Tarone up to speed as they went inside. The Airbnb was just as it had been left. Corey expected the place to have been either robbed or at least shows signs that someone had been trying to break in, but there wasn't anything of the sort. For Corey, it was just a quick in and out. He even packed a few things for himself in the event that he would be spending the night elsewhere. Then again, considering what he and Eddie went through these past few days, he wasn't sure if he wanted to come back to this place. He'd rather be close to Eddie.

On their way back to the hospital, Tarone stopped by a Digicel store so that they could each get new burner phones. They then went to the address listed on the sticky note. When they got there, Corey was able to retrieve the parcel using his own ID. Along with the smartphone was a note from Craig Beinecke at TekDry International, wishing Eddie a speedy recovery. Corey figured that Beinecke must have seen the news of Denton's and Weiss's arrests and had the foresight to add Corey's name as a contingent receiver.

Once they were in the car, Corey opened the parcel and took out the smartphone. "I wonder if Eddie's hunch was right about

Dwayne recording his final moments."

"You want to see Ellis to give it to him?" asked Tarone. "He should know colleagues who could unlock the phone and find out."

"Yeah, but the problem is the prosecutor assigned to the case would already know that Eddie and I found Dwayne's purse. If we hand this over to Ellis then the prosecutor will know that we were withholding evidence to a murder case. We could be charged with obstruction."

Tarone smirked. "Who said they need to know it was you who returned it?"

Corey pondered what Tarone just said and looked at him with a grin. "I met a bredgren who sold cold drinks and snow cones at the taxi stand where we first met."

"I know who you're talking about."

"You're in the mood for a snow cone?"

"Yes, sah!"

***

Roughly a little over half an hour later, Tarone dropped off Corey back at the hospital. They waved their goodbyes before Corey swallowed the last bit of sweet pineapple-flavored ice and evaporated milk, then tossed the cone-shaped container in the trash before entering the hospital.

He arrived at Eddie's room, where he found him and Candace talking. His best friend looked up at him in excitement as he entered.

"You hear about Judge Stewart?"

"Tarone and I were there." Corey nodded as he placed the bag with Eddie's belongings on the table next to his bed. "We saw the whole thing. Even Delroy woke up on time to see it. It's been all over the radio since we left to get your things."

Corey then described the whole incident from the moment Judge and his wife showed up, to the point Ellis surprised everyone with the DNA paternity results.

"Who would've thought?" said Candace. "Delroy must be

devastated. I mean, he had a right to know. But for him to find out like this and after so many years."

"He'll need time. At least Lucille's there to keep him company."

"Lucille?" asked Eddie.

Corey reminded him who she was and how she had helped him.

"How's Tarone?" asked Eddie.

"I know he's still hurting from the loss of his brother," said Corey. "But I think him watching Judge Stewart getting arrested gave him hope that he'll finally get justice."

Eddie reached for his belongings, but Corey handed them to him when he saw that the bag was out of reach. After Eddie thanked him, he felt inside and took out Dwayne's scrapbook.

Corey smirked. "I thought you'd brush your teeth first."

***

"Something's on my mind and I need to check it out," said Eddie.

"What is it?" asked Candace.

Eddie turned to the page, which was not a dress design but the picture of the flying fish.

Candace chuckled. "I remember when Dwayne drew that. He told me that it was his inspiration for a collection he called *Sunrise Over Barbados*."

"A collection?"

"Yeah, he once talked about producing his own fashion show," said Candace. "The dresses in the collection weren't meant for normal casual wear but were designed specifically for the show. The models would each wear a dress that displayed a part of the fish. Later during the show, they would stand side by side to form the complete flying fish. They would also blend in with the background display."

A collection. Eddie grabbed the tablet from the table and logged into his cloud to access the photographs he had saved, then found the one of Dwayne appearing as Shenice at the Citrusville Bar, when he took the selfie with Pusey's niece. He studied the picture for a few moments before something jumped out at him.

So that's what Dwayne was after. He turned to Candace. "Around what time did Dwayne begin designing this collection?"

Candace tilted her head to the side as though she was searching for the answer. "At least a year ago."

"Before he met Pusey for the first time, right?" asked Eddie.

"For sure, long before then," said Candace. "He always preferred drawing the designs by hand rather than on the computer."

"That's right," said Corey. "On bristol board. Eddie and I saw a roll in his room when we visited Wesley's house."

"Bristol board," said Eddie as he nodded slowly. "Bristle board…paper."

Eddie rested the tablet on his lap as he stared blankly ahead and grabbed both Corey and Candace by their arms. Several thoughts raced through his mind at once.

"What's wrong?" asked Candace.

Corey calmly turned to Candace. "Just wait for it."

Eddie released them, grabbed the tablet, and wrote a specific question on Google. A list of links appeared, and the one he was most interested in appeared near the top. Speedreading through the article he found his answer.

"Your phone." Eddie turned to Corey. "Give me your phone, quick."

"Are you going to tell us what's going on?" asked Candace.

Corey handed Eddie his phone and turned to Candace. "Wait for it."

Eddie dialed Ellis's number. He answered after the first ring.

"Detective Inspector Ellis."

"Detective Inspector, it's me," said Eddie. "You told me about your colleague's son who works at a paper mill in British Columbia. Didn't you say the fire occurred more than a year ago and that Jamaica's been getting practically all its paper from Quebec ever since?"

"Yeah, I think so. What's this about?"

"I need you to call a Doctor Thomas Young. He's a scientist who specializes in timber authentication in Great Britain. As for his contact info, all I have are some details from an article he wrote."

"What? Why do you want me to do that?"

"Because Vanessa Pusey stole Dwayne Pottinger's designs. There's a slight chance, but I know how to prove it. But we need to act fast."

Lang run, shat ketch

—Jamaican Proverb

Long run, short catch

People that get away with wrongdoing will eventually be held accountable and be punished for their actions.

Chapter 67

Usain Bolt's Tracks and Records Sports Bar, 7 Jimmy Cliff Boulevard, Montego Bay, The next day, 12:17PM

Freedom.

It's all Eddie had wanted for the past three days since he was admitted. He made it clear that he didn't want to stay, however, he was warned that if he felt any dizziness or headaches then he should head back as soon as possible. It took him a few phone calls, but he was able to track down Vanessa Pusey to this restaurant as she frequented it for lunch, sometimes with friends and other times alone. He wore a cap on his way to the restaurant to cover the bandages but chose to leave it in the car, entering the restaurant with nothing else but a bag with Dwayne Pottinger's scrapbook.

On entering, he saw two yellow mock clocks that one would see at the finish line of Olympic and World Track and Field Championships. They both proudly displayed Bolt's world record times of 9.58 and 19.19 he did in Berlin at the Worlds.

Above it was a window to the kitchen with the Tracks & Records restaurant logo on it. Surrounding it was a bright green wall decorated with real vinyl records.

He took the stairs on his left to the second floor to a room that was more than half full. He was greeted by a petite yet attractive female maître d'.

"Good afternoon," she said. "Welcome to Tracks and Records. Table for how many?"

"I'm here to meet Ms. Pusey."

She smiled and gestured to a spot in the corner away from the bar, where a European football game was shown on the massive screen. "She's over there."

"Thanks." Eddie walked off thinking that he had gotten away with his little white lie, until she called out to him.

"Excuse me, sir. Do I know you? You look familiar."

Eddie turned to her. "I don't think so. It's my first time here."

She showed off a flawless smile as she rubbed her forehead with a finger—possibly to draw attention to her Marcel waves. "Really? My name's Saroya."

"I'm Eddie," he answered returning the smile.

"Well, Eddie, you know where to find me if you need anything."

His gut told him that she knew who he was and was playing hard to get. "For sure."

Eddie walked to Pusey's table. She dined alone, with a tablet in one hand and a fork in the other. "Mind if I join you?"

"Now isn't the time..." She then looked up and saw Eddie. Any remaining warmth faded from her face. "Oh, it's you."

Eddie grabbed a chair and rested the bag beside him. "I just want to talk."

"Are you going to make more frivolous allegations about me?" she asked. "Because I'm warning you, if this what you came here for, I can have you thrown out of here, followed up with a phone call from my attorneys. And believe me when I tell you they will not limit themselves to getting a restraining order against you for harassment."

"I admit, we got off on the wrong foot," said Eddie as he noticed her eating while staring at her tablet. "I just want a fresh start."

Without taking her eyes off her tablet, she took a sip of her water. "Do you?"

"Sure, I suspected that you had something to do with Dwayne Pottinger's murder. You responded by putting out a bounty, sorry, a *reward* for my capture after I was falsely accused of a stabbing."

Pusey sighed as she looked at him. "I was only doing what I thought was best, given what was known at the time."

Eddie pretended that he needed to rub the bandage. "I'm sure you were."

Pusey rolled her eyes and took another bite from her salad. "I heard about the arrests. A VP from an American steel manufacturer and a movie producer. There are rumors that you were involved in exposing them. Is that true?"

"There are many rumors about me. Some of them are true."

"Well, if it's true, congratulations. Is that what you wanted to hear from me?"

"Actually," said Eddie as he took out his tablet and rested it on the table in front of Pusey. "There's something else I want to discuss with you."

"Is this going to take long? Because I have a very busy schedule this afternoon."

"Oh, you're not going to be late." Eddie smiled and shook his head. "I can promise you that."

Eddie tapped a side button on the tablet to activate the screen from sleep mode. The selfie picture that Shenice took with Pusey's niece at Citrusville appeared. "You saw this picture before, right?"

Pusey crossed her arms and narrowed her eyes. "You already showed me this."

"It's a nice picture. Both Dwayne—or should I say, *Shenice*—and your niece are ridiculously photogenic. She's also a good sport, hugging Shenice to congratulate her on her win."

"You seem to have forgotten that my niece was dancing against a man and not a woman."

"Naw, I didn't forget. After all, Dwayne found the perfect disguise that allowed him to get next to your niece. No one knew that it was him. Not your niece, hell, I didn't even know that Shenice was a guy."

"He went very far, just to get a picture with my niece. It's not like she's a celebrity."

Eddie relaxed into the back of the chair as he nodded. "It bothered me too, why Dwayne would take the chance of showing up as Shenice. It took me a while to figure it out. I mean, let's face it. A man in drag who shows up at a straight dance club in a very homophobic environment? Not the smartest thing for someone to do, right? Let's be honest, that's suicide. Unless the person was desperate."

Pusey held a palm out at Eddie. "Okay, you're going to have to pause for a moment because I think what you're about to say next is going to be something my lawyers will want to hear. In fact, I'll post this live so that my eleven million followers can be entertained."

Eddie stared at her with half-lidded eyes as Pusey took out her mobile and began filming. "Be my guest."

"Besides, your publisher dumped you and I also heard through the grapevine that your restaurant burned down. You haven't been having a good week, have you, Mister Barrow?"

"It's a coffee shop, not quite the traditional restaurant," said Eddie.

"Anyhow, you were saying..." Pusey chuckled. "Dwayne Pottinger showed up to a straight club, dressed up as woman, because you thought he was desperate?"

"It's not a secret that there was bad blood between the two of you," said Eddie. "He alleged that you infringed on his intellectual property rights by copying his designs from the scrapbooks he left with you and then presenting them to the *House of Grace* as your own. His only problem was that he couldn't prove it, or so you thought."

Pusey nodded. "Go on."

Eddie held up the tablet with the selfie photograph so that Pusey could film it. He then tapped his finger next to the dress Pusey's niece wore. "That was until your niece wore *this* dress. I'm not sure how Dwayne learned in advance that your niece would be wearing this specific one." Eddie then opened another picture from the photograph gallery that he had screenshot. It was a picture of Pusey's niece showing off her dress earlier that evening, stating that she'd be wearing it during the dancehall competition. He showed it to Pusey. "But I believe that he saw *this* picture on her social media page."

Eddie turned the tablet toward him very briefly to catch a glimpse of the picture. "Sure, the picture quality isn't too great. But Dwayne, presumably, recognized it as one of his."

Pusey put her free hand to her mouth as she yawned. "Are you going to be done soon?"

"I'm getting there." Eddie smiled. "As I was saying, once Dwayne presumably recognized your niece wearing one of his dresses, he had to act fast. So, he put on a dress of his own, wore the right wig, add a bit of makeup, and *voilà,* he transformed into Shenice. He then showed up at Citrusville to get a clearer picture than the one she posted. Getting a selfie with her was a great way to do so."

"If that were true, then why would he dance with you?" asked Pusey. "If he was simply there to see my niece, why would Dwayne draw so much attention to himself and then take part in the dance competition."

"Those are fair questions," said Eddie. "To answer the first one, Dwayne was a fan of mine. According to his sister, he was going to attend my book signing the next day. When he saw me at the club, it's reasonable to assume that he recognized me and probably couldn't contain his excitement. Once he got his kicks, he took off to find your niece. It would explain why he didn't hang around to talk to me."

Eddie crossed his legs. "To answer your second question, he wasn't planning on participating in the dance competition. In fact, I saw that he was trying to leave right after he took the selfie, but the crowd wouldn't let him and pushed him to join the competition. I'm sure Dwayne realized the mistake he'd made by dancing with me."

"Where are you going with this? There's over three million and counting who are currently watching. I'm sure they want to know."

"The thing is this." Eddie uncrossed his legs and leaned toward the table, rested the tablet on the surface and slid it closer to Pusey. "I looked at this picture several times trying to figure out why it was so important for Dwayne to take this selfie, then try to leave. Then it hit me. The whole time I was focusing on the dress rather than what was *on* it."

Eddie then opened another picture from the photo gallery to show her the image of the flying fish.

Pusey rested an elbow on the table to prop her head while she kept filming with the other. "A fish? Wow, you find plenty of fish in the sea around Jamaica."

"It's a flying fish, a national dish of Barbados. I know that because it's one of my favorite meals, especially with coconut bread for dessert," said Eddie with a smile. He then opened a new photograph from the gallery which juxtaposed the picture of the flying fish next to the dress that Pusey's niece wore in the selfie. "Do you notice anything familiar?"

Pusey took the tablet, glanced at the pictures, shook her head, then let the tablet drop onto the table. "No. What am I supposed to be seeing?"

Eddie slid the tablet back toward her. "Look again."

She looked at the pictures again while pointing her mobile at it. "Oh, look at that, I'm up to over six million viewers."

"Let me help you and your viewers see what both Dwayne and I spotted." Eddie then pointed to a pattern on Pusey's niece's dress, then zoomed in on the tail end of the fish drawing to show the similarities. "Now do you see it?"

Eddie watched as Pusey leaned closer to the tablet for a moment. Suddenly her eyes jolted open even wider, followed by her pointing the phone away from the tablet. She rapidly shook her head at first, then closed her eyes as she looked away from Eddie. "No, I don't see it."

"I think you did," said Eddie. "And I'm sure you fear that some of your more observant viewers saw it too, judging at how quickly you pointed your phone away from the tablet."

"Then tell me, Barrow. What is it that you think I saw?"

"You just saw a mistake that you made. In fact, I believe Dwayne made the mistake first." Eddie then switched back to the selfie. "According to one of Dwayne's friends, the flying fish pattern was a part of a collection that was to be shared on more than one dress. It was supposed to be part of a fashion show project Dwayne was working on. This dress was designed exclusively for the show. The day he first met you with his scrapbook, I believe the drawing of *this* dress was put inside one of the scrapbooks he gave you in error. You wouldn't have known that, of course. Actually, I wouldn't be surprised if the only reason you showed up at the club was to scold your niece for making off with this dress without your permission."

"And where is this so-called collection of Dwayne's?"

Eddie reached into the bag beside him, took out Dwayne's

scrapbook and opened it up on the table to a page he had already marked, placing his index finger on it. It was one of several pages that were damaged. Pusey pointed her mobile to it.

"It's sad, but I was told that some of Dwayne's scrapbooks were severely damaged when he was kicked out of his family's home. Those drawings, unfortunately, were the same ones he showed you several weeks before—practically guaranteeing that it would be impossible for him to prove that he was a victim of intellectual theft. When I visited the last place he lived a few days ago, I noticed that he had another scrapbook. It was only after I was given this damaged one that I realized that Dwayne redrew his designs from memory. Then *that* one was destroyed after a Molotov cocktail was thrown into the house. I know because Dwayne's former roommate, my friend, and I were there when it happened. We barely escaped with our lives."

Eddie removed his finger from the page and sat back in his chair. "It was only several months after he took his scrapbook back from you that he saw what he alleged were his designs in store catalogues—credited to you as a signature design of the *House of Grace,* based in London. I can imagine how he must've felt betrayed, knowing that you'd increased your net worth more than tenfold with his creation. It would've been his ticket out of extreme poverty. I mean, he was once homeless like other gay teenagers who were also thrown out of their homes, just for who they are."

"As I said before and I'll say again," said Pusey, "it's very unfortunate what Dwayne went through. I feel sorry for him, I really do. And the way he was murdered, unacceptable. He didn't deserve that and I'm glad that his killers were caught. I'm curious—and I'm sure my…uh…five million viewers are too, there hasn't been any details about the case, what do you know about it?"

"I'm not at liberty to say as the investigation is still ongoing," said Eddie noticing how Pusey was trying to divert from the subject at hand. "But as I was saying before, Dwayne had very little chance of proving that his intellectual property was stolen."

"And as I also said before and I'll say it again, my designs are mine and mine alone. It's unfortunate that Dwayne believed that he was a victim, but the truth is he wasn't. *I* was. And based on what's transpired over the last few minutes, I still am." Pusey then gestured to the damaged drawing that was opened in front of her. "As you just said, this doesn't prove anything. And as my lawyer pointed out, Dwayne's drawings don't even have dates written on them. He'd never be able to prove to a judge they were his designs."

"You're right," said Eddie. "But you have to admit, *this* drawing—even though it's damaged, if you look carefully, you'll see that it has another section of the flying fish. The tail end, in fact, the one that's found in the selfie."

Eddie then flipped the page. "As well as this. Do you see the wing?"

He flipped another page. "And this. Yeah, this one's damaged pretty badly with mud stains and all. But look closely enough, you'll see the head of the fish."

Pusey shook her head. "I don't see it."

"Yeah, you're right. It's not very visible. It's too badly damaged." He then flipped to another page, one that was torn as though it were violently ripped out of another scrapbook. "You must recognize this one, don't you?"

"Of course, it's mine. This is one which Dwayne made off with when he threw his childish temper tantrum in my office and accused me of stealing." She then pointed to the lower corner of the page. "As you can see, it's an original and it's dated several months before Dwayne and I even met. That being said, I don't understand how he could accuse me of having stolen something that I created long before I ever even met him. And I don't know why you're showing me this. Everything you've shown me so far doesn't prove that I did anything illegal—if that's what you're trying to imply. If anything, you've just corroborated what everyone's been saying all along—that Dwayne was disgruntled that I did not believe his designs would ever sell. His false accusations against me were just a way for him to get back at me."

Pusey then flipped her phone around briefly to show to Eddie. "There are over nine million viewers watching right now, Mister

Barrow. You still haven't proven anything. Not one thing."

"I'm not done yet." Eddie reached in the bag and took out an envelope. He opened it and held it up for Pusey's smartphone. "These are lab results from a stable isotope ratio analysis I requested, or, SIRA for short. The test was performed at an independent laboratory with the assistance of the Royal Botanic Gardens at Kew in Richmond. That's in Great Britain in case you were wondering. For those of you who aren't familiar with SIRA, this technology is used in the fight against illegal logging. Through this type of validation process, one can determine where a piece of lumber originated. The process relies heavily on the availability of reference samples from forests or plantations. Fortunately, wood samples are available in the World Forest ID collection in Kew. Allow me to explain how SIRA works. It compares the ratios of isotopes of common elements such as oxygen, carbon, hydrogen, nitrogen, and even sulfur. The ratios of these elements vary from one location to another. What's interesting is that SIRA can also be used to identify the origin of the tree used to create bristol board."

"In other words," Pusey chuckled, "you're telling me and my audience that paper comes from trees. But go on, I'm enjoying this."

Eddie placed the lab analysis document on the table next to the scrapbook while he turned the pages of each of Dwayne's damaged drawings as well as Pusey's. "You'll notice that there are pieces torn from each of these pages. Those samples were all labeled and sent to the UK by overnight courier for a SIRA analysis."

Eddie then pointed to the lab analysis sheet. "The SIRA signatures produced were compared to the reference samples in Kew. Guess what? The comparison revealed that your paper and Dwayne's came from softwood lumber found in two different locations."

"So what?" Pusey rolled her eyes with a halfhearted smile. "A tree is a tree."

"Allow me to be more specific." Eddie spoke directly into Pusey's camera. "I asked if the World Forest ID collection contains wood samples from British Columbia and from Quebec. They did."

"You're boring me, Eddie."

Eddie raised a palm. "Just bear with me. As I was about to say, trees in western Canada have different SIRA signatures than those in the eastern Canada. Therefore, in comparing the signatures from the tests with known samples from the World Forest ID collection, the lab technicians were able to conclude that Dwayne's paper originated in British Columbia. Yours, on the other hand, originated from the other side of Canada in Quebec."

A waiter stopped by their table and turned to Pusey. "Would you like anything else?"

Pusey reached into her purse and gave him her credit card. "Just the bill, thanks."

When the waiter turned to him, Eddie smiled. "Just water, thanks."

When the waiter left, Pusey lowered her head and took a deep breath as though she was losing her patience. "Are you going to get to the point?"

"I was just getting to that," said Eddie. "I found out a few days ago that Jamaica imports a lot of their paper products from Canada. Almost all of it once came from British Columbia. It was only recently that Jamaica's paper products came from Quebec."

Eddie pointed to the date written at the bottom of Pusey's design. "This is the date you created this design. From what I see, it's from nearly two years ago, right?"

Pusey sighed. "Yes, that's what the date says."

"And during the press conference you held, you displayed all your drawings Dwayne claimed you stole, where you specified that they were *all* created more than a year ago. Am I correct?"

Pusey held up one hand as though she were inspecting her nails. "That's correct."

"In that case," said Eddie as he relaxed in his chair with a grin while crossing his arms. "Please be so kind as to explain *how* designs you said were yours, which—based on your claim—were created more than a year ago, were drawn on bristol board that was only imported to Jamaica within the last ten months?"

Eddie watched as Pusey's eyebrows raised in a sudden jerk followed by rapid blinking. "I...I purchase paper from other places. There's—"

"I already met with your vendors," Eddie interrupted. "You order your paper from the same three stores here in Montego Bay. I spoke with the owners, and they told me that you prefer to only support local Jamaican businesses as your way of giving back. And I'm sure your credit card statements will demonstrate that too."

Eddie watched as Pusey avoided eye contact with him as she drank from her glass, putting down her mobile. She was so blindsided that she obviously didn't realize that it was still on.

"Before you came here for your lunch break, a warrant was obtained to search your home and your office. While we've been here chatting, those other drawings were seized, and paper samples will be sent in for analysis. Would you prefer to wait on the lab results, or would you rather come clean and tell us *when* you actually drew those designs?" Eddie then nodded to her phone. "By the way, how many viewers are you up to now?"

Pusey snatched her phone so quickly that she fumbled over the controls to stop the recording. She then slammed it on the surface. With an elbow on the table she held her head as she stared wide-eyed onto the surface.

"As I mentioned to you a few nights ago, sales of your designs were spiraling downward. When you were introduced to Dwayne and saw his work, you saw an opportunity to increase your brand's popularity once again—based on an error he made. You could've worked together and helped each other out. After all, you know the importance of giving back. That was your biggest opportunity to practice what you preach. But you chose to exploit this young man's mistake and you profited from it. Why? Were you afraid that the *House of Grace* would drop you in favor of him?"

The waiter returned and handed Pusey her credit card. "I'm sorry, Ms. Pusey. But the card was declined."

She shot him a glance through narrowed eyes. "What? That's impossible."

"I'm sorry, but we tried three times," said the waiter. "This card has been cancelled."

Eddie took out his wallet and handed the waiter his credit card. "Here you go."

The waiter nodded and walked away.

Eddie turned back to Pusey. "Let me guess, *that* credit card was given to you from the *House of Grace* for your business expenses. Your broadcast must've caught their attention. And I expect that they'll be calling you any second—"

Eddie was interrupted by the ringing of Pusey's phone.

"—Now."

Pusey sank back in her chair, closed her eyes, and swallowed as her phone rang three more times. It stopped, as it obviously switched to voicemail.

Eddie rested an elbow on the table as he pinched the bridge of his nose. "You know, I don't think they're going to give up. Something tells me that you'll be getting another call—"

Pusey's phone rang again.

"—Right now."

Pusey took a deep breath, then sighed as she reached for the phone and answered it. She slowly raised it to her ear as beads of sweat formed on her face. "Yes…no, no, no, it's not true, Missus Grace. I can expl—if you just…hello…hello?" Her voice ended in a crack. She inhaled to clear her nose then put the phone down.

Eddie watched as Pusey rested her elbows on the table and let her head fall into her hands. "I don't know much about the fashion industry, but I know that it's competitive." Eddie closed the scrapbook but left the lab analysis sheet in front of her. He had another copy. "From what I learned from his sister and his best friend Dwayne would never have allowed the *House of Grace* to drop you in favor of him. He would've done everything to help you regain your inspiration because he looked up to you. Many people hated Dwayne because he was gay. But Dwayne didn't hate, nor did he ever wish harm on anyone—even to those who persecuted him. He just wanted to live his life and pursue his dreams like the rest of us."

Eddie was about to get up when he noticed that many patrons had their mobile phones out and were filming them. For how long, he didn't know, but it was as though he and Pusey were being watched by a silent paparazzi. He would've noticed them had he not been so focused on Pusey.

It was only then that Pusey turned and spotted the numerous smartphones pointing at her. She stood up, nearly stumbling, as her breathing intensified. Her jaw dropped, it appeared as though she struggled to find her words as she raised a shaking hand and then pointed to herself.

"Those...those are my designs," she stuttered as she looked from one section of the restaurant to another. "Mine. I drew them. They're mine."

She took a step forward, this time not only pointing but jabbing herself in her sternum. "They're mine, all mine. I designed those outfits, me alone." Her voice began to crack even more as she fought back the tears.

Eddie saw no use staying any longer. He observed the expressions on the faces of the other patrons as many of them shook their heads in what appeared to be disgust and disappointment. He grabbed his bag and headed out, retrieving his credit card from the waiter on his way out of the dining area. As he walked down the stairs, he passed two policewomen who nodded to him as they made their way up.

When he stepped outside, not only did he get a blast of heat, transitioning from the air-conditioned restaurant, but he was also immediately mobbed by journalists with their smartphones throwing so many questions to him at once that all he heard was noise. He waved his free hand to calm them down.

"I can't say anything right now. Everything you need was filmed live. As for the rest, you'll have to wait until the police release an official statement. Thank you." He was still mobbed with questions as he walked away from the crowd, but he ignored them. Once Pusey would be led outside in handcuffs, the vultures would swoop in to feast on the main course.

As expected, Eddie found Corey leaning against their car which was parked on Jimmy Cliff Boulevard. He watched the entire incident on his mobile phone.

"Nice stuff. I watched Pusey's live video. You knew she'd film you," said Corey. "What you did in there is blowing up all over the internet. Even TSN and ESPN didn't waste time getting in on the scoop. How did you convince the police to let you talk to her first before they arrested her?"

"Ellis felt bad about misjudging us." Eddie got into the passenger seat while Corey slid behind the wheel. "He thought letting me have this moment was the best way to make up for it."

"I should hope so," said Corey. "Thanks to you, Dwayne's killers are going to prison and you were able to prove that Pusey stole his dress designs. They never would've solved those cases had it not been for you. You got justice for Dwayne."

"Don't sell yourself short," said Eddie. "You got justice for Tarone and Chevelle."

Eddie turned to a ruckus in front of the restaurant entrance. Pusey was being marched in cuffs through the gauntlet of reporters. They watched the vultures have a field day.

"She's looking at around two to five years in prison, not to mention a potential lawsuit from the *House of Grace*," said Eddie. "Even if she were to get a reduced sentence, her reputation's taken a big hit. Who knows how she'll bounce back, or if she ever will."

"As the saying goes," said Corey as he drove off, "you reap what you sow."

"True," said Eddie. "But a part of me feels sorry for her."

Chapter 68

Kingdom Pathway Ministries Church.
143 Albion Road, Montego Bay.

Pastor Green sat on the front pew on the far left of his church. The police took away Judge Stewart the day before, and from what he'd learned so far, Stewart had been arrested for rape and incest.

My God, Delroy wasn't my son, it was his. And he was the one who wore the condom. How did this happen?

Stewart had all the inner connections to the police. He knew who could be bought and would do as he pleased. No one would care if a battyman got shot, stabbed, or burned alive. Jamaica didn't need those sinners. Why didn't everyone understand that? Now these so-called human rights organizations were sticking their noses where they didn't belong, telling them how to govern themselves. All they were doing was poisoning and confusing children into believing that homosexuality was normal. It wasn't. It never was and never will be.

As for those children he'd *helped* over the years, they themselves needed to be purged of their homosexuality demons. That was something that had to be done, and he would do it again if another parent ever requested it.

But he was sure the police would be coming for him next. Those fools would never understand that God's law rules above any and every law of the land.

When he heard the door open behind him, he did not even look back. "Everyone's welcome in the house of the Lord. Speak, the Lord is listening."

There wasn't any answer. He was expecting the police to at least identify themselves or call him by his name. He took a deep breath and then stood.

"As I said, everyone's welcome in the house of the Lord." Green then turned around. "Speak, the Lord is—"

Green's chest tightened when he saw four masked men who had split up and walked down each aisle toward him. One of them was holding a petrol container.

He spun around to run through a side door, only to see another masked man blocking his escape. The blow to his lower spine sent waves of pain which extended down the back of his legs, causing him to fall backward onto the floor—screaming and writhing in agony.

"Pastor Green," said the masked man who blocked the side entrance, kneeling down and pressing his knee to Green's chest, while covering his mouth with his hand. "I have a message for you." The masked man then showed him a cellphone and played a video.

It was Chevelle at a press conference in the company of a woman Green assumed was her attorney, along with Ellis, and an advocate for the intellectually disabled. She was speaking out against sexual abuse of intellectually disabled people, that it's real, and that the world needs to have a conversation. She then mentioned how she was raped—naming him—and how he and her own father gangraped her because they thought she was a lesbian. She said he had raped her several times. She begged his other victims to come forward and speak out.

"Wait," the masked man said. "It gets better." What Green saw next was a compilation, where many intellectually disabled women and men each called out him and his church for sexually abusing them when they were children.

Green tried to say something, but it was muffled under the masked man's hand. The man lifted his hand.

"That's not true," cried Green. "It's not abuse because I was doing the Lord's work. I wasn't doing anything wrong. No one in my church did."

"One of your former sheep don't agree with you," said the masked man. "She told me that she left she husband after she learned what you and her husband did to her daughter. Now her daughter's parted ways with her. You probably heard that her husband got arrested at the hospital."

Henrietta?

"She sent a message to me to take care of you. This will be the last community service I'll be doing in a long time. I was going to cut off your arms and legs." The man then removed his mask. Green's eyes bulged as he opened his mouth to scream, but Brutus clamped back down on it. "But since I'm pressed for time, I'd rather burn this place down to the ground with you in it."

While he kept the weight of his knee on him, Brutus grabbed a Smith and Wesson Model 19 revolver.

"You want to know what's good about this gun?" Brutus smirked as he watched Green shake his head slowly. "It doesn't leave any shell casings. And that makes it next to impossible to match a bullet to it. But it also gets the job done." He then popped off a round into each of Green's kneecaps. Pastor's howling echoed throughout the church as an explosion of pain was left in the wake of the .38 special ammo that tore through bone, ligaments, and flesh in each kneecap. The agony was so unbearable that he did not notice that a liquid was being splashed on him, until some splashed into his mouth, causing him to choke. It then occurred to him what was happening.

That smell. Oh Lord, the petrol.

He opened his eyes to see Brutus standing over him and striking a match.

"I was doing the Lord's work," screamed Green. "Those children were abominations. I had to do what I did."

"Now it's my turn," said Brutus. "Raping children makes *you* the abomination."

Green screamed as he watched Brutus drop the match.

Chapter 69

Dovecot Memorial Park and Cemetery,
Montego Bay, The Next Morning

A slight drizzle turned into a light shower as Eddie and Corey watched Jalissa throw the last bit of earth on top of the coffin as Dwayne was slowly lowered into the ground. But even though the rain poured, the bright yellow sun still shone. About a handful of the fifty-plus in attendance had umbrellas. No sooner had they rushed to open them, the rain simmered down to a drizzle.

On arriving, if Eddie had not been told this was a burial ground, he would not have believed it. Besides the well-manicured lawn, the park stretched over a few acres of hills and valleys—a paradise of palm and fruit trees. Since the rain just fell, ponds even formed, not even appearing out of place.

Nancy Bevins had flown down after the FBI confirmed that it would be safe for her to travel. She stood behind Eddie and Corey, with Tarone and Candace on either side of them.

Two Members of Parliament from the Saint James Parish were in attendance. A police presence, led by Ellis, was also there to ensure no repeat of Dwayne's previous funeral. Alongside Dwayne's grave were those of Charlene, Shirley, and Wesley. Several members of the LGBTQ community were there, most of whom had attended previously. Milly, Delva, Lucille, and Amancia were also gathered. Father Andrew was the celebrant. Eddie had heard him debating against Pastor Green on the radio a few days before.

However, the biggest surprise was Lady Grace herself. She'd flown in from London with her husband, and couldn't be missed, wearing an African-styled dress and hat that rivaled the one worn by Angela Bassett while playing Queen Ramonda in the Black Panther movies. She was accompanied by two young brothas who appeared to be her assistants. One held an umbrella above her while the other pushed her husband's wheelchair. Her husband and Ms. Bevins were the only Caucasians, not surprising, considering where they were. Equally predictable was that neither Dwayne's, Shirley's, nor Charlene's parents were in attendance.

After Father Andrew said his final words, and the crowd began to disperse slowly, Eddie heard a familiar voice.

"Eddie, Corey." They turned to see Jalissa walking quickly toward them. "Thank you for coming."

Eddie nodded toward Corey. "We wouldn't miss this, not after everything's that's happened."

Eddie saw that Jalissa couldn't maintain her composure as she broke down and hugged him. "It's okay." He patted her lightly as he returned the hug.

"I'm so sorry for what I put both of you through," said Jalissa as she coughed on her own tears.

Corey put a hand on her shoulder. "It's okay. You couldn't have possibly known what was going on."

"Dwayne was brave and bold." Eddie turned to Candace as she dabbed her eyes with a tissue. "And he was looking out for his best friend."

Jalissa sniffed as she wiped her nose with a tissue then turned to Dwayne's grave. "My brother can finally rest in peace. So can his friends." She then turned to Eddie and Corey with a teary smile. "I don't know how I can ever repay you for what you've done. You were up against near impossible odds, yet you still kept your promise." She hugged Eddie and Corey once more.

"Eddie?" He turned to the British-Jamaican accented English and saw Lady Grace prancing toward him with outstretched arms with one of her assistants close behind with the umbrella. "Eddie Barrow, darling, I've been dying to meet you." She pulled him in and kissed him on each cheek. He couldn't believe how a seventy-four-year-old woman could be so fit.

She gestured to her husband in the wheelchair, who waved to them. "That's my husband, Christian Walken. Such a darling he is, flying with me all the way over here from London. We used to be so much more adventurous when we were your age. Unfortunately, a bad fall left him permanently asleep below the waist ever since."

She then winked at Eddie before she pranced toward Jalissa with the same greeting.

Eddie turned to Corey. "Did she just make a pass at me?"

"Damn right," Corey whispered. "You better watch your ass, 'cause that cougar will maul you in the sack."

"Eddie, darling." Lady Grace had her arm around Jalissa's shoulder. "Come. And bring your deliciously handsome friend."

She turned to Jalissa. "First, I'd like to express my utmost sympathy and my sincerest apologies for any trouble that the *House of Grace* has caused. I'm so embarrassed at what happened. None of us had *any* idea that we were selling your brother's stolen designs. But I want to make it up to you. Since we found out, we have removed Vanessa Pusey's name from everything that she sent to us since last year, where we will compare them to your brother's designs, before releasing them. I understand that Mister Pottinger had a will, didn't he?"

"Yes, he did," said Jalissa. "His will said that if his designs ever made it, then the proceeds should go toward building a shelter for sexually abused and battered people. It will also serve as a shelter for the homeless LGBTQ community."

Lady Grace nodded. "Then his wish is our command. The *House of Grace* will help establish the *House of Dwayne,* unless you prefer that it be called the *House of Shenice*. Once we find the land, we'll start building."

Jalissa's face lit up before she threw her arms around Lady Grace and thanked her. She then looked at Eddie and Corey, not containing her excitement.

"It looks like you gave Jalissa something else," said Candace as she approached and stood next to him. "Hope."

Eddie watched as Milly, Amancia, and Lucille acknowledged them with a smile and nod.

"Are you going to the reception?" asked Candace.

"Sure," said Eddie as he turned to Corey. "You going to the

reception?"

"You go ahead. Tarone and I will catch up later." Corey walked away with Tarone.

Eddie went with Candace toward his car, when she stopped and pointed away from the parking lot.

"What's that?" she asked.

"What's what?" replied Eddie.

Eddie watched her walk up an incline as she pointed. "That."

Eddie caught up to her and saw that she was referring to what appeared to be the landscaper's shed. She stopped in front of the door and turned around.

"What's going on?" asked Eddie.

"Well," Candace said as she gently held both of his hands. "Everyone else got a chance to thank you...except me."

Oh!

It started with a kiss on his lips, which they held momentarily before she opened her mouth, allowing their tongues to touch as their lips locked. As Eddie let Candace force her tongue past his teeth, he did the same. She pressed harder against him, his heart raced and blood rushed to his groin. He was hard, and Eddie knew that Candace felt it, yet she did not push him away.

As five fingers dug deep into his back, he heard the latch to the door open. Her doing obviously.

Eddie pulled his head away a few inches. "Are you sure?"

Her eyes flashed with passion and she answered him by flinging the door open and kissed him again. Their lips pressed hard together, their tongues wrestling, they stumbled inside and stopped, leaning against a potting table. They came up for air long enough for Eddie to lift her up on top of the wooden bench. Candace glanced over his shoulder and kicked the door, slamming it shut and blowing a wave of hot air over them.

Thoughts raced through Eddie's mind. She certainly *seemed* to want this. But he didn't want to be the cause of any more trauma in this woman's life. He asked her one more time. "You're sure?"

"Yes. I'm ready for this. I want it to be you, Eddie. Is that what you need to hear?" She grabbed him by the shirt collar. Her hands were quick as she unbuttoned his shirt. He felt his erection wanting to break free. Soon after, his pants and drawers were down, and she snapped the condom on him before he even had his wallet closed.

Then he felt the wet, warmness of being inside her. He grabbed her ass, and she wrapped her legs around his waist, as she rode him up and down. From deep down inside was stress, fear, and frustration that begged to be released as he thrust his hips into her—matching her growing frequency. There was no light, just darkness, heat, humidity, and their heavy breathing.

Eddie squeezed her ass tighter as the buildup was too intense for him to hold in. He lost control of his body as the sweet release exploded out of him—causing him to scream.

"Bumboclaaaaaaat!"

Chapter 70

Corey rode in the passenger seat as Tarone took very little time making it to the highway. "How are you and your mother holding up?" asked Corey.

"Trust in God one day at a time," answered Tarone. "The rest of the extended family a guh pass by. Di funeral is next week."

"I wish I could be there."

"That's okay," said Tarone as he overtook a truck. "Mi tell mi madda."

"Huh?"

"I told my mother the truth about me."

Shit. He came out to her. "How did she react?"

"She told me that she already knew. She's always known it since I was four years old." Tarone glanced at Corey and laughed. "She was the one who told my brother to teach me how to fight. It had nothing to do with turning me into a man, as my brother used to say. It was so that I would learn to defend myself against anyone who found out my secret. I also told her why I chose prison. If people found out about me and Nesta, they wouldn't only come to kill us, but they may try to hurt her and Garfield also. I couldn't bear to have that on my conscience. Now you understand?"

Corey nodded. "I'm glad that it worked out for you. You're a good man, Tarone."

"I also heard from INDECOM. They told me that they identified the men who shot my brother. A di police dem who was paid by Judge Stewart and Pastor Green. They caught three others, including the lab chemist who lied in court that my DNA matched Delroy's and that he's my son. Since she was the one who did the test, she tampered with my DNA to get the results she wanted."

"Let me guess," said Corey. "They paid her off too."

Tarone nodded. "Yes, sah. Mi talked to mi lawyer. With all the evidence against Judge Stewart and Pastor Green, she's confident that she could get the government to agree to an out-of-court settlement for the wrongful imprisonment, assault and battery by the arresting officers, and other damages."

"That's great. I'm happy that you're getting your life back," said Corey. "But after this happens, what will you do then? You're not going to still be driving a taxi, are you?"

"No, sah," said Tarone. "Mi talk to mi madda. She said I should explore the world while I'm still young. Now that I'm out, it might not be safe for me to stay. I could immigrate to England or to Canada. I haven't made up my mind yet."

"Wherever you go, I'm sure you'll adapt quickly."

They traveled for a good distance until they arrived at the tall grass-lined driveway to Karlos's house. They had called him three times and didn't get an answer. They were concerned because he said that he'd be at the funeral but was a no show.

Corey's door was halfway open before Tarone had even come to a full stop. He ran up the steps onto the porch with Tarone close behind.

Corey knocked loudly on the door. "Karlos?"

No answer, but Corey heard the television. He turned the doorknob and saw that it was unlocked. "Karlos. You home?"

Corey and Tarone walked into the living room and saw him sitting in his recliner, staring blankly at the television. But he wasn't responsive.

"Oh rass," said Tarone as they both walked around and stood in front of Karlos. Corey glanced at the television and saw that it was the local news station. The anchorwoman was speaking about Karlos, how in two days he managed to contact over sixty of Pastor Green's victims across the Caribbean and got them to come forward. This resulted from Chevelle's press conference which had been broadcast all over the West Indies, as well as going viral on the internet. Currently, Pastor Green's church was under investigation. Child and Disabled Children's advocates across the Caribbean were in an uproar as to how such flagrant and egregious abuses were kept hidden for so many years.

The news then replayed earlier footage of Pastor Green's church in a blaze—catching Corey and Tarone off guard. The authorities believed that the cause was arson, considering firefighters found a body which they believed was Pastor Green's. Corey then felt Tarone tap him on the arm and point to the bottle and glass on the table beside him.

Corey saw that the glass was mostly water from melted ice. As for the bottle, it had been opened, as the cap sat beside it.

"Karlos said that he was saving that bottle for the day that Pastor Green faced justice," said Corey.

"He didn't only live long enough to see Pastor Green face justice, he also got a chance to see his victims come forward. They're finally going to get justice too," said Tarone.

Corey knelt beside Karlos, staring into his face as he swallowed hard to soothe the dryness at the back of his throat. He then nodded once. "We all did."

Chapter 71

Montego Bay, six blocks away from Cornwall Regional Hospital

Ever since Eddie and Corey left the Airbnb for the last time, the news had overplayed the arrests of Denton and Weiss—which overshadowed the massacre at Guava Hill, as both incidents became international news. Eddie heard his name mentioned so many times that he got tired of it.

"Please change the station," said Eddie as he scratched behind his left ear.

"Sure." Corey used the controls on the steering wheel to scan each station. He stopped when he heard a familiar song by Soul II Soul. "Yes! Old school hip-hop, and you like this song."

Corey nudged Eddie with his elbow. "Sing along with me. 'Back to life, back to reality. Back to—'"

Eddie's hand shot out to the dash's controls where he hit the power button, killing the radio.

Corey turned to him. "What's wrong?"

Eddie was puzzled as he stared into space. "I...I don't know. For some strange reason that song just rubs me the wrong way. Come to think of it, I don't think I want to hear that song anymore."

Corey scrunched up his face. "What? I thought you liked that song."

"I did, I mean, I used to. It just feels weird hearing it."

"Another mystery for you to solve."

"Perhaps," said Eddie. "But my gut tells me that whatever I find out I'll want to keep to myself."

"Whatever you say, bruh." Corey swung the car toward the entrance to the hospital's parking lot.

Minutes later, Eddie and Corey exited the elevator and found their way to Delroy's room. The good news was that he was finally out of the ICU and was talking again. When they arrived, Lucille and Chevelle were with him, as expected.

Chevelle waved to them. "Oh. You came to say goodbye."

"We fly home later this evening," said Eddie as he nodded to Delroy, who responded the same way to both of them.

Corey then turned to Lucille. "You said it was urgent."

"Yes," said Lucille with a nod. "When Delroy woke up, he said he wanted to see both of you."

"Sure, what about?" asked Eddie.

"He'll tell you." Lucille turned to Chevelle. "Why don't we go for a walk. Your son doesn't need all of us crowding around him."

"Okay." Chevelle exited the room behind Lucille. She paused and turned to Eddie. "It was nice meeting you. Corey's a great person, and I hope that you're great friends for a very long time."

Corey wiped an imaginary tear with the back of his hand. "Damn, Chevelle. You're going to make me cry."

"No. I'm sorry," said Chevelle. "I didn't mean to do that."

"It's okay," said Lucille. "He was just joking."

Corey smiled. "I'm fine. You don't need to worry."

Chevelle relaxed her shoulders and smiled as she waved. "Okay, bye. And please don't forget us."

Eddie and Corey waved back as Chevelle and Lucille left.

"Waah gwaan?" said Delroy. He still appeared to be weak, but much better than before.

"Hey," said Corey as he nodded to Eddie. "This is my friend, Eddie. I don't believe you two really met."

"I remember you from Citrusville," said Delroy as he grabbed his cup and sipped the water through the straw. "I saw both of you on the news."

"We're glad that you're recovering," said Corey. "How much longer are you in here for?"

"Who knows. A few days, maybe another week."

"No sense in rushing your release if you haven't recovered," said Eddie. "What's so urgent that you needed to see us?"

"Mi want to make sure mi talk to yuh before yuh leave." Delroy looked past them and nodded. "Shut the door."

Eddie walked over to the door and closed it, leaving them in silence. He felt the sweat on his palms as he released the handle.

"We're listening," said Corey.

"I want to tell you what I saw at Citrusville the night Dwayne got killed." Delroy then nodded to the three chairs against the wall. "You'll want to grab one."

Corey and Eddie each dragged over a chair and sat.

"What did you see?" asked Eddie.

"During the dancehall contest, I went to the bathroom. When I got inside, I saw a man on his phone, but I didn't pay him much attention. Once he saw me, he hung up and bolted. After I left, I went looking for the friends I came with, but I couldn't find them. All I knew was that the contest ended." Delroy then turned to Eddie. "That's when I saw you calling for Shenice, or Dwayne."

Delroy began shaking his head. "I saw you heading to the parking lot, so I figured that my friends were out there because they said earlier that they would be looking for Shenice too. That's when I thought the worst because I know how Scuba can get when he wants something bad enough. And Jucee will do anything to help him. So, I headed out to the parking lot." Delroy then looked at Eddie. "When I got outside, the first thing I saw was you yelling at them to stop, but then a man attacked you from behind. He had his back to me, but there was enough light that I saw the clothes he wore. It was the same man I saw inside the bathroom earlier. So, I ducked quickly behind a car before he saw me."

"Did he come looking for you?" asked Corey.

"Let me finish," said Delroy. "I stayed hidden behind the car because something about that man didn't seem right. I knew that Scuba and Jucee were going to do something bad to Shenice, so I crawled to where I last saw them, keeping low so that the creepy man don't see me. Then I heard Jucee scream and Scuba cry out. When I found them, Jucee was rubbing his eyes—complaining that Shenice sprayed him with pepper spray. Scuba was on the ground naked from the waist down, clutching his balls. But Shenice was gone. I assumed that she was okay because I didn't see her anywhere. So, mi help mi boys back to mi car. I had to help Jucee to the front seat while Scuba managed to get around on his own."

Delroy took a sip of water.

"I just wanted to get away as far and as fast as I could because I didn't know where that man was. I take off so fast that I nearly hit you." He glanced at Eddie. "Once you got out of the way, I bolted."

"Did you ever tell this to the police?" asked Eddie.

Delroy's eyes widened as he shook his head in short shakes. "No, sah. Mi couldn't tell di police bout weh mi si. My gran…I mean, *that man* who rape mi madda always tell me never to inform pon anyone. I know that Scuba and Jucee were bad people, but the judge always ordered me not to inform on them because it could ruin their lives over something he claimed was just 'young men having fun.' But when it came to Dwayne, I didn't dare say anything. The next morning at work, I got up from my desk because I was told someone wanted to see me. When I went to the counter, I saw the same man from Citrusville standing near the entrance, staring at me. He didn't say anything, he kept staring at me. He even looked over his shoulder at me as he left."

Eddie glanced at Corey who responded with the same look. *Hansel was stalking Delroy to intimidate him into keeping quiet.*

They turned back to Delroy.

"I got home on time to see Jucee's and Scuba's fathers with the judge in his office. Dwayne's murder was all over the news and about how someone set him on fire. I knew neither Scuba nor Jucee killed him because Dwayne got away. I pretended I didn't see them and ran upstairs to my bedroom. I heard Jucee's and Scuba's fathers leave and the judge came knocking on my door soon after. He asked me what I knew about Dwayne Pottinger. I told him that I didn't know anything, and *that* was the honest truth. He then asked me if there's anything else I wasn't telling him. I lied when I told him no. He seemed satisfied with my answer, even though I knew that he didn't believe me."

Delroy took another sip of water. "When the judge left, I received a text on my phone, telling me to look under my pillow. So, I did, and found a picture of my mother as she was leaving the group home."

Eddie gasped as he glanced at Corey, who met his brief gaze.

Delroy took a deep breath and let it out slowly. "The person texted me again, telling me to look out my window. When I did, I saw a car parked out on the street. The driver flashed his headlights twice, then sped off. I knew that it was the same man. It was as though he found some way to listen inside my house, like he planted bugs. I looked all over my room right away but couldn't find anything."

"Did you see him again?" asked Eddie.

"Yes, sah," answered Delroy. "The next day when I left work. The moment I stepped outside I saw him on the other side of the square. Several people walked in front of him. When they passed, he was gone. Disappeared. Like a ninja."

"So, when I saw you at the poolhall looking all spooked, that was why," said Corey as he turned to Eddie. "I waited outside the bank to follow Delroy. The brotha would've been standing behind me across the street."

"You were there too?" asked Delroy.

Corey nodded. "Why didn't you go home? That's the first thing I would've done."

"I panicked," said Delroy. "I knew Scuba and Jucee would be waiting for me at the poolhall. I felt safer around them. But after that evening I never met them at the bar. I just go to work and then come home. I never saw that man again."

Corey put a hand on his shoulder. "He wanted to intimidate you and it worked. I understand why you kept quiet."

Eddie patted him on the leg. "You're going to be fine. When the police come, just tell them what you told us."

Delroy stared straight ahead. Eddie could tell that something else was on his mind.

"What's wrong?" Eddie asked.

Delroy turned to him. "There's something from that night at Citrusville."

"What else do you remember?" asked Corey.

"That same man I saw in the bathroom? I overheard a bit of what he said on the phone," said Delroy.

Eddie looked at Corey, who did the same in return. He then

turned to Delroy. "What did he say?"

Delroy bit his lower lip. "I only heard a name. I don't know what it means."

"Tell us," said Corey. "What did you hear him say?"

Delroy blinked rapidly before turning to Eddie and Corey. "I heard him say…*Ares*."

Eddie and Corey looked at each other briefly before simultaneously staring back at Delroy.

"Ares?" asked Eddie. "Like the god of war?"

"I'm sure that's what I heard," said Delroy.

Eddie looked at Corey to see if he had anything to say. Corey read him and responded by shaking his head. Eddie then sighed and turned to Delroy. "Do yourself a favor and don't mention that last part to anyone. Let's keep it between us three."

"Not even the police?" asked Delroy.

Eddie and Corey leaned toward Delroy. "Especially them."

Chapter 72

As they exited the hospital and walked toward the parking lot, they saw Ellis approaching from the opposite direction.

"Mister Barrow and Mister Stephenson."

"Hey, Detective Inspector Ellis," said Eddie.

"What brought you two here?"

"We came to say goodbye to Delroy, Lucille, and to Chevelle before we head to the airport," said Eddie.

"I guess you came to get your statement from Delroy," said Corey.

"Just doing my job," said Ellis. "And hopefully both of you will be available to testify against Weiss and Denton."

"Via videoconferencing, I hope," said Eddie.

"That's what we'd all prefer," said Ellis. "By the way, you didn't hear this from me. PennSteel is suing Denton's company for a whopping thirty-four million dollars US, Weiss is being sued for around thirteen million, which is the amount that PennSteel's auditors estimated that he received in kickbacks. All of that while both Denton and Weiss are looking at life imprisonment for murder and conspiracy to commit murder. However, it's highly likely that they'll be extradited back to the US, where they'll serve their sentences."

"What about the assassins Denton hired?" asked Corey.

Ellis shook his head. "We still haven't identified the bodies of the two women we found. As for the male member of the trio, still nothing. He could be anywhere in the world by now."

"Before I forget, I'm sorry about your friend, Karlos," said Corey.

"Yeah, you have our sympathy," said Eddie.

"Thanks." Ellis turned to Corey. "Before he passed, Karlos told me that you and Tarone helped him remember why he became a detective. He never felt so alive in years. The medical examiner said that he had heart failure, but the truth is I knew a long time ago that his health was on the decline—ever since he retired. But all I can say is he really put his heart into his work, and thanks to you both, his biggest case was finally put to rest. Now he can rest in peace knowing that he made a difference. I guess you heard about Pastor Green and his church."

Eddie and Corey nodded.

"We can expect to press other charges on Judge Stewart and other members of Pastor's church," said Ellis. "Oh, another thing. The two men you probably know as Scuba and Jucee were just arrested."

"Really?" asked Eddie.

"What for?" asked Corey.

"You won't believe this," said Ellis. "Someone passed by the station and left a cell phone and said that I would know what to do with it. With some help from the phone's provider, we were able to get it unlocked. It turns out that it belonged to Dwayne Pottinger. And on it we found a video of him filming himself leaving Citrusville with Scuba and Jucee harassing him right before they attacked him."

"They were actually filmed attacking him?"

"Yes, sah." Ellis nodded. "The phone was dropped during the scuffle, but somehow Dwayne managed to escape."

"But we already know that they weren't the ones who killed Dwayne," said Corey.

"True," said Eddie. "However, the video is enough to arrest them for lying about Dwayne being the one who attacked them." Eddie then turned to Ellis. "Lying on a deposition is a violation of Jamaica's Perjury Act, isn't it?"

Ellis sighed. "How do you know so much about Jamaican law?"

Eddie shrugged his shoulders. "I read a lot."

Ellis then turned to Corey as he made a side nod to Eddie. "Don't you get annoyed hanging around this human encyclopedia?"

"You get used to it."

"You may want to mention the phone video to Delroy," said Eddie. "I'm sure he'll be able to fill in the gaps."

"Really?" said Ellis. "What else did he tell you?"

"Besides thanking us, nothing else," Corey answered.

Ellis tilted his head to the side as he looked at them with slanted eyes. "You sure?"

Eddie raised both palms in surrender. "As I said, anything that you need to know, I'm sure he'll tell you."

Ellis let go of the gaze and nodded. He then held out his hand. "I was wrong about you two. Everything from solving the Pottinger murder, exposing a foreign criminal conspiracy, sex crimes committed by a church, bringing down a superior court judge. Lord, even our prime minister's on thin ice right now. None of it would've happened had it not been for you guys."

Eddie shook his hand. "Thanks for not throwing us in prison."

Corey shook Ellis's hand. "Thanks again for saving my life the other night."

"Just doing my job." He nodded to them. "Have a safe flight home. And don't take too long to come back and visit. Just remember, you'll always have a friend in the Jamaican Constabulary Force."

They said their final goodbyes and were on their way back to their car when Eddie's phone rang. He picked it up and saw that it was Bevins.

"Hey, Nancy," said Eddie.

"I have great news." The excitement in her voice was clear.

"What is it?"

"After your publisher dropped you, I took the liberty to upload your books to Amazon where they can be purchased in both eBook as well as the paperback format. I'm glad I did, because since Vanessa Pusey's live video blew up in her face, in addition to the rumors that you helped bring down Denton and Weiss, *all* your books have climbed into the top ten spots in Canada, the US, and in the UK. Your royalties are significantly higher than what your previous publisher was paying you."

Eddie nearly dropped the phone as he laughed. "Oh my God! Nancy, you're a lifesaver."

"No problem," she answered. "It gets better. Your old publisher wants you back. I saw what they're offering you, it's very tempting."

"Really?" Eddie chuckled as he shook his head. "Tell them that I'll think about it."

"I knew you'd say that. Are you on the way to the airport?"

"Yeah, Corey and I are about to head out there right now. I can't wait to get home."

"My flight to Boston leaves in two hours. We can still see each other if you hurry up."

"I'll tell Corey to step on it. Some new friends we made these past few days told us they'll be there. I believe you may have met them at the cemetery."

"They're already here," said Bevins. "Amancia and Lucille brought baked goods they called rock cake, rum cake, and I believe something called bulla. They look good, they even made enough for me. I hope you can fit them all in your suitcases."

Eddie chuckled. West Indians will always make sure that you're well fed. "Excellent. Corey and I will see you soon."

Eddie put away his phone and was about to get inside the car. It was then that he noticed that Corey was missing. He could've sworn that he was right in front of him. He did a complete 360, no Corey.

"Corey?" He looked around again. "Corey?"

An arm wrapped around his neck, locking it in the crook of his captor's arm while a fist pressed into the small of his back. Eddie had no control over his movements as he felt himself being dragged backward.

"Don't move, you bloodclaat!"

Wait a second. "Corey?"

Eddie was released and he turned around to see Corey standing with his arms crossed. "Jesus! Why'd you do that?"

"To test you."

"What for?"

"No one should ever be able to ambush you so easily," said Corey. "If you're going to make a habit of being a Black Sherlock Holmes, then you're going to need to learn to defend yourself.

You're my best bro. But seeing how many close shaves we both had while we were here, we need to do better."

"We?"

"Damn right." Corey walked around to the passenger side, while Eddie removed his phone from his back pocket before sitting down behind the wheel. "As soon as we get back home, we're both signing up for martial arts classes. We're going to learn Karate, Tae-Kwon-Do, Krav-Maga, you name it."

"You can't be serious. It'll take us years to master those disciplines."

"I know," said Corey. "Look at it this way, the better you master your self-defense skills, the better you'll be able to write realistic fight scenes."

Eddie smiled as he looked at his best friend. "You're really serious about this."

"Damn right I am. We're in this together, you and me. Everything you do affects me, and vice versa. If you fall, I'll be there to pick you up. And if I fall, I know you'll be there to do the same."

"You'll never stop being there for me, will you?" said Eddie.

Corey smiled back at him and grabbed his shoulder. "We'll always be there for each other."

Epilogue

Palais Garnier, Place de l'Opéra, Paris, France
(Two nights later)

The asset known as Hansel chilled in his private box as he watched renown operatic soprano, Kathleen Battle, unleash some of the most powerful yet soothing, vocals he'd heard in weeks. He'd heard enough reggae and dancehall music to last him a lifetime. What graced his ears now was serenity.

It'd been five days since he left Jamaica and he was ready to lose the sling. As for the person responsible for it, that was a lucky shot. He was fortunate that he had hit him at all, as the bullet passed through his shoulder without leaving any permanent damage. He'd heal in no time. Switching from one plane to the next while island hopping was not only tiring but frustrating.

He turned to the vibrations he felt in the floor behind him. Someone was approaching, and quick. But not as quick as Hansel clutched his steel pen from the upper pocket of his blazer—ready to gouge out the eyes of whoever was going to rush in here. If they'd managed to get past security with a weapon, then he'd disarm and neutralize his assailant, popping off a single head and chest shot in the same breath. Ms. Battle and the Paris Opera Orchestra would drown out the kill shots—especially if his would-be assailant brought a noise-suppressed gun. A shot from a regular gun may go unnoticed, but only an amateur would be dumb enough to use one. Then again, an amateur wouldn't even get past the security.

The curtains drew, and Hansel relaxed his grip on his pen when he saw that it was one of the female ushers whom he had already analyzed and determined not to be a threat.

"Pardon, Monsieur," said the young woman who handed him

an envelope.

Hansel took the envelope and nodded. "Merci."

It was so good to be able to speak again in public. That one screw-up at Citrusville was a potential hazard. Never let anyone hear you mention Ares in public while on the job. And when Delroy surprised him by showing up in the men's room while he was in mid-sentence, it was a potential hazard to the mission. He did what he had to, to let Delroy think that the Grim Reaper was coming for him—especially after the second *visual* intimidation when he stood outside his workplace where he could be seen the moment Delroy exited. He only did the visit outside his home as a third visual intimidation because he was a sucker for doing things in threes. He could've killed him, but that would've turned too many heads—even more so than Eddie Barrow's. Sure, it was an exaggeration resisting the urge to speak unless he was addressing his own associates, but there wasn't a need to chance it and screw up twice.

Once the usher left, he opened the envelope and removed a single card with an address which read: 1 Rue de Vaugirard.

He left his private box and was soon walking down the majestic grand staircase. He only thought of where he would be sent to next. He wouldn't mind being sent to a slightly cooler climate for his next assignment. He couldn't stay grounded for too long before the urge to be back out in the field caught up to him.

Minutes later, Hansel exited the subbasement parking lot and onto Rue de l'Opéra in his black Aston Martin Vantage V8, where he headed south. After roughly sixteen minutes, he parked his car a stone's throw from the address. The six-story renaissance building had seen its share of changes over the centuries. Today there was a Crédit Mutuel on the ground floor as the building sat on the corner of Rue de Vaugirard and Boulevard Saint Michel.

Even though he was alone as he rode the elevator to the sixth floor, he had spotted at least four CCTV cameras on the way, as well as two plain-clothed operatives outside across the street. They would've alerted the people upstairs to his arrival. He exited the elevator and walked down the hall to the door at the end, where he let himself in.

There, he walked into a conference room complete with a long table, where eight people, predominantly men, sat.

"Welcome to Paris," said a man who wasn't less than sixty, and who spoke with a German accent. "We were just reviewing the report you sent to us. You look like you could use a break and let that shoulder heal."

As Hansel sat in the empty seat that was closest to him, the German turned to the rest of the group. "With regard to infiltrating the entertainment industry, I vote that we abandon this experiment and invest our resources in more familiar territory. All in favor?"

The others unanimously tapped the screens of their tablets to register their vote in a secure app.

"As for the other matter at hand," continued the German as he turned to Hansel. "You wrote that even though Eddie Barrow's not a major threat and should be left alone, he's unpredictable and should not be underestimated."

The German then chuckled. "Are you serious? We're speaking of someone who writes books for a living. He's your typical mild-mannered next-door neighbor."

Hansel eyed the German, holding a cold, expressionless stare. He did not have to warn the German that he did not appreciate being mocked, the stare was enough to send a clear message that made the man quickly lose the smile.

"I agree with the asset," came a woman's voice as she entered the room. She took her seat at the opposite end of the table. There was no limit to this former Mossad operative's expensive tastes, as was demonstrated in her navy tweed short-suit by Chanel, designed to show off her toned legs while accentuating the Gianvito Rossi pointed gold pumps. Her burgundy hair—a change from her natural brunette—was tied into a ponytail.

"Ms. Erela Ganz," said the German. "Nice of you to join us."

"Always a pleasure to be back in Paris," said Ganz as she eyed Hansel. "As I said, I agree with the asset. As much as it pains me to admit this, we cannot ignore the fact that Barrow eluded our assets for as long as he did. As a result, our client and his business partner will be spending the rest of their lives in prison. We lost millions—a drop in the ocean, but we need to move on."

"And you're positive that Denton doesn't know who we are?" asked the German.

"Didn't you read the asset's report?" asked Ganz. The German did not reply. "I ordered him to eliminate the problem."

Ganz then turned to Hansel. "It's fixed, so no one knows about us." She reached into her handbag and took out her tablet. She went to Eddie Barrow's website, where she glanced at his biography. "In the meantime, I'd like to learn more about Eddie Barrow."

The End

A Note of Thanks from Russell

Thanks again for purchasing *Jam Run*. I hope you were sitting on the edge of your seats throughout Eddie and Corey's wildest adventure. If you want to stay updated on when my next book will be released, the best way is to join my newsletter. You can do so by visiting my website at: russellparkway.com. If you're having difficulty doing so, please write me at russell@russellparkway.com.

Finally, I need your help. If you're so inclined, I'd love a review of *Jam Run*. Loved it, hated it, I would appreciate your feedback.

Reviews are very difficult to obtain and for Indie authors, such as myself, they are vital for us in order to gain exposure. If you may spare a few moments of your time, please visit my author page on Amazon where you can find all my books. I'm also on Goodreads and on Bookbub.

If you're not camera shy, please email me a selfie with you holding your copy of *Jam Run* so I may share it on social media.

Thanks again,

Russell

March 3, 2023

Acknowledgements

Writing *Jam Run* was an arduous task that required several hours of research. The project was too big to accomplish on my own. I wanted to create a Jamaican crime thriller, not a stereotype nor a caricature of Jamaica. My original plan was to visit Montego Bay to see the locations where the story took place. However, COVID-19 changed that. As a result, I was introduced to "Chuck" Norris Douglas, the CEO of RealTours Jamaica. He and I spent several hours on ZOOM, where he helped me fact-check the Jamaican content. This included the geography, food, history, Jamaican Patois, and local expressions.

Norris also helped me confirm the location of where the fictional town of Guava Hill would be located. He also helped me located where The Drought would be located if it was a real village.

In January 2023, I finally had my chance to visit Montego Bay, where I met Norris. He drove me to the locations where *Jam Run* took place. This allowed me to experience Jamaica in a way that cannot be done virtually or online. The benefit was that it allowed me to correct several scenes to make them more accurate.

I also travelled to Kingston, where I had the chance to visit the Assistant Director of Prosecutions, Judi-Ann Edwards. At the same time, I met her mother, Nordia Sweeney—a schoolteacher specializing in intellectually disabled students. Judi-Ann was essential in helping me fact-check the legal content and the police procedures in the story. Nordia helped me improve Chevelle's character.

Before I wrote the first chapter or even completed the plot, I needed more information on the murder of Dwayne Jones—who inspired the character of Dwayne Pottinger. I virtually met Dane Lewis—the former executive director of the Jamaica Forum for

Lesbians, All-Sexuals and Gays (J-Flag). He helped bring me up to speed on the current relationships between the LGBTQ+ community in Jamaica and the police.

I also want to acknowledge my friend, Doctor Myrna Lashley—a psychologist. Having a rape victim as a character meant me being careful about how they're presented. Furthermore, the final hospital scene involving Chevelle and her father could not have been written so realistically had it not been for her input.

From Barbados, I'd also like to thank my cousin, Doctor Makeba Cummins—a medical doctor. She helped Eddie and Corey find their way around the hospital.

In an earlier draft, Eddie Barrow kept Dwayne Pottinger's wet phone in a bag of desiccant packets. My gut told me this may not be the most efficient way to dry a phone. Through further investigation, I found an article about Craig Beinecke—the co-founder of TekDry International Inc. I took a chance writing him and was surprised at how quick he replied and how friendly he was. He explained why dumping a wet cell phone in a bag of desiccants or rice is useless. I rewrote those scenes and asked Craig if he would mind having a cameo appearance in *Jam Run*. He accepted. If the name Craig Beinecke rang a bell, it's because he was on the TV Show Shark Tank.

As with my previous novels, Wim Demeere—a martial arts teacher from Belgium—assisted me in writing realistic fight scenes.

Once again, Jeff Meek of Carry On Colorado offered his help selecting guns for my characters.

When I found an article about the illegal logging industry written by Aisling Irwin, I knew that Eddie Barrow would need to understand how it works to prove that Vanessa Pusey had infringed on Dwayne Pottinger's intellectual property right. I contacted Mrs. Irwin who referred me to Roger Young, the CEO of Agroisolab in the United Kingdom. His help made it possible for Barrow to identify Pusey's error and get justice for Dwayne Pottinger.

The year leading up to the release of *Jam Run* I participated in book fairs and pop-ups in Montreal, Ottawa, and Toronto. My friend, Michael Smith, always loaned Jamaican art sculptures to help me decorate my table. I also received additional help from Sharon Nelson—the first vice president of the Jamaica Association of Montreal. She loaned other items to help me create a Jamaican-themed table at my events. I also want to thank her for organizing my first book club meeting, including members from the Caribbean Coalition of Montreal.

I also want to thank my brother, Randall, and his partner, Niki, for their continued moral support and assistance.

This was the first time I worked with a publicist. Janis Kirchner was professional and got me interviews that I never thought possible.

I also want to thank Penny Sansieveri and Amy Cornell of Authors Marketing Experts for their hard work in helping me promote *Jam Run*.

A huge thanks goes to my publishing team. My editor, Lisa Martinez, who has spent countless hours revising *Jam Run*. Jeroen ten Berge who keeps designing kick-ass book covers. Signe Nichols who formats my manuscripts into eBook and paperback formats.

I want to also thank journalist Richard "Bugs" Burnett. Ever since I told him that I was writing an LGBTQ crime thriller, he immediately took an interest. He informed me of the first LGBTQ book fair in Montreal and encouraged me to participate. His advice paid off. Burnett was also the first major media personality to interview me.

I was hoping to consult with Eric Jerome Dickie, who's a NYT Bestselling author. He helped me previously by revising the sex scene in *The Demeter Code*. I was looking forward to his input for this story. Unfortunately, I was saddened when I learned he passed away on January 3, 2021. I'm positive he would've enjoyed reading *Jam Run* as he did with *The Demeter Code*.

Even though he never gave me feedback, my cat Clinton loved to sit beside my laptop whenever I worked. For countless hours he was great company. Sadly, he became ill from cancer. As devastating as it was, I chose to put him down. He passed away peacefully on December 5, 2022.

Lastly, I want to thank everyone who contributed to my crowdfunding campaign. Without your donations, it would not have been easy finishing this project. However, I want to give special attention to Sandra Stephenson, Hannah Rosenfeld, David Bontemps, Randall Brooks, Niki Koloudas, Suzanne Duciaume, Nancy Greene Gregoire, Frederick Francis, Oswin Foster, Sheila Alleyne, Gabriella Pomponi, Renee Cummins, Emanuel Da Costa, Seymour Walden, and Renee Jordan.

References

1. "Dwayne Jones (Gully Queen)," unresolved.me, accessed April 21, 2019 https://unresolved.me/dwayne-jones,
2. "Transgender teen killed by mob in Jamaica," The Associated Press, August 11, 2013, https://www.cbc.ca/news/world/transgender-teen-killed-by-mob-in-jamaica-1.1366239
3. Eric Campbell, "One love, one hate, one hope: Tackling homophobia in Jamaica," ABC News, July 21, 2017, https://www.abc.net.au/news/2017-07-22/homophobia-in-jamaican-music-one-love-one-hate-one-hope/8711620,
4. Kimberly Engels, "Anti-Gay Laws and State Complicity with violence against LGBT People," Antillean.org, June 1, 2016, https://www.antillean.org/jamaica-buggery-law-complicity-violence-876/
5. Sheila Veléz Martínez, "Government shouldn't let Dwayne Jones' Death go in vain," Jamaica-gleaner.com, August 13, 2013, https://jamaica-gleaner.com/gleaner/20130813/cleisure/cleisure3.html,
6. Colin Stewart, "This must stop: Jamaican Homophobia leads to two murders," 76Crimes.com, May 27, 2016, https://76crimes.com/2016/05/27/this-must-stop-jamaican-homophobia-leads-to-2-murders/
7. Richard Ammon, "Gay Jamaica: Crime and Punishment," GlobalGayz.com, April 2008, https://www.globalgayz.com/gay-jamaica-crime-and-punishment/
8. Joseph Shapiro, "The Sexual Assault Epidemic No One Talks About," NPR.org, January 8, 2018, https://www.npr.org/2018/01/08/570224090/the-sexual-assault-epidemic-no-one-talks-about
9. Nadine Wilson Harris, "My baby's baby! - Eleven-year-old pregnant after sexually assaulted by two adult men," Jamaica-gleaner.com, March 14, 2015, https://jamaica-gleaner.com/article/lead-stories/20150315/my-babys-baby-eleven-year-old-pregnant-after-sexually-assaulted-two

10. Kate Chappell, "Devout Jamaica debates green light for abortion after rape, incest," Reuters.com, February 25, 2019, https://www.reuters.com/article/us-jamaica-women-abortion/devout-jamaica-debates-green-light-for-abortion-after-rape-incest-idUSKCN1QE0OF
11. Mark Dent, "Bill Cosby Accuser Gives Graphic Testimony, Gets Grilled About Contradictions On Cross-Examination – Update," Deadline.com, April 13, 2018, https://deadline.com/2018/04/bill-cosby-rape-trial-accuser-takes-witness-stand-graphic-details-andrea-constand-1202363874/
12. Jen Kirby, "Cosby lawyers press Andrea Constand on her motives in pursuing a $3.4 million settlement," Vox.com, Apr 16, 2018, https://www.vox.com/2018/4/16/17236580/bill-cosby-andrea-constand-testimony-cross-examination
13. Janet Silvera, "'WE WON' - 'Dad raped us' sisters get day in court," https://jamaica-gleaner.com/gleaner/20110717/lead/lead7.html, Jamaica-Gleaner.com, July 17, 2011
14. Vidya Rao, "Memory Loss after Sexual Assault is Real," HealthyWomen.com, September 15, 2021, https://www.healthywomen.org/your-wellness/self-care--mental-health/memory-loss-sexual-assault-real
15. Sammy Caiola, "How Rape affects Memory and the Brain, And Why More Police Need to know about this," NPR.com, August 22, 2021, https://www.npr.org/sections/health-shots/2021/08/22/1028236197/how-rape-affects-memory-and-the-brain-and-why-more-police-need-to-know-about-thi
16. Jane Sims, "Man gets prison for incest after baby's DNA reveals secret sex with daughter," lfpress.com, February 20, 2020, https://lfpress.com/news/local-news/man-gets-prison-for-incest-after-babys-dna-reveals-secret-sex-with-daughter
17. "'Bishop' charged with rape in St. Mary," Jamaica.loopnews.com, July 13, 2021, https://jamaica.loopnews.com/content/bishop-charged-rape-st-mary?fbclid=IwAR0NfM0ArCoCn9Axbn3B5_qJjWC7W4fwleiUPgjnecBywPAnfxnxa5S6gFs
18. Rochelle Clayton, "Years of Cult Shame," jamaicaobserver.com, October 21, 2021, https://www.jamaicaobserver.com/news/years-of-cult-shame/
19. Chris McGreal, "Christopher 'Dudus' Coke tells US court: 'I'm pleading guilty because I am'," TheGuardian.com, September 1, 2011, https://www.theguardian.com/world/2011/sep/01/christopher-dudus-coke-us-court

20. Mattathias Schwartz, "As Jamaican Drug Lord is Sentenced, U.S. Still Silent on Massacre," NewYorker.com, June 7, 2012 https://www.newyorker.com/news/news-desk/as-jamaican-drug-lord-is-sentenced-u-s-still-silent-on-massacre
21. Sandra Laville, "Jamaica police commit 'hundreds of unlawful killings' yearly, Amnesty says," Guardian.com, November 23, 2016, https://www.theguardian.com/world/2016/nov/23/jamaica-police-killings-amnesty-report
22. "Jamaica: Illegal police tactics fuel scores of murders and sow culture of fear," Amnesty.org, November 23, 2016, https://www.amnesty.org/en/latest/news/2016/11/jamaica-illegal-police-tactics-fuel-scores-of-murders-and-sow-culture-of-fear/
23. Jon Schuppe, "Epic Drug Lab Scandal Results in More Than 20,000 Convictions Dropped," NBCNews.com, April 18, 2017, https://www.nbcnews.com/news/us-news/epic-drug-lab-scandal-results-more-20-000-convictions-dropped-n747891
24. Todd South, "This device could help soldiers see through walls in the urban fight," Armytimes.com, October 24, 2019, https://www.armytimes.com/news/your-army/2019/10/24/this-device-could-help-soldiers-see-through-walls-in-the-urban-fight/
25. "The Dark Side of Privacy: How ISIS Communications go undetected," PSMAG.com, June 14, 2017, HTTPS://PSMAG.COM/NEWS/THE-DARK-SIDE-OF-PRIVACY-HOW-ISIS-COMMUNICATIONS-GO-UNDETECTED
26. Robert Tie, "Preventing Kickback Schemes, Know How to Stop Bribery in its Tracks" Fraud-Magazine.com, June 2010, https://www.fraud-magazine.com/article.aspx?id=4294967730
27. Robert Snell, "Witness gives bite-by-bite insight into Detroit airport kickback scheme," Detroitnews.com, May 30, 2019, https://www.detroitnews.com/story/news/local/detroit-city/2019/05/30/detroit-metro-airport-contractor-testifies-james-Weiss-trial/1288552001/
28. Jen Kirby, "The US has made its biggest anti-money-laundering changes in years," Vox.com, January 4, 2021, https://www.vox.com/22188223/congress-anti-money-laundering-anonymous-shell-companies-ban-defense-bill

29. Randy Bennett, "Former Minister found Culpable in Money Laundering Case," Barbadostoday.com, January 17, 2020, https://barbadostoday.bb/2020/01/17/former-minister-found-culpable-in-money-laundering-case/?fbclid=IwAR06WjYEUNdRRggd_bmM-ha8fsPdA7hg93sjGy9ly34XG6yGeUHe2Vqt5Z4
30. "Christopher Hitchens Get Waterboarded," Vanity Fair, accessed March 3, 2022, https://www.youtube.com/watch?v=4LPubUCJv58
31. "HAMMEL Recyclingtechnik GmbH presents RED GIANT in a new version," Hammel.de, accessed September 1, 2020, https://www.hammel.de/index.php/en/aktuelles-8/pressemeldungen/275-hammel-recyclingtechnik-gmbh-presents-red-giant-in-a-new-version
32. "VB 950 DK (RED GIANT) - Autos / cars," Hammelbasa, accessed September 1, 2020, https://www.youtube.com/watch?v=L7eKMgrwo1A
33. Drew Anderson, "City puts pressure on scrap yard to end explosions," CBC.ca, January 24, 2018, https://www.cbc.ca/news/canada/calgary/evraz-navajo-explosions-scrap-yard-calgary-1.4498895
34. "J'can gov't to pay man J$2.4m for false imprisonment," jamaica-gleaner.com, April 10, 2016, https://jamaica-gleaner.com/article/news/20160410/jcan-govt-pay-man-j24m-false-imprisonment
35. Carmen Drahl, "What You Need To Know About Captagon, The Drug Of Choice In War-Torn Syria," Forbes.com, November 21, 2015, https://www.forbes.com/sites/carmendrahl/2015/11/21/what-you-need-to-know-about-captagon-the-drug-of-choice-in-war-torn-syria/?sh=20b716263c82
36. Aisling Irwin, "Tree sleuths are using DNA tests and machine vision to crack timber crimes," Nature.com, April 3, 2019.
37. CNNwire, "Suspected bank thief arrested after flashing stacks of cash on social media," Foxnews.com, December 16, 2019, https://fox5sandiego.com/news/suspected-bank-robber-arrested-after-bragging-about-cash-online/

Also from Russell Brooks

The Ridley Fox/Nita Parris Series

PANDORA'S SUCCESSION
The Deadliest Weapon Against Mankind has been Unleashed

UNSAVORY DELICACIES
Three Short Stories of Suspense

THE DEMETER CODE
Crack the Code and You'll Save Lives...
Knowing it Exists Will get You Killed

The Eddie Barrow Series

CHILL RUN
You Know a Publicity Stunt Has Backfired When Someone Dies

Find out more at:

www.russellparkway.com

Manufactured by Amazon.ca
Bolton, ON